College life 401;

Senior Experience

J.B. Vample

Book Seven

The College Life Series

COLLEGE LIFE 401-Senior Experience

Copyright © 2019 by Jessyca B. Vample

Printed in the United States of America

First Printing, 2019

ISBN-10: 1-7323178-3-6 (eBook edition)
ISBN-13: 978-1-7323178-3-3 (eBook edition)

ISBN-10: 1-7323178-2-8 (Paperback edition)
ISBN-13: 978-1-7323178-2-6 (Paperback edition)

For information contact; email: JBVample@yahoo.com

Website: www.jbvample.com

Book cover design by: Najla Qamber Designs

Dedicated to that quiet, awkward young girl who used to write stories as a hobby. To that high school teenager with the overactive imagination, who one day thought up a story concept simply while imagining what her own college life would be like. She didn't think anything would ever come of her talent; she didn't even think that she *had* talent. She wrote simply because it made her happy...To my younger self...you finally saw your potential. You finally realized that you need to do what has always made you happy...and now you're doing it.

Chapter 1

"Damn, they finished these new campus houses fast," Alex Chisolm mused, pushing open the door to her new campus dwellings and setting an overnight bag on the tan couch.

"Yeah well, I guess they figured with the number of new students they get each year, they needed the space," Eric Wendell pointed out, setting Alex's large brown suitcase on the floor.

Alex smiled as she looked around. The new Winfield houses of Paradise Valley University certainly were a step up from the dorms and clusters. The two-story house featured one double and three single bedrooms, and came equipped with one bathroom, a modern kitchen, living room, and dining area. *What a great way to start my senior year*, Alex thought.

"Do you know who your housemates are?" Eric asked, snapping Alex out of her thoughts.

Alex nodded. "My girls," she smiled.

"Oh yeah?" he replied. "That's good."

"Yeah, we made sure we put our names on the list to be in the same house," Alex informed, running a hand along the back of her neck. "They should be arriving soon." She then began to laugh. "We were all trying to beat each other here because there are only three single rooms, so the last two to arrive, have to share. "

Eric chuckled. "Oh, that should be interesting."

Alex was about to speak, when she peered out of the window and noticed a familiar black car pull into the first parking spot in front of the house. A smile formed on her dark brown face. "And here comes one of them now," she beamed.

Alex moved away from the door as the young lady, who'd jumped out of the car carrying only her pocketbook, ran into the house.

"Hey sis!" Alex exclaimed, arms outstretched.

Chasity Parker eyed Alex with suspicion. "Before I give your hype ass a hug, please tell me I'm not the last one to get here," she said.

Alex put her arms down in a huff and sucked her teeth. "No Chasity, you're not the last one... In fact, you're only the second," she confirmed.

Chasity let out a sigh of relief as she put her hand on her chest. "Okay good," she said before giving Alex her hug.

"So damn rude," Alex laughed as they parted. As Chasity gave a slight wave to Eric, Alex looked at her. She'd barely spoken to Chasity since her Aunt Brenda passed away over a month ago. "So...how are you?"

Chasity looked at her, then as she went to speak, Eric put his hands up. "Umm, I'll let you two catch up," he said. "I'll call you later, Alex?"

"Sure," Alex confirmed. Once Eric walked out of the house, Alex lightly tapped Chasity's arm. "Well? How are you?" she pressed. "Except for our group text this morning, I haven't really talked to you."

Chasity pulled on her long ponytail with two hands to tighten it. "I know... Sorry I've been distant," she said.

"I understand why you *have* been," Alex assured. "I couldn't imagine what you've had to deal with."

Chasity glanced away briefly. She did feel bad for being distant from her friends when they only wanted to know how she was doing. But she needed the space. Having Brenda show up after all that time, with the news that she was dying, was a lot for Chasity to handle. She not only struggled with her own feelings about the woman, but was in the room when Brenda took her last breath. Then Chasity had planned Brenda's funeral due to her mother's inability to do so because of her own grief. That, on top of a heartfelt memento left behind for her from Brenda, caused an emotional breakdown. The breakdown was hard on Chasity, but she needed it.

"Yeah well…I'm okay though," she answered.

Alex tilted her head. "You sure?"

Chasity nodded slightly. "Yeah. Just needed some time."

Alex smiled. Normally she would press Chasity for more details, but for now her answer satisfied Alex. "Okay…good to hear," she said, giving Chasity another hug. "Love you."

"Still not with the mushy shit," Chasity jeered, prompting Alex to release her.

"Fine," she laughed.

Chasity looked around; she liked the look of the new place. "This is cute…looks better than it does online," she said.

"Wait, there are pictures on the school website?" Alex asked.

Chasity raised an arched eyebrow. "Yeah Alex…hence why I said—never mind," she dismissed, waving her hand. "You pick your room yet?"

Alex shook her head. "I just got in a few moments before *you* did."

"Okay," Chasity mumbled, before taking off up the stairs. "I got first dibs."

"Damn it Chasity!" Alex yelled, running after her. "I got here first, so I get to *pick* first."

"Bullshit," Chasity shot back.

Malajia Simmons pushed the door open and stuck her head inside the house. "Hello?" she called. When no one answered, she stepped inside.

Mark Johnson walked in behind her, carrying two of Malajia's massive suitcases. "Why do you always have so much shit?" he griped, sitting them on the floor by the couch.

"Less complaining, more getting the rest of my shit out of your car," she demanded.

Mark shook his head.

Malajia looked around as she stretched. "This is cuuuute," she squealed. "*Way* better than the clusters. It's all shiny and new, *and* I get my own room."

"You hype you get to have your own room," Mark chortled.

"You damn right," she replied, flinging her long, curly dark brown hair over her shoulder. "I love Sidra to death, but the prissy neat freak worked my nerves last year with her complaining. 'Clean up your stuff Malajia', 'Will you shut up, I'm trying to study Malajia', 'Stop stealing my stuff, Malajia.'"

Mark stared at her. After driving for hours through traffic, he was tired. "Yeah, I didn't need to hear all that."

Malajia made a face and sucked her teeth at his tone. "Fix your attitude," she ground out.

"No, I had to listen to your dry, bum ass playlist all the way down here *and* you ate my fries," he barked back.

Malajia fought the urge to laugh. "You still mad about those fries?"

"You goddamn right, you ate mine *after* you said you didn't *want* any," he fussed. "You fucked up my lunch."

Malajia shook her head. "You're such a baby." Mark sucked his teeth, prompting Malajia to laugh. She walked over to him. "I'm sorry about your fries," she pacified, wrapping her arms around his toned waist. "You still mad?"

Mark looked away. "Yup."

Malajia stared up at him. "You want me to make it up to you?" she crooned.

Mark's attitude immediately vanished. "Yup," he smiled. As he leaned in for a kiss, Chasity walked down the steps.

"Gross," she scoffed.

Mark and Malajia parted. "Where the hell did *you* come from?" Malajia asked.

Chasity looked at her. "Did I *not* just come from upstairs?" she bristled. "This must be 'stupid ass question day' or something."

Malajia waved a dismissive hand at her. "Oh shut up and hug me," she said, walking over to Chasity.

"What's up Chaz?" Mark said.

"What's up Mark?" Chasity threw back.

"Me and Mel, got it in," Mark revealed. Malajia snickered and Chasity looked disgusted.

"Yeah, I heard," Chasity scoffed. "Please spare me the details, I just ate."

Mark shrugged. "Very well," he chuckled, grabbing Malajia's suitcases from the floor. "Mel, go pick your room so I can take these heavy ass bags upstairs."

Malajia smiled. "Okay." She skipped to the steps, then stopped. "Wait, who else is here?"

"Alex, was earlier," Chasity answered.

"Okay, well Mark, you can put the stuff in the empty single room," Malajia said, moving away from the steps.

"Really, you're not gonna go up with me?" Mark asked.

Confusion set in on Malajia's face. "*Why*? It's a room with one bed. What do you need *me* for?" she sneered. "Don't embarrass me by being simple."

Mark shot her a glare, then proceeded to take the bags up the steps, mumbling in the process.

Malajia ignored him and turned her attention back to Chasity, who sat on the couch. "Yooo, Sidra's gonna be pissed, she *swore* she was gonna beat me here," Malajia said, amused.

"Yeah, she was talking all kinds of shit in the group text," Chasity dryly put out.

"Yup, and for that, I'm not even gonna tell her that the single rooms are taken… I want to see her face," Malajia laughed, flopping down on the couch next to her.

Mark trotted down the steps. "Alright, I'm out."

"I still got more stuff in your car," Malajia pointed out.

Mark tossed his head back and let out a loud groan.

"Why you always gotta be so loud?!" Malajia barked at him as he walked out the door.

Chasity shot Malajia a side-glance. "*Him?*" she sniped.

Malajia snickered.

Mark walked in with the rest of Malajia's stuff and took it upstairs. "Thank you, Chocolate Daddy," she said to him as he headed back down the steps.

"Wow," Chasity muttered.

"No problem. I'll see y'all later," Mark said. "I hope there's a single room left in *my* house."

"You don't seem that pressed," Chasity observed.

"Nope. 'Cause I'll be over *here* most of the time anyway," he smiled at Malajia. "Isn't that right, Sugar walls?"

Malajia smiled and nodded.

Chasity's glossed lips curled in disgust. "Ugh."

As Mark left the house, Malajia let out a happy sigh. "Senior year light skin, we made it," she mused, giving Chasity a slight nudge.

"Yeah, let's hope we can make it *through* without bullshit," Chasity said.

"Well, we won't *now* 'cause you probably jinxed us," Malajia joked.

Chasity winced. "Shit, you're probably right."

Malajia giggled. She looked over at Chasity, then opened her mouth to speak.

"I'm fine," Chasity said, before Malajia could get a word out.

Malajia scrunched her face up. "*Damn*, mind reader."

"When you get quiet before you say something, it means you're gonna ask me something serious," Chasity explained. "I knew your question would be 'are you okay'."

Malajia stared at her. "You know me so well," she drew out.

"Unfortunately," Chasity teased; Malajia, playfully nudged her. "Glad you worked things out with Mark," she added after a moment.

Malajia smiled. "Really?"

"Yes…you two are weird as a couple but you seem happy, so…"

Malajia's big brown eyes became slits. "Always gotta throw a bitchy comment in, huh?" Chasity chuckled. "But thanks, I *am*…for the first time in a long time." Malajia smiled to herself. The past few weeks, Malajia's mood had been much lighter. Ever since she came clean to her family about her past abusive relationship with Tyrone, and opened up to Mark about her feelings and about her abortion, she felt like a weight had been lifted from her shoulders. The truth brought them even closer together, so much so that they finally took the next step in their relationship and slept together.

"Feels good, you know," Malajia added. She glanced at the blank space on the entertainment stand in front of them. "We need a TV down here," she scoffed. "Bring yours down."

Chasity shot Malajia a glare. "No," she replied bluntly.

"What are we gonna do about a TV?" Malajia harped.

"Emily said she's bringing *hers*," Chasity replied.

"Don't nobody wanna watch Emily's smedium ass TV," Malajia griped. "It looks like a tablet."

"*You're* one to talk, when yours got a fuckin' black stripe running across the top of it."

"That was my Dad's fault," Malajia barked, clapping her hands with each word. "His bad knee having ass dropped it when he was moving it one time," she argued. "Hence why I'm not bringing it down here. *Yours* got the good shit on it and it's the biggest."

"No, Malajia."

"So you gonna be stingy?" Malajia fussed.

"Yes," Chasity replied, resting her head against the cushions.

Malajia adjusted her position on the couch to face Chasity. "So you're *not* gonna bring your TV down here?" she pressed.

"Malajia, get your annoying ass away from me please," Chasity bit out, examining the black polish on her nails.

Malajia stared at her as she slowly folded her arms. "Okay," she relented. "You feeling strong today?" she asked, much to Chasity's confusion.

"What?"

"You been lifting weights or anything recently?" Malajia asked.

Chasity held a confused look on her pretty face. "What the fuck are you talking about?"

Malajia shrugged. "I guess I'll find out," she mumbled, before suddenly jumping on Chasity, grabbing her hands so she couldn't swing on her.

"Bitch are you crazy?!" Chasity yelled, struggling to get free. "Get off me." She almost got her hands free, but Malajia put her knee in Chasity's side as she straddled her.

"Bring your TV down!" Malajia hollered as Chasity screamed.

"I'm gonna fuck you up when I get up," Chasity fumed. She got her hand free again, then punched Malajia on the arm.

"Ouch!" Malajia shrieked. "Fine, you asked for it," she said, struggling to keep Chasity pinned. "Now I'm gonna give you all the details about me and Mark's sex life."

"Eww! I swear to God, you better not," Chasity protested, as Malajia laid on Chasity with all of her body weight.

"Too late," Malajia laughed. "You have *no* idea how big his penis is—"

"Shut up!" Chasity screamed, as Malajia kept talking. "Malajia, please I swear my stomach hurts."

"He can work the hell out of his tongue too, it's like a damn tornado. And when I ride him, I can feel every—"

Alex walked through the door just as Chasity started

screaming at the top of her lungs. Confused, she stopped and took in the awkward scene.

"What the hell is going on?" Alex asked. "Malajia, why are you sitting on Chaz like that?"

"Alex, Alex kill me please," Chasity begged as Malajia cracked up laughing. "She's telling me about Mark's dick."

"Ugh *why*?" Alex grimaced.

Malajia looked up at her. "You wanna hear about it too?"

Alex put her hand up. "No, I'm good, thank you," she scoffed. "Get off of her."

Chasity maneuvered her arm and was able to pinch Malajia's side.

"Ow! You always gotta go overboard," Malajia screeched, jumping off of Chasity. She lifted her red tank top and examined the red mark, which was prominent on her brown skin. "Childish *and* violent."

Chasity sat up and smoothed her hair back with her hands "It's on," she promised, hazel eyes burrowing through Malajia like a laser. "I'm gonna fuck Jason right on your damn bed."

Malajia shrugged. "Can I watch?" she asked.

Chasity rolled her eyes as she rubbed her side. "Heavy ass bitch," she grunted.

Malajia pointed her finger in Chasity's face and Chasity immediately slapped it down. "I'm *not* heavy," Malajia protested. "I'm damn near the same size as *your* ass."

Alex looked confused. "Malajia, just because you're slender in size, it doesn't mean that you're not heavy," she pointed out.

"Shut up Alex," Malajia spat. "You just mad 'cause you *look* as heavy as you actually *are*."

Alex shook her head. "First off, I *love* my *heaviness*," she boasted, giving her ample behind a smack. Malajia rolled her eyes. "Second…despite your ignorant comment, I actually missed you."

"Nobody cares," Malajia bluntly said.

Alex sucked her teeth, then flagged her with her hand. There was no point in continuing with the back and forth.

Sidra Howard bolted into the house, a hopeful look on her face. The girls locked eyes with her. That hope left Sidra's face as she came to a realization. "Shit!" she fumed, stomping her wedge-covered foot on the floor.

"Ahhh, you salty you gotta share a room," Malajia taunted, pointing at her.

Sidra folded her arms in a huff. "Stupid traffic," she grunted.

Chapter 2

Emily Harris flung some of her long, light brown, individual braids over her shoulder as she placed several folded items into her drawer. She'd arrived on campus nearly two hours ago and went to her new dwellings to find it empty. Already finding out from Alex via text that she was the last to arrive, she put her stuff in the double room and began to unpack.

Hearing a noise, she closed her dresser and made her way down the steps. Emily smiled as she saw the girls. "Where were you guys?" she asked, greeting them with hugs.

"At the grocery store," Alex informed, putting one of several plastic grocery bags on the kitchen counter. "We're going to have a little impromptu 'first day back on campus as a senior' cookout."

Alex dissolved into a fit of laugher as Chasity and Malajia stared at her with disgust.

"Nobody said all that," Chasity sneered, shaking her hand in Alex's direction.

"I know right," Malajia added. "You were told on the way home to shut the hell up."

Alex frowned as she watched Malajia flip her hair over her shoulder. "How many bundles did it take to do your weave?" she hissed.

"About as many packs of cheap ass fabric it took to

make that ugly ass shirt your big ass got on," Malajia shot back.

Alex flipped Malajia off; Chasity spat out the water that she was drinking with laughter. Alex shrieked as she felt droplets of water hit her on the face. "Chasity!" she exclaimed, wiping her face with her shirt.

Chasity couldn't even apologize, she was laughing so hard.

"How come every time you spit some damn water out, it's near my face?!" Alex barked.

"Oh shut up Alex, you should be grateful," Malajia mocked, examining her nails. "She was only trying to wash that shirt." She caught the nasty look from Alex. "Don't ever come for my weave," Malajia threw back, shaking her finger in Alex's face.

"So Sidra, you're stuck rooming with me this year, huh?" Emily cut in, trying to diffuse the tension.

Sidra smiled. "Sweetie, don't say it like it's a problem," she said. "It's gonna be cool. Welcome to my freakishly neat world."

"Fine with me," Emily shrugged.

Malajia tapped Emily on the arm, prompting her to look over; Malajia leaned in. "It's not gonna be cool at all," she muttered.

Emily snickered; Sidra on the other hand wasn't amused. "I heard you," Sidra hissed.

"I know," Malajia laughed, before rummaging through the bags.

"Loving the braids Em," Alex complimented.

Emily ran her hand over them. "Yeah?"

"Of course," Alex confirmed. She ran a hand through her thick, brown wavy shoulder length hair. "I might get some myself."

"Alex, ain't nobody gonna sit there and braid that nappy mess on your head," Malajia jeered, opening a bag of chips.

"I'm gonna punch her before the day is over, I swear," Alex hissed through clenched teeth.

Jason Adams barged through the door, carrying a brown paper bag. He walked into the kitchen and set it on the counter. "Here's y'all coolers," he announced, wiping his face with his hand. "That damn liquor store was crowded."

"Thanks babe," Chasity said, giving him a quick kiss on the lips.

Malajia skipped over to the bag and removed a few bottles. "Why did you get *this* nasty kind?" she scoffed, holding up a bottle of the orange liquid.

Jason pointed at her. "Malajia, don't start with me," he warned, "I had to damn near fight for *those*."

Malajia made a face. "Eww, *stank* you for going," she scoffed of his attitude.

Jason waved his hand at her dismissively.

Mark opened the door and stepped in, yet still focusing his attention outside. "David, how you gonna walk over without the electric grill dawg?!" he yelled out the door.

"*You* were supposed to bring it!" David Summers could be heard yelling from across the lot.

"*Obviously* I forgot it," Mark yelled back. Laughter erupted as loud profane-ridden rambles could be heard from David.

Josh Hampton moved around Mark as he walked into the house. "David is cussing you out man," he chuckled at Mark.

"Yeah? His ass is going back to get that grill, ain't he?" Mark returned, shutting the door behind him.

"Keep messing with him, he's gonna punch you in your face like he did *last* semester," Alex joked, rinsing a head of lettuce in the sink.

Mark narrowed his eyes at her, then slowly walked over. He pointed at Alex's shirt. "Alex, what's that?" he asked. When Alex looked down, he ran his finger up her face.

"Asshole!" she screeched, slapping him on the arm. "Don't touch my face, I don't know where your fingers been."

"They've only been in Malajia," he shot back, walking away.

"Oh my God!" Alex yelled, frantically wiping her face with her shirt.

Sidra frowned her face in disgust. "That's gross, Mark."

Malajia laughed. "Good one babe," she approved, giving Mark a high five.

"You two are fucking disgusting," Alex seethed.

"Ooh, she said the 'f' word, she's pissed," Chasity mocked.

"Kill it Chasity," Alex barked.

Chasity calmly opened a wine cooler. "Don't get mad at *me* 'cause you got *juices* on your lip," she shot back.

"Oh wow," Emily laughed.

Alex tossed her hands up in frustration as laughter resonated through the room. *I should've requested to live in a different house,* she fumed.

"Yo, who bought these cheap ass burgers?" Mark asked, flipping the patties on a small portable, electric grill; which sat on the girls' kitchen counter.

Sidra stopped stirring her potato salad and pointed at Alex, laughing in the process. "*She* did."

Alex sucked her teeth. "Look, we had a lot of stuff to buy for this thing. I had to budget in everything," she bit back. "Besides, there's nothing wrong with those burgers."

Mark pointed the spatula at the burgers on the grill. "Alex, *clearly* these things are melting!" he exclaimed.

Alex glanced over at the thin, flimsy patties sizzling on the grill and fought the urge to laugh. "Look, put some condiments and veggies on the thing and it won't taste any different than the more expensive ones."

Mark sucked his teeth as he went back to tending to the grill. "Paper thin ass burgers and shit," he muttered.

Sidra finished fussing with her salad, covered it with plastic wrap, then took it outside. Walking over to a plastic tablecloth-covered foldout table, she set it down with the other sides.

Malajia walked up to her. "Sidra, that better taste like your mom's salad," she warned, pointing to it. "I'm not fuckin' around with you."

"Girl, if you don't get away from me," Sidra ground out. "That pasta salad *you* made better taste like *your* mom's."

"Oh, I don't think you want that," Malajia laughed. "You remember her stuffing?"

Sidra scrunched her face up. "Eww, good point."

Josh opened a can of soda as he sat on a plastic foldout chair. "I'm sure the salad will taste just fine Sidra," he assured, taking a sip.

"Please, I'm not thinking about Malajia and her pointless comments," Sidra dismissed with a wave her hand. Sidra looked at Josh as she sat down next to him. "So…how's things?" she asked.

Josh looked at her. "Good."

"Yeah?" Sidra pressed. "You and Sarah talking more?"

Josh paused his sips and looked out ahead of him. Despite being estranged from his older sister for years, Josh, after some prompting from his friends and family, finally talked to her over summer break.

"Things are…progressing," he answered. "I mean, my guard isn't all the way down yet but…."

"But you're giving things a chance," Sidra finished

"Yeah," Josh replied.

Sidra reached out and touched his arm. "I'm proud of you," she smiled.

Josh returned her smile with one of his own. "Sidra, listen," he began. "About you and the guys paying my—"

"Nope, we're not discussing that," Sidra cut in, standing up.

"I can't say 'thank you'?" he asked, confused.

"You *have* and I told you that you don't have to keep saying it," she replied. "I don't want you to feel like you owe us anything."

Josh put his hands up. "Okay," he relented. When Mark revealed over summer break that he, Sidra, and David pulled money from their college funds to cover the three-thousand-dollar tuition payment that Sarah had stolen from him, Mark didn't do so to throw anything in Josh's face, or to make him feel bad. Mark just wanted to let Josh know that no matter what happened with his sister, that they would always be there for him and have his back. Josh was grateful, but being who he was, he also wanted to pay it back. Still, he would keep that to himself, for now.

Sidra gave him a nod, before tending to the table of food.

A few hours had passed, and the heat had waned just a bit, giving way to a light breeze. The food, which consisted of burgers, hotdogs, potato salad, pasta salad, corn on the cob, and tossed salad, drew a small crowd. Other returning students couldn't pass up an opportunity to get a meal, listen to some music, and hang out with the well-known clique of Paradise Valley University.

"Where did all these greedy ass people come from, and why is all the potato salad gone?" Malajia fussed, slamming the empty bowl that she held back down on the table.

"Malajia, that salad has been gone for like an hour already," Alex chuckled, fixing herself another hamburger.

"Right, I wish she'd shut up about it," Chasity added.

"Says the person who still has some on her plate," Malajia threw back, pointing to the food on Chasity's plate. "Just *eat* it already."

"Nah, I think I'll wait," Chasity taunted. "I like how angry it's making you."

"Fuck you," Malajia grunted, earning a snicker from Chasity. She then looked at Sidra who was busy throwing some soiled paper plates in a trash bag. "You," she barked, poking Sidra on the arm

"Ouch! Girl, what?" Sidra snapped, rubbing her arm.

"You were supposed to make some more earlier," Malajia ground out.

"No, I was *not*," Sidra argued, walking back into the

house. "I told you to leave me alone."

Malajia sucked her teeth at Sidra, then seeing a familiar person trot up to them, she sucked her teeth louder.

The guy grabbed a plate off the table. "Aye sexy, how about you fix me a burger?" he smiled.

"Fuck outta here Carl," Malajia hissed at the stocky, dark-skinned football linebacker; Carl just laughed in return.

"Fine, I'll do it myself," he relented as he began to prepare himself a plate.

Malajia smacked his hand down. "Don't touch our goddamn food," she barked. "You didn't contribute no money to this."

"Oh, come on Malajia, help a hungry brother out," Carl pleaded.

"You over here starting trouble already, Carl?" Jason asked, giving his teammate a handshake.

"Now when have you ever known me to start trouble?" Carl joked.

"Please," Chasity muttered.

"Damn, *still* ain't get no nicer, huh beautiful?" Carl jeered to Chasity.

"No but *you* damn sure got uglier…ugly," Chasity returned, earning a snicker from Jason.

Carl looked at Jason. "Really bro?"

"She's my woman, and it was funny," Jason shrugged.

Carl shook his head. "Anyway," he said, sitting his plate down. "You playing this season?"

Jason nodded. After suffering an injury at the hands of two players from a rival team last fall, Jason was ordered to sit out the rest of the season. Fully healed and rested, Jason was eager to get back to his beloved sport. "Yeah man, I'm looking forward to it."

"Yeah, the team is too," Carl informed. "We sucked without you."

"Now, I wouldn't say—" Jason began.

"*I* would, y'all sucked," Chasity cut in, sipping her soda.

Jason glanced at her. "Be nice babe."

"No," she refused. Jason shook his head.

Spotting someone in the distance, Carl smiled and waved for the guy to come over. "Ooh, I want y'all to meet my cousin," he said.

Malajia sucked her teeth. "Don't nobody wanna meet your damn family," she ground out. "And how you just gonna invite someone to a cookout that you didn't throw?"

Carl waved his hand at Malajia as the guy approached. "This is my cousin Will," he introduced. "He just moved up here from North Carolina."

Jason smiled and shook the man's hand as the rest of the introductions were made; Malajia and Chasity sized him up. They had to admit that the tall, dark-skinned man with the short cut and fine beard was attractive.

"You go to school here?" Malajia asked, handing him a burger.

Before Will could answer, Carl's mouth dropped open. "Damn Malajia, how come you fixed *him* one and not me?" he asked.

"'Cause I don't *like you!*" Malajia snapped, flicking her hand in his direction. The instant outburst caused Chasity to bust out laughing, as Jason put his hand over his face to avoid laughing in his teammate's stunned face.

Will chuckled a bit. "No, I don't go to school here. I just came to help my cousin move his stuff in."

Nice deep voice, Malajia thought. "Okay, okay," she said.

"I took time off of school to work," he added, before taking a bite of burger.

Before Malajia could interrogate him further, Emily came over holding a small container of salad. "Malajia, Sidra said take this salad and don't say nothing to her for the rest of the day," she informed, pushing some of her braids over her shoulder.

Malajia grabbed the bowl of potato salad and threw her head back. "Yeeeesssssss!" she groaned in satisfaction. "My little lying ponytail. She stashed some for me."

"No, that was *her* stash," Emily giggled. She was about to walk off, when she locked eyes with Will, who just smiled at her. Emily shyly looked down at the ground before returning his smile. *He's so cute,* she thought.

Malajia and Chasity caught the exchange. They glanced at each other, then Malajia nudged Chasity.

"Hey, Will," Chasity called, causing him to snap out of his trance.

"Huh?" he answered.

"This is Emily," she said, giving Emily a slight nudge.

Emily let out a nervous laugh as she stiffly put her hand out for Will to shake. "Hi...I'm Emily."

Chasity rolled her eyes and shook her head. "I *just* said that," Chasity huffed. Malajia snickered.

Will shook her hand. "Nice to meet you, I'm Will."

"Hi," Emily muttered, glancing back down to the ground.

Carl, noticing the shy interaction, patted his cousin on the shoulder. "Okay cuz, come on, before you drool all over the burgers," he teased, guiding him away.

Emily followed his progress, before the sound of her name being called snapped her back to reality. "What did you say?" she asked Malajia.

"Let me find out you think he's cute," Malajia teased.

Embarrassed, Emily pushed a braid behind her ear. "I don't know what you're talking about?" she denied.

Malajia pursed her full lips together. "Em, you know you light, we can tell when you're blushing," she teased.

"I'm gonna go get some food," Emily said, tuning back towards the house.

"The food is right here, crazy," Chasity reminded, pointing to the table.

Emily looked at the table full of food. "I knew that," she said before walking away.

Jason laughed. "Baby girl has a crush," he mused. "It's about time."

"Lucky for her, he looks a hell of a lot better than his

big-headed ass cousin," Malajia commented.

Chapter 3

"Whatchu' mean I gotta take Spanish 201!" Malajia exclaimed, eyeing the words on the paper in her hand.
"Miss Simmons, you are required to take three language classes for your major."
Malajia rolled her eyes at the head of the Business department. Malajia went to meet with him to register for her senior classes and to discuss her goals for the semester. She had no idea that she would need to take another Spanish class.
"Dr. Fairway, no disrespect, but I'm not taking that class," she refused, folding her arms. "I already took Spanish 101 *twice* and I don't even wanna *talk* about Spanish 102."
Dr. Fairway shook his head as he shuffled some papers on his desk. "I am aware of your struggles with your Spanish classes," he stated. Malajia sucked her teeth. "However, a requirement is a requirement. Now either you take Spanish or another foreign language," he offered, looking at a large book. "How about Chinese?"
"How about naw," Malajia answered, instantaneously.
"Excuse me?" Dr. Fairway frowned.
Malajia gave a nervous laugh. "Nothing... I'll take Spanish," she conceded, slinging her pocket book strap over her shoulder and rising from her seat.
Dr. Fairway proceeded to type on his laptop. "You're all set," he stated, shooting her a smile. "Good luck."

"Thanks," Malajia returned with a phony smile before walking out of the office. "You bald headed bastard," she mumbled to herself as she proceeded down the hallway. She pushed the door to the building open with force and let out a loud groan as she trotted down the steps. The other girls were waiting for her by the benches.

"What's *your* face all screwed up for?" Alex chuckled, noticing the disgusted look on Malajia's face.

Malajia shot Alex a death stare. "Alex, I told you earlier not to talk to me until you take those hot ass flare jeans off!" she erupted, earning a snicker from Sidra and Emily, and outright laughter from Chasity. "It's like a hundred degrees out this bitch and you got on all that denim."

Alex turned to Chasity, who was still laughing. "It's not that damn funny," she bit out.

Chasity immediately stopped laughing and glared at Alex. "Why you always gotta direct your damn attitude towards *me* when Malajia plays the shit outta you?" Chasity shot back, pushing some of her long, straight black hair behind her ears. "We *all* told you that it was too fuckin' hot to be wearing those thick ass jeans."

"Whatever Chasity," Alex spat, pushing some of her hair off of her forehead.

"Yeah whatever," Chasity returned.

Malajia busted out laughing at the look on Alex's face. "Ahhhh, Alex got cussed out over jeans and shit," she teased.

Alex shook her head. "Y'all make me sick," she fussed. "And I'm *not* hot."

"You *smell* hot," Malajia joked.

"Malajia, I swear to God—"

Sidra tried to contain her laughter as she put her arm out to block Alex from stepping towards the laughing Malajia. "Okay, okay, relax you two," she said, voice laced with amusement. "Malajia you didn't have to get smart though; she was only asking why you were looking mad."

"I just didn't like the way she asked me," Malajia fussed. "And I *hate* those jeans. She wears 'em like five times a week."

"Keep insulting my clothes, hear?" Alex warned, pointing at her.

Malajia flagged Alex with her hand. "Anyway, I just came from a meeting with the Business department head, and that damn fool had the nerve to tell me that I have to take Spanish 201," she groused as the girls began to amble through the campus.

Chasity looked baffled. "Aaaaand, you didn't know that you needed to take it *before* now?"

"Nope. I thought I only needed to fulfil *two* language classes," she sulked. "I hate this shit... Chaz can you tutor me this semester?" she asked, shooting Chasity a hopeful look.

"Fuck out my face Malajia," Chasity returned, nonchalantly.

"Seriously?!" Malajia exclaimed. "How you not gonna help me when *you've* gotten help for your Math before?"

"'Cause you *play* too damn much," Chasity argued, remembering the last time that she tried to tutor Malajia in Spanish during their sophomore year. Malajia's lack of focus and insistence on making up her own phrases that made no sense was not something that Chasity wanted to go through again. "If you remember, I quit helping you after like two tries."

"And that's why her butt had to repeat that class," Alex grunted.

Malajia shot a sideway glance at Alex, resisting the urge to fire off another smart remark. "I'm focused now," she promised. "Trust me, I'm not trying to repeat a class my last year here. If I don't graduate on time, everybody in my *family* will kick my black ass...even on down to my *baby* sister, and she's about to be five."

Chasity threw her head back in frustration. "Fine Malajia," she reluctantly agreed. "But I swear to God, play with my time and you and me are gonna fight."

"Wouldn't be the first time," Malajia joked, shrugging.

"*I* actually found out some interesting news about my senior curriculum today," Emily put in.

"I hope it consists of sewing Alex some new clothes," Malajia mocked, and ducked as a fed-up Alex tried to grab the strap of her tank top.

"No," Emily giggled. "I get to do student teaching at the local elementary school," she informed, excited. "It won't be until *next* semester, but I'm pretty excited about it."

"Oh that's so cool," Sidra smiled.

"Yeah, maybe you can find out that cute guy Will's number and call him to tell him about it," Malajia added, much to the confusion of Alex and Sidra, and the annoyance of Chasity.

"What kind of out-of-nowhere shit is that to say?" Chasity sneered. Malajia shrugged as Emily smiled shyly.

"Wait, who's Will?" Alex asked, curious.

"Football Carl's cousin," Malajia announced. "He came to our cookout the other day and Emily has a crush on him."

"Oh really?" Sidra mused, glancing at Emily; the girl shook her head in embarrassment. "It's about *time* you started liking someone."

"Wait, you mean *player* Carl?" Alex asked, putting her hand up. She wasn't too happy to hear of this. "Slept with half the cheerleading squad Carl? Tries to hit on every girl on the campus Carl?"

"You keep asking those dumb ass questions and you already *know* that's the Carl she's talking about," Chasity ground out.

Alex ignored Chasity's smart comment as she focused her attention on Emily. "Em, you make sure that his *cousin* isn't like that before you start talking to him. The apple doesn't fall far from the tree you know."

Emily just looked away as she pondered Alex's warning. She barely had a conversation with him, and now she was thinking if she even should.

Malajia sucked her teeth. "Only *your* greedy ass would bring up a damn apple," she snarled at Alex. "And why you always gotta go straight to the negative? You don't know that man and you're already spewing your man-hating garbage."

Alex took a deep breath. "Malajia, you're dancing on my last damn nerve, girl," she fumed.

"And?" Malajia shot back.

"Is this conversation even necessary?" Emily cut in. "I mean, I don't have his number to even *talk* to him. It was just a quick meet."

"Don't worry, *I'll* get the number for you," Malajia promised. "I'll ask Carl. All I gotta do is push my boobs up and he'll give up anything I ask for."

"You might have better luck with *Chaz* doing that," Sidra laughed. "He's always liked her more. I've caught him staring at her on *more* than one occasion."

"Ugh," Chasity grimaced at the thought

Malajia shrugged. "Don't make me no difference," she said. "Chaz, go put that shirt on that accentuates your boobs, and go ask Carl for his cousin's number for Emily."

Chasity looked at Malajia as if she was crazy. "I wish the fuck I *would*," she griped.

"Come on Chasity," Malajia pressed, putting a hand on Emily's shoulder. "Go bat those light eyes and fling that pretty weave-less hair at that corny man to help our shy friend out."

Chasity rolled her eyes, before looking at Emily who was staring at her, eyes hopeful. She let out a loud huff. "Fine, I'll ask," she relented. "But I won't be nice about it."

"We would expect nothing *less* from the Ice Queen," Malajia replied. "But just to be on the safe side," she added, eyeing Chasity's outfit of black shorts paired with a black and gold tank top. "Hike those shorts you got on, up some more."

Chasity flipped Malajia the finger.

"Yo, this back to campus night is wack bee," Mark complained later that evening from the balcony of the

Student Development Center.

"You just got here," Josh chuckled. "How are you complaining already?"

"'Cause man, they got those corny ass games downstairs," Mark griped. "Don't nobody wanna play no table tennis. We did that shit *last* semester."

Josh shook his head. "Then don't play it," he said, walking away. On his way down the steps to where the event was being held, he passed Malajia, who was heading up. "Mel, Mark is bitchin' again."

"What *else* is new?" she giggled, walking up to Mark. "What are you doing up here? Everybody is down on the main floor."

"It's dry as shit down there," Mark groused.

Malajia nodded. "I know right," she agreed. "We can go get the others and go skating at the rink near the mall."

Mark flagged her with his hand. "Naw."

Malajia looked around the room and pointed to a large covered pool table. "Ooh, look," she said, walking over. She pulled the cover off.

"What? You wanna do it on the pool table?" Mark asked, a huge smile plastered to his face.

Malajia narrowed her eyes at him. "No fool," she shot back. "Come on, let's play pool. You can show me what to do."

Mark let out a loud groan. "Fine," he huffed, walking over and grabbing a pool cue from a hook on a wall. "But you gotta *pay attention*. This takes skill."

"Just set it up," she spat, pointing to the triangle full of balls.

Mark quickly set the table up and positioned the cue in his hand for his first shot. "You gotta focus 'cause you wanna make sure you hit the ball in the right spot." He closed one eye. Malajia watched in anticipation as Mark was about to shoot.

"Come on dawg, you taking all long," Malajia urged, nudging him.

"Hey hush, you can't rush perfection woman," Mark boasted, before taking his shot. "Ooh!" he exclaimed as he lost his grip, pushing the white ball off the table, creating a large scratch on the table in the process.

Malajia's mouth dropped open as she looked at the scratch. "Oooooh," she gasped, pointing at him. Those tables looked expensive, and she knew that the school would not appreciate having it marked up.

Mark quickly set the pool cue on the table. "Come on, let's go get the others and go skating," he deflected, signaling for her to come with him.

"Oh *now* you wanna go skating?" she jeered, walking over to him.

"Come on, don't bring up old shit," he threw back, looking around to make sure no one was looking.

"Are you at *least* gonna put the cover back on the table?"

"Just shut up and keep walking," Mark urged, hurrying down the steps with Malajia trailing close behind.

"Whose idea was this?" Chasity asked, lacing up her skates.

"Malajia's," Mark answered, grabbing his drink off the counter.

Malajia shot him a glance. "Oh, you wanna throw this on *me*?" she shot back, pointing to herself. "*You're* the one who suggested we do it *after* you scratched the damn pool table at the SDC."

Mark quickly put his finger to his lips. "Shhh, you loud as shit," he panicked, frantically looking around the skating rink.

Mark and Malajia quickly rounded up the others, who were none too eager to leave the SDC, and headed to the skating rink off campus. Luckily for them it was after eight in the evening, which meant that the bar was open and the good music was playing.

"Boy, ain't nobody paying you no mind in here,"

Malajia scoffed, grabbing his drink from him and taking a sip.

Sidra wobbled over to them on her skates. "I hate skates," she complained, grabbing onto Chasity for support. "Suddenly my ice-skating fiasco is coming back to me."

"Girl move, I'm trying not to fall myself," Chasity hissed, nudging Sidra off of her.

Malajia laughed at the sight of Sidra reaching for Mark. "Sidra, stop being dramatic," she teased.

"Leave me alone Malajia," Sidra huffed. "I hate this shit. I feel like I'm not in control when I wear skates... I *hate* not being in control."

"Yes, we know," Malajia ground out, skating around Sidra with ease. She looked over at Chasity, who was trying to balance herself on the skates. "You got control issues too?"

"No bitch, I just don't know how to skate," Chasity spat.

"Chaz, stalling is not gonna get you out of skating," Jason said, voice filled with amusement as he skated up to her.

Chasity let out a loud sigh. "Yes, I know," she said, picking up her drink and finishing it. "Maybe if I'm drunk enough, I won't feel the pain when I bust my ass on this floor," she conceded, before allowing herself to be led away by Jason.

"Last one to the floor buys a round of drinks," Mark quickly proposed, before making a dash for the floor in his skates. Before anybody could respond, Mark stumbled in an effort to not collide with another skater, and went falling to the floor.

"Are you fuckin' *kidding* me?" Malajia snapped, annoyed at the sight of Mark sprawled out on the floor.

"I dropped my drink!" Mark yelled.

"That's *your* man," Alex teased.

"Don't remind me," Malajia sneered, skating off.

"Baby, help me up," Mark requested, holding his hand out.

"I don't know you right now," Malajia refused, skating by him.

Sidra groaned and tiptoed off to the side, after trying for the past fifteen minutes to skate without falling. "I quit," she ground out, sitting on a step.

"You corny Sidra," Malajia taunted, skating past her. Malajia was approaching Chasity, who seemed to be getting the hang of the skates. "Get it Parker," she encouraged, skating next to her.

"Don't talk to me, I'm trying to focus," Chasity hissed at her.

Malajia listened as a new song began to play through the rink along with an announcement over the loud speaker that only ladies should be skating through the song. "Ooh, this is my song! Come on, let's skate fast," she said, grabbing Chasity's arm and pulling her along.

"Malajia, I swear to God!" Chasity screamed as she was being pulled.

Alex was gliding with ease alongside Emily, when she heard Malajia's mouth behind her.

"Alex, you better move," Malajia warned as she and Chasity skated closer.

Alex turned around. "Girl, you better skate around me," she threw back.

"I said move!" Malajia yelled. When Alex didn't listen, Malajia let go of Chasity's arm and they parted to pass Alex and Emily. As Chasity passed, she felt herself wobble and grabbed onto Emily for support.

"Don't hurt yourself," Emily teased.

"Funny, I fall, you fall," Chasity retorted as she held on.

Alex, frazzled by the close encounter from Malajia skating next to her, wobbled and fell. As she slid across the floor, she bumped into Malajia, who was attempting to skate backwards. The impact sent Malajia falling on top of Alex.

"Why your big ass gotta slide near *me*?!" Malajia

hollered, trying to roll off Alex.

"This is *your* fault," Alex fumed, nudging Malajia off of her. "*You* made me fall."

"*How?*" Malajia argued. "I didn't even *touch* you. I skated *around* your goofy ass. And why do you *still* have those hot ass *jeans* on?"

As Malajia and Alex continued their argument, Emily and Chasity who were making their way back around the rink for another lap, approached.

"Y'all look stupid," Chasity laughed at the sight of the two girls laying on the floor smacking each other.

"She always falling and shit," Malajia complained, trying to stand up.

"Shut the hell up, Malajia," Alex seethed.

"Come on, this is supposed to be fun," Emily reminded, reaching her hand out for Alex to grab. "Try not to kill each other."

"Move, moooooovvvvveeee!" they heard Sidra scream. Before anybody could react, Sidra came plowing into Chasity and Emily at top speed, sending both girls falling into Malajia and Alex, who were just rising from their initial spill. Sidra landed in a heap on top of them.

"Sidra, I thought your whining ass quit skating," Chasity barked, shoving Sidra off of her.

"I wanted to try one more time," Sidra explained, flicking her long-curled brown hair over her shoulder.

"Y'all suck!" Mark yelled from the sidelines.

Song now over, the announcer informed the crowd that it was now time for the ladies to leave the floor and for the guys to skate.

"Let us show you how it's done," Josh teased as he and the other guys approached the floor. The girls sat at a nearby table to watch.

"Y'all gonna bust y'all asses too," Chasity bit out.

"I know right," Malajia chimed in. "Don't talk shit until the song is over *Joshua.*"

Josh made a face at them as he began skating.

Mark, who was familiar with the popular rap song, began rapping along with the lyrics. He was loud as usual.

"Those aren't even the right words," Jason laughed as he skated past him.

"Stop hatin' dawg," Mark threw back, dancing around the rink, "I'm killin' it," he boasted.

David shook his head as he glided across the floor. A familiar face caught his attention; he smiled as he noticed the short, brown-skinned, curvy woman standing off near the bar with some friends. *Her*, he thought. Losing focus, he stumbled forward. He tried to catch his balance, but his efforts were in vain. David heard laughter as he went tumbling to the floor.

"Ahhh, David bust his ass!" Mark laughed from across the room.

David, ignoring Mark's outburst, pushed his crooked glasses up on his nose and craned his neck to see if he still saw her. His hopeful face fell when he realized that she was gone.

"You cool man?" Jason asked, stopping in front of David. He reached a hand down to help him.

David groaned as he was helped to his feet. "I'll live," he concluded, rubbing his lower back.

Once the announcer stated that it was time for everyone to get back on the floor, a new song began playing, much to Mark's delight. "Yoooo, they jammin' in here tonight," he mused, trying to dance on his skates. While trying to get the move down, he tripped over his own foot and fell.

Malajia smacked her forehead with her hand. "I *can't* with him," she groaned to Sidra. "He is so freakin' embarrassing."

Sidra giggled. "Well, he's *your* responsibility now."

Malajia rolled her eyes as she stood up from her seat. "Can y'all stop reminding me? Shit," she jeered, slamming her hand on the table.

"Baby!" Mark yelled for Malajia. "Come help me up."

Malajia put her hand over her face and shook her head.

Sidra laughed.

Chapter 4

Alex stretched her neck from side to side as she examined the textbooks on the shelves of the campus bookstore. "Why are these damn books so expensive?" Alex asked aloud, eyeing the price of the African History textbook in front of her. Letting out a heavy sigh, she grabbed the book. "No reason in complaining, I still have to get it," she muttered.

Turning to make her way to the cashier, she nearly bumped into someone. "Oh my God, I'm so sorry," she panicked, putting a hand up.

"It's okay," the person reassured her.

Alex smiled when she saw who it was. "Stacey," she beamed, giving her a hug.

Stacey Addison returned Alex's smile with a small one of her own as the two women embraced. Alex pulled away and gave her high school friend a once over. Her curvy frame had filled out a bit more since the last time Alex saw her. "Looking good sis," Alex mused, adjusting her book bag on her shoulder. "Loving the hair by the way."

Stacey giggled as she pushed some of her long purple ombre colored hair over her shoulders. The color looked nice against her light brown skin. "Thanks," she replied. "I figured I'll get my color experiments out of the way while I'm in school."

Alex nodded. "I feel like I haven't seen you in so long."

"Well, you *haven't*," Stacey said, reaching for a textbook. "I think the last time we hung out together on campus was...my freshman year."

Alex thought for a moment. "My God, has it been *that* long?"

Stacey nodded slightly. "I'm a Junior now."

Alex looked down at the floor. "Wow..." she sighed. "I take full blame," she admitted. "I've just been so caught up with—"

"Your other friends," Stacey finished; she chuckled seeing the guilty look on Alex's face. "Alex, don't worry, I'm not mad at you. I've made some new friends here too, so I get it."

"No, we've been friends a long time. We should *still* hang out with each other," Alex said.

Stacey nodded. "Well...when you get some time, hit me up," she proposed, making her way to another aisle. "My cell number is still the same."

"I will," Alex promised, smiling.

"Oh, and tell the other girls I said hey," Stacey smiled, before disappearing around the corner.

Alex's smile faded. Despite what Stacey said, she felt guilty for not spending any time with her friend. Sighing again, Alex made her way up to the cashier to pay for her book.

"Sidra, please kill me," Chasity whined as she rolled around on Sidra's bed.

Sidra sat at her desk, laughing at the sight. "Girl, what is wrong with you?" she asked, thumbing through her textbook.

Chasity sat up on the bed and ran her hand through her disheveled hair. "I have been trying to tutor that *idiot* for the past two hours," she complained.

"Oh God. I almost forgot that you agreed to tutor Malajia in Spanish," Sidra remembered. "Damn, she's acting up already? Classes haven't even been in session a full *week* yet."

Chasity put her hand up. "She's so damn stupid. I can't deal—" She paused as the door opened and Malajia walked in, textbook in hand.

"Why did you leave, Chaz?" Malajia asked, shocked.

"Get the hell away from me, Malajia," Chasity hissed.

Malajia, put her hand on her hip. "You're a rude bitch," she sneered. "I'm tryna learn and shit and you just get up and walk out?"

"You're not trying to learn *shit*," Chasity barked. "You're trying to get on my fuckin' nerves."

"How so?" Malajia questioned.

Chasity looked like she wanted to scream. "When I told you to say 'take me to the store' in Spanish, what did you say?" she asked, drawing her words out slowly.

Malajia tried not to laugh. "I don't see what the problem was."

"What did you say?!" Chasity yelled, startling Malajia.

Malajia held a straight face. "I said, 'takea me toda el storeo."

Sidra busted out laughing as Chasity held an angry gaze. "And you thought that was an appropriate answer?" Chasity seethed.

"Malajia, come on," Sidra laughed as Malajia shrugged. "That is basic stuff. How did you pass Spanish 101 *and* 102?"

"I have *no* idea," Malajia admitted, voice filled with amusement. She looked at Chasity who just shook her head. "Come on Chaz, I have a quiz coming up soon. Help me, I'll be serious this time."

"I'm not for this bullshit," Chasity refused, standing up. "I have my own quiz to study for and a damn website to create, so fuck you and your Spanish."

"No seriously, I was paying attention," Malajia insisted, blocking the door. "Ask me a question."

Chasity rubbed her face before looking at Malajia. "Fine,

how do you say 'can I have change for a dollar?' in Spanish?"

Malajia sucked her teeth. "Oh foreal?" she scoffed, then put her hand up in surrender as Chasity went to walk out of the room. "Okay okay," she relented, looking at her textbook. "Um okay…I would say…fuckayou el bitcho," she joked, then busted out laughing as an angry Chasity pushed her aside and stormed out.

"Malajia, she's gonna kill you," Sidra chortled.

"No wait, Chaz I'm just playing!" Malajia yelled after her.

"Fuck you Malajia!" Chasity shouted back.

"Okay listen, it's 'cana I hava el quarto quartatoes.'" Malajia laughed again when she heard Chasity's door slam.

"Go ahead and fail," Sidra warned.

"I ain't failing *shit*," Malajia confidentially stated, walking out the room.

Sidra shook her head, then sighed as she turned on her laptop. "Might as well get started on my paper," she said to herself. As her fingernails tapped on the letter keys, her cell phone rang. Eyeing the name on the caller ID, her grey eyes lit up as she answered. "Hi James," she crooned into the phone.

"Good afternoon sweetheart," James Grant returned. "How is everything going so far? How are your classes?"

Sidra smiled. She was glad to hear her boyfriend's voice. It'd been almost a year since they decided to just stop talking and give a relationship a go. Even though they didn't see as much of each other as Sidra would like—due to him working as a lawyer in Washington DC—she spoke to him often. And even though he was seven years her senior, Sidra felt that she could relate to him. "Things are fine," she answered. "Except for the fact that I have a paper due already… A *small* one, but still a damn paper nonetheless."

A deep chuckle came through the phone. "Yeah, I remember those paper days," he mused. "Hell, I *still* write a ton in my line of work."

"Yeah, I'm sure," Sidra returned, leaning back in her seat. "So I guess I better stop whining, huh?"

"You're not whining, sweetheart," James placated.

Sidra smiled again. "I really like when you call me that."

"Then I'll make sure to do it more often," James crooned.

Sidra blushed. "When am I going to see you?"

"*About* that," he began. "I wanted to run something by you."

"Oh yeah? What's that?" Sidra asked, curious.

"Well, with your birthday coming up, I thought that it would be a good idea to go away together," he suggested. "Just a nice little weekend getaway."

Sidra was silent as she held a blank expression on her face. "Oh...okay," she finally sputtered.

"You don't sound too enthusiastic about that," he said, picking up on her hesitation.

"Oh no, that's not it," she assured, nervously tapping her fingers on her desk. "Something on my laptop caught my attention," she lied. "So umm...where did you have in mind?"

"I was thinking that I'd take you to New York," he revealed. "We can go see a play, go to dinner, do some sightseeing and some shopping. Everything is on me of course."

Sidra could register his smile through the phone. "That sounds nice," she said.

"Good to hear. Well, I have to get going, but I'll call you later," he said.

"Okay," she mumbled.

"Bye sweetheart."

"Bye." Sidra's mind raced once she hung up. *A weekend trip? Together? Alone?* were the questions that screamed in her head. She'd never spent the night alone with a man that she considered a boyfriend, let alone an entire weekend. She knew what he was going to expect, and she wasn't sure if she was ready for it.

She put her head on her desk. "Ugh, as if I'm not stressed enough," she groaned to herself.

Emily looked at her watch as she made a mad dash down the library steps. "Crap, I can't believe I lost track of time like that," she complained, jogging down the path.

Emily had been in the library with her study group for over two hours. She almost forgot that she was supposed to meet her friends so that they could go to a movie. As she darted through the gates of the Winfield houses, she was stopped suddenly by the sound of Carl calling her name.

She spun around. "Huh?" she panted.

Carl chuckled as he approached her. "In a rush?"

"Uh yeah, kind of," Emily giggled, fanning herself with her hand. "What's going on?"

"Well, I tried to give your girl my cousin's number for you a few days ago," he revealed.

Emily looked embarrassed. She'd almost forgotten that Chasity was supposed to get Will's phone number for her. She just figured that she never got around to it. "Oh?" was all that she could say.

"Yeah and she said... Let me see if I can remember the exact words," Carl began, tapping his cheek with his finger in an effort to remember. "Oh yeah she said, 'fuck that phone number, if he wants to talk to Emily, then he needs to call *her*.'"

Emily snickered. "Yeah, that sounds like Chasity alright."

"I asked him if he wanted your number and he said yes... So I'm here to get your number for him."

Emily's eyes widened with surprise. "He wants to call me?"

"Yes," Carl confirmed. "But after this, no more go-betweens. You two are on your own."

Emily nodded, then grabbed a piece of paper from her notebook and quickly jotted down her cell phone number.

She smiled brightly as she handed Carl the paper.

"Cool, see ya later," he said. "Oh and can you *please* tell Malajia to stop calling me 'big head ass Carl' every time she sees me? It's old now."

"Yeah I don't think I can stop her," Emily chortled.

Carl sighed. "It was worth a try," he sulked, walking off.

Emily let out a long happy sigh as she made her way to the house. Upon opening the door, she heard chatter. "Hey ladies," she greeted, shutting the door behind her.

Malajia quickly pointed to Alex. "Emily, Alex ate all the hot chips!" she yelled, much to Alex's irritation.

"What the hell are you *talking* about?" Alex frowned. "We didn't even *have* any hot chips."

"Oh, my bad," Malajia laughed.

Alex shook her head and flagged her with her hand. "Over you," she grumbled, grabbing a bottle of juice out of the refrigerator.

"Guess what?" Emily beamed, setting her book bag on the floor. "I just gave Carl my number to give to Will."

Chasity shook her head in amusement at Emily's giddiness. "You're acting real corny right now," she teased.

"Oh, come on, be nice Chasity," Emily returned, amused. "I'm just excited that he wants to talk to me."

"Why are you surprised that he *would*?" Sidra wondered. "Do you have any idea how beautiful you are?"

Glancing at the ground, Emily pushed some braids over her shoulder. "To be honest, no not really," she admitted. "…still working on that confidence thing."

"Well, you better work on it fast," Malajia urged, flopping down on the couch. "'Cause men can smell insecurities a mile away. Ignorant ass *boys* feed off it."

Emily just stood there, pondering what was just said.

"Emily, remember what I said, just make sure he's a good guy before you get serious with him," Alex warned.

Emily rolled her eyes slightly. *Yes, I know that Alex, God.* "I hear you," she replied, sitting on the arm of the accent chair.

"Alex, who said she wants to get serious with him?" Chasity chimed in, annoyed by Alex's negativity. "*Maybe* she just wants a fuck buddy," she mocked.

Emily put her hands over her face in embarrassment, as Alex shot Chasity a glare.

"I'm sure that Emily doesn't just want a *sex* buddy," Alex groused. "You need to think before you open your damn mouth and stop being so damn vulgar. You don't have to say the 'f' word all the damn time... You're too rich not to have class."

Chasity stared at Alex for several seconds, then her lips curled into a sly smile. "Would you look at that? The girl who sucked some guy who's *not* her boyfriend's *dick*, is telling *me* that I have no class," she taunted.

"Oh wow," Sidra muttered as Emily winced at the harsh words.

Alex's eyes widened in shock as Malajia busted out laughing. "Oooh Alex, maybe you should think before you battle *that* one," Malajia laughed, pointing to Chasity.

Sidra shook her head. "I really hope that you two don't end up killing each other before we graduate," she said.

"Sorry Sidra, I can't make any promises," Alex fumed, staring Chasity down.

"How can you talk with Eric's dick in your mouth?" Chasity threw back, earning a loud scream from Malajia.

"*Seriously* Malajia?! It wasn't funny," Alex exclaimed at the sight of Malajia flopping around in her seat.

"It was *hilarious*!" Malajia howled.

Emily put her hand up as she rose from her seat. "Okay, everybody calm down," she softly suggested.

"I'm *quite* calm actually," Chasity assured, nonchalant.

Alex, on the other hand, was still annoyed. "I'm fine Em," she bit out.

"I'm gonna go freshen up so we can go to this movie," Emily said, making her way up the steps.

Chapter 5

"It's about time y'all showed up," Mark griped, making room on a large blanket on the grass.

"Oh shut up. The movie didn't even start yet," Malajia threw back, sitting down next to him. The warm, summer evening proved to be ideal for the outdoor movie event on campus. The front of the Student Development Center was the perfect location for the oversized projection screen.

"Damn, everybody and their mother is out here tonight," Chasity commented, trying to get comfortable on the blanket.

"Did y'all bring the snacks?" Josh asked, craning his neck to see if he saw any bags in the girls' hands.

"Um no, *you guys* were supposed to bring the snacks," Sidra reminded.

"No, the *deal* was that *we* were supposed to hold the spots while you girls get the snacks." Mark contradicted.

"Oh my God, does it *matter*? They have popcorn out here, so let's just eat *that*," Alex huffed, fed up with the pointless bickering. Truth was, she wasn't really in the mood to be watching a movie. She was still highly annoyed with Chasity from earlier.

David hopped up from the ground and dusted off his jeans. "I'll go grab some bags," he announced.

"You might as well grab something to drink too, 'cause you know that popcorn is gonna be dry," Malajia said to him.

"I won't be able to carry all of that," David mumbled, walking off in the direction of the outdoor popcorn stand. He sighed when he saw the long line. *I knew I should have come over here earlier*, he thought as he ambled over and stood behind the last person.

He adjusted his glasses on his face as he glanced over to where his friends were sitting. Turning back around, he was bumped by a guy who was sprinting past him. The bump sent him colliding into the woman who stood in front of him. "Seriously dude?!" he hollered at the culprit.

"My fault bruh!" the guy hollered over his shoulder, continuing on his way.

David cursed to himself, then turned to face the person he bumped into. "I'm so sorry," he said to her. His eyes widened when she faced him.

"It's okay, I know it wasn't your fault," she smiled.

David stared at her. This was the second time that he had seen her in a week. The same woman that he was instantly attracted to last semester, the one who he never worked up the nerve to speak to.

Noticing the blank expression on his face, she giggled. With a warm smile, she held out her hand. "Hi, I'm Nicole," she introduced.

David eagerly but gently shook her hand. "I'm David," he smiled.

"Nice to meet you David," she returned, pushing some of her shoulder length brown hair twists away from her face. "Waiting on this popcorn too huh?"

"Yeah," he shyly answered. *She's even more beautiful up close,* he thought as he ran his hand over the back of his neck. Her smooth brown skin, bright smile, and curvy figure were incredible. Her height was perfect to him; she came up to his chest. He always had a thing for shorter women. He remembered being intrigued with her ever since he first saw her, when they were out celebrating Chasity's birthday at a lounge last semester. He couldn't stop thinking about her after that.

Stop staring at her you idiot, he scolded himself.

"Um…so have you seen this movie before?" he sputtered.

"No, this will be my first time."

"Yeah me too… I'm here with my friends," he replied, pointing in their direction. "They're over there."

Nicole craned her neck to see. "Oh yeah, I see you around… You hang out with them a lot," she mused.

"Yeah…" he pushed his glasses up on his nose. "So um…are *you* here with anybody?" he hesitantly asked. "'Cause if you aren't, then maybe you can….um…sit with *us*," he suggested, voice full of hope. When she didn't respond right away, he panicked. "I mean you don't *have* to, I just wasn't sure if—"

Nicole, noticing the embarrassment on his face, put her hand on his arm. "No, no it's not that I don't *want* to," she assured. "It's just that I'm here with someone already and it would be rude to leave them."

David nodded as he came to a realization. He remembered that Mark told him last semester that she had a boyfriend. "Oh, I'm sorry. I didn't realize that you had a boyfriend," he stammered. "I meant no disrespect."

Nicole shook her head. "No, David—"

"I'm gonna get back to my friends," he said, cutting her off. "It was nice to finally meet you Nicole," he added before hurrying off.

She followed his progress with his eyes. "Nice to meet you too, David," she quietly said to herself.

David quickly made his way back to his spot on the grass and plopped down, then put his head in his hands.

"Yo man, where's the popcorn?" Mark asked, noticing David's empty hands.

"I don't have it," he answered, voice muffled by his hands.

"Clearly," Sidra teased. "Are you okay?"

"Somebody *please* go get some food, I'm starving," Mark complained before David could answer.

"Boy shut up," Chasity hissed.

Mark pointed at her. "Jason, tame your girl," he ordered.

Chasity sucked her teeth as Jason smirked. "I'll tame mine, when you tame *yours*," he shot back.

Mark quickly looked at Malajia, who shot him a warning look. "Boy, I'll punch you in your Adam's apple. You ain't taming shit over *here*," she ground out.

Mark flagged her with his hand.

"David, what's wrong?" Sidra pressed, getting back to the original topic.

David lifted his head up and rested his arms on his knees. "Oh nothing, I just made myself look like a corny, thirsty dude in front of one of the most beautiful women on this campus," he revealed, voice dripping with sarcasm.

"Who's more beautiful than *me*?" Malajia questioned. "...Oh and Chasity...and maybe Sidra... Emily you cute too."

David rolled his eyes as Sidra frowned in confusion. "*First* of all, you are *not* every damn man's type," Sidra snarled.

"Never said that, next," Malajia countered.

"*Second*," Sidra sniped, making a face. "You left out Alex, and *third* what do you mean *maybe* me?"

Malajia laughed. "I'm just messing with you Sid, with your sexy self."

Sidra stared at Malajia, amused.

"And Alex's clothes trump her looks," Malajia joked, flinging hair over her shoulder.

Alex let out a huff, then backhanded Malajia on the arm.

"Sike naw," Malajia chortled. "You know you cute Alex. Your looks are very...hobo-ish."

Alex sucked her teeth then stood up; she was tired of Malajia's running commentary. "I'm gonna go get the popcorn," she announced, storming off.

"You play too much, Malajia," Sidra scolded.

Malajia tossed her head back and let out a loud sigh. "You *all* know this, yet you *still* get in your feelings," she huffed.

David shook his head at the banter. "Anyway," he

sighed. "I *finally* got a chance to talk to her and I sounded like an idiot." He plucked a piece of grass from the lawn. "I forgot that she has a boyfriend."

"Who?" Malajia asked.

"The girl that was in Chasity's computer class last semester…Nicole," he answered.

"Oh," Sidra said, voice full of sympathy. "I'm sorry sweetie." She gave his hand a pat.

David let out a sigh. "Yeah, thanks."

"No offense," Mark began after a moment of silence. "But I'm not tryna hear David bitchin' all night," he jeered.

David pulled up a few more blades of grass and tossed the blades at Mark. "Shut up," he bit out.

"Yeah, kill the grass, that's nice," Mark sarcastically spat, brushing the grass from his t-shirt.

A collective sigh was met when the credits began to roll on the screen over an hour and a half later. "Who picked that wack ass movie?" Chasity asked, stretching.

"Somebody who thought that bullshit was gonna be funny," Malajia answered, brushing popcorn kernels from her skirt.

"What do y'all wanna do now?" Mark asked, propping himself up on his elbows.

Josh looked at his watch then gasped. "Ooh!"

"What's wrong with *you*?" Sidra chuckled, looking over at him.

"I was supposed to call December back before the movie started," he stated, jumping up.

"Damn Josh, you *just now* remembering?" Malajia chortled. "That's triflin'."

"I know," Josh sighed. "Now I gotta go show up at her room with a peace offering."

Mark sucked his teeth. "Man, just give her the D, she'll be a'ight," he joked.

Josh couldn't help but let out a laugh. "Gotta go," he

said, then hurried off.

David rose to his feet, exhaling loudly in the process. "I guess I'll take my salty self back to my room."

"David, don't feel bad," Sidra consoled, standing up along with the others. "There will be other girls,"

David just shrugged as he shoved his hands in to his jeans pocket.

"Come on David, I got something that'll take your mind off your lonely ass problems," Mark assured.

"Oh yeah?" David spat. "And what would *that* be?"

Mark stretched his neck from side to side. "Tag," he blurted out, touching Chasity's shoulder then running off. "Chaz you're it!"

"What the hell?" Chasity belted out, watching her friends running away, laughing. "I'm not playing tag, you morons!" When nobody stopped running, she let out a loud sigh. "Shit," she huffed, taking off running after them.

Chasity knew she would have no problem catching up to them; she was a fast runner. Quickening her pace, she focused on Malajia, who was struggling to run in her high-heeled sandals.

"Keep the pace, keep the pace," Malajia coached herself. Glancing behind her, she saw Chasity's hasty approach. "Oh shit!" she screeched, trying to run faster. Seeing people in her way she yelled, "Move, mooooove!"

Chasity slapped Malajia on her back. "You're it," she announced, running past.

"You didn't have to slap me that damn hard!" Malajia yelled after her.

"I know," Chasity laughed.

Malajia ran along the path and through the gates of the Winfield houses. When she saw her friends take off behind other houses, she stopped running and stomped her foot on the ground. "No, to hell with that," she barked, causing everyone to stop.

"Stop trying to get out of tagging somebody, Malajia," Alex chided, putting her hands on her voluptuous hips.

Malajia sucked her teeth. "Alex, shut your slow running ass up," she hurled, annoyed.

"How are you calling *me* slow and *you're* the one who got caught first?" Alex threw back.

"That's not the point—" Malajia pinched the bridge of her nose in an effort to calm herself down. "Look, this is a big ass complex. Nobody is gonna be running around these damn houses chasing y'all all night. So we need to stay between *our* two houses."

"Does that include the back?" David asked.

"Yes," Malajia agreed, placing her hands on her hips.

"You mean where that duck pond is?" Jason asked, pointing in that direction.

Malajia nodded. "Yup, if you fall in it that's on you."

Chasity looked at her watch. "Are we done talking?" she bit out.

Malajia ran her hands over her hair as she slowly walked up to the group, who was clustered together. "No...not yet," she said.

"She's lying, she's tryna cheat. Run," Mark warned.

Malajia watched as the group took off running again. "Mark, shut the hell up sometimes!" she shouted at him.

Malajia ran behind Sidra and Emily, who were making their way behind their house. When Sidra saw that Malajia was closing in on them, she purposely bumped into Emily, causing her to stumble and allowing Malajia to tag her.

"You're it," Malajia laughed, running off.

"Sidra!" Emily exclaimed, shocked.

"Sorry, everyone for themselves," Sidra threw over her shoulder, turning a corner.

"Clearly," Emily sniped. She looked around as she pulled her braids into a ponytail. She walked around the property. Seeing a shadow illuminated by the moonlit sky, she darted behind her house to the grassy area to find Chasity, Jason, Mark, David, and Malajia trying to creep around the other side of the house.

"I can see you guys, you know," Emily announced,

running.

"Shit! Jason and Chasity get y'all bright asses away from us, all illuminating the group and shit," Malajia joked, trotting away.

Ignoring Malajia's comment, Chasity took off running towards the pond with Jason and David. As Emily chased them, Chasity and Jason made their way around the pond and ran back toward the house. David wasn't so lucky; he slipped on some wet grass and slid down into the shallow pond. "Damn it!" he yelped as laughter erupted around him.

"Ahhh! David fell in the pond," Mark laughed.

"Are you okay, David?" Emily asked, running up to him.

David let out a loud groan as he struggled to get up. "Well—"

Emily tagged him. "That's nice, you're it," she giggled, darting away.

David sucked his teeth as he stood up from the pond. "I just bought these sneakers," he fumed, stepping onto the grass.

"Stop bitchin'." Mark mocked.

David opened his mouth to respond; however, hearing splashing in the pond, he turned around. Seeing several ducks wadding their way towards him, he frowned. "The hell?"

"David disturbed the ducks," Malajia announced, watching David back away from the pond. "They're turning on him."

"I'm sorry! I'm sorry," David yelped, jogging away.

Malajia laughed as she watched David round the corner toward the front of the house. Hearing a scream, Malajia turned to find Emily running; there was a goose chasing after her. "Emily what did you do to the damn bird?" Malajia asked, confused.

"I bumped into it when I was trying to hide," Emily panicked.

Malajia, trying to focus in the dark, noticed that the goose stopped moving.

"Malajia, I think it sees you," Mark's voice warned.

Malajia saw it waddling in her direction. "Shit! Mark come help me," she demanded, backing up.

"Naw bruh," Mark refused.

"Asshole," Malajia fumed. Hearing commotion around the corner, she made her way around. Seeing that the goose was no longer after her, she stopped running. "Emily, what the hell?" she huffed, walking over to her.

"I didn't know it lived back there," Emily panted, fanning herself. "Oh, and Mark's it."

Malajia looked at Mark. "*How?*"

Jason busted out laughed. "He tripped over a shrub and David tagged him."

"I thought it was a duck," Mark defended.

"Looked *nothing* like one," Chasity ground out.

"Shut *up*, Chasity," Mark spat at her.

"I wish it *was* a duck and that it would've bitten your ignorant ass," Malajia hissed. "You were gonna let the goose eat me and shit."

"I would've missed you though," Mark jeered.

Malajia sucked her teeth.

Watching everybody take off again, Mark ran his hands over his face and sighed, then started sprinting after them.

He chased them through the lot, and in between the houses. Seeing that his sneaker was untied, he bent down to tie it, only to look up and see them running into the girls' house. "Hey! Y'all can't run in the house, that's not fair," he barked.

"Should've said that in the beginning," Jason taunted, shutting the door.

Mark walked up to the house and stared at his friends through the window; they were staring back, taunting him.

"Open the goddamn door, you cheating jackasses," he fumed, banging on the door. When they wouldn't comply, Mark sucked his teeth. Then they started making faces at him. He turned around to find Josh walking through the gates. Mark smiled slyly as he walked toward him. "Yo Josh, what you doing back so soon?"

Josh looked up from his phone. "December put me out. She has a test to study—" He paused, then frowned when he noticed the others gesturing to him from the window.

Mark continued his stride. "Damn, that's a shame," he said, feigning interest.

Skeptical, Josh backed up. "What's going on?"

The front door opened. "Josh run, we're playing tag and Mark is it!" Sidra bellowed, then shut the door again.

"Damn it, Sidra!" Mark barked as Josh took off running in the opposite direction. "Josh, you can't run out the gate you cheatin'!" he belted out, running after him.

Chapter 6

Standing outside of the English building, Alex fussed with her mp3 player. "Ugh, come on, I know this didn't break," she fussed, tapping it. When it didn't come on, she sucked her teeth and stuffed it into the pocket of her jeans.

"Hey you," Eric said, approaching.

Alex glanced up at him, face void of a smile. "Hi."

"You cool?" he asked, giving her a hug.

She nodded as they parted. "I'm fine," she replied. "My music player just gave out on me, but things could be worse you know."

"Damn, sorry to hear that," Eric sympathized. Alex shrugged. "Well...you ready to get going?"

"Not really," she returned, tone lackluster. The thought of having to spend money that she already didn't have on a new music player, paired with the long day of classes that she'd endured, Alex wasn't in the mood to work her shift at the Pizza Shack.

"What's wrong?" Eric asked, concerned.

"I'm already tired," she complained, "I have to write a five-page story without dialogue for my Creative Writing class, *plus* study for this African History exam that's coming up on Thursday. On top of doing a mock edit for my Editorial Studies class."

Eric winced. "Whoa, your professors aren't playing any

games this year huh?"

She started walking, Eric keeping in step with her. "Tell me about it," she said, adjusting her book bag on her shoulder.

"You want me to carry that?" Eric asked, holding his hand out.

Alex shook her head. "No, it's okay," she assured. "Thanks for walking me to work."

"No problem, you know that this is our routine," he smiled. "I even brought my homework so I can sit and wait for you."

"Eric, you don't have to stay," Alex said, glancing at him. "I've told you before, four hours is a long time to wait."

"It's fine, these Advanced Statistics problems will keep me occupied," he joked. "Besides, it's our routine, remember?"

Alex was silent as she continued walking along the tree lined street; Eric too was silent. He didn't have to talk; he just enjoyed being in her presence. But there was a question that had been plaguing him, something that he desperately wanted an answer to.

"Can I ask you something?" he asked, breaking the silence.

"Sure."

"Are you going to let me take you out this semester?"

Alex stopped in her tracks. *Ugh, not now with this Eric,* she thought. "Eric, we've discussed this."

Eric stopped and faced her. "Come on Alex, it's just dinner," he pointed out.

"I know that, but with everything that I have going on right now, I don't have *time* for dates," she explained. "You just heard about everything that I have to do for some of my classes, and that is just the stuff due *this week*...I have to focus."

"And *one dinner* is going to make you lose focus?" he questioned, bite in his voice.

Alex narrowed her eyes at him. "I'm sorry, are you

catching an attitude with me?"

Eric quickly shook his head. "Not at all," he lied. Eric had so much that he wanted to say to Alex. But knowing the stress that she was under, he didn't want to add to it. "Come on, you don't want to be late." His tone was flat.

Feeling a little bad, Alex touched his arm. "Look...you know that I care about you right?" she asked. He looked at her. "I don't want you to think otherwise... Me not dating isn't about you, it really is because I don't have the time."

Eric held his gaze. He wasn't sure if he believed her, but he wanted to. "I know," he said.

"Good," she smiled, patting him on the arm.

They approached the front of the parlor, and Alex opened the door to walk inside. Eric called her, causing her to turn around. "What's up?" she wondered.

"On second thought, I think I'll be better off solving these Statistics problems in the library," he said.

Alex looked a little disappointed. "Oh...okay, whatever works for you."

Eric gave a slight nod. "I'll call you later."

"Okay." Alex followed his progress down the block before heading inside.

Emily rubbed her temple with one hand, flipping a page in her book with the other. She had been working on her homework assignment for over an hour, and the words were starting to run together. The cell phone ringing offered a welcome distraction. Grabbing it from her desk, she looked at the caller ID. Not recognizing the number, her brow furrowed. "Wonder who this is," she muttered to herself. She put it to her ear. "Hello?"

"Hi, can I speak to Emily?" a deep male voice answered.

Not recognizing the voice, Emily frowned slightly. "Um, this is Emily."

"Hi...this is Will."

Emily's eyes widened, and her breath got caught in her

throat. When she gave Carl her number to give to Will a few days ago, she never expected that he would *actually* call.

She moved the phone away from her ear as she tried to calm herself down. She was both excited and nervous. Fanning herself, she put the phone back to her ear.

"Um…hi," She wondered if the fact that she was smiling from ear to ear could register through the phone.

"Sorry for calling so late."

Emily looked at the clock on her desk. It was only eight thirty; she hardly considered that late. "That's okay, I wasn't asleep or anything," she replied. "Studying and all."

"Oh, am I disturbing you?" Will panicked. "Sorry, I'll just call back—"

"No!" she belted out, immediately berating herself for being so hype. *Geez, calm it down, girl.* "I mean…you weren't disturbing me," she amended. "I needed a break anyway."

"Well, glad to be of service," Will chortled.

Emily giggled, twirling a braid around her finger.

"Emily, let me first say that I admit that it was really corny that I didn't ask for your number myself," he admitted. "I know how middle school that whole thing was."

Emily laughed. "Well, nobody ever *had* my number in middle school, so I wouldn't even know what that's like."

"Hell, who am I kidding, nobody had mine either," he returned. "Except for my teacher…I was a talkative kid."

Emily laughed again.

"No seriously, it was weird I know, but I've been tied up at work a lot and wasn't able to make it back to your campus," he explained.

"It's *really* okay," she assured, sincere. "I'm just glad that you *wanted* my number." As soon as the words left her lips, she smacked herself in the forehead. *Nice, you sound desperate and corny.*

"Why *wouldn't* I?" he asked.

Emily shrugged even though he couldn't see her. "I don't know…don't even know why I said that."

"Well…I wanted your number so that I could talk to you," he said. "I would like to get to know you."

Emily smiled. "Yeah?"

"Sure," he assured. "As a matter of fact, I'd like for you to go out with me."

Emily was floored. "You mean like a *date?*" she asked. This was the first time that she'd been asked out the entire time at college; the proposition had her a little frazzled.

"Well…yeah," he chuckled. "We can maybe do a lunch date, on Saturday. Is that okay with you?"

"Uh—yeah, sure, that umm...that sounds fine…sure," she sputtered.

"Cool, there's a nice little place not too far from the park that would be perfect I think," he suggested.

Emily didn't care if it was the Pizza Shack, she was just happy that Will was asking her out. "Okay sounds cool."

"Cool…well, I'll let you get back to studying. I have to take care of some stuff right now," he said. "Can I call you tomorrow?"

"Sure," she beamed.

"Great and good luck with whatever you're studying by the way."

"Thanks, you too—I mean—" Emily put her head on her desk. *Why would you say you too? Idiot.* "Have a good night, Will."

"You too Emily."

Once Emily hung up the phone, she set it on her desk and stared at it for a minute. She couldn't believe what had just happened. She went from studying Curriculum development, to being asked out on a date. She smiled to herself; she felt the urge to run and tell the girls, but decided against it for now. She figured if she left her desk, she'd never finish studying. She was fine with waiting.

Letting out a happy sigh, she went back to her textbook.

The next few days went fast for Emily as she anticipated

her lunch date with Will. Just like the first time Will called her, she was nervous and excited at the same time. Standing in her fluffy pink robe, she searched through her closet for something to wear. Letting out a loud sigh, she shut the closet door.

Walking to her room door, she opened it and stood in the hallway. "Girls, can you come help me please?" she called.

"No, you hurt our feelings," Malajia bit out from her room. "You told us to leave you alone."

"I did *not*," Emily contradicted. "All I said was can you please stop asking me what time my date was."

"I kept forgetting," Malajia argued.

"Eight times?!" Emily exclaimed.

Malajia busted out laughing.

"You should've said more than *that* to her," Chasity said from her room. "You know she's a moron."

Emily giggled. She was elated when she saw the girls make their way into the hallway. "Come, come," she urged, signaling them to come into the room.

Malajia flopped down on Sidra's bed. "So, what time is your date?" She snickered when Emily shot her a glare.

"Will you leave her alone?" Alex charged, sitting on Emily's bed. "I'm sure she's nervous *enough*, don't need *you* upsetting her."

Malajia scrunched her face up. "Alex—just shut up," she huffed, not having anything else to say.

Emily flopped on her bed and sighed.

Sidra tilted her head. "What's wrong Em?"

Emily twisted some of her braids around her finger. "I'm *really* nervous."

"It's *okay* to be nervous," Alex assured.

"Is it *also* okay that I'm twenty and this is my first date?" Emily asked.

"Absolutely," Alex returned, confident. She glanced over and cut her eye at Chasity. "You better not start."

Chasity looked around shocked. "I *literally* said nothing."

Emily sighed again. "I also have nothing to wear," she added. "Unless you count college sweatshirts and sweatpants as proper date attire."

"Not in *this* hot ass weather, it isn't," Chasity commented, earning a snicker from Malajia.

Malajia stood up. "Em, don't even worry about it, we're not gonna let you go out like that. We'll find you something to wear," she assured. She held her hand out in Emily's direction. "Come on, let's go through Chasity's closet."

"Malajia, don't get slapped," Chasity warned.

Putting her hand on her hip, Malajia sucked her teeth. "*Still?* You *still* being stingy with your clothes?" she sneered.

Chasity narrowed her eyes at Malajia as she kept talking.

"Our fashion victim of a friend has nothing to wear for her date—"

"Seriously Malajia?" Sidra cut in.

"Oh wow," Emily muttered, insulted.

"Em, shut up, I'm trying to help you," Malajia ground out, putting a hand up. She looked back at Chasity. "Chasity you have way too many clothes in that closet and in those drawers, so I know you have *something* in there for her to borrow… I mean, her stomach ain't as toned as yours, but she can squeeze—"

"Malajia, please stop trying to help," Emily begged. "It's doing *nothing* for my confidence right now."

Ignoring Emily, Malajia held her gaze on Chasity. "Help the girl, will you?"

Chasity abruptly flicked her hand in Malajia's face, startling her. She then let out a groan. "Fine," she agreed, through clenched teeth. "I'll be back."

Malajia looked shocked. "Shit…I wasn't expecting that," she admitted, amused.

"*You?*" Sidra joked. "I just *knew* she was gonna slap you first."

Alex jumped up and followed Chasity out of the room. "Chaz, since you're sharing, can—"

"Alex, get your big ass away from me," Chasity spat,

halting Alex's steps.

"Oh my God, that was uncalled for," Alex bristled. When Chasity ignored her, Alex spun around to find Malajia laughing out loud, while Sidra and Emily had their heads turned in an effort to not laugh in her face. Having nothing to say, Alex walked back over to Emily's bed and sat down. "Emily, if you want my opinion, I say you should just wear what's in your closet."

"Why?" Emily wondered.

"Well, you need to be yourself, and wearing anybody else's clothes other than your *own*, isn't being true to yourself." She was met with confused looks.

Malajia squinted. "What kind of bullshit?" she ground out. "Since when does borrowing a damn *shirt* mean you're not being yourself?"

Sidra scratched her head. "Yeah Alex, I'm a little confused myself," she admitted.

"You know what I meant," Alex huffed, folding her arms.

Emily quickly shook her head. "No, no not really," she softly put out.

Alex ran her hands over her wild hair. "I'm just saying if you feel like you have to wear someone else's style just to impress this guy—"

"It's a date, why *wouldn't* she want to impress him?" Sidra cut in.

"So, she has to change her style because of *him*?"

"I'm not changing my *style* Alex, I just don't want to wear a baggy t-shirt on a date," Emily explained, "I have nothing dressy—"

Malajia sucked her teeth. "Emily, you don't gotta explain nothing to her ass," she bit out.

Alex tossed her arms in the air in frustration. "I'm not trying to sound—"

"What the fuck are you even *talking* about?" Chasity sniped, walking into her room, clutching pink fabric in her hand.

"*Excuse* me?" Alex hissed.

"I heard your loud ass from my damn room," Chasity threw back. "You sound dumb."

Alex opened her mouth to retaliate, but Sidra stepped forward, putting her hands up in the process. "Emily is the focus right now, okay," she placated. "Kill each other later." She looked at Emily. "Go get in the shower sweetie, we'll put your outfit together for you."

Emily smiled up at her. "Thanks."

Seeing that Emily had yet to move, Malajia snapped her fingers. "You gonna sit there or get your sweaty ass in the shower?" she jeered.

Emily jumped up. "Oh, right," she chortled, running for the bathroom.

"You know you hot as shit in that long ass robe," Malajia hurled after her.

"I am," Emily laughed from the bathroom.

Chapter 7

"Don't you want to put a little bit more lipstick on her lips, Sid?" Malajia asked, peering over Sidra's shoulder to examine Sidra's makeup skills a half hour later.

Sidra nudged her away. "No, I *don't*," she ground out. "Dramatic lips are *your* thing. Em just wanted something simple and soft."

"Fine," Malajia shrugged. "At least put some more gloss on her damn lips, they all dry," she teased, earning a giggle from Emily.

Sidra shook her head. "Pay her no mind Emily, she's lying," she assured. When she finished, she signaled for Emily to stand up and give herself a look in the floor length mirror.

Emily almost didn't recognize herself. "I look so...pretty," she smiled.

The pink short sleeve, skater dress which fell mid-thigh, fit her nicely. That, paired with the nude pumps, modest rose gold toned jewelry, soft makeup and her styled braids which she had pushed back over her shoulders, completed the look.

"You *always* look pretty, Em," Alex complimented.

"Not in the morning," Malajia chuckled.

Alex cut her eye at Malajia, then looked back at Emily. "You sure you're comfortable in that dress?"

Emily rolled her eyes.

"It's not too short?" Alex pressed.

"No, I'm fine Alex," Emily replied, fiddling with her bracelet. *God, stop treating me like a child.*

"This outfit is perfect," Sidra chimed in, placing the top on her lip-gloss. She then handed it to Emily. "It's still warm outside, so you'll be comfortable."

"Chasity, *why* did you have that pink dress in your closet?" Malajia asked, laughter in her voice. "You hate pink."

"*I* didn't buy that shit," Chasity sneered, leaning up against the wall. "My grandmom said she's tired of seeing me in black all the time, so she bought that for me."

"Does she really think you'll wear it?" Sidra wondered, amused.

"I *told* her I wasn't," Chasity ground out. "But if she wants to waste her money, so be it."

"Well, I'm glad that you had it. Pink is my favorite color," Emily mused.

"Yes, I know," Chasity scoffed, glancing at Emily's side of the room. "Everything on your side is pink."

A knock on the door froze Emily in place.

"Ooh, he's here. Interrogation time," Malajia announced, darting out of the room and towards the stairs.

"Malajia, don't scare the boy off!" Sidra shouted after her.

"I'm with Mel, I have some questions too," Alex added, heading out of the room, she looked back at Emily. "You okay walking in those heels?"

Emily let out a quick sigh.

Chasity nudged Alex out the door. "Out, hoverboard," she ordered, following her out.

Sidra put both hands on Emily's shoulders. "You look nervous. Just breathe, it'll be okay," she assured.

Emily nodded. "Okay."

Sidra smiled, then grabbed Emily's hand. "Come on, he awaits."

Emily walked down the steps to find Will standing by

the door. Alex and Malajia were standing in front of him, talking.

Will smiled at her; he was also dressed casually. He'd paired a crisp grey button-down shirt with a pair of black khakis and black shoes. "You look pretty," he said.

Emily glanced down at the floor, blushing. "Thank you."

"Don't worry, we already got on him about not bringing you flowers," Alex said, looking at Emily.

"Don't drag me into that, *you* did," Malajia contradicted, pointing to Alex.

"That's fine, I don't really like flowers anyway," Emily said to Will.

"That's good because I bought you candy instead," he grinned, handing her a small square box.

Emily was smiling from ear to ear.

"Aww look, he bought her candy," Malajia directed at Alex.

Will held his arm out for Emily to grab. "*Shall* we?" Emily nodded as she took hold of his arm.

"Have her back at a decent hour Will, we don't want to have to come find you," Alex joked.

Chasity rolled her eyes as they headed out of the door. "Y'all better go before Alex asks for the address to where you're going."

Once the pair walked out of the house, Alex darted to the window and peered out of it.

"What are you looking at, you stalker?" Malajia bristled.

"I'm just seeing if he opens the car door for her," Alex answered, still watching.

"Alex, get your hype ass away from the window," Chasity ordered.

Alex looked at them with shock. "What? I'm just making sure he's doing the right thing."

"She's not *five*, she doesn't need for you to watch over her like that," Sidra threw back, stern. "So do like Chasity *said*, and come away from the window."

Alex sucked her teeth, then looked back outside. Seeing that they had pulled off, she walked to the couch. "I don't appreciate you three treating me like I'm wrong for making sure that she's okay."

"You've been nitpicking and *nagging* her all damn day," Malajia pointed out, flopping down on the couch.

"*You* call it nagging, *I* call it looking out for her," Alex argued.

"Go look for that flip phone and call Eric," Malajia threw back. "Go bother *him*."

Alex rolled her eyes as she grabbed the TV remote off of the coffee table.

Emily played with one of her braids as she glanced at the menu. The small, quiet restaurant; which sat on a tree-lined street between a book store and coffee shop certainly was intimate enough; maybe it being intimate was what had Emily feeling uncomfortable. She wasn't saying much. Then again, she didn't say much during the car ride either.

"Anything look good to you?" Will asked, looking up from his menu.

Emily shrugged. "The ravioli looks good," she muttered.

"Yeah, I was looking at that too," he said. "Either that or the squid."

Emily made a face. "Eww," she scoffed.

Will let out a small laugh. "I was joking," he said. "Just trying to get a smile out of you."

Emily didn't have the heart to tell him that that was a poor attempt at a joke; nevertheless, it was cute that he tried. "Oh," she said, feigning a giggle.

Once the waiter came to the table, they placed their food orders. Will glanced at Emily; "You want to order something to drink?"

Emily shook her head as she folded her arms across her chest. "I don't drink," she declined. "Thanks though."

"Not even *iced tea* or *lemonade*?" Will asked.

Emily put her hand over her face, embarrassed that she had jumped to conclusions. "Sorry, yes, lemonade will be fine, thank you."

Will nodded, then placed his drink order. Once the waiter left the table, Will chuckled. "Tough crowd," he teased of her tense demeanor.

"I'm sorry," she sputtered. "When I hear 'drink,' I automatically think of alcohol."

"It's okay," he replied, putting a hand up. "I should've been more clear…but that's cool that you don't drink. I don't do it much myself."

Emily played with a napkin on the table. "Yeah," she said, voice low. She didn't want to stay on the topic of alcohol; she didn't know him well enough to share her past experiences with the substance.

Will looked around, almost as if he was trying to search for something to say. "So…do you like the candy?"

"I'm sorry?" she asked, confused.

"The candy that I gave you," he clarified. "Do you like that kind?"

"Oh," she breathed. "Yes."

Will nodded. "Cool."

Fifteen awkward minutes later, their food arrived. It was silent as Will began to devour his meal. Emily poked at hers; her nerves were ruining her appetite. *This is going horrible. I'm ruining everything*, she thought.

Will, noticing that she was staring at her food, frowned in concern. "You okay?"

Emily looked up, eyes wide. "Huh?"

He chuckled at the look on her face. She looked like a deer caught in headlights. "Are you okay?"

"Oh yeah, I'm fine…just not that hungry," she admitted, rubbing her arm.

He grabbed his glass of water and took a sip. "Emily, am I making you nervous?" he wondered, voice calm.

Yes! Emily gave a nervous laugh. "No," she lied.

Moving her arm, she accidentally knocked her glass of

lemonade on the floor, causing the juice to spill and the glass to shatter. Mortified, she put her hands over her face as the hostess darted over to clean up the mess. *Way to go, stupid!*

"God, I can't believe I just did that," she whined, voice muffled by her hands. If she didn't think that she would fall in Sidra's high heels, she would have gotten up and run right out of the restaurant.

Will reached over and touched her hand. "Don't worry about it," he assured, voice laced with amusement.

She removed her hands from her face; she'd had enough. "I'm sorry Will," she began. "I know I've been acting like...a social reject—"

"I wouldn't say that," he placated.

"*I* would," she stressed, placing her hand on her chest. "It's not because I don't want to be here. It's because I'm just not good at this."

"Good at *what*?"

"*This*," she emphasized, gesturing to the surroundings. "This dating thing...I look like a complete idiot."

"You don't look like an idiot," Will disagreed. "And what do you mean? You've never been on a date before?"

Emily sighed and shook her head.

Will raised his eyebrow. "Like...*never*?"

She once again shook her head. "I just never got a chance to," she admitted hesitantly. She was so coddled and smothered growing up that she could barely breathe, let alone date. But that wasn't something that she was going to reveal to Will. She wasn't even sure that he would ever want to see her again after this awkward date.

Will shrugged. "That's okay," he replied, much to Emily's surprise.

"You mean, you don't think it's weird?"

"No...I mean if you were in your *thirties*, maybe," he joked. She managed a giggle. "Come on, let's get out of here," he suggested, signaling for the waiter.

Emily sighed. "Okay."

"The park is around the corner, you want to go for a

walk?"

Emily looked up at him, smiling slightly. "Sure," she nodded, grabbing her small handbag from the arm of the chair. Maybe the fresh air would do her some good.

"Is this better?" Will asked. The pair were walking in perfect stride through the well-kept park of Paradise Valley fifteen minutes later.

Emily smiled up at him. "Yes," she said. "Thanks."

"What do you say next time we try to do something a little less formal," Will suggested. "Maybe something fun."

Emily looked surprised. "You...you actually *want* to go out with me again?"

Will looked at her. "Of course," he assured. "I like you."

Emily blushed as she glanced down at the ground.

"What, you think that an awkward lunch is going to scare me off?"

Emily shrugged, gazing back up at him. "It would scare most."

Will held his gaze on her. "Well...I'm not most," he smiled. "And I understand. We probably should've talked on the phone a little more before I asked you out. That way you would feel more comfortable."

"Listen, you don't have to feel bad about anything," she said. "You didn't do anything wrong, I still would've acted the same way... A first date is a first date."

Will nodded. "Good point."

"So," she began after a few moments. "What do you do?" she asked. "Are you in school?"

"Not at the moment," he answered. "I mean I *was*, but I left."

"What happened?"

He hesitated for a moment. "Life," he replied. "I had to take some time off to work," he added, shoving a hand in his pants pocket. "I just need to stack some money, you know... I'm a manager at the movie theater in the mall and I live about ten minutes from there."

"Oh yeah?" she said. "My friends and I have been to that theater many times; don't think I've ever seen you."

"I only started working there not too long ago," he replied.

"Oh... So you said you don't live too far from the mall?" Will shook his head. "No, which is fine for now."

"What do you mean, for now?" she wondered. "Bad neighborhood or something?"

"No..." Will paused for a moment, wondering if he even wanted to share what he was about to say. But for some reason, he felt comfortable talking to her now that she seemed to loosen up a bit. "I'm living with my parents at the moment," he revealed. Emily just looked at him. "But that's only because I just left school last semester. I'll be getting my own spot soon enough, which is why I'm trying to save."

"There's nothing wrong with staying with your parents while you get yourself together," she said, pushing some of her braids over her shoulder.

He shrugged. "Most girls think so."

"I'm not most," she smiled, he smiled back. "And those girls probably never dated a guy in college or *just out* of college," she added. "Not everybody can get their own place so soon."

"Thanks for that," he said.

"For what?"

"For not making me feel like a loser," he chortled.

She touched his arm briefly. "You're *not* one," she said.

"So," Will breathed. "Tell me about *you*."

"There's nothing to tell, really," she replied, kicking a stone off to the side as she walked. "I'm a senior majoring in early childhood education. I'm the youngest child in my family and I live with my father in North Carolina...when I'm not *here* of course."

His eyes lit up. "Oh, nice major. You like kids?"

"I *love* children," she enthusiastically returned. "They're just smart, little people who want to be understood...and they're adorable."

He nodded in satisfaction. "Yeah, kids are great," he agreed, staring off in front of him. "Um, you said that you live with your father...is your mother still around? If you don't mind me asking."

Emily resisted the urge to roll her eyes or frown at the mention of her mother. The woman who hadn't had any desire to interact with her daughter ever since she made the decision to move out of her mother's house the end of sophomore year. The last time that Emily saw or spoke to her mother was at her grandmother's funeral last semester, where Emily finally let her mother know that she was no longer going to feel guilty or try to gain the woman's approval.

Sure, Emily missed her mother, but she refused to beg her to talk to her. "Um...she's alive," was all that she could say.

The bite in Emily's tone told Will not to press any further. "There's a bench over there by that tree, if you want to give your feet a rest," he suggested, pointing to the bench in question. "Or, do you want me to take you back to campus?"

"No, we can go sit," she replied. She was finally loosening up and she didn't want their conversation to end just yet. Will offered his arm for her to take hold of as they walked along the grass.

Chapter 8

Sidra eyed the rectangular box in her hand with anticipation. Opening it, she smiled at the perfume in front of her. "Aww, so sweet," she gushed. Grabbing the item, she pulled the top off of the three-ounce glass bottle and put it to her nose. "Ooh, this smells good."

Grabbing her cell phone, she hit the number on speed dial. She paced the carpeted living room floor as she waited for an answer. "Ugh, machine," she griped to herself. "Hi James, it's me. I just got the perfume in the mail. I love it," she cooed. "Thank you. Talk to you later." As she ended her message, the door opened and Malajia darted inside, tossing her book bag on the floor and giving it a kick.

Sidra eyed the book bag as it landed right in front of her slipper covered feet. "You must be mad because you're abusing your book bag again," she teased.

"Fuck that old ass book bag," Malajia fumed, pointing to it and earning a giggle from Sidra. "Girl, that Finance class is gonna be the death of me," she complained, making her way into the kitchen. "Damn Professor with his same-orange-suit-jacket-and-green-tie everyday wearing ass, gonna tell us that we have two quizzes this week on dividends and repurchases…Who gives a shit about a dividend?"

Sidra shook her head at Malajia as she watched her rummage through the cabinets. "Well *you* should, Miss Business major," she commented.

"Well, I *don't*," Malajia hissed. "Where are all the damn snacks?" she barked, slamming the cabinet door. "I bet Alex's fat ass has them hidden in her bra."

Sidra shot her a warning look. "Malajia, stop it."

"Fine," Malajia huffed, leaning up against the counter. "But I still know she ate 'em." She pointed to the bottle in Sidra's hand. "Whatchu' got there?"

"Oh! One of my birthday presents from James," Sidra gushed, showing Malajia.

"Oooooh," she squealed, grabbing the bottle from Sidra's hand. She took a whiff. "Ooh, this smells *way* better than that vanilla body spay you keep using."

Sidra made a face. "Funny, coming from the person who keeps *borrowing* it."

Malajia shrugged. "And I will *continue* to borrow it," she boasted. "You're almost out by the way."

Sidra waved a dismissive hand at her. "Anyway, I just got it in the mail today."

"Your birthday isn't for another two weeks," Malajia pointed out.

"I know. He's doing this thing where he's sending me a gift every few days until my *actual* birthday," Sidra responded. "This is the second one."

"Well, what was the *first*?"

"That vase of flowers that's on my dresser," she revealed.

"You mean them ugly ass blue hydrangeas?"

Sidra sucked her teeth. "Just because *you* don't like them, it doesn't mean they're ugly," she bit out. "They happen to be my favorite."

"Yes, I know." Malajia chuckled a bit. "But damn bitch. He's spoiling your little uppity ass, huh?" she said, folding her arms.

Sidra narrowed her eyes. "You could've left the 'bitch' out of that," she hissed.

"Nah, it called for it," Malajia maintained. "Let me borrow this," she added, spraying some of the perfume on her wrist.

"No," Sidra refused, snatching the bottle from Malajia's clutches. "Keep your hands off of it."

Malajia laughed. "Okay fine, I won't touch it," she promised.

"Mmm hmm," Sidra muttered.

"Must be nice to have a boyfriend who spoils you like that," Malajia said, pushing hair over her shoulder.

"You jealous?" Sidra jeered.

"A little bit," Malajia returned before breaking into a smile. "No, I'm joking. I'm happy for you, he's treating you like you deserve to be treated."

Sidra smiled back. "Thank you Malajia," she said, sincere.

Malajia gave a slight nod. "What's he going to do for your *actual* birthday?"

Sidra ran her hand through her hair. "He's taking me to New York for the weekend," she revealed. She neglected to mention that to the girls when she first learned of his plans a few weeks ago.

Malajia's eyes widened. "Well damn, he's not playing no games," she said. "Y'all are coming up on a year of being a couple, right?"

Sidra nodded. "Yep."

"Why does it sound like you're not excited for your trip?" Malajia asked, noticing the bland tone in Sidra's voice.

Sidra's eyes shifted; she didn't know if she wanted to tell Malajia, or anyone for that matter, that she was nervous. "No, no, I'm excited about it," she said.

Malajia eyed her skeptically. "You're lying Princess."

Shit! "I am *not*," Sidra sneered.

"Yeah, okay," Malajia replied, examining her nails.

Sidra rolled her eyes. "Okay, well maybe I'm a little nervous," she admitted. "I haven't taken a trip with a boyfriend before."

"You haven't *had* a boyfriend before him," Malajia pointed out.

"Yes, Malajia, I am aware," Sidra sniped.

Malajia put her hands up in surrender. "No need to get your slacks in a bunch," she mocked. Sidra sucked her teeth. "Look, just loosen up for *once*. Go spend up his money...buy *me* something and have fun."

Sidra frowned. "I'm not buying you *shit*," she assured, causing Malajia to bust out laughing.

"David, if you don't come on, I *will* leave you," Chasity urged, looking at her phone as she stood against the wall. Having class in the Science building that let out the same time as David's, she agreed to wait for him so that they could walk back home together.

David, notebook in hand, rushed out. "I had to go back for my notebook," he said, adjusting the book bag on his shoulder. "I'd hate to lose this, too many notes."

Chasity let out a sigh as they made their way down the hall.

David glanced at her as they walked through the halls. "You look annoyed, something wrong?" he observed.

"Oh nothing, just wanted to smack my professor in the neck," she jeered.

David chuckled a little. "Oh wow."

"No, his dumbass gonna call me to the board to solve a goddamn problem that I *told* him I didn't understand...ugly bastard."

David shook his head. "Don't worry, just this last year to go and it'll be over," he comforted, putting his arm on her shoulder.

"That bullshit isn't helping me *now*," she griped.

Walking out of the building, David was about to respond, when something caught his eye. He began staring. Chasity, noticing that he'd stopped walking, glanced at him and frowned at the look on his face.

"What did you stop for?" she asked, annoyed. "And what are you looking at? You look crazy."

"Uh...."

Chasity sucked her teeth when he wouldn't form a full sentence. Looking in the direction of his stare, she relaxed her frown and smirked. "Oh okay," she said, pointing to Nicole.

David cleared his throat. "Damn, it sucks that she has a boyfriend," he complained. Ever since he had embarrassed himself a few weeks ago after working up the nerve to talk to her, David made it a point to avoid talking to Nicole again. But he couldn't help but stare when he saw her from afar.

When David kept staring, Chasity waved her hand in his face. "Stop that," she demanded.

He laughed a little. "I'm looking like a stalker huh?"

"A little," Chasity agreed. "Anyway, how do you know for a fact that she has a boyfriend?"

"Mark told me last semester. Her boyfriend plays basketball with him sometimes," he sighed.

Chasity sucked her teeth. "Mark's stupid ass don't know shit," she sneered, heading off in Nicole's direction.

David started to panic. "Chasity, what are you doing?"

Chasity looked back at him as she continued walking. "Relax, I'm trying to help you out."

David shook his head frantically. "No, no, don't go over there," he urged. He put his hands on his head when Chasity ignored him and kept walking. He looked away the moment Chasity began chatting with a smiling Nicole.

David looked up as Chasity headed back over to him after a few moments. He looked nervous.

"You wanna chill the hell out?" she ground out.

David put a hand up. "Sorry, sorry." He took a deep breath. "Well?"

Chasity pushed some of her hair behind her ear. "She doesn't have a boyfriend," she confirmed after a few seconds.

David's eyes widened in shock. "Wait what? How do you know that?"

"She told me."

David was in disbelief. "You mean she just *told* you?" he probed. "Did you tell her that *I* wanted to know?"

"No boy," Chasity sneered, much to David's relief. "I saw a bracelet on her wrist and said that it was cute and that my boyfriend gave me one just like it," she explained. "She said 'I wish *I* had a boyfriend,' then started to tell me how her aunt gave it to her. Then I cut the conversation short 'cause I no longer cared."

David laughed a little. "*Please* tell me you were nice about it."

"Yeah, sure," she dismissed.

David smiled brightly. "So...no boyfriend, huh?"

Chasity narrowed her eyes at him. "You smile any harder and I'll be able to see your damn wisdom teeth," she jeered, earning a laugh from him.

David grabbed her hand and gave a quick kiss to it. "Thank you," he said, grateful.

"Sure," she replied.

"Now, to just get the nerve to actually go talk to her again," he muttered as they continued on their way. "Wait, did Jason really give you a bracelet like hers?"

"Fuck no, that thing was tacky looking," she scoffed.

David shook his head.

"I'm glad that we finally got a chance to hang out," Alex mused, squirting some mustard onto her turkey burger.

Stacey pushed some hair over her shoulder as she picked up her slice of pizza. "I know right," she agreed before taking a bite. Alex, needing a break from her studies, decided to call Stacey up to meet her for lunch at the cafeteria. It'd been a while since Alex had shared a meal with her old friend.

"How are your classes coming?" Alex asked in between bites.

Stacey shrugged. "They're fine...*tougher*, but fine."

"Yeah? Well, wait until you become a senior, they'll almost *kill* you," Alex joked. "But you've always been smart;

you'll be able to handle them."

"Maybe," Stacey returned, reaching for her drink. After taking a sip, she set her cup down and looked at Alex. "So…a lot has changed over the past two years," she began.

Alex looked up from her burger. "Like what?" she asked, curious. "Is something wrong?"

"Not with *me*," Stacey assured, shaking her hand in Alex's direction.

Alex let out a sigh of relief. "Oh good." She took another bite of her sandwich. "So what's changed? And with who?"

Stacey folded her arms on the table top. She hesitated for a moment, and Alex took notice.

"Seriously…what's going on?" Alex asked, worried.

"It has to do with umm…Victoria," Stacey blurted out.

A frown masked Alex's face. The last name that she wanted to hear was her ex-best friend's. Ever since Alex found out the beginning of sophomore year that Victoria had slept with her boyfriend Paul while she was away at college, Alex completely wrote Victoria off and vowed never to speak to her again.

"I don't want to hear anything that has to do with that conniving bitch," Alex hissed.

"Well, you should probably know what I'm about to tell you," Stacey responded. "Especially before you go back home for Thanksgiving…you know how people talk."

"Well, they didn't say *shit* when Victoria was screwing Paul behind my back," Alex spat.

"Didn't say they would talk about it to *you*," Stacey clarified.

"Fine," Alex rolled her eyes. "Spill it."

"Victoria is pregnant," Stacey revealed, hesitantly.

Alex's eyes widened with shock. "Wait *what*?" She leaned back in her seat. "That girl is so *stupid*," she condemned. "She drops out of college when she didn't *have* to in the *first* place, then she goes and gets herself pregnant."

"You haven't heard the worst part," Stacey alluded.

Alex stared at Stacey and shook her head. "Please don't

tell me what I think you're about to tell me," she pleaded. When Stacey looked down at the table, Alex closed her eyes and sighed. "It's Paul's isn't it?"

"Yeah," Stacey confirmed.

Alex slammed her napkin on the table. "Why would you think that I wanted to know that?" she snapped. "Why would you *tell* me that?"

"Because I made the mistake of keeping things from you before, and I didn't want to do that again," Stacey reasoned. "I didn't want you to be caught off guard."

"Yeah well, like you waited to tell me last time, you could've done that *this* time," Alex spat out.

Stacey was taken aback by Alex's tone. "Are you mad at me right now?" she frowned.

Alex put her hand up. "No, I'm not," she said. "I'm mad at *them*... You know what, no I'm not. I'm over it, that's what they get. They can live miserably-ever-after for all I care."

Stacey eyed Alex sympathetically. "Alex, I'm sorry."

Alex felt like screaming on the inside. "It's fine," she lied.

It was like she couldn't escape this Paul and Victoria mess. The initial betrayal embarrassed her, and now she had to relive it again because now they were having a baby. She felt betrayed all over again. *I hate men*, she fumed to herself. Another student approached the table and interrupted her thoughts.

"What!" she snapped at the startled student.

"Um, I'm sorry, I just wanted to know if I can use your ketchup," he stammered. "The one on my table is empty."

"Sure, take it," Stacey intervened, handing him the red bottle. She looked at Alex as the young man scurried off. "Sis, relax," she urged.

Alex rolled her eyes. "I gotta go," she huffed, standing from the booth.

"Um...okay," Stacey said.

"Look, I meant what I said. I'm not mad at you," Alex

assured, gathering her trash. "But I'm just left to wonder why you're still talking to her."

"I'm *not* talking to her," Stacey promised.

"Yeah? Well how *else* did you find out?"

Stacey shook her head. "My *mother* told me," she informed. "*She* still talks to Victoria's mother."

Alex felt bad and it showed when she looked at the floor. "I'm sorry," she apologized. "I really gotta go, I'll call you later." Alex hurried off without another word.

Alex fumed silently as she made her way through the campus towards her destination. As she approached the steps to the campus apartments, her thoughts wandered.

So not only does he cheat on me and completely humiliate me, he goes and gets that bitch pregnant? Why did he do that? Why are men so damn selfish? They just do what they want to do without caring who gets hurt.

She approached the first door in the apartment and knocked. Eric opened the door and frowned, concerned at the tense look on her face. "Alex? What are you doing here? Is everything okay?"

Alex stared at him. She didn't know why she was there, what made her go to him instead of back to her house. She was disgusted with men at the moment and knew that she should be alone to calm herself down. But then she figured, why not let *him* calm her down?

"I'm fine...you busy?" she responded.

"No not really, was just studying," he said.

Eric was confused; Alex hadn't been to his apartment in weeks. She'd seemed a bit standoffish to him lately.

"Oh...well I've got like fifteen minutes before I have to start on my paper, so you wanna get it in real quick?" she causally asked, shocking him.

Eric backed away from the door as Alex walked in, shutting it with her foot. "Um...so what does this mean?" he asked as she walked towards him, removing her shirt. "I thought you didn't want to do the causal thing anymore?"

"Are you gonna talk, or are you gonna fuck me?" she barked. She didn't want to hear him talk; she just wanted to relieve the stress and be on her way.

Eric put his hands up in surrender. "You sure you wanna do this?"

Alex unbuttoned her jeans. "Does it look like it?" she threw back.

Eric didn't say another word as he grabbed her hand, pulling her to the bed.

Alex left her inhibitions at the door. She no longer questioned why she wanted to be with Eric in that moment. As he passionately and aggressively took her body as only he could, her mind was no longer on Paul, or Victoria, or their love child; it was focused only on Eric and the pleasure that he was making her feel. The pleasure that she remembered.

God, why did I ever stop sleeping with him? she wondered, gripping on to him.

Eric kissed her neck. "Alex," he whispered in her ear.

"Shhhh," she whispered back. She meant it. She didn't want to hear him talk; she just wanted his body. She wanted her release.

Physically spent, Alex laid on her back, staring at the ceiling. She'd been staring at that same spot since Eric rolled off of her nearly ten minutes ago. Finally glancing at her watch, she sat up. "I should go," she said.

Eric too sat up. "You don't *have* to," he said, reaching for her hand.

She subtly moved it out of his reach. "Yes, I do," she insisted. "I have stuff I gotta do."

Eric frowned. "Oh…okay then." He watched her get out of bed and get dressed. "Yo, seriously, what was that about?"

She snapped her head towards him. "Eric, it—" Alex felt her temper rising with each word that he spoke. She just wanted to get out of there, before she said something that she'd regret. "It was just…" she let out a quick sigh. "Like I said, I gotta go…I'll call you."

"Yeah," Eric moped, watching her as she headed for the door. When the door closed behind her, he just shook his head before laying back down.

Chasity leaned back against Jason as she concentrated on writing in her notebook. Jason focused his attention on reading the textbook in his hands.

She held the completed answer to his face. "Is this right?" she asked him.

Jason peered at the book for a brief second, before shaking his head. "Chasity, stop playing. You know good and well that's not right," he chided, much to her annoyance.

She sucked her teeth and flipped the book closed. "Well tough shit 'cause I'm not doing it again," she mumbled.

Jason rolled his eyes. "Chasity, we go through this every time it's time for you to do any sort of math," he said. "The sooner you stop complaining, the better off we'll *both* be."

Chasity made a face, even though Jason couldn't see it. "Yeah well, the sooner you realize that I'm gonna complain each and every time, the better off *you'll* be," she shot back.

"Chasity, kill the backtalk and redo the problem," Jason commanded, voice stern but calm.

"Whatever," she mumbled, flipping open the notebook.

Jason shook his head and suppressed a chuckle. *Always gotta get the last word, smart ass*, he mused to himself.

A noise from her cell phone interrupted her work. "What?" she sighed, picking up the phone. She sucked her teeth and slammed the phone down once she looked at the message. "I don't feel like this shit right now."

Curious as to what got her so riled up, Jason set his textbook down. "What's wrong?" he asked.

Without saying a word, she showed him the phone. Jason sighed. "You're not going to respond?" he asked once he read the message.

"Nope," she bit out.

Jason guided the phone back in front of her face. "Chaz,

just respond," he urged, voice caring.

"No. Why?" she fussed.

"Because he's your father."

Chasity sat up and looked at him. "*And?*" she hissed. "I already told him the day of Brenda's funeral that I don't want to communicate with him," she tossed the phone on the couch cushion next to her. "He's fuckin' hard headed."

"Well, at least I know where you get it from," Jason said at a sad attempt to lighten the mood. Chasity was not amused; it showed on her face when she glared daggers at him. He cleared his throat as he sat up. "Baby listen—"

"No, don't *baby* me Jason, I'm not for it today," she angrily replied.

"I know."

"No, you *don't*," she bit back. "*You've* always had a relationship with your father. *I* haven't. And now that I'm a grown ass woman, he wants to get back in the picture? For what? No, fuck him."

Jason looked down at the floor. *She's right*, he thought. Jason's father was a huge presence in his life; he couldn't image his life without his dad. He couldn't understand how a father could willingly not be a part of his child's life, especially his daughter's. As far as he was concerned, a father was supposed to be the first example of a man to his daughter, and her father was a terrible one to Chasity. It explained why Jason had to jump through hoops in order for her to even give him the time of day in the beginning.

"I hear you," he said, holding his gaze on her.

She let out a loud huff. "But?" she questioned, knowing that it was coming.

"I'm not telling you what to do. I honestly don't blame you for not wanting to talk to him... No bullshit, I kinda want to punch him in the face one good time for you."

Chasity managed a smirk.

"But...I just feel that one day, maybe not any time *soon*...but *someday*, you will need your father, every girl *does*," he said. "So, all I'm saying is just *think* about hearing him out."

Chasity frowned slightly as she pondered Jason's words. Seeing that she was thinking about it gave him enough satisfaction. He gave her a kiss on the cheek before standing from the couch and heading into the kitchen. She grabbed her phone and stared at it for several seconds, before letting out a sigh and responding to the message.

Chapter 9

Emily giggled as she hurried down the steps with her cell phone cradled between her neck and her shoulder. Sidra glanced at her as Emily walked into the kitchen to grab a bag of chips out of the cabinet. She was happy for Emily; it'd been over a week since her first date with Will and although they haven't been out again yet, they had plenty of phone conversations—one of which was going on right at that moment.

"Okay, I'll talk to you later…bye."

Sidra smiled as Emily ended the call and let out a pleased sigh. "Your cheeks must hurt with all that smiling you're doing," she teased.

Emily blushed as she opened the bags of chips. "Yeah well…he makes me smile," she cooed.

"That's a good thing," Sidra confirmed, voice filled with amusement. "When are you two going out again?"

"Soon," Emily replied. "He's been working a lot of double shifts lately. I know he's been tired."

Sidra was about to respond, when Alex walked through the door, dropped her book bag down at the steps, and headed over to the kitchen. Emily and Sidra glanced at each other when Alex brushed past them without a word and opened the refrigerator door.

"Something wrong with you, Alex?" Sidra asked, folding her arms.

Alex looked up, eyes tired. "I'm fine, why?"

"Well for one, you look like you're worn out," Sidra pointed out. "Second, you were kind of rude just now."

Alex looked surprised. "Was I?"

Emily nodded. "Yeah, you walked right past and didn't say anything," she added. "That's not like you."

Alex ran her hand over her hair. It'd been a few days since she had learned of Victoria and Paul's child, and she neglected to tell the girls in hopes that she could shake the sick feeling that she had. She realized at that moment that holding it in wasn't in her best interest. "Do you know where Chasity and Malajia are?"

"Um, Chaz was studying with Jason when I last spoke to her, and Malajia should be on her way back from class," Sidra answered, looking at her watch. "Why? What's the matter?"

"I promise I'll tell you, I just want to tell you all at once, so I don't have to repeat it," Alex answered.

"*That* bad huh?" Sidra assumed.

Alex nodded. "Nice necklace by the way," she acknowledged, pointing to the crystal drop pendant hanging onto a dainty silver chain, around Sidra's slender neck.

"Thank you, it's another gift from James," Sidra said, touching the pendant.

Alex managed a smile. Although she was happy for Sidra, she really wasn't feeling too happy with men in general at the moment, so a conversation about Sidra's generous boyfriend wasn't on her preferred list of topics.

"Um, I'm gonna head up to my room for a bit. When Mel and Chaz get in, can you all come up?" Alex said as she made her way to the steps.

"Sure," Emily agreed, following Alex's progress with a sympathetic look.

"You want me to bring up some food or something when we come up?" Sidra offered.

"No, but thanks," Alex threw down the steps.

Sidra and Emily looked at each other. "It must be bad,"

Emily figured.

"Yeah," Sidra sighed.

Alex removed her sneakers and tossed them into her closet. As she crossed the room, she removed her grey sweatshirt and tossed it into the hamper. She pulled her white tank top down and ran her hands over her hair. Sitting down on her bed, she felt tears well up in her eyes. *God, why can't this bullshit just be over?* she thought, wiping her eyes with the back of her hand. She let out a loud sigh as she put her head in her hands.

Hearing a light tap on her room door nearly fifteen minutes later, Alex sat up and wiped the remaining tears with her shirt. "Come in." She smiled slightly when she saw the girls walk into her room. "Hey."

"What's going on?" Malajia asked, sitting on the bed next to her as the other girls made themselves comfortable around the room. "Emily said that you wanted to talk to us about something."

"I do," Alex confirmed, voice shaky. "You girls remember Paul, right?"

"Your ex?" Emily asked, sitting on the other side of the bed next to Alex.

Alex nodded.

"Your sorry ass, cheating with your best friend, ex?" Chasity added, looking at her nails.

"Your non-graduating on time, whining 'cause you went to college without him, ex?" Malajia chimed in.

Alex rolled her eyes. "Can you not make jokes? This is serious," she hissed.

"They're sorry," Sidra assured, cutting her eyes at both Chasity and Malajia.

"Anyway, I talked to Stacey a few days ago and she told me that...not *only* are Paul and Victoria still dealing with each other, they..." she ran her hands along the back of her neck as she tried to gather up the strength to say it. "They're about to have a baby together," she revealed.

The girls stared in shock.

"Wait, what?!" Sidra exclaimed.

"Oh shit," Chasity added.

"Ooh they're so damn *triflin'*," Malajia scoffed.

"Exactly!" Alex wailed. "I can't *believe* this shit. It's like being punched in the damn face by them over and over again." Emily rubbed Alex's shoulder as Alex began to tear up again. "*First*, I find out he cheated. *Then*, I find out that, not *only* did he cheat on me, but it was with Victoria. Someone who was supposed to be one of my best friends. And *now*, I find out that they're about to have a fuckin' *baby* together... Really? A *baby!*"

"Alex..." Sidra leaned forward in her seat as she searched for the right words to say to her friend, who was clearly hurting. "I'm sorry sweetie."

"I don't understand why they kept on *dealing* with each other," Alex seethed. "I can't believe that they *did* this."

Chasity rubbed her face as she sat back in her seat. She let Alex vent, but felt that she needed to say something. "Alex, um...I feel *really* bad that that happened, but can I ask you a question?"

Alex looked at her. "Yeah, sure."

"And don't think I'm being a bitch right now, because that's not my intention," Chasity disclaimed. "But...why do you *care?*"

"Chasity!" Emily exclaimed.

"Chaz, seriously, not now with this okay?" Sidra chastised.

"I *promise* I'm not being a smart ass," Chasity reasoned, putting her hand up. "I'm seriously asking."

Alex glared at her. "What do you mean 'why do I care'?" she hissed. "Because it's fucked up, *that's* why, Chasity. Seriously? The *queen* of holding a grudge is asking *me* why I care?"

Chasity sucked her teeth, putting her hands up in the air in surrender. "It's fine, you're right," she relented, refusing to be sucked into an argument with Alex at that moment.

"I kind of get what she's asking Alex," Malajia put in.

Alex gave a phony laugh. "Of *course* you would," she ground out.

Malajia resisted the urge to roll her eyes at Alex's snarky tone; she knew that it came from a place of hurt. "Look, all she's asking is why are you letting this affect you, Alex?" she replied, voice sincere. "It's been *years* since you were done with Paul *and* Victoria. You moved on from that, so like Chasity asked…why do you care?"

Tears spilled from Alex's eyes. "I guess it just brought up the old memories of being cheated on in the *first* place," she admitted. "When you trust somebody with your heart and they break it… It's hard to get over…" She looked around at her friends. "I mean, I know you get that."

"That may be true," Malajia agreed. "But you holding on to that isn't good for *you* or any relationship you plan on getting into."

Alex let out a loud huff. *They're not getting it.*

"Look, cry about it, vent about it, do what you need to do—"

"You really wanna feel better? I say punch the bitch in her face once she drops that kid," Chasity commented. "Slash his tires…throw a brick through his window… Or punch him in his face with it."

"Are you done, Parker?" Malajia asked, looking at her.

Chasity caught her eye. "For now," she bit out.

"No Alex, don't go to jail over them, they're not worth it," Sidra cut in.

"What I was *saying* was, do what you need to do to get over it, but make sure you *get* over it," Malajia said. "Don't let it make you bitter."

"She has a point Alex," Sidra chimed in. "It's okay to feel hurt, but don't let those two idiots ruin your outlook on relationships… Not all men are like that. Hell, *Eric* isn't."

Alex shook her head. The last thing that she wanted to hear about was relationships…or Eric, whom she hadn't

spoken to since she showed up at his door for sex days ago.
She'd neglected to keep her promise about calling him; she
dodged every call that he made to her and every attempt he
made to see her on campus. She wasn't in the mood for any
companionship. "I hear you," she said after a few moments
of silence.

It was the half-truth.

"How are you liking your gifts so far?" James asked as
he wrote on a piece of paper at his desk.

Sidra paced the floor in her room as she held her phone
to her ear. "All of them were beautiful, thank you," she
smiled. Her birthday was merely days away and James
fulfilled on his promise to send her a gift every few days.
From the flowers, to the perfume, to the necklace to the gift
certificate to the spa; he was truly generous and she was
welcoming it.

"I'm glad and you're welcome," he returned. "So,
everything is set for our trip to New York this weekend.
We're going to be staying right in Times Square. The hotel is
amazing."

Sidra stopped pacing. She was excited about the trip. She
was looking forward to spending some quality time with
James. She hadn't seen him since the summer and she missed
him. But she still couldn't help but feel a bit of pressure.

"Sidra," he called, noticing that she had fallen silent.
"Yes?"

"Why is it that every time I mention our trip, you get
quiet?" he asked. "Do you not want to go? We can do
something else if you want."

Sidra sat on her bed. "No, no that's not it. I *do* want to
go, it's just…" she let out a long sigh. "James can I ask you a
serious question?"

James picked up his mug and began to take a sip of his
coffee. "Sure, you can."

"Are you going to expect me to sleep with you on this

trip?" she asked point blank. The blunt question caused James to spit out his coffee. Sidra frowned in concern when she heard him cough over the phone. "Are you okay?"

"I'm fine," he coughed. "What do you mean, am I going to *expect* you to sleep with me?" he asked once he composed himself.

"I think it's a pretty clear question," Sidra returned, some bite to her tone.

"Sidra, of *course* I don't expect you to sleep with me," James assured. "The only thing that I expect of you is to relax and have a good time. Have I given you any indication that this was the reason why I want to take you away?"

Sidra shook her head as if James could see her. "No, you haven't," she answered. "But...I guess I just thought that because this is our first trip as a couple...and most couples...you know, have sex when they go away together—"

"Sweetheart, we've talked about this before. I know that you are a virgin and aren't ready to have sex yet. I respect that and as much as I would love to take our relationship to the next level and make love to you, I would never pressure you to do so," he said. "Trust me when I say that this trip is just for you to enjoy yourself for your birthday...nothing more."

Sidra smiled. She felt like a weight had been lifted off her shoulders. Deep down, she knew that James would never pressure her to do something that she wasn't ready for, but hearing him say it made her feel that much better. "Okay," she said. "I have to get to class, got a test. I'll talk to you later."

"Good luck on your test," he replied.

"Thank you." Sidra ended the call and quickly grabbed her book bag from the floor and darted out of the room.

Chapter 10

Sidra quickened her pace through campus on her way to the Criminal Justice building. *God, please let me pass this test*, she thought as she rounded the corner.

"Sidra," a female voice called, halting her in her tracks.

Sidra spun around, frowning. The voice didn't sound familiar. Her frown softened when she saw Josh's friend December Harley walking over to her. "What's up?"

"Do you have a minute?" December asked.

Sidra looked at the silver watch on her wrist. "A quick one," she replied as politely as possible. "I have a test to get to."

"Okay," December said, adjusting the book bag on her shoulder. The tall, dark-skinned, wavy-haired beauty looked like she had something on her mind. "It's about Josh."

Sidra frowned in confusion. "What *about* him?" she asked. "Is he okay?"

"Um, he's fine I guess. I wouldn't really *know* because he's not talking to me so much right now," December hesitantly revealed. "I feel like he's pushing me away nowadays."

Sidra was confused. "Uh...I don't mean to sound rude but...why are you telling *me* this?" she asked. "I mean, this is a conversation that you need to have with *him*. He's your boyfriend after all."

"He's *not* my boyfriend actually," December corrected, smoothing a few tendrils up into her high bun. "He's my friend and...I actually *want* him to be my boyfriend. I mean I really like him. I care for him and I thought that..." She looked down at her grey sneakers momentarily. The look on Sidra's face told December that maybe she shouldn't have said anything, but it was too late to take it back. "I don't know. I tried talking to him, but he just seems so vague... It's like he's holding back for some reason."

Maybe he just doesn't like you, Sidra thought, then immediately regretted it. Even though December couldn't hear her thoughts, she felt bad for thinking it. The girl was always so sweet. "December I really don't know what you want me to do or say," she said, voice sympathetic.

"I know that you're his best friend... I know that he talks to you all the time. I was just hoping that maybe—"

"I'm sorry, but I have to cut you off. If you're asking me if I can talk to Josh for you...no. I'm sorry, I can't. It's not my place," Sidra replied. "Or, if you're trying to ask me to tell you what he talks *about*...I won't do that either. I mean, he hasn't mentioned any of *this* to me, but even if he *did*, I wouldn't repeat it... Again, it's not my place."

December let out a sigh.

"Look, all I can suggest is that you try to talk to him again. Josh is usually a pretty good communicator, but you just need to drag things out of him sometimes," Sidra advised.

December stared at Sidra for a moment. She had to admit that she was feeling a little uneasy about this entire conversation, even though she initiated it. She stared at Sidra and took in how pretty she was. This brown-skinned, long-haired, grey-eyed, well dressed woman was the best friend of the man that she was trying to be in a relationship with. In her mind, Josh probably spent more time with Sidra than anybody. A thought popped in her head. "Can I ask you a personal question?" she asked.

Sidra once again glanced at her watch. "December, I really have to get going," she said, voice beginning to show her lack of patience. *Come on girl, I have to get to this damn test before I forget everything.*

"Just this last thing, I promise," December insisted, putting her hand up.

"Fine…what's your question?"

December hesitated; she wondered if she should ask. "Have you and Josh ever been in a relationship before?"

That question took Sidra back and it showed on her face. "*Excuse* me?"

"I'm just curious. I mean he's around you all the time, he talks to you more than anyone… I'm just wondering if I'm in competition with you for him," December explained. "I'm not mad, I just want to know."

Sidra put her hand up. "Listen, Josh and I are just friends. Nothing more," Sidra assured. "We have never been in a relationship and we never *will* be. He is like my brother… You have nothing to worry about."

December smiled and breathed a sigh of relief. "Thank you for that," she said. "I'll take your advice and try talking to him again. Thanks again, and sorry I held you up. Good luck on your test Sidra," she added, turning to walk off.

Sidra smiled in return and as she headed off in the other direction, her smile faded. She had withheld the fact that Josh was once in love with her. If December knew, she would be crushed.

Alex bundled her coat up to her neck as she and Emily walked through campus. "Damn this weather changed real quick," Alex complained of the crisp fall weather. "And this rain isn't helping."

"I guess it's making up for all of the unusually warm days that we had," Emily chuckled as she held onto her umbrella.

"Yeah well, I want to hurry up and grab this mail from

the post office and get back to the room. My hair can't take this," Alex joked.

Emily looked over at Alex. "You seem to be in a better mood," she observed. "I take it that you're feeling better about the whole…" she paused as Alex looked at her. Emily wondered if she should even mention it. After all, it had only been a few days since Alex revealed the baby issue to the girls.

"The whole Paul and Victoria situation?" Alex finished.

"Yeah," Emily answered.

"I'm *not* really," Alex admitted as she switched her umbrella from one hand to the other. "But I'm trying to put it out of my mind… It's hard though."

"I know," Emily sympathized. "And I'm sorry, I shouldn't have brought it up. I know it's still pretty fresh."

"It's okay," Alex smiled, putting her arm around Emily. "But enough about that, how are things going with Will?" As far as Alex was concerned, any topic of discussion was better than Paul, Victoria and their baby.

Emily blushed at the sound of his name. "Things are good. I enjoy his conversation," she gushed. "I just wish that we could see each other a little more often you know," she confided.

Alex frowned. "When was the last time that you *actually* saw each other?"

"Um…not since our first date," she admitted hesitantly.

Alex rolled her eyes. "That was *weeks* ago," she sneered.

Emily frowned slightly. "Just *two*," she clarified.

"So what, that's long *enough*. What is his excuse for not seeing you?"

Emily noticed that Alex's tone had a bite to it, but she resisted the urge to mention it. "Well Alex, he's been working a lot of hours at his job. Doing a lot of doubles," she answered. "He's been tired. But we talk all the time."

Alex shook her head. *This girl is clueless.* "Emily, you need to make sure that he doesn't have a girlfriend somewhere," she advised, point blank.

This time Emily did show her annoyance. "Why would you say that to me?"

"Em, what man who claims that he likes you and wants to see you, wouldn't *make time* to do so?" Alex was agitated with Emily. After everything that Alex had gone through in the past with her relationship with Paul, she hoped that Emily would pay attention to certain signs. Alex put her hand on Emily's arm when the girl turned away from her. "I don't mean to upset you sweetie," she said, voice calmer.

Are you sure? Emily thought as she kept her eyes focused ahead of her.

"I just don't want you to get hurt," Alex said. "You have to pay attention to these guys and what they do. I'm sure that Will is a nice guy, but something just seems off about him."

Emily sighed. "Alex, I get why you would feel that way but—"

"Listen, I'm only looking out for you," Alex interrupted as they approached the front of the post office door. "I mean, I would hope that you'd notice certain things, but I guess with you being so sheltered your whole life, you wouldn't know what to look for."

Emily stopped walking and turned to Alex, a stern look on her face. Alex in so many words had just called her an inexperienced, naïve child. That didn't sit well with her.

"Whoa, this rain is getting heavy, I'm gonna go and check this mail," Alex declared before Emily had a chance to respond. "Don't you have class right now?"

Emily continued to hold the same look on her face. "Yes," she answered, some bite to her voice.

"Girl, you better get going then," Alex smiled, completely unaware of what Emily was feeling. "I'll see you back at the house later."

Emily looked down at the ground as Alex walked inside.

"Yeah," she muttered, heading off to her class.

Sidra knocked on the door to Josh's room, only to hear him groan loudly. "Come in," he called. She opened the door to find Josh sitting at his desk, surrounded by balled up pieces of paper on the desk and the floor.

She giggled. "Struggling with homework huh?"

Josh spun around in his chair, smiling at the sight of her. "Yes. I'm working on this damn homework for Accounting, and my balance sheet isn't coming out right," he complained, scratching his head.

"Let me see, I took that class last year," she said, walking over. Sidra leaned over his shoulder, touching it with her hand to brace herself from toppling while she peered at his paper. "Uh sweetie, I'm no expert at this, but I don't believe you are using the right equation," she observed.

Josh snapped out of whatever trance he was in. "What?"

Sidra pointed to an equation in his textbook. "See?"

Josh leaned forward and read what she pointed to. Realizing his mistake, he smacked his hand against his face. "Shit!" he belted out, ripping another page out of his notebook and balling it up.

Sidra laughed a little as she sat on his bed. "That was the *one* thing that I actually took from that class," she joked.

"Thanks," Josh replied, writing in his notebook. "What brings you by?"

Sidra rubbed her hands on her dark blue pants as she paused for a moment. The conversation with December from the day before still plagued her. Although Sidra told December that she wasn't going to get involved in her and Josh's personal business, Sidra still felt that she needed to tell him what had happened. She couldn't keep things from Josh for very long. "Um…well, I actually wanted to talk to you about December," she revealed.

"What *about* her?" Josh asked, still focused on redoing his homework.

"She stopped me on my way to class yesterday to talk to me...about *you*."

Josh halted his writing and looked up at Sidra, a frown on his face. "She did *what*?"

Sidra nodded slowly. "Yeah... She was telling me how she felt that you were pulling away from her...she didn't talk to you?"

Josh was clearly irritated. He ran his hand over his freshly cut hair. "No, she didn't. And why the hell would she talk to *you* about that?"

Sidra shrugged as she put her hands up. "I have no idea. I guess people think that because we're close that they can get through to you through *me*," she figured. "Sarah did the same thing."

"Yeah, I know, and I didn't like it when *she* did that," Josh bit out. "December shouldn't have gone to you. That was out of line, and I'll talk to her about it."

"Josh, I didn't tell you that to start an argument between you two," Sidra said after a few seconds of silence.

"We're not going to argue."

"And I don't think she meant any harm by it," Sidra added. "She seems to genuinely care about you and I think she just wants to know where she stands with you."

Josh rolled his eyes. "Please don't lecture me on my relationship."

Sidra frowned. "I'm not *trying* to" she bit back. "But I *will* say that as a woman, I can't imagine feeling like the guy that I thought I had a connection with is pulling away without an explanation."

"You have no idea what you're talking about Sidra," Josh shot back.

Sidra folded her arms. "No?" she challenged. "I know that when I see you two together that you seem happy. I know that you're not the type of guy who hangs out with random chicks, so I know you must care for her."

Josh was silent for a moment. "Yeah," was all he said as he rubbed the back of his neck. Josh admitted that he did care for December. While they were talking about pursuing a more romantic relationship, something was holding him back from taking their friendship to the next level. "So...I know that you'll be going on your trip this weekend," he said, looking back at his notebook.

Sidra rolled her eyes. "Joshua, don't deflect," she chided.

"I'm *not*. I'm going to talk to her," Josh promised, looking back at her. "So...are you excited?"

Sidra smiled. "Yeah, I am."

Josh paused, considering if he should ask his next question, or not. He didn't know if he could handle the answer, but he needed to say it. "Are you going to sleep with him?"

The question rocked Sidra. "What?"

"I know you heard me," Josh replied, tone even.

"I'm not going to discuss this with you."

"Why not?" he pressed.

"Because!" she exclaimed. "Because of how you...." she trailed off.

"Because of how I felt about you?" he finished. Sidra nodded. "Sid, at the end of the day, you and I are friends. It doesn't matter how I feel—*felt*... You don't feel the same and...I'm okay with that now. I don't want you to feel weird talking to me about anything."

Sidra stared back at him. She heard what he was saying, but still couldn't help but feel that it would be wrong to talk about James to him, let alone *sex* with James.

When she didn't respond, Josh let out a quick sigh. "Look Sidra...I'm sure James is a good dude... He seems to make you happy," he said sincerely. "I'll just say that if you *do* decide to sleep with him..." Josh took a deep breath. "Just make sure that you be careful and don't do it unless you really want to."

"I know," was all that Sidra could say. She didn't know if she was going to sleep with James or not, but she knew that she needed to talk through her feelings with someone, and it wasn't going to be Josh. She stood from the bed. "I'm gonna get going," she announced. Josh followed her progress to the door with his eyes. "Good luck on your homework."

"Thanks," he mumbled as she walked out.

When the door shut, he put his head in his hands and let out a long sigh. *God, please don't sleep with him* he thought, hoping that the words screaming in his head could be transported to Sidra somehow.

Just that brief conversation about the possibility of Sidra giving her virginity to James made all the feelings for her that he tried to force back down, come bubbling back up. He now knew what was holding him back from getting into a relationship with December. He was unconsciously holding out for the slightest possibility that Sidra might realize that she had feelings for him.

"Stop Josh, it's never going to happen," he told himself. "Let her go man."

Chapter 11

Sidra walked into the house to find Malajia sitting on the couch, watching TV. "What's up Mel?" she solemnly greeted. When Malajia didn't immediately answer, Sidra walked over to her. "Mel what are you—" She rolled her eyes when she looked at the screen, and saw that Malajia was watching an explicit sex scene. "Seriously Malajia?"

"Shhh!" Malajia admonished, gesturing for Sidra to get away from her. "This is the best part of the movie."

Sidra nudged her with her hand. "God, you are so gross," she sneered. Sidra stared at the screen and found herself drawn into it. Watching the scene made her feel hot and bothered. That was not what she wanted to feel when she was about to make the biggest decision of her life in two days. She wanted to make it with a clear head. "Turn it off Malajia," she ordered, voice almost to a whisper.

Malajia nudged her. "No, girl move," she fussed.

Sidra snapped out of her thoughts when Chasity walked down the stairs. "Malajia, turn the fuckin' porno off," Chasity commanded. "Nobody wants to see you rubbing one out on the goddamn couch, you nasty bitch."

Malajia sucked her teeth as her head snapped toward Chasity. "Damn why I gotta be all that?!"

Sidra eyed Malajia in disgust. "Eww, is that what you were doing?"

Malajia narrowed her eyes at Sidra. "Oh sure," she sneered, voice dripping with sarcasm. "I was doing it right here on the couch, where people can just walk in and catch me."

Sidra rolled her eyes. "Simple 'no' would have done just fine," she bristled.

"No, I wanted you to hear how stupid your question was," Malajia threw back, pointing the remote in Sidra's direction.

Emily ran down the steps. "Ooh, did I burn the lasagna?" she panicked, running over to the stove.

Chasity opened the oven and peered inside. "No," she answered. "It's done actually."

Emily breathed a sigh of relief. "Thank God. I got so caught up in my homework," she chuckled. "I almost forgot it was in there."

Sidra sat on the couch. "What are you girls about to do?"

"Eat this food Emily cooked and play some spades," Malajia answered, turning the television off. She walked over to Emily and peered over her shoulder, as Emily pulled the aluminum pan filled with lasagna out of the oven. "That better be good," she commented.

Emily giggled. "Well it's my first one, so I hope it *is*," she replied, setting it on the counter.

As the girls were setting the table, Alex walked into the house holding a pizza. "Y'all cooked?" she observed, eyeing the pan on the table.

Malajia looked at her. "You hype as shit with that pizza," she laughed. Alex rolled her eyes.

"Yeah, I cooked," Emily responded unenthused. Even though Emily never said anything to Alex, she was still annoyed with her for talking down to her about Will.

Alex groaned as she set the pizza on the arm of the loveseat. "Damn, if I would've known I wouldn't have lugged this thing back."

"Alex, nobody *asked* you to bring that, first of all," Chasity sniped, sitting down at the table. "Second, Malajia texted you and told you that Emily was making something tonight."

Alex removed her hat and scarf. "Malajia never texted me," she spat.

"I *did* actually. If you had a better damn phone, then you would've *gotten* it," Malajia confirmed, showing Alex the text that she sent earlier that afternoon.

Alex looked at it and waved her hand dismissively. "Whatever, we'll just have it tomorrow," she huffed.

"Please take that shit to the guys' house, we don't want it," Chasity scoffed.

Alex sighed as she grabbed the box from the chair and headed for the refrigerator. "Chasity you can't speak for everybody. Somebody in this house will eat it tomorrow."

"Actually she *can* this time," Sidra confirmed, voice filled with laughter. "We don't want that."

Alex looked around shocked. "Nobody?" she asked. The girls vigorously shook their heads no. Alex shrugged and set the box on the counter. "Fine, I'll tell one of the guys to come get it later."

After eating and cleaning the mess up, the girls sat back down at the dining room table for a game of spades. Emily, who hadn't played before, was spectator and score keeper.

"Who keeps buying these nasty orange wine coolers?" Malajia sneered, eyeing a bottle while she arranged the cards in her hand.

"Your man," Chasity laughed, eyeing her cards.

Malajia sucked her teeth. "Damn, I keep telling Mark's ass not to get these. I told him to get any kind *but* these... He don't listen."

Alex shook her head. "Men never *do*," she complained, taking a sip of her cooler. She looked up and saw that Emily was getting ready to open one. "Em, do you really want to drink that?" she asked.

Emily paused and looked at Alex. "Yes," she simply answered.

"Alex, leave the girl alone," Chasity chimed in, annoyed.

Alex put her hands up. "Look, I just don't think it's a good idea," she maintained.

"It's a *wine cooler*," Emily muttered.

"It's still *alcohol*," Alex pressed. "You shouldn't have *any*, especially since you had a problem with drinking—"

"Sophomore year. It was *sophomore* year and I appreciate the fact that you keep reminding me," Emily bit out, pushing the drink away from her. She was almost at the end of her rope with Alex the know-it-all.

Malajia pushed the drink back in front of Emily. "Girl, don't let mop-n-boots stop you from doing what you want to do," she griped.

Alex shot Malajia a glare.

"Wine coolers are like *juice*," Malajia added.

"No, I'm fine," Emily mumbled, writing the score system on a piece of paper.

Chasity laughed at her partner. "Wait, did you just call Alex mop-n-boots?"

"I sure did," Malajia laughed back, then ducked as Alex tossed the bottle top from the wine cooler at her. "Missed, you dusty hag." Malajia's remark earned her snickers from Sidra and Emily. Alex wasn't amused as she held her angry gaze upon Malajia.

"Chaz, if you lose us another goddamn hand to Alex and Sidra, I swear I'll smack you with Mark's dick," Malajia jeered, causing Emily to nearly choke on the juice that she was drinking.

Chasity eyed her cards. "Yeah, I don't think me being smacked with a pencil sized instrument will do any damage," she flashed back, voice filled with sarcasm.

Malajia chuckled. "Yeah okay, I already told you once how big it was," she shot back. "Do I need to repeat the details?"

"No, I'd prefer to keep my food down," Chasity returned, tone even.

"Malajia, I'm going to need you to stop taking every opportunity to mention penises," Alex grumbled.

Malajia let out a huff. "I only mention *one* penis, stop exaggerating."

Sidra eyed Malajia with disgust as she shook her head. "God Malajia, Alex is right," she chimed in. "Everything with you is about sex, or something sex *related*."

"And here goes the uptight queen, offering her dry ass two cents," Malajia mocked, rolling her eyes. "Not my fault you have no sex life."

Sidra made a face. "Just saying," she muttered. "And you don't have to remind me that I have no sex life. I remember, trust me."

"You sound pretty bitter there, Princess," Chasity laughed.

"I'm not bitter," Sidra hissed.

Malajia gestured to Sidra as she looked at Chasity. "Aye Chaz."

"What?" Chasity dryly asked.

"She mad 'cause her fingers be cramping and shit," Malajia joked.

Chasity shook her head. "Don't call me if you're just gonna say corny shit like that," she grunted.

Sidra slammed her hand on the table. "Malajia!" she belted out as Malajia laughed. "That was uncalled for."

"Wow," Emily commented, putting her hand over her face.

Alex shot Malajia a glower. "Will you just stop it?"

Malajia put her hand up in surrender. "Fine, I'll chill," she said to Sidra. "But you started with me first."

Sidra sucked her teeth. "Whatever," she grumbled as she shuffled her cards around in her hands. After a few moments of silence, Sidra looked up. "Okay, can I ask you ladies a personal question?" she then glanced at Malajia. "Without you making a joke about it?"

Malajia looked around shocked. "I am offended."

"Are you really?" Sidra jeered.

Malajia chuckled. "No, not really."

Alex flagged Malajia with her hand. "Sidra, of *course* you can," she replied, sincere. "Ask away."

"Okay...sorry Em, this one doesn't apply to you," Sidra said.

Emily just shrugged.

Sidra took a deep breath. "How..." she hesitated for a moment. "Okay, how did you know that you were ready to lose your virginity?" she finished, feeling a little embarrassed. Her question was met with stares and silence.

"Well damn," Chasity chortled.

"I know right?" Malajia added.

Alex adjusted her position on her seat. "Sid, that's a great question," she praised. "And to *answer* it... at the time I just *knew*. I was sixteen and in love...or I *thought* I was anyway." Alex looked at the table briefly. "Paul and I both wanted to be each other firsts, so we just decided to do it."

Malajia paused for a moment, unsure if she wanted to answer. She'd worked hard on putting her past experiences with her ex behind her—that included losing her virginity—but her friend was asking for honesty, so she knew she needed to share. "Sid, I'm not gonna lie..." she began, pushing hair over her shoulder. "I *wasn't* ready to lose mine," she admitted.

While Chasity's facial expression hadn't changed, as she knew the situation, Sidra, Alex, and Emily couldn't hide their shock.

"Are you serious?" Sidra asked. Malajia nodded. "But, you never said—"

"It's not something that I felt like sharing," Malajia cut in. "When you fantasize about the ideal situation, and it turns out to be the opposite...you tend to not want to celebrate it."

Emily glanced down at the table in silence, fiddling with the pencil in her hand.

"Truth is, I *talked* myself into having sex with...*him* the first time, because I thought it would make things better between us," Malajia revealed. "It was stupid and I regretted it."

Sidra eyed Malajia sympathetically. "I'm sorry," she said. "If I had known, I wouldn't have asked you."

"It's okay," Malajia assured. "I've moved on to better experiences so…"

"Wow Malajia," Alex commented. "I can't—"

"Chasity is trying to avoid eye contact with you, Sidra," Malajia quickly deflected, cutting Alex off. She already knew that Alex was going to harp on the fact that she didn't tell them before this, and Malajia didn't want to hear it.

Sidra looked at Chasity "Yeah, you, spill," she said. "How did you know that you were ready to lose your virginity?"

"Fine," Chasity relented. She thought for a moment. "Um… Honestly it was—I think I was just…" She looked at the ceiling as if the words were up there.

"I don't think I actually remember a time where you were tongue tied," Malajia teased.

Chasity flipped her off in retaliation. "Honestly Sidra, although it wasn't *planned*, at that moment I kind of just knew that I *wanted* to," Chasity finished.

"So, you just wanted to lose it in *general* or to Jason specifically?" Sidra asked.

"To *Jason*," Chasity assured, folding her arms. "Please, who *else* would I have considered?"

Malajia leaned in and stared intently at Chasity. "So, your hot ass, wanted it to be him *before* you were actually in that situation," she pressed.

Alex leaned forward. "How soon after you met him, Chasity?" she asked.

"Yeah, how soon?" Sidra added, intrigued.

Chasity looked around. "If y'all don't get out my damn face," she hissed.

"Nah, confess," Malajia harped, shaking her hand in Chasity's direction. "How soon?"

Chasity ran her hand over her face. "Why are y'all lingering on *me*?" she fussed.

"'Cause, you obviously been holding out on some details," Malajia explained, tapping her finger nails on the table.

Chasity narrowed her eyes at them. "Fine," she grunted through clenched teeth. "I started *thinking* about it...freshman year," she confessed.

Malajia tossed her hands in the air. "I knew it!"

"You ain't know shit. I said I was *thinking* about it, I never said I was actually gonna *do* it," Chasity argued.

"Nope, that doesn't matter," Alex laughed. Chasity flagged Alex with her hand.

"Drawls was probably all wet and shit when Jason would call her," Malajia joked. "He'd be like 'hey beautiful' and bam, water falls."

Chasity busted out laughing. "Fuck you Malajia," she hurled, tossing a balled-up napkin at her.

Sidra shook her head in amusement. "Well, this has been enlightening," she chortled. "Thank you all for being honest."

Alex looked at her. "Of course," she said. "But what made you ask in the first place?"

"'Cause she wanted to know, *duh*," Malajia mumbled. Alex ignored her.

Sidra shrugged. "Was curious."

Alex held her gaze. "Sidra... are you planning on having sex with James when you go on your trip this weekend?"

Sidra fidgeted in her seat as all sets of eyes focused on her. "I don't know," she answered finally. "Maybe...I mean... I've been *thinking* about it." She tapped her finger nails on the table. "I have feelings for him and...I mean isn't that what you do when you have feelings for someone?"

"Not necessarily," Chasity said. "Just because you care about someone, doesn't mean that you have to sleep with them if you're not ready to."

"That's just the thing, I think I *am* ready," Sidra stressed.

"You think, or you *know*?" Chasity asked.

Sidra opened her mouth to speak but closed it when she

couldn't decide. "Not sure," she admitted. "I *do* know that I've been feeling..."

"Horny?" Malajia jumped in. Sidra covered her face from embarrassment. "Girl, there's nothing wrong with admitting that."

Sidra shook her head. "Yeah well, Malajia and all her pornos and *loudness* whenever Mark is over, doesn't help," she grunted.

Malajia clutched the necklace on her neck. "You hear me?" she asked, feigning shock.

Sidra glared at her. "You *know* you're loud," she bit out.

"Yes, *always*," Alex confirmed, spiteful.

"This barrage of hate coming my way is unnecessary," Malajia threw back, trying to hold in her laughter.

"Bottom line is," Alex began, putting her hand up. "Malajia, you need to either be more discrete or have sex in *his* room," she said.

Malajia sucked her teeth. "You got me chopped," she flashed back. "And why is this about me—"

"Malajia, just shut up already," Chasity jumped in, annoyed.

Malajia sucked her teeth once again. "Don't nobody say *shit* when Chasity's headboard be—"

"I said shut up," Chasity barked, causing Malajia to snicker.

Alex kept her focus on Sidra. "Listen sweetie, *whenever* you decide to lose your virginity, just make sure it's really what you want..." she said, sincere. "If you have to second guess yourself, then you're not ready."

Sidra rubbed her arm as she pondered Alex's words. "I hear you...I get it."

Alex smiled at Sidra, then looked over at Emily, who was quiet during the entire conversation. "That goes for you *too*, Emily," she said. "You make sure you only lose it when you're ready."

Emily hesitated to speak as she rubbed the back of her neck. She'd been quiet for a reason, and it wasn't the reason everyone thought. "Um…" she began, letting her hand linger on the back of her neck. "I kinda sorta…already—"

"Already what? Stopped listening to Alex?" Malajia chuckled. "Don't worry, so did I."

"You're not funny, I hope you know that Malajia," Alex ground out.

"No," Emily answered, tone low. "I mean that…I already lost…it," she revealed.

The girls fell quiet; confusion set in.

"You lost *what* Em?" Sidra asked.

Emily glanced down at the table. "My virginity." She glanced up; saying that her friends were shocked was an understatement.

"Say *what* now?" Chasity managed to get out after a few moments of stunned silence.

"I'm not a virgin," Emily confirmed.

"The fuck?" Chasity muttered; that was the only thing that she could think to say. That certainly wasn't what she expected to hear.

"Wait, wait," Malajia protested, waving her arms. "So…" she was in complete disbelief over Emily's revelation. The shy, quiet one? The innocent, naïve one? The baby? Not a virgin. "So, you mean to tell us that you actually had *sex*?"

Emily slowly nodded.

"*You*?" Malajia pressed, pointing at her. "Emily, my-mommy-never-let-me-play-in-the-snow Harris had, *actual* sex?"

Emily once again nodded.

Malajia tossed her hands up and leaned back in her seat. "Well ain't this some bullshit," she conceded.

"Yeah," Emily mumbled, pushing some braids over her shoulder.

"Whoa," was all that Sidra could get out. She, like the other girls, didn't know what to think. Here, they thought that Emily didn't even know what sex *was* when they first met her.

The person in the most shock was Alex, who sat there with her mouth wide open. She and Emily had had many personal conversations, how could she not mention this? "Wait," Alex began, rubbing her forehead. "You didn't sleep with *Will,* did you?"

Emily shot Alex a side glance. "No, I didn't," she replied.

"So...did it happen while you were here at school?" Alex pressed.

Emily shook her head. "No... I was fifteen."

"Fifteen!" the girls exclaimed in unison.

"Are you serious?" Sidra wailed, leaning forward.

"How did you get off your mom's lap long enough to do *that?*" Chasity jeered.

Emily shot Chasity a warning look. "Chasity," she said.

Chasity put her hand up. "Sorry, it was so easy," she teased.

"Chasity, that was funny and we shall laugh together later," Malajia directed to Chasity, then looked back to Emily. "Baby girl, you better start spilling some damn details," she added, fully anticipating Emily's story.

Emily pointed to the scores on the notebook. "Don't you want to finish your game first?" she asked.

"Fuck that game," Malajia barked.

Emily let out a sigh as she set the pencil down. "Okay," she relented. She wished she hadn't said anything. But now that it was out, Emily knew she had to talk about it. "Well...like I said, I was fifteen," she began. "There was this boy that I..." she took a deep breath. "Do I *have* to?"

"Yes," the girls answered in unison. There was no way that Emily could reveal something this big about herself and not share the details.

Emily put her hands up in surrender. "He was in some of my classes, Damien was his name... I thought he was cute," she began. "Didn't really think that he paid me any mind... I mean, nobody really *did* to be honest." She rubbed her arm. "Anyway, one day we were assigned to be partners for a project in one of our classes… I was pretty excited because I knew that he had no choice *but* to talk to me… And to my surprise, after the project was over, he still wanted to talk to me, so he asked me for my phone number."

"Did you give it to him?" Sidra asked.

"Sidra, shut up with your stupid questions, let her finish," Malajia snapped, flinging her hand in Sidra's direction.

"*You* shut up, it was a valid question," Sidra hurled back. Malajia flagged her with her hand.

"To answer your question Sidra, yes I did," Emily said. "Luckily at that time, my mom started working as a night school teacher, so I was able to talk to him while she was gone… I never thought that it would go anywhere, but it was nice to have a friend, you know." Emily played with the pencil on the table as she recalled more. "He actually asked me out to a movie one day and I couldn't believe it… Like he really wanted to go out with weird, awkward, quiet little me—"

The girls were quiet as they listened, faces were masked with sympathy. The fact that Emily didn't even think that she was worthy of being asked to something as simple as a movie was disheartening.

"I begged my mom to let me go and of course she said 'no'," Emily remembered. "It was always *'no'* to *everything*. It was never an explanation as to why her answer was 'no', it was never a conversation about my feelings, it was just always 'no'," her voice grew bitter. "Needless to say, I was mad at her… I went to my room and she went to work…then Damien called me. I started venting to him about not being able to go with him and he suggested that I sneak out to meet him…"

"You didn't really *go*, did you?" Alex asked.

Chasity slammed her hand on the table in frustration. "Oh my—Alex, shut up," she snapped, earning a snicker from Malajia.

"Yes, Alex, I did," Emily confirmed. "Mom was at

work, my brothers and sister didn't care about me enough to check on me, so it wasn't as hard as I thought it would be... I just wanted to get out of the house—I just wanted to go to the movies...but he suggested that we go to his house instead. He snuck me in through his basement and we played video games and talked... Then after a while, he talked *me* into having sex with him." Emily let out a sigh. "I was naïve and stupid, so I did it...in the basement on an ugly worn-down couch... He didn't say anything afterwards, he just got up and went back to playing his stupid game, so I just left... Made it back home before Mom got in and that was that." She shrugged as regret filled her. "Imagine my surprise the next day when he wouldn't even *look* at me. He treated me like he didn't even *know* me, I was so confused... By the time the semester had ended, he moved away."

Alex reached across the small table and grabbed Emily's hand, holding it.

"I thought that it meant something to him...that *I* meant something to him and it turned out that he was just a stupid boy trying to get *one* thing...and I was the stupid girl who *gave* it to him," Emily sulked.

"Wow..." Alex commented. She would never have imagined that Emily would have gone through something like that. "Did you guys at least use protection?"

Emily looked at her. "I told you, I was stupid," she reiterated, giving Alex the answer. "Luckily, God looks out for fools because I didn't end up pregnant or with any disease..." she sighed again. "You girls are the first ones to hear about this."

"You've been carrying that since you were fifteen?" Sidra asked, sympathetic. "Poor baby."

Emily nodded. "I could *never* have told my mother what I'd done," she stressed. "She almost pulled me out of school over my friendship with *you* guys. And I was *nineteen* at the time," she pointed out. "Can you imagine what she would have done if she found out that her fifteen-year-old actually had *sex*? I would be in a boarding school somewhere."

"You got a point there," Malajia muttered. Although her own first-time experience happened when she was twenty, and wasn't exactly the same as Emily's, Malajia still understood what it felt like to regret it.

"That's fucked up Em," Chasity said. "Sorry you went through that."

Emily smiled slightly. "Thanks…" she said. "I'm okay though. I know that it's not something that can be undone, so I've just chosen to learn from it."

"He's an asshole for doing that to you and I hope his balls get rotten and fall off," Malajia fumed, earning a giggle from Emily. "And that an elephant comes past and *steps* on them raggedy balls while he's trying to pick them up off the ground…*and* I hope the elephant kicks him in the face with his ball-juice-covered foot."

"What?" Chasity barked at Malajia's rant.

"Yeah, you and me *both*," Emily laughed.

Emily then turned to Sidra, who looked like someone had just died. "Sid, Alex is right. Make sure you're *really* ready," she said, tone serious. "You don't want to look back and wish that you'd waited."

Sidra just nodded before giving Emily a hug.

Chapter 12

Sidra stood in the lobby of the luxury hotel, taking in the high ceiling, chandeliers and antique furniture. She watched as James chatted up the clerk at the front desk. Her conversation with the girls about sex two days ago played over and over in her head; she was on edge that entire morning.

But when James had showed up at her house in a limo nearly six hours ago, a bouquet of flowers in hand, and a smile on his face, she had felt her tension ease a bit. When he had enveloped her in a strong embrace and placed a kiss on her lips, she was able to let go of her apprehension all together. They'd spent the long luxurious ride up to New York talking, laughing and cuddling.

Sidra was all smiles as James approached her, room keys in hand.

"All set," he announced, extending his arm for her to loop her arm through.

"What about the bags?" Sidra wondered, pointing to two small suitcases by the desk.

"Oh, the bellhop will bring them up," James smiled.

"Ah, the perks of a high-end hotel," Sidra grinned. "I can get used to this."

"I sure hope so," James chuckled, leading the way to the

elevators. "We have reservations at seven for dinner," he informed. "How does Italian sound?"

"Sounds good to me," Sidra cooed, stepping into the elevator.

"Good," James returned. "After that, I have a little surprise for you."

Sidra clapped her hands together in excitement as they arrived on their floor. "Really?" she beamed. He nodded.

James stuck the key card in the door to their assigned room and pushed it open. Stepping inside, Sidra looked around the massive room in awe. Sure, she'd been in nice hotels on several occasions, but this one-bedroom suite was immaculate. She took a walk around while James made his way to the well-stocked mini bar. Peering into the bedroom, she noticed the two queen beds.

She stepped back into the main room. "Two beds?" she asked, gesturing to the door.

James nodded as he made himself a drink of rum and cola. "Yes," he answered. "I meant what I said to you before, there are *no* expectations this weekend."

Sidra nodded slowly. *And here I was stressing over nothing.* "I appreciate your understanding."

"Come on Sidra, there is no need to thank me."

Sidra smiled, then peered out of the window, taking in the view.

"We have a few hours until dinner; you want to go check out some stores, or do you want to rest for a bit?" he asked, breaking her out of her trance.

"Umm…I kind of want to do *both*," she quipped. "I didn't get much sleep last night, so I am a little tired, but…*stores*."

James laughed. "Okay, tell you what, you rest for now and tomorrow, after breakfast, I'll take you shopping," he proposed.

Sidra's smile could have lit the hotel room had the lights not already been on. She offered an enthused nod, then retreated to the bedroom.

The two-hour nap refreshed Sidra. She was glowing while she sat across from James at the restaurant.

"You look well rested," James observed, taking a sip of champagne.

Sidra reached for her glass. "I *am*," she confirmed, taking a long sip. "I didn't realize how tired I really was."

"Yeah, that's usually how that goes," James chuckled. He stared at her. "Did I tell you how beautiful you look?"

Sidra glanced down at the linen cloth on the table, blushing. "You *did*, but thank you again."

"Of course," James replied.

Sidra smiled at him. James was already a handsome man, but he looked even more handsome through the candlelight. She pushed some of her curled hair over her shoulder. "And thank you again for this weekend and all the gifts that you've given to me," she added, grateful. "You're really making my birthday special."

James reached across the small table and gently grabbed her hand, holding it. "You don't have to keep thanking me, it's my pleasure to treat you like a princess," he crooned.

God, can he get any damn sexier? "My parents would be happy to hear you say that," Sidra chortled. "I've always been their princess."

"And now you're *mine*," he returned. Sidra blushed again, causing him to laugh. "Am I embarrassing you?"

"No, you're not," she smiled back. She couldn't decide if the funny feeling in her stomach was her hunger pangs or butterflies. Luckily, she didn't have to wonder much longer because their food had arrived.

Once the server set the entrees in front of them, Sidra grabbed the burgundy linen napkin in front of her and unfolded it as James reached into his pocket to retrieve something. "I hope this tastes as good as it *looks*," Sidra mused, picking up her fork.

"Before you start eating, I have another gift for you," James announced, holding something in his hand.

Sidra looked up at him, surprised. "Really?"

James nodded. "It's only right to get you something *on* your birthday," he chuckled, holding out the small square royal blue box.

Sidra glanced down at it, anticipating what could be inside. The box was a little too wide to be a ring—not that she was expecting one. She cared for him, but she knew she was nowhere *near* ready for a proposal.

"You going to keep staring at it, or are you going to take it?" James teased.

Sidra put her hand over her face in embarrassment. "The second option," she joked in return. He placed the box into her open hand. She untied the white ribbon and opened the box. A shriek left her throat. "Oh my God!" she exclaimed, eyeing the pair of princess cut solitaire diamond studs, set in white gold.

James sat there beaming as she held the box close to her face.

She looked up at him, eyes wide. "James...are these—"

"Real diamond?" he finished. "Yes, they are."

Sidra put her hand on her chest, then signaled James to come forward. When he did, she leaned in and kissed him. She was glad that she was in a restaurant and not in their room, because she didn't know if she would have been able to keep the sweet gesture from turning to something R-rated. "I love them," she gushed once they parted.

Sidra stared at the sparkling studs; they were so beautiful that she just couldn't wait to get them in her ears. She began removing the silver hoop earrings from her lobes.

"You're putting them on *now*?" James laughed, cutting into his veal parmesan.

"Oh *absolutely*," she confirmed, carefully putting the studs in. Once finished, she pushed her hair behind her ears.

James picked up his glass and tilted it towards her.

"Perfect."

Sidra was on cloud nine as she walked hand in hand with James out of the restaurant. She let out a happy sigh. "I'm stuffed." She glanced down at her silver stiletto pumps. "And I should *not* have worn these shoes."

James glanced over at her. "Feet hurting?"

Sidra nodded. "Unfortunately," she griped. "They felt fine when I tried them on in the store, but now that I've had them on all this time, not so much."

James nodded, signaling to something, "Well, it's a good thing you don't have to walk."

Before Sidra had a chance to respond, she saw a white horse drawn carriage pull in front of the restaurant. Her mouth dropped open. Though she was physically speechless, her mind wasn't. *Whaaaaat?! He got me a freakin' horse and carriage, this man is everything!*

"I figured, why not try another mode of transportation for the evening," James said, leading her to the carriage.

Excited, Sidra allowed him to help her inside. Once seated comfortably, the carriage started moving. As they rode through the streets, James placed his arm around her, and she leaned her head on his shoulder. Though they rode in silence, it was a comfortable silence. Entering the park and glancing up at the moonlight peering through the trees, Sidra grabbed James's hand and held it. She was filled with adoration for the man who sat beside her. James had gone above and beyond to make her twenty-second birthday special, and it was for no other reason than wanting to see her happy. The evening and this man were everything that she'd dreamed of and in that moment, she didn't feel apprehension, she didn't feel unsure; she felt…ready.

"James, what are we doing after this?" Sidra asked, breaking the silence.

"Whatever you want," he returned, looking at her.

Sidra moved her head from his shoulder and stared into

his eyes. "Can…can we go back to the room?"

"Sure."

"I mean *now*," she clarified.

He frowned slightly. "Are you tired?"

Sidra held her longing gaze as her body started to tingle. She slowly shook her head.

James stared at her the same way that she looked at him: full of what he felt was lust. He hadn't expected it, but he welcomed it. "You sure?"

"Yes," she breathed. "Let's go."

If Sidra's hormones were on high during her carriage ride, they were certainly in overdrive now that they were back at the hotel. James had successfully waited and held his desires back while they were making their way back to the hotel. Now that they were in their suite, he could no longer resist, and neither could she.

Kicking off her shoes and dropping her purse to the floor, Sidra fully welcomed James kissing her lips and her neck. The feeling of his hands roaming her slender body riled her up even more. Making their way to the bed, he removed his clothes then helped her out of her dress, sending it to the floor.

As James gently guided Sidra down on the bed, her mind began racing. She tried to keep herself relaxed while James continued to kiss down her body. She closed her eyes and tried to stay in the moment, but for some reason her racing thoughts wouldn't stop. *Sidra, what are you doing?* The more that James kissed and touched her, the more the voice in her head spoke.

You know this doesn't feel right, she thought. Trying to ignore the voice, Sidra put her hands above her head as James gripped the delicate fabric of her lace underwear with his fingers. She squeezed her eyes shut when James's tongue touched her skin. Even though what James was doing to her felt good—*really* good, she couldn't focus; the voice in her head was screaming too loudly. *I can't do this! I can't— I'm not ready.*

Sidra grabbed his hand, "James...wait..." she panted.

James was so focused on trying to please her that he didn't hear her.

"Stop," she said, a little louder. "Stop, James *stop.*"

James halted and looked at her. "What's wrong, are you okay?" he asked.

"I'm sorry," she stammered, voice cracking. "I—I can't—"

He moved up, coming face to face with her. Seeing the look of uncertainty in Sidra's eyes, he touched her face. "Sidra, what's wrong?"

"I can't. I can't sleep with you," she answered, tears filling her eyes. "I'm sorry. I thought I was ready and I'm not... I'm so sorry." Sidra put her hands over her face and sobbed quietly. She was embarrassed.

James closed his eyes briefly in an effort to hide his disappointment. He was looking forward to showing Sidra just how much she meant to him, but he would never want her to go all the way before she was ready. He grabbed her hands from her face. "It's okay," he assured, tone caring.

"No, it's *not* okay," Sidra whimpered. "I didn't mean to lead you on—"

"I *promise* you, it's okay," he insisted, wiping the tears from her cheeks. "If you're not ready, you're not ready... You're entitled to change your mind."

Sidra wiped more tears from her eyes. She appreciated the fact that James was trying to comfort her, but she was frustrated with herself. She was so sure during the carriage ride; she couldn't understand what within her changed in such a short amount of time. "Are you mad?" she asked after a few seconds of silence.

James leaned forward and kissed her cheek then glanced back at her. "I'm *horny*, I'm not mad," he joked.

Sidra managed a slight chuckle, though she found the situation far from amusing.

James moved off of her and laid down beside her. Pulling the covers over them, he just held her as they drifted off to sleep.

Josh stared at his cell phone, where he'd left it on his bed. He didn't know exactly how long he'd be staring at it, but he knew for sure it was over ten minutes. *Don't do it. Don't call*, kept playing in his mind.

Frustrated, Josh rubbed his face with both of his hands. It had been a day since Sidra left for New York with James, and he couldn't stop thinking about her…most importantly what she was *doing*. It was *all* that he had been thinking about.

He snatched the phone up, and, ignoring his inner voice, dialed Sidra's number. He waited in anticipation as it rang. When it went to voicemail, he rubbed the bridge of his nose with his fingers. Letting out a long, frustrated sigh, he ended the call and tossed the phone back on the bed. *Dumbass*, he chided himself.

Staring out in front of him, he felt the walls closing in. He picked the phone back up and dialed another number. "Hey," he greeted once the line picked up. "It's Josh… What are you doing right now?... Do you mind if I come over?... Okay, see you in a few." Rising from his chair, he grabbed his coat from the back of his chair and headed out.

Josh walked through the cluster gates and headed towards a familiar house. Knocking on the door, he shoved his hands in his pockets while waiting. He smiled when the door opened. "Hi."

December stood in the doorway, clad in pajama shorts and a tank top. Her long hair fell to her elbows. "Hi," she replied in a curt tone. "What brings you over?" She hadn't spoken to him in days and her irritation with him was quite clear.

"I um…I wanted to talk to you," Josh sputtered.

"Why *now*?" she hissed.

"Can I come in please?" he pleaded, feeling the brisk air brush over him.

December rolled her eyes and moved aside to let him in.

"You look cute," he complimented.

"Yeah right," she snarled, leading the way up to her room. When Josh walked in, he shut the door behind him.

"Your roommate isn't here?" Josh asked, removing his coat and hanging it on the back of December's chair.

She flopped down on her bed, removing her white fluffy slippers. "No, she went home for the weekend," she ground out, running her hand through her hair. "You said you wanted to talk Josh, so…what do you want to talk about?"

Josh turned the chair around to face her and sat down. "First off, I want to apologize," he began.

"*For?*"

"For being distant," he responded.

"Distant?" she repeated.

Josh nodded. "That *is* why you're angry with me isn't it?" he asked, tone calm.

"Josh you haven't just been distant," December argued. "You've *completely* shut me out. I thought we were trying to build something."

"We *are*," he insisted.

"That is *not* how you treat someone who you're trying to build something with, Joshua," she spat, folding her arms.

Josh rubbed his face with his hand. She had a point, he knew that. "Look…I've had a lot on my mind lately—"

"That's no damn excuse—"

"I *know* that," he cut in. "I was wrong. I shouldn't have shut you out." She rolled her eyes. "Just like *you* shouldn't have gone to Sidra with your issues with me."

December's eyes widened slightly. *She told him.* "Josh…" she looked down at her hands briefly. "I didn't know who else to talk to… *You* weren't talking to me," she explained.

Josh sat back in his seat, sighing in the process.

"I figured that your best friend would be able to get through to you…since *I* couldn't seem to," she added. "I just—I just wanted some insight…some *advice*."

Josh sighed once again. "I guess I get it," he said after a moment. "I messed up, but I promise to do better… I really like you, December."

"I like you *too* Josh," she replied, bite in her voice. "I really *do*. But I'm not gonna just sit around and be *played* by you."

Josh looked at her. "I wouldn't play you," he promised. "I'm not like that."

She shook her head. "I want to believe that."

Josh stood from the seat and sat next to December on the bed. He could see that he had hurt her feelings, and that was the last thing that he wanted to do. He wasn't lying; he really did like her and thought that December was someone who he could try being with. "I'm sorry that I made you question how I felt about you," he apologized, sincere. "I'm still the same guy that you first started talking to…can you give me another chance?"

December stared into his eyes and couldn't help but let some of her guard down. She cared for this man sitting in front of her. Even though she was frustrated with him, she wanted to be with him. Always had, but before she could allow herself to take that step, she needed to know something. "Before—" she paused for a moment. "I need to ask you something first."

He tilted his head. "What is it?"

December took a deep breath. "Is the reason why you pulled away from me…because you really want someone else?"

Josh looked confused.

She didn't know if she wanted to ask the rest of her question, but she had to. "Namely…*Sidra*?"

Josh's eyes widened. "What made you ask me that?"

"Because she's a woman, Josh," she explained. "The

only woman that I've seen you cling to… Your face lights up when you talk about her…you don't even *realize* it, but it does."

Josh held his same gaze, he was panicking on the inside. He thought that he was doing a good job of hiding how he still felt about Sidra, but clearly, he wasn't. If this was obvious to December, then it had to still be obvious to Sidra.

"You say that she's just your best friend, but I'm just wondering if she is or has *ever* been more than that." December continued. "I asked *her* the same question."

Josh ran his hand over his hair. *Why didn't Sidra mention that part of the conversation to me?* Josh stared in December's eyes as he gathered his thoughts. He was still in love with Sidra, and as much as he wished that she would return his feelings, he knew that that would never happen. As far as he was concerned, Sidra was giving herself to James right at that very moment.

"No…Sidra is *just* my friend," he answered. "I don't have any feelings for her other than that," he lied. "*You* are who I want to be with."

His answer seemed to satisfy December, who planted a kiss on him and threw her arms around him. As Josh hugged her, he couldn't help but feel terrible. After all, he did lie to December about his feelings for his best friend. But for the sake of his new-found relationship with December, and more importantly his sanity, he would get over them… At least, he would try.

Chapter 13

"Yo, I hope they have some fun shit for us to do for homecoming like *last* year," Mark said, walking out of the Business building, books in hand.

"Aww," Emily pouted, adjusting the zipper on her coat.

David looked confused. "What's the matter, Em?" he wondered.

"This is gonna be our last homecoming as students," she answered. "It's sad when you actually think about it."

Mark shook his head. "Shit, no the hell it's *not*," he threw back. "I can't *wait* to get out of here."

David chuckled. "You know its family weekend coming up," he informed, adjusting his book bag on his shoulder. "Anybody ready for *that*?"

"Yeah, good luck with that," Mark laughed. "My parents aren't coming up this time around."

"You laugh *now*, but you'll be missing out on all the food and supplies they would've bought you had they came up," David joked.

"Nope, not sweating it," Mark boasted. "We live in the same house, so I'll just use y'all shit."

David sucked his teeth, earning a laugh from Mark.

Emily just stood there, listening to the banter. She hated to admit it, but the mention of family weekend brought her mood down. "I need to get to the library," she announced. "See you guys later."

"You hype as shit to get started on your homework," Mark teased.

Emily just giggled, then waved as she walked off.

"David man, you wanna go play some ball?" Mark asked as the two made their way down the building steps.

David sighed. "Mark, it's like eleven in the morning, don't you think it's too early for that?"

Mark frowned in confusion. "It's *never* too early for basketball," he threw back. "Stop being corny."

David shook his head. "The answer is no."

Mark sucked his teeth. "Fine... Do my auditing homework then," he proposed.

David was about to fire off a retort, when the sight of Nicole, emerging from the cafeteria a few feet from him, stopped the words from coming out.

Mark, noticing that David stopped walking, looked at him. "What did you stop for?" he wondered. When David didn't respond, Mark craned his neck to see what had him in such a daze. Mark smirked when he saw Nicole. "Man, you *still* drooling over that girl?" he teased, giving David a nudge.

Snapping out of his daze, David quickly backhanded him.

"Yo, what was *that* for?" Mark griped, rubbing his arm.

"You told me that she had a boyfriend last semester," David snapped. "Had me looking all stupid when I talked to her that night at the movie."

"*First* off all I thought she *did*," Mark replied. "Second, you should have asked her *yourself*. Nobody told you to take my word for it."

David rolled his eyes. "Whatever."

"So, you still gonna stand here looking stupid, or are you gonna talk to her?" Mark pressed.

David quickly shook his head. "I have to get to the library," he reasoned.

Mark made a face. "The *library*—Yeah, you trippin'," he barked. He then shouted Nicole's name, much to David's astonishment.

Seeing Nicole glance in their direction, made David panic. "Asshole," he grunted at Mark through clenched teeth, as he hurried off.

Mark laughed, watching David's hasty retreat. "Yo David, stop being a punk!" he belted out, jogging after him.

"Sidra, we've been in this damn dish liquid aisle for way too long," Malajia huffed, standing in the Mega-Mart aisle. "They all make the same bubbles, just pick one and let's get to the snack aisle."

Sidra shot her a side-glance. "I was fine coming here by myself, you know that right?" she threw back.

"No, I didn't trust you to get the right ice cream," Malajia argued, shaking her hand in Sidra's direction. "You always buy that bougie ass pistachio bullshit, we need *rocky road* in the house."

Sidra rolled her eyes, but decided not to argue with Malajia any further; it was always pointless. "Anyway," she relented, grabbing a bottle of dish liquid and placing it into her half-filled cart. "Are your parents coming down this weekend for family weekend?" she asked, making her way down the aisle with Malajia in tow.

Malajia let out a quick sigh. "Yeah," she grunted.

Sidra looked at her. "Why so disgusted?" she wondered, voice filled with amusement. "I thought you actually *liked* being around your family now."

"I mean they *a'ight* and all, but don't nobody wanna hang with their old asses all on campus," Malajia complained, folding her arms. "All in my space and shit."

Sidra shook her head. "You act like you have something *important* to do," she said, stopping in another aisle.

Malajia watched as Sidra picked up a plug-in air freshener.

"Ooh, look at the design—"

"Sidra no, put it down. The house already smells like a

lavender field threw up in it," Malajia ground out, taking the freshener from Sidra's hand.

"But it's so pretty," Sidra laughed.

"I said no," Malajia insisted, then nudged Sidra out of the aisle. "Snack aisle, let's go."

"Fine," Sidra sighed, walking yet again.

"Anyway, it's not like I wouldn't *mind* seeing them," Malajia confessed, pushing some hair over her shoulder. "But my dad has been on some extra overprotective shit since he found out about the abuse," she said.

"Well sweetie, can you *blame* him?" Sidra questioned. "He's your father and he just wants to protect you. I'm sure he already feels guilty about not being able to protect you *then*."

Malajia grabbed a bottle of soda from a shelf. "Yeah, I get that and all, but he needs to chill," she maintained. "I don't want him trying to intimidate Mark and shit."

"Mark will be fine," Sidra assured with a wave of her hand.

"All I'm saying is that if my dad slaps Mark, I'm riding with my man," Malajia joked. Sidra busted out laughing. "Together we're gonna take them bad knees out."

Sidra gave Malajia's arm a playful tap. "Stop it, crazy," she laughed.

Malajia giggled as she began placing snack items in the cart. "Are *your* parents coming down?"

"Just my mom," Sidra replied, examining her nails. "My dad is going fishing with my uncles this weekend... It's cool. I'm looking forward to the one on one time with her anyway."

Malajia gave Sidra a long look. "Did you tell her about what *almost* happened with James?"

Sidra looked at the floor momentarily. When she returned from her weekend trip a few weeks ago, Sidra remembered feeling the need to talk about what had happened. She didn't hesitate in confiding in her girls about it. She pushed her hair over her shoulder. "No, not yet."

"That's surprising," Malajia replied. "You tell Mother Howard *everything*."

"Yeah, I know," Sidra agreed. "I guess I'm still trying to wrap my head around everything."

"Why do I get the feeling that you feel *bad* about not going through with it?" Malajia hesitantly put out.

Sidra shrugged slightly. "Because I *do*," she slowly answered.

Malajia looked confused. "*Why* though?" she pressed. "You weren't *ready*, it's that simple."

"I don't really know," she confessed; she tried to gather her thoughts.

"James isn't making you feel bad, *is* he?"

Sidra's hand jerked up. "Absolutely *not*," she frowned. "No, like I told you before he was a total gentleman about it… He hasn't even brought up the subject again."

Malajia looked at her, eyes caring. "I didn't mean to come at his character," she assured. "I just had to ask."

"I know, I appreciate the concern."

Malajia nodded. "You want to get some of that green ass ice cream you like?" she offered.

Sidra chuckled. "No thank you, it's a *rocky road* kind of day."

Emily trotted down the steps, book bag in hand, then headed for the kitchen. Alex, who was sitting at the table, looked up from her plate of waffles and smiled.

"If you're hungry, there's waffles done on the counter," Alex offered, pointing to a paper towel-covered plate.

Emily gabbed a small bottle of juice from the refrigerator. "Thanks. But I ate one too many pieces of bacon for breakfast and now I don't wanna *look* at food," she declined.

Alex laughed a little. "That's how I was last night with those buffalo wings that I had at work."

Emily opened her juice and chuckled as she took a sip.

Alex, cut a piece of waffle and speared it with her fork. "So…" she began as Emily made her way back into the living room. "Still haven't seen Will around."

Emily paused in the middle of drinking her juice. She stared at Alex. *Really?!* "We still talk every day," she said. Her tone was calm, although she was heated on the inside. She was tired of Alex mentioning Will's absence.

Alex let out a sigh. "Em…talking is fine if you're *also seeing* each other," she reasoned.

"Alex…" Emily took a deep breath. "Like I told you before, Will works a lot of hours—"

"And *you* are a full-time college student," Alex cut in. "A *senior* at that."

Emily frowned slightly.

"*You* have time to do things, I just wonder how come *he* doesn't," Alex pressed. She took a bite of her waffle and chewed it as Emily just stood there. "I don't mean to keep bringing it up. I'm just looking out for you."

You sure don't seem like you don't mean it. Emily thought. "And I appreciate that Alex, but I'm okay with how things are for right now," she explained.

Alex rolled her eyes; she hated how naïve Emily was being. "I know you don't mean that, Emily," she contradicted. "And I *know* that you don't want to hear me say this again, but you need to make sure he doesn't have someone else."

This time Emily couldn't help but roll her eyes. She slung her book bag over her shoulder. "I gotta get to the library," she ground out.

Alex followed her progress to the door, the bite in her tone wasn't missed. "You're not mad at me, are you?" she asked.

Emily grabbed the door handle. "Nope, not mad, just in a hurry," she quickly spat, before walking out of the door, shutting it behind her.

Alex shook her head as she went back to her food. "Poor baby, what would she do without me?" she muttered to herself.

Emily sat at the library table, studying her notes diligently. With a major test coming up the next day, she was stressed out to say the least. Unable to concentrate, Emily closed her eyes and rubbed her temple with her finger tips.

"I'm sick of this crap," she mumbled to herself. "I can't wait to freakin' graduate." The sound of her ringtone snapped her out of her thoughts. *Crap, I thought I put this thing on silent,* she thought, scrambling to retrieve the phone from her bag.

Seeing Will's number on the caller ID made her roll her eyes, though she didn't mean to. She hated to admit it, but Alex's comments about Will still rang in Emily's head. Alex had a point. Even though they still communicated via phone calls, Emily did wonder why he hadn't made an effort to see her again.

She contemplated ignoring the call, but decided against it. Letting out a loud sigh, Emily rose from her seat and walked off to an area behind the stacks. "Hi Will," she curtly answered.

Will chuckled at her tone. "Wow, you sound mad," he teased. "You okay?"

She ran her hand through her braids. "I'm studying for a big test tomorrow so...I'm stressed," she deflected.

"Well, maybe you could use a break," Will suggested. "I'm about five minutes from your campus. I was thinking that I could stop through and see you before I have to head to work."

Great, I get five measly minutes of your time today. "Um hmm," she muttered, looking at her watch. "That's fine, you can meet me outside of the library."

When he agreed, Emily abruptly ended the call. Afterwards, she leaned her head against the wall and sighed.

The next ten minutes passed by quickly. Emily sat on the cool concrete steps of the library and bundled her coat up to her neck. It wasn't too cold, but chilly enough—the typical October weather. Seeing him approach, she didn't even crack a smile.

Will, completely unaware of what Emily was feeling toward him, sat next to her.

"It's good to see you," he smiled.

Yeah right. "You too," Emily returned.

"It's chilly out here," he observed, shivering. Emily just stared at him. "You sure you don't want to sit inside?"

Emily slowly shook her head. "No...I'm fine here."

Will shrugged. "That's fine," he replied, nonchalant. "So, what's going on with you?" he asked.

Emily wasn't in the mood for Will's small talk; he could have stayed on the phone if that's all he wanted. She just stared at him, face void of any pleasantries. It was when she pictured herself kicking him off the step, that she figured it was time to find her voice and say something.

"Will, do you have a girlfriend?" Emily asked, point blank.

The question caught him off guard. "Excuse me?"

"I don't really have to repeat the question, do I?" she ground out. "Please, if you do just tell me."

"Emily, I don't have a girlfriend," he promised, offended. "I already told you that."

Emily looked confused. "I know what you *told* me."

"Then why would you *ask* me that?" he countered.

"Because...I don't see you," she explained.

"I know that, but we *talk* every day."

"I don't *see* you," she reiterated, tone sharp. "You can talk to me every day and *still* have a girlfriend... Guys do it *all* the time."

Will shifted to face Emily more easily. "Emily, I promise you, I don't have a girlfriend," he assured, voice calm. "I haven't been able to see you because I've been working like crazy. I've told you that *also.*"

Emily let out a sigh. "Yeah well, to be honest even if you *did*, I guess I can't get mad... We're only *talking* anyway," she bit out.

Will held his gaze. "Listen, I'm not dating or talking to anyone else," he stressed. "I just…look between work and other things, I don't get a lot of down time to do much hanging out. Which is why I make it a point to talk to you often. I don't want you feeling like I'm forgetting about you."

Emily just looked off to the side.

Will was trying his best to reassure her. "Hell, I practically *live* at work, feel free to come up there," he offered. "I'll give you my schedule and will even give you free food…the *good* stuff, not that raggedy popcorn."

Emily rolled her eyes, not at Will, but at herself. She was annoyed that she'd let Alex's reservations make her feel insecure. "I'm sorry," she said, now calm. "You've been honest with me to this point, I don't see why you would lie now."

Will looked ahead of him for a moment as he rubbed the top of his head. "Yeah," he sighed. "I don't blame you for questioning though… I understand how it looks."

Emily nodded in agreement.

"So that being said, I will try to make more of an effort to see you," he promised.

"Okay."

"I have a few hours between shifts on Saturday, you want to go bowling?" he smiled.

Emily thought for a moment. "Shoot, I can't," she declined. "It's 'family weekend' this weekend and my dad is coming down."

Will successfully hid his disappointment. "Okay then… How about this," he began, touching her arm. "Let me know when you're free, and I'll make sure that I schedule time for you. I promise."

Emily looked at him, then smiled. "Okay," she agreed.

Satisfied, Will stood from the steps and held his hand out for Emily to grab. He pulled her to her feet, then held his arms out. "Can I have a hug?" Emily nodded, prompting him to embrace her. "I'll let you get back to studying," he said parting. "See you soon."

"See you," Emily returned before heading back inside.

Chapter 14

Chasity propped a pillow behind her back and curled up on the couch as she flipped through the channels on the TV. Grabbing a handful of grapes from a bowl on the arm of the couch, she sucked her teeth. "All this tuition they charge, and they *still* got this basic ass cable," she griped to herself.

If that didn't annoy her, the knock on the door did. "It's open," she called, without taking her eyes away from the TV. She popped a grape in her mouth just as the door opened.

"You should really lock your door," a woman's voice advised.

Recognizing the voice, Chasity looked up and nearly choked on her grape. "Mom?" she sputtered between coughs.

Trisha Duvall rushed over and began patting Chasity's back as she stood up. "Are you okay?"

Chasity put her finger up as she stood, composing herself. "I'm fine," she said after a few seconds.

Trisha's face was masked with concern. "You sure?" Chasity nodded. Trisha threw her arms around her, drawing her into a long hug. She squeezed Chasity tight. "Hi honey," she said.

"Hi," Chasity replied, parting from her. She was shocked to say the least. Trisha was the last person she expected to walk through that door. Sure, they'd communicated through texts and a few brief phone calls, but Trisha had been distant since her sister died. "Not that I'm not happy to see you but...what are you *doing* here?" Chasity wondered.

"Well, its family weekend, isn't it?" Trisha shrugged.

Chasity raised an eyebrow. "Yes, yes it is," she replied, folding her arms. "Today is *Thursday* though."

"I am aware," Trisha confirmed, removing her coat. She draped it over the arm of the couch, then sat down. Trisha patted the cushion next to her, prompting Chasity to sit next to her. "I'm showing a house Saturday afternoon, so I'll have to leave at the crack of dawn that morning."

"You know that you didn't have to come in the *first* place," Chasity pointed out. "I don't care about this school shit anyway."

Trisha chuckled slightly. "Trust me, I know that," she said. "But, I wanted to see you."

"Okay then." Chasity stared at her. As much as her mother tried to put on a brave face and make jokes, she could tell that Trisha was still sad. "How are you?" Chasity asked, point blank.

Trisha took a deep breath, hesitating for a moment. "I'm...I'm doing okay," she answered. "I mean, as okay as I *can* be right now." She fiddled with the diamond ring on her index finger. "Taking time away was—I needed to clear my head."

"Yeah, you did," Chasity agreed.

"But...I realize that I was taking time away from you too, and that's not what I meant to do," Trisha explained.

Chasity shook her head briefly. "It's okay."

"No, no it's *not*," Trisha disagreed, adjusting her position to face her daughter. "Look, another reason why I came here to see you is because what I need to say to you, I need to say in person."

Chasity's face took on a concerned gaze. *Oh God, please don't let this be serious.* She had no idea what Trisha was about to say; she was panicking on the inside. She couldn't take any more bad news. "What is it?" Chasity calmly asked.

Trisha ran her hand through her bobbed hair. "I need to tell you how sorry I am," she confessed.

"Sorry for what?"

"For how I handled everything over these past months," her mother continued. "I constantly put you in situations that made you feel like your back was against the wall and I—I know I was wrong for that." Chasity didn't say anything; she just listened. "I was so focused on giving my sister what she wanted, that I didn't think of your feelings… Setting you up to see her wasn't how I should've handled it; I should have talked to you and let you make your own decision."

"I think we both know what my decision would've been, had I been given that choice," Chasity replied.

"I know, and I would have just had to live with that," Trisha said. "You're entitled to feel how you want."

Chasity sighed. "Look, what happened, happened," she said. "I was mad, yes but…now that she's gone and I had time to deal with it, I realize that seeing her—the closure was necessary…for me."

Trisha felt tears prick her eyes. She took hold of Chasity's hand and squeezed it. "I should've been there when you read that letter."

"I'm glad you weren't," Chasity said. Reading the letter that Brenda had written to Chasity before she died, the day of her funeral, caused Chasity to have an emotional breakdown. Something that she would not have wanted her mother to see, given Trisha's state of mind after Brenda's death.

Trisha wiped a tear from her eye. "She told me that she wrote you a few days before she died, but she didn't tell me what was in the letter," she said. She looked at her. "Do you want to tell me what she said?"

"Not right now," Chasity answered.

Trisha just nodded as she reached for her purse. "You know, Brenda didn't have much money," she began, rummaging through the designer bag. "Even though she had insurance, the medical bills alone, tore through that. I offered to pay them, but she told me no." She pulled an envelope from the bag. "There was only one thing that she wanted me to handle."

Chasity looked confused when Trisha handed her the envelope. "What's this?" she wondered.

"It's for you," Trisha said.

Chasity eyed the envelope skeptically, then after a moment, she opened it. Removing the folded-up piece of paper, her eyes skimmed over the words. Disbelief showed on her face. "It's the deed to the house in Tucson," she said.

"Yeah," Trisha confirmed. Chasity looked at her. "She still owed a balance on the house. I told her I'd pay it off for her and she agreed only if I made sure that the house would go to you."

"What?" Chasity was overwhelmed. She had left that house when she was eighteen—on bad terms with Brenda—and never looked back. Now she held that house in her hands. "Why?"

"She wanted to leave you *something*," Trisha explained. "The house was all she had left, and…she just wanted you to have it." When Chasity looked back down at the paper, Trisha leaned forward. "Baby, I don't want you to feel pressured to keep it," she said. "I know that house doesn't hold the best memories for you, so I understand if you don't want it… Just let me know what you want me to do. I can sell it, rent it out so that you have steady money coming in, or…whatever you want. Just tell me."

Chasity slowly folded the paper. She had no idea what she wanted to do. It was a decision that would not be made right then and there. "Can I think about it?"

"Of course you can, take all the time you need," Trisha said.

Chasity handed the deed back to Trisha. "Hold on to it for me."

"You know I will," she smiled. She placed the envelope back into her purse. "So…you still mind if your mess of a mother hangs around for a day or two?"

"As long as you're not staying in my room, I'm fine with

it," Chasity teased.

Trisha chuckled. She reached over and gave Chasity another hug. "I love you."

"Love you too."

"I missed you," Trisha gushed.

"Missed you too," Chasity replied.

"You're my best friend, you know that?" Trisha added

"Eww, Mom, don't be weird," Chasity jeered.

Trisha just laughed.

Sidra snatched open the front door and jumped into her mother's arms as the woman walked through.

Mrs. Howard chuckled. "Sidra, as happy as I am to see you, I'm going to need for you not to knock me over," she joked, returning her daughter's eager hug.

Sidra giggled, parting. "Sorry Mama." Sidra didn't care how any of the other students of Paradise Valley University felt about family weekend; she was excited to see her mother. "How was your drive up here?"

"Not bad," Mrs. Howard answered, removing her coat. "I arrived a little earlier, but I checked into my hotel room first."

"You're staying at the same one?" Sidra asked. Her mother nodded. "Ooh, can we go get a manicure at their spa?"

Mrs. Howard glanced down at Sidra's hands. "From the looks of those nails, you don't *need* a manicure," she commented on Sidra's perfect polish.

"But…I *want* one," she pouted, earning a laugh from Mrs. Howard.

"My girl," she praised, giving Sidra's smooth face a soft pat. Setting her coat down, she scanned the living space with her eyes. "Ooh, this is nice," she mused. "Much bigger *and* nicer than the house you stayed at last year."

"Yeah well, that's only because it's brand new," Sidra replied. "Give it time." She headed for the kitchen. "I made some iced tea earlier; do you want some?"

Mrs. Howard followed her. "Yes, thank you." She watched as Sidra grabbed the plastic pitcher of tea from the refrigerator. "So what's going on with you Princess? How's your classes? How's *James*?" she pressed, leaning against the counter. "I feel like we haven't spoken in ages."

Sidra grabbed two glasses from the cabinet. "I know. I'm sorry about the lack of calls," she sighed. "I've just had a lot going on."

Mrs. Howard put her hands up. "You don't have to apologize, you're not *obligated* to call me every other day," she chortled.

"I know, but still…" Sidra poured some tea into the glasses, sighing again. "Anyway, classes are okay and James is good… We're doing well."

Her mother grinned from ear to ear. "That's great to hear. I know that I had my reservations about him at first because of the age difference, but I'm happy that you two are together. I love the way that he treats you," she gushed. "*Speaking* of which, you never told me how your birthday trip went."

Sidra opened her mouth to speak, but the front door opened, grabbing both women's attention.

"Damn Chasity, if you would've stuck that key in the door any harder, you would have broken that thing," Malajia hissed as she and Chasity walked inside the house.

"Fuck you *and* this raggedy door," Chasity bit back.

Sidra loudly cleared her throat, gaining the bickering girls' attention.

Malajia quickly pointed to Chasity. "Oooh, you cussed in front of Mother Howard," she teased.

Chasity's eyes widened; she had no idea that Mrs. Howard was there. "Sorry," she put out.

"You should smack her," Malajia joked to Mrs. Howard. Chasity just cut her eye at Malajia.

Mrs. Howard chuckled. "Good to see you again, girls." Both Chasity and Malajia walked over and gave her a hug.

"Chasity, I remember when I first met you freshman year, you barely hugged me back," Mrs. Howard recalled, amused. "Now you give hugs willingly?"

"Don't be fooled by that, she's still Satan," Malajia jeered, earning a side glare from Chasity.

"Did your parents come down for the weekend too?" Mrs. Howard asked, picking up her glass of tea.

"Not yet, but they'll be slithering around later on," Malajia jeered. She looked at Chasity. "Ooh, aren't you and Ms. Trisha going out later on?"

Chasity pinched the bridge of her nose, and let out a frustrated sigh. "You already *know* the answer to that question, because I *told* you that *earlier*." Her tone did not mask her frustration. Malajia had been running her mouth and working her nerves since they left the house together a few hours ago. Chasity was tired of her.

"Well, you should let me come along," Malajia proposed, ignoring Chasity's tone. "I *know* y'all are going somewhere expensive."

"Shut up. Shut up," Chasity bit out, exasperated.

Sidra shook her head. "Malajia, leave her alone before she busts a blood vessel."

Malajia cut her eye at Sidra. "Worry less about me, and worry more about putting some more sugar in that bland mess you call iced tea," she griped.

Sidra sucked her teeth. "You're the *only* one who has a problem with the amount of sugar I use," she argued, folding her arms.

"Wrong," Malajia barked back. "Chasity spit *hers* out just this morning."

Sidra regarded Chasity with shock. "Did you *really*?"

"It just tasted too much like dirty water," Chasity commented, causing Malajia to bust out laughing, and Mrs. Howard to snicker.

Sidra looked at her mother; she was not amused. Mrs. Howard put the glass to her lips. "I'm sure it's not bad sweetie," she said, taking a sip. The girls watched as she swallowed the liquid. Mrs. Howard struggled not to make a face.

"You can admit it's nasty," Malajia prompted.

"It just needs...a little something," Mrs. Howard placated, placing a hand on Sidra's shoulder.

"Yeah, *sugar*," Chasity muttered.

Sidra sucked her teeth yet again. "Whatever, can y'all go away so I can talk to my mother please?" she grunted, pointing to the stairs.

Chasity looked at Sidra as if she were crazy. "Girl—" she put a hand up. "Nope, I'll save it until after your mom leaves," she ground out, then headed for the stairs.

Malajia let out a loud sigh. "I gotta go clean my damn room anyway before they get here," she chimed in, opening the cabinet. "Gotta hide my condoms."

Sidra backhanded Malajia on the arm, causing her to snicker; Sidra didn't find it funny. "Keep it to yourself, freak," she grunted.

Malajia was unfazed. She just grabbed a pack of cookies from the cabinet and walked away.

"Don't eat them all," Sidra called after her.

Malajia let out a huff. "Mother Howard, can you tell Sidra to start wearing her ponytails again?" she spat, pausing at the bottom of the stair case. "Ever since she started wearing her hair down, she's been minding way too much of people's business."

"Maybe you need to put that burgundy back in *your* head," Sidra threw back. "Now that you don't have it, you've gotten even *more* annoying."

Malajia held a blank stare. "You should've kept that comeback to yourself," she mocked.

"Just go," Sidra demanded.

Malajia flagged Sidra with her hand as she headed up the steps. "Chasity!" she yelled. "You still didn't give me an answer about going out with y'all later."

"Leave me the *fuck* alone, Malajia!" Chasity screamed through her closed door.

"Hey! There's still a parent down here, you rude ass bitch!" Malajia shouted back.

Sidra turned to her mother, shaking her head in the process. "I would apologize for their ignorant behinds, but it'll just be a waste of time," she bit out.

Mrs. Howard just giggled.

Chapter 15

"Ma, you sure you're okay with waiting?" Alex asked, sitting down at a small table across from her mother and sister. "If not, feel free to go after you finish eating. I get off in like an hour."

Alex was shocked to see her mother and sister walk into The Pizza Shack nearly an hour ago, while she was in the middle of working her mid-morning shift. When she had spoken to them earlier after they had arrived in town, they had said that they would wait at their motel room until she got off work; they never mentioned meeting her there. However, she was happy that they had.

Mrs. Chisolm smiled at her daughter. "Please child, I don't mind," she assured with a wave of her hand. "And neither does your sister, who acts like she's the *only* one who wants some of that pizza you brought out," she added, smacking her second child's hand away from grabbing her fourth slice of Hawaiian pizza.

Alex glanced at her baby sister, whom she could hardly call a "baby" anymore. Sahara Chisolm was merely weeks away from turning eighteen years old and certainly looked it. Her once thin frame filled out to a curvy one that rivaled her big sister. *Damn, where did the time go?* Alex thought, running her hands over her wild hair.

"Ma, you already said you weren't hungry," Sahara reasoned, reaching for the slice again.

"Girl," her mother barked, before waving her hand dismissively. "Child, just eat it. Sheesh."

Alex shook her head, smirking at the interaction. "Sahara, how's school?" she asked. "You'll be graduating next year, I'm sure you're excited."

Sahara shrugged, biting her slice. "School's fine," she answered, nonchalant. "Everybody there is on my nerves though...so immature. You're right, I can't wait to graduate."

"Where are you thinking about going to college?" Alex probed, rubbing the back of her neck.

"Where do you *think*?" Mrs. Chisolm asked, voice filled with amusement. "You already know that she's going to want to follow in your footsteps and come down here to Paradise Valley University."

Alex smiled. "Yeah well, they'll be lucky to have you," she approved. "Just make sure you keep up your high average so you can get a scholarship... If you can get a full ride, that'll be perfect."

"It sure *would* be," Sahara agreed, reaching for her cup of soda. "The less loans I need to take out, the better." She took a sip. "And if I don't have to *work*, it'll be even *better*."

Alex glanced over at her mother, who looked sullen. She sensed that her mother still felt guilty over the fact that Alex had to work while going to school. "There's nothing wrong with working while in school, Sahara," Alex said.

"Never said that there *was*," Sahara shrugged. "*I* just don't want to work."

Alex put her hands up in surrender. "Very well," she relented.

"But I'll tell you *one* thing though, Alex," Sahara began, looking at her.

Alex played with a piece of napkin on the table. "What's that?"

"I wouldn't mind going to work on Victoria's *face* with my fist after she has that baby."

"Sahara!" Mrs. Chisolm exclaimed, horrified.

Alex sat back in her seat, letting out a sigh. "Damn, y'all know about that?"

"Alex, you know how people talk around our neighborhood," Sahara said. "Besides, Stacey's mom told Ma."

Alex leaned forward, rubbing her face with both hands. "God, this is so humiliating," she grumbled.

"Alex, don't you even bother yourself with that mess," Mrs. Chisolm urged, stern. "Don't let it take your focus."

"Ma, that's easier said than done," Alex explained. "I mean yeah, I don't have to deal with it here at school but when I come *home*? ...I mean this is going to be constantly shoved in my face. Victoria lives on the next *block* for God sakes."

Mrs. Chisolm regarded her troubled daughter sympathetically. She couldn't imagine what Alex was feeling. "I know sweetie," she sighed. "I really don't know what to say to make you feel better."

"*I* know what to say," Sahara jumped in.

"You've said *enough*," Mrs. Chisolm scolded.

"Let me tag that chin in nine months," Sahara pressed, ignoring her mother's comment. "I never liked her petty, jealous butt anyway."

Alex shook her head. "You're starting to sound like my friends."

"Well...them I *do* like," Sahara chortled. "When can we go see the girls anyway?"

Alex looked at her watch. "Let me see if I can get off now," she said, rising from her seat. Alex sighed as she walked toward the back of the pizza parlor. The only thing that she wanted to do was go home, crawl under her covers, and sleep her feelings away.

Emily sat at her desk, sipping hot chocolate and writing in her notebook. Her mood was low—so low that she was spending Friday evening in her room alone working on an essay that wasn't due until the following week. Not that a quiet Friday wasn't the norm for her, but she didn't expect to be alone the first night of family weekend. She almost cried when her father called to say that he wasn't going to be able to make it down due to being called away for work at the last minute. With all of her friends being out, the loneliness hit Emily like a ton of bricks.

Frustrated with her essay, she slammed her notebook closed and rested her head in her hands. A soft knock on the door made her look up. "Come in," she called. Seeing Malajia open the door and stick her head in, Emily feigned a smile. "Hey."

"Hey," Malajia returned. "Sooo, I'm about to go out to dinner with my peoples… You wanna come with me?"

Emily scratched her head. "Thanks but, don't you want to spend some alone time with your family?"

Malajia waved a dismissive hand. "Girl please," she joked.

Emily giggled softly.

Malajia walked all the way in the room and leaned her back against the wall. "Look, I know you're sad that your dad couldn't make it, so I figured you could use some company."

Emily glanced at the floor briefly. "That's really nice of you, Malajia," she said, standing from her seat. "But I'll be fine. You go ahead."

Malajia frowned slightly. "You sure?" she pressed. "You look pitiful in here all by yourself."

Emily chuckled. "It wouldn't be the *first* time."

"True," Malajia agreed. "No but seriously, I'm not fuckin' around with you Emily. They're waiting outside, so bring your depressed ass on and get this free food."

Emily busted out laughing. "Oh wow."

"Yeah, I was tryna be sweet about it, but I ain't got time," Malajia replied, shaking her hand in Emily's direction.

Emily had a thought. "Wait, how long have they been

out there waiting?"

Malajia gave a hard shrug. "Girl, I don't know," she dismissed. "Just move your ass 'cause I'm hungry."

Amused, Emily grabbed her coat from the closet. "Okay," she relented.

"Good," Malajia rejoiced. "Now I don't have to talk to Maria, *you* can do that."

Emily busted out laughing, putting her coat on. "Oh, so *that's* the real reason why you wanted me to come with you, huh?"

"Come on Em, you've met her before. You *know* she's boring," Malajia joked, walking out of the room.

As the two women walked down the steps, Emily heard her cell phone ring. "It's probably my dad," she mumbled.

"Ooh, tell Daddy Harris I said 'heeeyyy Daddy'," Malajia crooned.

Emily shot Malajia a side-glance while grabbing her phone from her jeans pocket. "Malajia, can you not get all hot and bothered over my father please?" she pleaded.

"I can't make no promises," Malajia teased.

Rolling her eyes, Emily put the phone to her ear without checking the caller ID. "Hello? ...Dru?" her eyes lit up at the sound of her brother's voice. "What's going on? ...Wait what? *Really?*"

Malajia studied the surprised look on Emily's face as she spoke on the phone. She was curious as to what shocked Emily so suddenly. When Emily hung up the phone, Malajia didn't hesitate to pounce. "What was that all about?"

Emily unzipped her coat. "My brothers are an hour away from campus. They're coming down to see me," she beamed.

Emily was floored. Up until last semester, she hadn't had much of a relationship with her brothers. But after their grandmother passed, they had decided to put whatever childhood grudges against their baby sister aside and had begun to build a relationship with her.

Malajia gave Emily a hug. "Aww, that's so sweet," she gushed. "Soooo, that means that you're *not* coming to dinner to talk to Maria for me?"

"Yes, that's what that means," Emily laughed.

A loud horn from outside startled the girls. "Malajia, if you don't come on!" Mr. Simmons boomed from outside.

Malajia sucked her teeth. "He loud as shit," she griped, yanking the door open. "You all hype, Dad!" she hollered at him. "I said I was coming."

"Malajia, don't get left!" he returned.

Malajia checked her tone. "Dad chill, you know I'm hungry."

Emily laughed as Malajia walked out of the door, closing it behind her.

Emily sat on the couch, reading a book someone had left on the coffee table. She'd been reading that book for the past two hours. *Come on guys, you said an hour*, she thought, walking over to the window. She peered through the blinds, sighing when she didn't see any cars pull through the gate.

"This better not have been a joke," Emily muttered, heading for the kitchen. She opened the refrigerator and sucked her teeth at the container of leftover take out. "I could've been eating something *good* right now."

She reached for the container, then heard a knock at the door. Emily shut the refrigerator with haste, then darted for the front door, opening it. "Finally," she beamed, hugging both of her older brothers.

"Sorry we're late," Dru Harris apologized, stepping inside. "There was an accident on the highway, so we were stuck for a while."

Emily waved her hand as they stepped inside the house. "That's okay, just glad that you made it."

Brad Harris put his hand on the door as Emily went to close it. "No wait, don't close that yet," he protested.

Emily looked confused. "Why?"

The two tall, handsome brown-skinned men exchanged glances. "We umm…we brought someone with us," Dru said.

Emily scratched her head. "Umm okay," she slowly replied. "Do I know this person?"

"Unfortunately." A female voice, said.

Startled, Emily turned around. Her eyes widened. "Jaz?"

Jazmine Harris stood in the doorway, arms folded, no traces of smile on her face.

"Uh…what are you doing here?" Emily asked cautiously. The last time that Jazmine and Emily had seen each other was at their grandmother's funeral months ago. It was there that the resentment that Jazmine felt had come to a head. A verbal confrontation had ensued between the two sisters, where Emily finally stood up to Jazmine. She was certain that Jazmine wanted nothing to do with her.

Jazmine walked in and sat on the arm of the couch. "Just wanted to come visit my baby sister," she replied. Her voice and smile were blatantly phony.

Emily frowned, looking at her brothers for answers.

"Dad threatened to not loan her any money if she didn't come," Brad revealed, earning an eye roll from Jazmine.

"How nice?" Emily bit out, eyeing Jazmine. "You didn't have to come here if you didn't *want* to… I would've *preferred* it actually."

Jazmine rose from the couch. "Yeah, well, I need the money 'cause Mommy is holding out, so are we going out to eat in this dry ass city or what?" she sneered, heading for the door. "Dru you're buying right?"

Emily shook her head as Brad followed Jazmine out the door. She turned to Dru. "I don't care *what* Daddy said, you should've left her in Jersey."

Dru put his arm around Emily. "It won't be that bad, she *has* to be nice. She has no choice," he consoled. "She knows I'll tell Dad if she doesn't."

Emily giggled. "And Brad and Jaz thought *I* was the tattle tale growing up."

"Nope, it was me," he joked.

Chapter 16

"Dad, I'm gonna need for you to stop acting childish," Malajia ground out.

Mr. Simmons held his stern gaze on Malajia. "*Mark*, of all people?" he griped. "I know you can do better than *him*."

Malajia rolled her eyes. Saturday afternoon brought students and their attending families to the Student Development Center for games and food. Malajia decided that being in a fun-filled crowded place was the perfect opportunity to tell her father about her relationship with Mark. Not surprisingly, her father wasn't taking the news well.

"Dad, cut it out," Malajia urged. "Come on, he's good for me. I mean you *know* Mark."

"*Exactly* and you know I always thought that he was goofy and stupid," Mr. Simmons harped. Seeing Mark approaching from across the room, he rolled his eyes. "Great, and here comes the walking fool now."

"Dad—" Malajia put her hand up. "I'm not about to argue with you. He's who I'm with so you'll have to just get over it," she threw back. "Now calm your old self down before you fall over."

"Yeah, I'll fall right in front of *you*," he spat back.

Malajia looked perplexed. "That didn't even make any *sense*," she commented, agitated.

"Hey, shut up," he demanded.

Malajia rolled her eyes. "Just don't say nothin' smart to him, alright."

He scoffed. "I'll do what I *feel* like, and you can't stop me."

"*Mom* can," Malajia threw back.

"Yeah well, your mother is over there talking to Vanessa Howard, so she's not over here to do it," Mr. Simmons grumbled.

Malajia pinched the bridge of her nose with two fingers. Arguing with her father was making her head hurt. Mark sidled up next to her, a big smile on his face. "Hey," she said to him.

"Hey," he returned, placing his arm around her shoulder. Mark looked at Mr. Simmons, extending his hand. "How's it going, sir?"

Mr. Simmons stomped his foot on the floor. "Don't 'sir' me," he snapped, much to Malajia's annoyance, which showed on her face.

"Umm, okay," Mark muttered, dropping his hand to his side.

"Did you just stomp your foot on the floor like a damn two-year-old?" Malajia was mortified at her father's behavior.

Ignoring his daughter, Mr. Simmons pointed his finger at Mark's stunned face. "Don't think that I've forgotten the foolish crap you've done."

Mark's face held a blank stare. "I'm not sure what you're referring to, sir," he said, calm.

"You asked me for a beer when you were clearly underaged," Mr. Simmons remembered. "*And* you took part in tearing up my damn living room."

Puzzled, Mark and Malajia glanced at one another. "Dad, you trippin' bringing up old mess from freshman year," Malajia fussed. "And it wasn't just *us*, who messed up the house."

"No, it…it kinda *was*," Mark contradicted. "You

remember that you—"

Malajia's head snapped in his direction. "Shut up, I'm tryna help you," she hissed through clenched teeth.

Mark shook his head at Malajia, then looked back at Mr. Simmons. "You know what, I apologize," he smiled. Mark wasn't surprised by his reaction to him; Malajia shot him a text warning him before he even came to the SDC. Mark refused to let Mr. Simmons rattle him. In a way, Mark understood where her father was coming from. Mark knew that with his history of antics, it was hard to take him seriously.

"Don't smile at me," Mr. Simmons barked, earning a small chuckle from Mark.

"I swear to *God*, I'm telling Mom," Malajia grumbled, flipping her hair over her shoulder. "She'll have you sleeping on that hard couch and you *know* it."

Mark chuckled again, earning a glare from Mr. Simmons. "That's funny?"

"A little," Mark admitted. When Mr. Simmons shot him a warning look, Mark wiped the humor from his face and put his hands up. "Mr. Simmons listen, I know why you have reservations about me dating Malajia," he began, sincere. "I know how I can come off at times, I know I've done a lot of silly stuff, but…I've grown a lot and I'm really trying to be a better person."

Mr. Simmons still held his stern gaze as Mark pleaded his case.

"I want to be a better person for *her*," he said, gesturing to Malajia. "I care about Malajia, I would *never* hurt her. You have my word."

Malajia glanced at Mark adoringly. "Aww, you're so cute when you're being sincere," she gushed. As she went to hug Mark, Mr. Simmons stuck his hand in between Malajia and Mark, preventing the hug.

"Stop that," he grunted, rolling up the sleeves of his sweater. "Yeah, what you said would be impressive to someone who *didn't* know you. You're still not off the hook,

Mark."

Mark put his hands up in surrender. "That's fine," he said. "It's the *truth*, though."

Mr. Simmons grunted.

Malajia was over it and she didn't want to subject Mark to her father's bad attitude any longer. She looked at him. "You wanna go throw darts at balloons and try to win those cheap prizes they got?" she asked him.

Mark chuckled. "You mean like that Paradise Valley University t-shirt that everybody already has?"

"Yeah, the one with the *old* design," she followed up, amusement in her voice.

Mark let out a laugh. "Bet."

Malajia turned to her father and was about to speak, when her mother approached. "Mom, Dad is being rude," she said.

Mrs. Simmons greeted Mark with a warm hug, before eyeing her husband with disgust. "And *why* are you doing that?" she asked him.

"Look—did you know that she was dating *him*?" Mr. Simmons sputtered, pointing to Mark.

"Yes," Mrs. Simmons answered. "She told me awhile go."

"And you're *okay* with this?"

Mark raised his hand. "Umm, hi, standing right here," he muttered.

"What? Why *wouldn't* I be?" Mrs. Simmons hurled at her husband. "Stop embarrassing yourself, Richard."

Malajia grabbed Mark's hand. "Let's go," she urged, pulling him away. "He's gonna regret it later when he's on that couch."

"Oh and he *will* be," Mrs. Simmons promised.

Mr. Simmons put his hand over his face and let out a loud sigh.

Mark and Malajia made their way over to Chasity and

Jason, who were playing darts.

Chasity held the red dart steady, before hurling it at her balloon target. She sucked her teeth when the dart popped off of the balloon. "Fuck!" she snapped. "That's the third time that happened. Cheatin' ass balloons."

Jason laughed. "Yeah, they aren't making it easy to win."

"Nobody wants this bullshit anyway," Chasity barked.

"How long you been trying to pop those balloons?" Malajia asked.

"*Too* damn long," Jason answered, rubbing the back of his neck.

Mark held his hand out. "Chaz, pass me some of those darts," he requested.

Frustrated, Chasity placed her darts in his hand. "Knock yourself out," she ground out.

Malajia watched, hands on her hips as Mark made his attempt at popping balloons. "How come your family didn't come down Jase?" she asked.

"Kyle wasn't feeling well," Jason answered. "Doesn't bother me. They'll be down for one of my games, so I'll see them eventually."

Chasity resisted the urge to roll her eyes.

"What time did Ms. Trisha leave earlier?" Malajia asked Chasity.

"Like six," Chasity answered. "She had to show a house."

Malajia nodded. "I wish *my* family would bounce today," she grumbled.

"Why?" Chasity asked, examining her nails.

"Goddamn it!" Mark blurted out, interrupting their conversation. "What the fuck are these bitches *made out* of, tire rubber?"

Malajia shook her head, then looked back at Chasity. "My dad is on my nerves," she complained. "Over there acting like an asshole."

"To who?" Jason wondered.

"To *me*," Mark cut in, throwing another dart. "He's not too thrilled that I'm with Mel."

"Yeah, I know how that feels," Chasity mumbled to herself. Jason, having heard her, gently grabbed her and leaned over, kissing her on the cheek. He hoped the silent gesture made her feel a little better in that moment. His mother had a dislike for Chasity and had no problem expressing it. Jason hated it and wished that his mother would cut it out.

"Like, he's all hung up on *stupid* shit," Malajia vented. "You would think after that *last* one, he'd welcome Mark with open arms."

"I'm not even worrying about it, Mel," Mark assured, throwing another dart. He sucked his teeth when it popped off the balloon. "What the fu—yo, come on man!"

Jason grabbed some darts. "I honestly don't know what's up with these parents and their hang ups," he said. "The sooner they realize that we're gonna be with who we *want*, the better everyone will be."

"If it were only that simple," Chasity ground out. She was glad that Jason's parents didn't make it to family weekend. "If y'all don't mind, can we change the 'parent not liking the significant other' subject?"

"How does your dad feel about Jason, Chaz?" Malajia asked.

Chasity glared at her. "Yeah, 'cause I didn't *just* request that we change the subject."

Malajia narrowed her eyes. "Still got them cramps from earlier, huh?" she mocked of Chasity's attitude.

"Nope, you're just annoying me," Chasity threw back. Malajia sucked her teeth. "And to answer your question, I don't know and don't care. Derrick's opinion either way don't mean shit."

"Fair enough," Malajia relented.

Hearing a loud pop, they looked over. "Got it!" Jason rejoiced, pumping his fist in the air.

Mark's mouth fell open. "Get the fuck outta here," he

barked. "You cheated."

Jason looked confused. "*How*?"

Mark had a stupid look on his face. "I don't know, but there's no way *you* popped that tough ass balloon and *I* couldn't."

Jason folded his arms, a smirk on his face. "You seem a bit bothered by that."

Malajia smacked her forehead with her hand. "God Mark, *please* don't turn this into some stupid man competition, that I'm gonna have to hear about later on, when you lose," she griped.

"Oh, so you don't think I can pop the balloon?" Mark asked, offended. Malajia tossed her hands in the air in frustration, but didn't respond. "Nah, Jase, get them darts. You got me out here looking like a loser in front of my woman."

"That takes no effort on my part," Jason joked, earning a phony laugh from Mark. "Look, I'm not doing this with you." He looked at Chasity. "You wanna get out of here baby?"

"Yeah," Chasity replied.

"Take me with you," Malajia called after them when they walked off hand in hand.

"No, you stay here and watch me pop this balloon," Mark demanded.

"Mark, I'm hungry," she bit out.

"Then you better hope I pop this shit soon 'cause I ain't leaving until I do."

Malajia folded her arms, shaking her head in the process. Mark threw a dart and missed. "Goddamn it!" he yelled.

"I'm glad that we finally got to come down and see your school Emily," Dru mused, taking a bite of his hoagie.

"I know right? It's only been four years," Emily joked, giving him a poke on his arm. Skipping the event in the SDC, Emily and her siblings hung out at the house, eating junk food and talking.

"Yeah, we were assholes to you for a long time, we know," Brad admitted, opening a bag of chips.

Hearing Jazmine suck her teeth, Emily cut her eye at her. But Emily just waved her hand at her brother dismissively. "It's okay," she assured.

"No, it's not," Brad insisted. "It wasn't right."

Emily sighed. "No...it wasn't," she agreed. "But you already apologized. I don't want to live in the past anymore okay? The important thing is that we're in a good place now." Emily, hearing another snide sound out of her sister's mouth, took a deep breath in an effort to remain calm. *She's on my nerves.*

"Okay, no living in the past," Dru agreed, taking a sip of his cup of juice. "So let's talk about the present. Any boyfriends that we should know about?"

Emily blushed, pushing braids behind her ears. "No, no boyfriend really," she answered. "Just a friend."

"Oh? Well, if he's a boy and your *friend,* then I would consider him a boyfriend," Dru stated. "So...who is he? Where does he live? I need to talk to him."

Emily playfully rolled her eyes. "His name is Will, he lives in the city and you're not going to be talking to him any time soon," she said. "But...he's nice...and smart—"

"Can't be *too* smart if he's talking to *you*," Jazmine mumbled.

Having heard her, and having had enough of the snarky comments and sounds, Emily's head snapped towards her sullen sister. "Jazmine, is there something that you want to say to me?" she asked, tone sharp.

"Nope," Jazmine replied, a phony smile plastered on her face.

"Are you sure?" Emily challenged. "Because you've been saying indirect stuff the entire time you've been here."

Brad and Dru exchanged glances. They'd never seen their sisters argue; it was always Jazmine picking on Emily, and Emily cowering away. They didn't even witness the exchange at their grandmother's funeral.

Jazmine let out a huff. "I don't think you *really* want me to say what I *want* to say to your face," she replied, tone nasty. "I don't think Brad and Dru want to see you cry like the baby you are."

Emily rolled her eyes.

Jazmine folded her arms. "Look, don't think because you said a few pointless words to me at Grandmom's funeral that you can get all hype with me *now*," she threatened. "Your body guards aren't here to back you."

Emily narrowed her eyes at her. "I'm not afraid of you anymore."

"Yeah okay, whatever," Jazmine mocked, turning to her brothers. "Take me back to the hotel, her presence is irritating me."

"Likewise," Emily muttered.

Dru held his hands up. "Okay, chill out *Jazmine*," he interjected.

Frustrated, Jazmine tossed her hands in the air. "Can we just go?"

Brad stood up. "You always ruin everything," he hissed at Jazmine. "Let's go."

Emily held an angered gaze on Jazmine as she headed for the door with haste.

Brad leaned over and gave Emily a kiss on her cheek. "We're going to head to Jersey early," he said.

Emily offered a solemn nod. "Have a safe trip."

"Y'all go ahead, I'll be out in a second," Dru said to his siblings. When they walked out the door, he turned to Emily. "Sorry about Jaz."

"I'm used to it," Emily grunted.

Dru let out a sigh as he reached into his pocket. Grabbing his wallet, he pulled something from it. "Here," he offered, handing it to her.

Emily looked down at his hand and saw five crisp twenty-dollar bills. "Dru, you don't have to give me any money," she said, pushing his hand away.

"Stop, just take it. It's the *least* a big brother can do." he insisted, smiling. "I'm proud of you. I want you to know that."

Emily smiled back. "Thank you," she said, taking the money from him.

Dru watched her pocket the bills. "Listen, I didn't want to say this in front of the others but…I think you should call Mom."

Emily looked confused. "Why?" she bit out. "She wouldn't answer anyway."

"Well, now that more time has passed, she might," he replied. "She's been asking about you… She misses you."

Emily shook her head. "I'm sorry Dru, but I'm not going to do that," she refused. "I spent *months* trying to talk to her after I moved out. I even tried to reason with her at the funeral and she just dismissed me, so…at this point if she wants to talk, she needs to call *me*."

Dru gave Emily a nod of approval. She was truly changing, standing up for herself, being more assertive; he was impressed. *About time little sis.* "I hear you loud and clear, I will relay that message," he promised, standing from his seat. "I'll call when we get home."

"Okay." Emily waved to him as he walked out the door. Now alone, Emily sat back in her seat. No matter what her brother said to their mother, Emily already knew that she wasn't going to receive a phone call. So, there was no point in even getting her hopes up.

"Do you think the school will let me apply early?" Sahara asked, eyes roaming, taking in the buildings on the beautifully landscaped campus. She was excited when Alex suggested that she and their mother take one last walk through campus before heading back to Philadelphia.

Alex chuckled. "Applying early is not going to get you in here any faster. You still have to graduate high school."

"Ugh, I just can't *wait* to go to college," Sahara gushed.

Eyeing an attractive young man walking past, she spun around to follow his progress. "Ooh, do you think *he'll* still be here when I'm a freshman?"

Mrs. Chisolm grabbed Sahara's coat collar. "Girl, focus," she hissed.

"I'm *trying* to," she joked.

"Not on *boys*."

"Ma, I'm just kidding," Sahara protested, when her mother pointed a warning finger at her.

Mrs. Chisolm shook her head. "Alex, you need to talk to your boy-crazed sister," she urged. "Too bad you'd already have graduated when she comes."

"She'll be fine Ma," Alex assured. "She's already doing better than *me*, by not having a boyfriend in high school... They're not worth the headache, trust me."

"Well, Paul is a bum," Sahara put out, earning a snicker from Alex and their mother. "You've upgraded just in the *friend* department alone... The guys you hang with, are cute."

"And off limits for *you* little sis," Alex ground out, giving Sahara a poke on the arm. "That *includes* the single ones."

"I know, I know...but that Mark though."

"Mark?!" Alex laughed. "Child go sit down somewhere. He's Malajia's...but even if he wasn't...*Mark* though?"

Sahara shrugged unapologetically. Sure, Alex thought that Mark was attractive; she couldn't lie, *all* of the guys were to her. But hearing her baby sister admit it was a little weird to her. It was *Mark*—the one who got on her nerves the most.

"Well, friends are all I *have* at the moment," Alex said, putting her hands up. "No boyfriends for me for a long time."

"I hear that, but I'm wondering why you're not open to having another boyfriend," Mrs. Chisolm wondered.

Alex scratched her head before fixing the scarf around her neck. "Well Ma, I'm just focused on school right now," she explained. "Trying to maintain my grades takes up a lot of time."

"What about *after* classes are over?" her mother pressed.

Alex shrugged. "Well, after I graduate I'll have to focus on my career," she reasoned. "That'll be time consuming as well."

Mrs. Chisolm too shrugged. "Makes sense."

Alex was silent for a moment. She knew she wasn't being honest with her mother or herself. "Okay can I be honest?"

Mrs. Chisolm glanced over at her. "You don't even have to ask that," she replied, tone caring. "What do you need to say?"

Alex hesitated for a moment, taking a deep breath. "So...*another* reason why I don't want a boyfriend is because... I don't feel like I can trust another man enough to be able to *be* in a relationship," she revealed hesitantly.

"*That's* the reason that I was afraid of," Mrs. Chisolm replied. She had an inkling that that was Alex's real reason. "Alexandra—"

"Ma, not the full name," Alex complained.

"I told you before, learn to love your name, it's your grandmother's," Mrs. Chisolm chided, Alex put her hands up in surrender. "Listen baby, you can't let your experience with *one* fool, make you jaded for the rest of your life."

Alex rolled her eyes. *I'm sick of people telling me that,* she fumed as her mother continued on.

"You're a smart woman, you know good and well that all men are not like Paul," she pointed out. "So why would you stop yourself from being with someone who could be good for you, because of your experience with one person?"

"Ma, I'm entitled to feel how I feel," Alex hissed, tone sharp. She wondered why she even told her mother the truth in the first place. She just knew she was going to get a lecture, something that she wasn't in the mood for.

Mrs. Chisolm put her hands up. "Fine, I'll drop it for now."

Alex glanced over at the sullen look on her mother's

face. She regretted snapping. "I'm sorry Ma," she
apologized, putting her arm around her mother. "I hear you,
but I just need to deal with this in my own way okay?"

Mrs. Chisolm smiled up at Alex. "Okay."

"Aww," Sahara gushed as the two women hugged.
"Okay now that that's done, can we go check out the
basketball players—I mean the basketball court?"

Alex shot Sahara an amused look. "What are we gonna
do with you?" she laughed.

Chapter 17

"So, are we participating in these homecoming activities this year or no?" Alex asked the girls as they cleaned up downstairs. With family weekend over, the campus was getting ready to celebrate homecoming week.

"Man, don't nobody wanna do these sorry ass activities," Malajia griped, reaching in the cabinet. She pulled out a container and examined it. "How long has this damn hot chocolate been in here?" she ground out.

"You try looking at the expiration date?" Chasity asked, washing dishes.

"Damn the date, I'm looking at this generic ass name," Malajia chuckled. "This shit is called 'non-dairy imitation chocolate drink powder'."

Chasity busted out laughing. "No the fuck it's not."

Malajia walked over and held the can in her face.

Reading it, Chasity laughed again. "What the fuck? Eww, throw that shit out."

Alex rolled her eyes. "There's nothing wrong with that cocoa," she grunted, wiping off the dining room table with a rag.

"*You* must've bought this bullshit," Malajia jeered, gesturing to Alex. "And it's not *cocoa*."

"Nah, it's 'non-dairy imitation chocolate colored dust'," Chasity teased; Malajia joined her in laughter. "The shit probably don't even blend right."

"Wait, don't forget about the 'gelatin squares O fun' that she got that were supposed to be marshmallows," Malajia added.

"Nothing is worse than those 'vanilla wafer circle disks 'N crème'," Chasity mocked.

Malajia screamed with laughter. "Yo, they tasted like straight card board," she remembered. "We told her ass *sandwich cookies* not no goddamn wafer disks."

Sidra swept the floor, laughing at the banter. She couldn't help it, Chasity and Malajia always made things funny with their comments. But seeing that Alex was clearly getting annoyed, she stopped. "Alright you two, back off," she urged. "Alex, there is nothing wrong with the stuff that you pick out. I'm sure the cocoa is just fine."

"You want me to make you a cup of it?" Malajia asked, holding the can up.

"No, thank you," Sidra quickly declined. She glanced at Alex. "Already had some umm, coffee earlier. Don't want to ruin my appetite with too many hot liquids," she sputtered.

Chasity smirked. "Good save," she mocked. Sidra made a face at her.

"Right," Malajia chuckled, tossing the can in the trash.

Alex pointed to it. "Hey—"

"Just let it go Alex," Chasity cut in.

Alex just flagged them with her hand. "Whatever," she grumbled. "Anyway, back to my question—"

"Back to our *answer*," Malajia commented. "Nobody's doing anything for homecoming."

Sidra shook her head at Malajia. "Let us look at the activities again Alex, and we'll decide... Hush up Malajia," she said when Malajia went to protest.

"Fine," Malajia huffed, reaching for something else in the cabinet. "'Fizzie fruity soda water'?" she blurted out, grabbing a six pack of canned sodas from the shelf. "Alex, you're banned from doing the shopping by yourself."

"Chaz, is Jason excited about playing in the game Sunday?" Sidra asked, changing the subject. "I know he hasn't played since last season."

"Yeah, he's pretty excited about it," Chasity answered, wiping the water from the counter.

She tried to block the last game that Jason played out of her mind. Chasity was distraught when Jason ended up hurt at the hands of two rival players. "He needed the break, but I know he missed playing."

"I sure hope he doesn't get hurt *again*," Alex commented.

Chasity shot Alex a glare. "Why would you even put that out there?" she spat.

Alex tossed her hands up in the air. "What?" she asked, shocked. "You act like I'm *wishing* for him to get hurt."

"Nobody asked you to mention anything *about* him getting hurt," Chasity returned.

"God, I get that that's your man and everything, but don't you think you're overacting just a bit Chasity?" Alex bit out.

"Nope," Chasity threw back. Alex rolled her eyes.

Emily barged through the door, interrupting the building argument. She looked around. "Ooh, it's cleaning day," she observed, sitting her books on the couch. "I'm sorry, I had some homework to finish."

"It's cool, you want some of this red number five colored soda water that Alex bought?" Malajia offered.

"Malajia stop it," Sidra cut in, trying not to laugh again.

Emily scratched her head. "I don't even know what that *is*," she said.

"Shit, neither do *we*," Chasity commented. Alex, over the topic in general, just sucked her teeth as she went back to cleaning.

"Anyway, guess what?" Emily beamed, clasping her hands together. The girls looked at her in anticipation. "I'm going out with Will again."

"That's great," Sidra gushed.

"Yeah, we're going out on Friday," Emily smiled.

"Well, glad he *finally* made time for you," Alex

muttered.

Emily frowned at the comment. "Thanks for that," she sneered.

Alex tossed her arms up. "What do you want me to say, Emily?"

"Not *that*," Emily replied, gathering her books. She was agitated; Alex went and ruined a happy moment with her sniping. "If the bathroom isn't cleaned yet, I'll do it."

Sidra followed Emily's progress up the steps. "We're happy for you sweetie."

"Thanks," Emily ground out, continuing upstairs.

Sidra waited until Emily disappeared up the steps. "That was nice, Alex," she hissed, sarcastic.

"Yeah, tell us how you *really* feel," Malajia added, pulling more items from the cabinet.

"*What?*" Alex barked, frustrated. "I don't think my *one* comment warrants being jumped on."

"Your miserable ass didn't even have to *say* that," Chasity jumped in. "I'm sure Emily is aware that it's been a while since she's seen Will...bitch."

Alex slammed her hand on the table. "Screw you," she snapped. "And calling me a bitch was unnecessary."

"Trust me, it *wasn't*," Chasity threw back.

Alex could have slapped Chasity right across her face. "I swear, lately it's like every time I say *anything* it's a damn problem."

"That's not true," Sidra calmly stated.

"No, it's just when you're being an *asshole*, that it's a problem," Malajia added. "Alex, your attitude been stank lately, not gonna lie."

Alex rolled her eyes. "*You* would know about stank, *wouldn't* you?" she threw back.

Malajia pointed at her. "Careful now," she warned. She wasn't about to let Alex drag her into an argument, for unlike Alex, she was in a good mood. But if Alex continued with her nonsense, Malajia wouldn't have a problem fighting her on it.

Alex folded her arms in a huff, storming towards the staircase. "Maybe I should just stay quiet."

"You promise?" Chasity sneered, earning a middle finger from Alex as she stomped up the steps.

"You already know where the fuck you can shove that," Chasity called after her.

Malajia pulled a box from the cabinet. "Hey Alex!" she yelled up the steps. "Come take this poor ass box of 'elbow noodles and powered cheese substitute' with you!"

Sidra put her hand over her face to avoid busting out laughing.

Alex took a quick break from jotting notes in her notebook. Letting out a sigh, she ran her hands over the back of her neck. "Just two more pages," she muttered. Over the past few days, besides work, the library had seen her more than her own room did. Sure, she had tons of assignments to complete and studying to do, but she found that the quiet was the reason she lingered. She hadn't been feeling like interacting too much with anyone lately.

Hearing her name being called, she glanced up. *Swore I wouldn't be bothered in here,* she thought, seeing the person standing in front of her. "Eric," she frowned, tone unenthused.

"What's going on Alex?" Eric replied.

Alex frowned at his sharp tone. "What's wrong with *you?*"

Eric set his book bag down and pulled the chair across from her out. "Can I sit?" he asked.

"Um, I'm actually trying to finish this homework right now," she protested. She had no interest in having any type of conversation.

"I think I'll sit anyway," Eric insisted, sitting. He pushed himself up to the table.

Alex let out a quick sigh. "Can you make this quick? I have work to do," she hissed, rubbing her eyes. "This assignment is due tomorrow."

"You know what, given the fact that I've seen you naked, I think that I deserve a little *less* of your attitude," he bit out.

Alex put her hand up, eyeing him as if he had lost his mind. "Excuse *you*," she spat. "*Your* attitude is the one that's showing."

Eric rubbed his head with his hand. "I've been calling you for *two* days straight and you haven't picked up," he stated, voice stern.

"I've been busy with school," she argued, tapping her books with her hand. "Don't be dramatic."

Eric frowned at her. "You weren't too busy to *fuck* three days ago," he snarled.

Alex gasped. "*That* was uncalled for," she hissed through clenched teeth. She was trying to keep her voice as low as possible.

"I'm sick and tired of you giving me the run around," Eric threw back.

"Again, you're being dramatic," she argued. "You already *know* I have a lot going on, so no I don't have time to sit and talk."

"You don't have time to answer the damn phone and talk to me for a few minutes, or even hang out, but you always find time when you want some," he scoffed. "Funny, I thought you weren't the casual sex type."

Alex ran her hand over her hair and let out a huff. Eric did have a point. Ever since Alex had gone to Eric's room for some sexual release after finding out about Paul and Victoria's baby over a month ago, she found herself going back to him whenever she felt on edge. Even as recently as three days ago, after the verbal back and forth with the girls over her comment about Emily's second date. While she could see where he was coming from in feeling like she was playing games, Alex wasn't in the place to care.

"I'm *not*," Alex seethed, glaring at him.

"Really? You could've fooled me," he threw back. "You

seem like a pro at this unattached sex thing. How many guys have you done this with?"

"Go to hell, Eric," Alex spat, voice raised. "I haven't done this *casual thing* with anybody *but* you."

"Yeah okay," Eric sneered.

"Whatever," Alex argued. "You're sitting over there throwing a temper tantrum because all you get from me is sex, poor baby," she mocked. "Men do this shit all the damn time, but when a woman does it, it's a problem." She folded her arms and sat back in her chair. "You guys are all hypocrites."

Eric stared at her. He had grown to have feelings for Alex, but her constant shoot downs and confusing behavior towards him was turning him off. "First of all, you're not a man," he pointed out. "So stop comparing yourself to one. Second, I'm not lik*e all* guys. I keep *telling* you that, but you obviously haven't heard me."

"Yeah, yeah," Alex huffed.

Eric rolled his eyes. "Point blank Alex," he began, fed up. "I don't mind chasing you…but not if I have no chance of ever catching you." He fixed an intense gaze on her. "Do you think that you can *ever* want more than just sex from me?"

Alex looked into his eyes. They were big, brown, and full of hope. She could see that he cared for her and wanted a real relationship; not just sex. But with the past betrayal weighing heavy on her, she just couldn't get past the pain enough to even *try* to be with Eric the way that he wanted.

"Eric…I just don't have time for a relationship," she maintained, cold.

Not getting anywhere, yet again, Eric lost all hope. He sat back in his seat, rubbing his face with his hands. "I'm done," he said after a moment.

It's about time, now I can get back to what I was doing. "What? You're done with the conversation?" she asked, watching him stand up.

He slung his book bag over his shoulder and fixed a

stern gaze. "No, I mean I'm *done*," he clarified. "You say you're not the casual sex type, well neither am *I*," he declared. "I only did it because it seemed to be what you wanted. But I can't do this anymore."

Alex was confused. "Are you kidding me right now?" she snapped.

"No," Eric confirmed. "You don't have time for a relationship, well I don't have time for your games."

Alex was in disbelief. "So basically we're not friends anymore is what you're standing there telling me," she spat.

"I never wanted to *just* be your friend Alex," Eric replied.

Alex couldn't care less about Eric's feelings at this point. As far as she was concerned, Eric was just like Paul. He couldn't get her to do what he wanted, so he was pulling away from her. "I don't even care Eric," she snarled, waving her hand at him dismissively. "Just go. It's a good thing that I *didn't* end up in a relationship with you."

"Oh really?" he challenged.

"Yes, *really*," she countered. "Clearly you're the type to step out when you can't get your way."

Eric just shook his head in disbelief at the woman in front of him. After all this time, she still looked at him like a typical doggish dude.

"God forbid I don't suck you off one time, you'd go find another whore to do it… Just go away," Alex waved her hand at him again. "Good riddance."

Eric rolled his eyes and walked off. "Have a nice life Alex," he threw over his shoulder.

"Yeah, kiss my big black ass Eric," she returned, flipping a page in her notebook. She didn't even make eye contact with him as he left. Not able to regain her concentration, Alex pushed the book across the table and put her face in her hands. If she could've screamed out her frustrations right there in the library, she would have.

Chapter 18

Mark barged through the front door of the girls' house. "Whatcha'll doin'?" he asked Sidra and Malajia, shutting the door behind him.

Sidra shot Mark a glare, handing Malajia a glass of lemonade. "Still haven't learned to knock, huh?" she spat.

Mark shot her a confused look. "Why *would* I when I know that y'all are gonna let me in *anyway?*" he reasoned. "Plus, it's always unlocked."

Malajia set her glass on the coffee table, then clapped her hands. "See, that's what I've been tryna tell her about *her* room door," she agreed. "See, *you* get me."

Mark pointed to Malajia. "I love it when we agree on how to be annoying," he joked through clenched teeth, holding his arms out. "Get over here with your sexy self."

Sidra watched as Malajia jumped up from the couch, darted over and jumped in Mark's arms. She frowned in disgust as the pair started kissing. "Eww," she complained. "You two need help."

Mark laughed as he parted from Malajia.

Sidra flopped on the couch. "What brings you by, Johnson?"

"The school set up a laser tag maze in the gym, y'all wanna roll?" he asked, sitting on the arm of the love seat. "It's part of the homecoming stuff."

"So, we're going to be running around a dark gym, in a maze...with laser guns?" Sidra questioned. "This spells another 'shooting my teammate' disaster."

"Naw, it'll be cool," Mark assured. "We know not to shoot at each other."

Malajia shot him a glance. "You mean like the time you shot David point blank with the paintball gun before he even got a chance to play?" she reminded.

Mark stared at her. "You still bringing up old shit?" he fussed.

"Was just making a point," Malajia explained, fighting to keep her laughter in.

"Naw, we're supposed to be on the same page," he argued. "You about to be on time out."

Malajia tossed her hands in the air. "We *still* doing that?" she griped. "If so, I missed like five opportunities to time out your ass just *last week*."

Mark pointed at Malajia. "We're not *talking* about last week," he countered. "See, still with the old shit."

Malajia sucked her teeth.

Sidra let out a loud huff. "God, help me," she muttered to herself.

Mark looked at Sidra. "Anyway, you going?" he asked.

"Sure, why not?" she shrugged, taking a sip of her lemonade. "It's not like I have anything *else* to do tonight."

"Cool," Mark beamed, rubbing his hands together. "Where's everybody else at? I thought we could go grab some burgers or something first."

"Chaz is out with Jason," Malajia answered.

"Oh, *that's* why Jase didn't answer his damn phone," Mark commented, looking at the call log on his phone screen.

"Emily is on her way back from her last class and I don't know where the hell Alex is," Malajia continued.

"Yeah, she left hours ago without even saying anything," Sidra put in. "I mean not that she *had* to."

"Naw, fuck that, she always asking us where *we're* going and shit," Malajia pointed out, shaking her hand at

Sidra. "But she don't want nobody to ask *her* anything."

Sidra shrugged; she knew that Alex had been on edge lately. She only wished that Alex would talk to them.

"A'ight then, when they get in just come over to our place and we can go together," Mark proposed, heading for the door. "Josh is already over there with December, and David is in his room nerdin' around as usual."

Sidra hadn't meant to, but she frowned slightly at the mention of Josh being with December. "Oh December's over there?"

"Yeah, she's been over a *lot* lately," Mark commented. "Eating up all the snacks and shit," he chuckled.

"Shit, now you know how *we* feel, about y'all eatin' up *our* shit," Malajia jeered, examining her nails. "Greedy asses."

Mark pointed at her again. "You on time out," he barked.

Malajia's mouth fell open. "Oh my God!"

Sidra was too preoccupied with her own thoughts to pay attention to the banter around her. *I wonder why he didn't tell me that they worked things out?* she thought. Josh hadn't mentioned anything about December ever since their last conversation about her, before Sidra went on her birthday trip with James.

"Sid, you alright?" Malajia asked, once Mark left the house. "You're looking all dry in the face."

"Oh, yeah I'm fine," she deflected. She peered out of the front window. "Here comes Alex," she announced. Before she could say anything, Alex busted through the door, slamming it shut behind her. "Alex, what's the matter sweetie?" Sidra charged, concerned.

"Nothing I'm fine," Alex grumbled, sprinting for the steps.

"Uh, time out slammy," Malajia ground out, halting Alex's progress.

"What is it Malajia?" Alex huffed.

Malajia turned her lip up. "Your attitude smells worse than those boots you got on," she bit out, folding her arms.

Alex was in no mood for Malajia's poking. She was still fuming from her conversation with Eric just hours ago. "I don't have time for this, what do you *want*?"

"Alex, what's *wrong*?" Sidra pressed, noticing the angered look on Alex's face. "And don't say nothing because *obviously* something is upsetting you."

Alex rolled her eyes. "Can I at *least* take a nap before you girls start hounding me with your questions?"

"Nope," Malajia rebuffed, grabbing her phone from the end table

"What are you doing?" Sidra asked Malajia, confused.

Malajia put her finger up, signaling for Sidra to be quiet as she placed the phone to her ear. "Bitch where are you?... How long?... Hurry up." Malajia looked at Alex as she disconnected her call. "Chasity is on her way back, so sit your ass down."

Alex once again rolled her eyes and walked over to the couch, flopping down on it. *I just want to be left alone.* She sat in annoyed silence for ten minutes until Chasity walked through the door, with Emily coming in a few moments after.

Emily set her book bag by the steps. "God, I'm glad that quiz is over," she said, exhausted.

"Nobody cares about that quiz," Malajia mocked, pointing to Alex. "*This* one over here is about to tell us why she got a damn attitude."

"What's going on?" Emily questioned, sitting down next to Alex. She might have still been annoyed with Alex, but that didn't mean Emily wasn't concerned about her.

The girls sat in anticipation, waiting for Alex to speak. "Can I just do this later?" Alex begged. "I'm not in the mood."

"No, 'cause we have laser tag to go to later and if your attitude sucks, we're all gonna shoot *you*, which will mess up our damn team spirit. So you might as well start talking," Malajia replied, folding her arms.

Malajia shut up! Alex fumed, standing from her seat, "I'm not doing this right now," she fussed.

"Oh *really?*" Chasity commented, voice filed with sarcasm. "The queen of force-talking people doesn't want to talk about *her* issues?"

Alex stared daggers at Chasity. "Shut the hell up Chasity," she barked.

Chasity raised an eyebrow.

"And thanks for always throwing shit in my damn face, I appreciate it," Alex ranted, heading for the stairs.

"Alex, sit your black ass down," Chasity snapped, pointing to the couch.

Alex paused at the steps and let out a long sigh.

"Yeah Alex, you need to really let whatever is going on in there, out," Sidra calmly put in. "I mean, we understand that you were upset about that whole thing with Paul and the baby, but this seems like something *new.*"

Alex stomped over to the couch and flopped back down, running her hands through her hair. She rubbed her eyes as she gathered her words. *Either I tell them or they won't leave me the hell alone.* "I got into an argument with Eric," she revealed after a moment.

"What did you do?" Malajia blurted out, earning a death stare from Alex. "What?" Malajia questioned. "Come on Alex, from what we know about Eric, he's always been a good guy... *You're* the one with the problems."

"Whatever Malajia," Alex hissed. "It wasn't me, it was *him*," she assured. "He caught an attitude because I don't want to date him... He already *knew* that though." She looked around at her friends' faces. "He basically in so many words told me to screw myself and that he was done with me." When the girls didn't immediately jump to her defense, she frowned. "What's with the silence?" she spat. "You wanted me to talk, now I'm talking... Interact, say *something.*"

"Um...I don't know what you want us to say to that, Alex," Sidra slowly drew out. "I mean, I have *something* to say as I'm sure the *rest* of us do on this, but... I'm not sure that you'll want to hear it."

Alex was confused. "What do you mean?" she pressed. "So...you *agree* with what he did?"

Sidra put her hands up in surrender as Alex's tone rose in anger. "I'll save it for another time."

"Alex, you're yelling at *us,* when you *should* be yelling at your damn self," Malajia cut in. "This is *your* fault."

"How so?" Alex seethed.

"Girl, we kept *telling* you to stop jerking that man around and you *know* that," Chasity threw out. She for one, was not fazed by Alex's anger; Alex needed to hear what they had to say. "You did the 'causal sex' thing, then decided *not* to because you said that you couldn't do stuff like that. *Then* you started fucking him *again*, sending him mixed signals and shit."

Alex just sat there, seething in silence, staring at Chasity as she kept going in on her.

"You were messing with his damn feelings and he finally got sick of your ass," Chasity bit out. "I'm surprised it took *this* long."

"Thanks a lot, Chasity," Alex sneered.

"Don't catch it with *me,* I'm just being honest," Chasity defended, pointing to herself.

"And her observation matches mine," Malajia confirmed. "Alex you were trippin' with Eric. Using him for sex...just like a damn dude."

"Exactly!" Alex boomed. "Men do it *all the time.*"

"So *what?*" Sidra threw back.

"All I'm saying Sid, is that when a guy does it, it's no damn problem," Alex argued. "When I, as a *woman* do it, then everybody is all up in arms."

"When *anybody* does it, it's a problem," Emily cut in, feeling her temper rise as she began remembering her own experience with being used for sex. "Using someone just for sex is plain *wrong*, no matter if it's a man *or* a woman. *Especially* if the other person is expecting *more* than that."

"Boom!" Malajia blurted out, slamming her hand on the arm of the chair.

Alex rolled her eyes at Malajia, before turning back to Emily. "Look Emily, I'm sorry about your experience, but this is not the same thing."

"How *isn't* it?" Chasity asked, confusion written on her face. "You sound stupid. You're trying to justify something that you *know* you're wrong for."

"And I thought you cared about Eric for more than just his damn penis," Malajia added. "At least that's what you told us at one point in time."

"Damn it, I still *do*," Alex fumed.

"You're not acting like it," Malajia pointed out. "Why *won't* you date him?"

"I just don't want a relationship with anybody, how hard is that to understand?!" Alex yelled, clapping her hands in frustration.

"That's fine Alex, but you can't get mad at *him* because *he* wants one," Sidra replied, tone calm.

Alex shook her head; she was so irritated. She couldn't believe how quickly her friends had sided with Eric. "I'm going to bed," she huffed, rising from the couch.

"It's like six o'clock!" Malajia exclaimed, looking at her watch. "Besides, we're supposed to go play laser tag."

"Count me out," Alex sneered, walking up the steps.

Sidra looked at the other girls once they heard Alex's door slam. "Do you think we were too hard on her?" she asked.

"Nope," Malajia and Chasity answered in unison as Emily shook her head.

"She needed to hear it," Chasity concluded.

"But we all know that it's gonna go in one ear and out the other," Malajia commented. "She don't listen to any of us. She thinks she's the only one who is the voice of reason in this group… It's gonna take someone to really hurt her damn feelings before she actually takes what we say to heart."

"Believe me, I've tried," Chasity jeered.

Malajia chuckled. "She's used to *you* tearing through

people's feelings, she just takes it as typical Chasity behavior," she replied. "Same with me and *my* comments."

"Look, let's just give her some space," Sidra suggested, stretching. "Come on, let's go get the guys so we can go eat."

"Thank God, nobody has to share a room with that," Malajia joked, heading for the door.

Chapter 19

"Oh we're about to win this game," Mark boasted, adjusting the target vest on his chest. "We got this in the bag. Just like we did the paintballing tournament."

"Are you going to shoot me this time?" David bit out, examining his laser gun.

Mark loudly sucked his teeth. "*Again*, with the old shit," he fumed as David laughed. "I already said sorry for that."

After filling up on fast food, the group, minus a sullen Alex, made their way to the gymnasium, which had been transformed into a maze using large partitions. Colorful strobe lights flashed along the walls and the floors, while neon light fixtures were hung in between the maze for added effect. Students gathered by the entrance, getting instructions along with their gear, which consisted of a tag vest with visual and audio sensors, and a laser gun.

"We're team Ninja Strike, we got this," Mark assured, rubbing his hands together. "We eight deep, everybody else might as well quit *now*."

Sidra, holding a flyer, tapped Mark on the shoulder. "Uh, Johnson, did you read this?" she asked, holding the paper in his face.

"Naw, what does it say?"

"That there are teams of *two* only," she informed, pointing to the highlighted line.

Mark paused for a moment as his eyes roamed over the group. "Every team for themselves," he quickly put out, pointing his gun at his friends.

"Shit," Chasity huffed, then took off running for the maze.

"Bitch wait! You know I'm on your team!" Malajia yelled, trailing after her.

Hearing laser guns going off in the distance, Josh took off running as Jason adjusted his gun.

"Jase, shoot Josh! I got David," Mark yelled to his partner as he chased a screaming David into the maze. "You can't hide David, I see the reflection off those glasses!"

"Damn it, it's true!" David agreed.

Sidra and Emily looked at each other. "Come on Em, not panicking will help us win this thing," Sidra said.

"Team roommate," Emily chuckled as the two girls made their way to the maze.

Chasity slowed her pace as she rounded a corner, then came to a complete stop. She peered around another corner, just as Malajia bumped into her. "Move," Chasity hissed, jerking her arm away from Malajia, who was holding on to it.

"Shut up," Malajia threw back, giving Chasity's arm a poke. "You got me running around this dumb ass maze, getting lost... How are we gonna get out, stupid?"

"Well, you followed *me through* this dumb ass maze, so who's *really* the stupid one?" Chasity retorted.

Malajia sucked her teeth. "Whatever," she mumbled. Peeking around the corner, the girls saw some other players sneaking their way through the maze. Chasity signaled for Malajia to move to the wall across from her. Malajia complied, and the girls stood with their guns positioned, waiting for the opportunity to attack. As the guy approached their opening, both girls fired their guns at his target, setting off his sensor.

"Damn it!" the guy griped. It was then that the girls

recognized the voice.

"Josh?" Malajia laughed, seeing him clearly in the light as he walked up to them. "Damn boy, you outta here *early*."

Josh removed his vest. "These damn neon lights are making my eyes hurt," he complained. "I can't focus." He wished the girls luck as he took off in search of the way out. "Oh. Watch your back. Mark took out like five people already and he's out for blood," he threw over his shoulder.

"You're outta here dawg!" Mark boasted, taking out yet another opponent. He laughed as the annoyed guy removed his vest and stormed off. "You mad as shit you can't shoot," he taunted. He crouched down and crept along the walls, scanning the area with his eyes. Seeing someone dart across from him, he took several shots, missing his target. "Damn! David I know that's you," he barked, chasing.

David ran through the maze in a desperate attempt to lose Mark. "No, no," he panicked as someone aimed for his vest. Being quick, David ducked as he returned fire, setting off the person's sensor.

"Well, it was fun while it lasted," the girl giggled.

David stood up. He stepped into the light as the young woman removed her vest. He smiled brightly. "Nicole."

She smiled back. "So, *you* were the one who took me out, huh?" she joked, giving him a soft poke on the arm.

"Sorry." He fixed his glasses on his face. "I feared for my life," he chortled. He stared at Nicole as she tucked the vest under her arm, then pushed some of her twists off of her neck. *Say something fool! What are you just staring at her for?* Here it was, she didn't have a boyfriend after all, and he still couldn't get up the nerve to ask this woman out. *David, come on, get it together man!*

He swallowed hard when she glanced up at him. It was almost as if she was waiting for him to say something. He opened his mouth to speak, but was stopped when she lightly touched his arm.

"These lights are tearing my eyes up, I'm going to head out," she announced. "I'll see you around."

"Oh o—okay," he sputtered, watching her saunter away. He was so focused on her that he didn't immediately notice that his sensor had gone off. He looked down and saw the red lights flash on his vest. "Crap," he huffed, turning around. He frowned; Mark was standing there holding his gun up. "You snuck me bro?" David bit out.

"I was standing there waiting for your scared ass to ask Nicole out," Mark admitted, scratching his head with the tip of the gun. "When you flaked per *usual*, I decided to put you out of your misery."

David stared at him, shaking his head.

"Besides, the back of your head was making me mad. You need a haircut man," Mark mocked.

David flagged Mark with his hand, then walked away, removing his vest.

Malajia took out an opponent as she and Chasity rounded another corner. "I swear, next time they do this, these lights gotta go," Malajia complained, rubbing her eyes.

Chasity shook her head, but kept her eyes focused. "How many people are left?" she asked.

Malajia scratched her head. "Girl, I don't know," she huffed. "Probably not too many. We took out a lot of 'em… Well *I* took out most of them."

"All you had to say was 'I don't know,'" Chasity bit out. "Nobody asked for all of that commentary."

Malajia sucked her teeth as she stood in Chasity's face. "Look, this is the *last* damn time I partner with you on any of these stupid games," she griped, pointing at Chasity. "You've been saying smart shit the *whole* time."

Chasity frowned at her. "What the fuck are you talking about?"

"Why can't we just shoot people and win?" Malajia harped. "Why you always gotta make smart remarks?"

"You just stood here and claimed to have done *all* of the work, which is a goddamn *lie*. But you catch attitude because *I* make a comment?" Chasity threw back. "And let's be clear, I didn't ask you to be my partner. You followed me."

"That's not the point," Malajia barked, moving her finger closer to Chasity's face.

Chasity glanced down at Malajia's finger, then back up at Malajia.

"I'm just trying to hurry up and win so I can get the fuck out of here," Malajia ranted. "It's hot in here, this vest is heavy, and these lights are about to give me a seizure—" She let out a gasp when her vest lit up and the sensors went off. Malajia turned around to see Jason standing there, a boastful smile on his face. "Shit!" she belted out, stomping her foot on the floor. "Chasity you saw him and didn't do shit?" Malajia accused, spinning around to face her.

"Well, I was going to warn you, but I was too distracted by your finger in my damn face," Chasity returned nonchalantly.

"Traitor ass heffa," Malajia spat out, storming away from a smirking Chasity and a laughing Jason. "Where's the damn exit?!" she yelled, rounding the corner.

Jason and Chasity stared at each other, before quickly raising their guns at one another. "Baby, you know you're my everything, but I *will* shoot you if you don't lower your gun," Jason warned.

"Save it Adams," Chasity returned, arm steady. "We both know you're not gonna shoot me."

Jason pointed the gun to different points on her vest. "Lower your gun and walk away," he urged. Chasity didn't budge and Jason lowered his gun, shaking his head. "Always so stubborn," he commented, before suddenly delivering a laser shot to her chest, setting her vest off.

Chasity narrowed her eyes at him, then looked down at her vest. "You actually shot me," she calmly realized.

"I warned you," Jason laughed. Her icy glare halted his laughter. Chasity started firing laser after laser at his chest, setting his vest off. Shocked, he backed up as she approached him, continuously firing. "Damn Chaz, you're gonna break the vest," Jason belted out, putting his hands up.

She stopped in front of him, then fired one last shot.

He laughed. "Okay, okay," he relented. Chasity yanked her vest off. "You're so beautiful when you're pissed," he teased.

"Shut the hell up," she hissed, walking away.

Mark rolled along the floor, before standing up and rounding a corner. He came face-to-face with Sidra and Emily. "Y'all out!" he boomed, firing a shot at both girls.

Sidra sucked her teeth as Emily dropped her gun. "You always take these games way too seriously," Sidra complained.

"You mad you out," Mark taunted.

Emily giggled. "I assume you took a lot of people out?"

"But of *course*," Mark boasted. "I'm a beast. There was no way I was gonna lose."

Sidra's eyes shifted for a moment. "So you think you took out *every* other opponent, huh?" she asked.

Mark shrugged. "Nearly," he answered. "There's a few nerds around here somewhere. But they're no threat." Mark looked back and forth between Sidra and Emily, who were standing before him, smiling. Mark nodded slowly as he came to a realization. "There're lasers pointed at my back aren't there?"

Several beams of light were directed at Mark's back. "Yeah," Sidra confirmed as Emily quickly nodded.

Mark lowered his head. "Shit," he huffed, holding his arms out awaiting his fate. Suddenly he raised his gun and pointed at his own chest. "I'll take my own self out like a G!" he yelled, before pulling the trigger, setting off his sensors.

The girls watched Mark fall to the floor in dramatic fashion and roll around while making pained noises.

They laughed as Malajia appeared around the corner. "I

can't find the fuckin' exit!" she hollered, grabbing everyone's attention. She frowned in confusion when she saw Mark on the floor. He looked up at her, a silly look on his face. "Boy!" she hollered. "Get up off the damn floor and let's get the hell out of here."

Chapter 20

Emily shifted her weight from one foot to the other, peering out of the living room window. Glancing at the pink watch on her wrist, she sighed. "Where is he?"

Friday evening was upon her, and she was eagerly anticipating her second official date with Will.

Malajia skipped down the steps and paused on her way to the kitchen. "You still here?" she observed.

"Yep," Emily sighed. "He's like twenty minutes late."

"Oh girl, that's nothing. Now if it was an hour, *then* you could panic," Malajia placated. Noticing the troubled look on Emily's face, Malajia walked over to her. "Em you're not thinking that he stood you up, are you?"

Emily looked at Malajia, giving her the answer that Malajia already knew.

"Girl, it's only twenty minutes. He could be stuck in traffic," Malajia said, trying to offer a bit of comfort.

"He hasn't called."

"Okay, he's probably *driving* sweetie," Malajia reasoned. "You know those stalking ass cops are just *waiting* to pull somebody over for being on the phone." she chortled. "Don't stress yourself about it, he'll be here."

Emily fixed the sleeve on her white button down top. "I don't know," she replied sullenly. "I guess I just have Alex's voice stuck in my head from earlier today."

Malajia frowned, recalling the comment that Alex had made to Emily as she was getting ready for her date, telling her to just be careful when it came to Will.

"Girl, Alex is bitter and miserable," Malajia dismissed with a wave of her hand. "Don't let her get to you... The girl needs to get over her *own* issues and mind her damn business."

Emily forced a smile. "Thanks Malajia."

Malajia nodded, then gave Emily a knowing look when a knock sounded at the door. "I bet you that's him," she assumed, going to the door. "I told you," Malajia beamed, opening the door and seeing Will standing on the other side. "Hey Will," she greeted, walking into the kitchen.

"Hey Malajia," Will returned, standing in the door way. "Sorry I'm late," he directed at Emily. "You ready?"

Emily nodded, then headed for the door.

Emily stared at Will as he cut his smothered chicken with his fork. He was silent; as a matter of fact, he hadn't said a word during the entire ride to the soul food restaurant. They planned on going bowling after they finished eating, however Emily wondered if they should have done the more fun activity first.

"Hey, is everything okay?" Emily asked after gathering the nerve.

He looked up from his food. "Sure. Why do you ask?"

Emily slowly spun her glass of soda around, looking down at the table. "You just seem a little quiet, that's all," she muttered. Emily couldn't stop her mind from wandering. *Is he bored with me? Is he regretting going out with me again? Am I more interesting over the phone?*

Will wiped his mouth with his napkin after swallowing a bite. "I don't mean to be quiet," he responded.

"Is...is it *me*?"

"Emily, it's not you," he assured. "Honestly, I just have something on my mind that's all."

Emily rested her elbows on the table. "Do you want to talk about it?" she probed. "I mean...your mood seemed to change since we talked yesterday. What happened?"

Will stared at Emily as if he wanted to say something. "Um..." he stammered. When Emily just sat there in anticipation, he quickly shook his head. "You know what, let's not worry about that," he dismissed. "Things are good. How did you do on that test that you took the other day?"

Emily didn't know whether to be relieved that Will was being more talkative now, or bothered that he was trying to hide what was wrong with him.

"I think I did good," she replied, confident.

"That's great, what class was that for again?" he asked, taking a sip of water from his glass.

"History of education."

Will smiled and nodded. "I know this is probably weird for me to say right now but, you're going to make a great teacher."

Emily's smile was bright. "That's not weird to say," she gushed. "It's really sweet...and *generous*," she giggled. "I have to get through my student teaching assignment next semester. *That* will be a test to see if I can actually *handle* it."

"Don't ever doubt yourself," he replied with seriousness. "You'll do great."

Emily wondered if her face was turning red with all of the blushing that she was doing. "Thank you."

The next fifteen minutes felt like one of their many phone conversations, laid back and relaxed. Emily took a long sip of soda as she listened to Will talk. His ringing phone interrupted their conversation.

Will looked down at his phone and frowned. "I'm sorry, this will only be a moment," he assured her, rising from his seat. Emily concentrated on her food as he walked off. He returned a few moments later in a hurry.

"Emily, I'm sorry but I have to go," he said, taking her by surprise.

Emily was baffled. Not only at his words, but at the

panicked look on his face. "What's the matter?"

"I have an emergency," he quickly put out, gathering his coat from the back of his chair.

Emily slowly gathered her belongings as Will signaled for the check. She didn't know what to think. He was being so vague. *What is he hiding?* She stood up from her seat. "Will, can you talk to me please?' she begged, seeing him fumble with his wallet. "Can you just tell me what happened?"

Will tossed some cash on the table in a huff. "Emily, I can't do this with you right now!" he snapped, earning a wide-eyed look from Emily as she clutched her coat and purse to her chest. He ran his hand over his hair, sighing. "I'm sorry, I didn't mean to snap at you. But I *really* have to go."

Emily shrugged her coat on in silence.

He reached out for her arm. "Come on, I'll take you back to campus," he offered, voice calm.

"No that's okay, I'll get on the bus," she declined, moving around him to get to the exit.

"Em—"

"I'll be fine," she quickly put out, cutting him off.

He let out a long sigh as he watched Emily walk out of the restaurant.

The quiet ride back to campus didn't do much to clear Emily's mind. She was irritated; Will was being secretive and that didn't sit well with her. She took a long walk around campus trying to process what happened. She would have continued walking, but the cold air made her head for the house. She opened the door to find the girls sitting in the living room, watching TV.

Malajia looked at her watch. "You're back early," she observed.

Emily was silent while removing her coat.

"What's wrong?" Sidra asked, noticing the sadness on

Emily's face.

Emily tucked her coat under her arm. "Will had to leave early," she muttered. "I took the bus home."

"Why the hell didn't he drop you off?" Alex pounced. "And what do you mean he had to leave early?"

"I didn't *want* him to drop me off," Emily answered, scratching her head. She was in no mood for Alex's questions and assumptions; she had enough of them herself. "He said he had an emergency, so I figured bringing me back would only slow him down."

"You should've called one of us to come get you," Alex scolded, folding her arms.

Emily rolled her eyes.

"One of *who*?" Chasity sneered, shooting Alex a glance. "'Cause you already know *your* ass don't have a car."

Alex made a face at Chasity. "I have a *license*, remember?" she threw back.

"A license does *not* equal car," Chasity ground out.

Alex rolled her eyes. "Fine, but I'm sure you or Sidra or even *Mark* wouldn't have minded going to get her. It's dark out, anything could have happened."

"I'm not *twelve* Alex," Emily spat. "I can take a bus."

"Ooohhh," Malajia instigated, then dissolved into laughter once she saw the irritated look on Alex's face.

"Shut up Malajia," Alex hissed, giving her a light nudge with one hand. "Anyway, did he tell you what the emergency was, Em?"

Emily shook her head, which annoyed Alex even further.

"So...he just up and said that he had to cut your date short for an emergency, but didn't say what it *was*?"

"Pretty much," Emily grunted.

Alex put her hands up as she shot the other girls glances. "Is it just me or does this smell like the guy is hiding something?"

"No, what it *smells* like is that nasty ass food you made," Chasity scoffed, examining the black polish on her nails. Malajia snickered loudly at the comment.

Alex gave Chasity the side-eye, but decided not to derail the topic at hand by arguing with her. "So, nobody else finds this concerning?"

Emily was irritated. *Will she shut the hell up?!* "I'm going to bed," she announced, somber.

"I'm sure he'll tell you what happened later," Sidra said to her.

"Yeah sure," Emily dismissed, heading up the steps.

Once they heard the door close, Malajia's head snapped toward Alex, backhanding her on the arm. "You ass," she bit out.

Alex looked surprised. "Me?!" she exclaimed, placing her hand on her chest.

"Alex, Emily felt bad enough," Sidra chided. "The last thing that she needed was to be reminded of the fact that he just up and left her."

"Unbelievable." Alex threw her hands up. "I *can't* be the only one who sees this stuff."

"*You're* the only one who keeps *harping* on it," Chasity put in, voice low. "The girl isn't stupid, I'm sure she sees shit… Even if there *was* something going on, she's not gonna listen to you because you sound bitter."

"I'm *not* bitter," Alex hissed through clenched teeth.

"Bull*shit*," Malajia mumbled, adjusting herself in her seat.

Chasity turned in her seat to make sure that she faced Alex. "I said you *sound* bitter," she reiterated, smartly. "But in all honesty, you *are* bitter."

"So because I'm looking out for my friend, I'm bitter." Alex said, voice filled with disdain. It was more of a statement than an actual question.

"The way that you're going about talking to Emily about Will isn't cool," Sidra chastised.

"I'm just offering her my opinion," Alex argued. "*Clearly* she needs it."

"She didn't fuckin' *ask* you for it!" Chasity snapped.

Alex folded her arms in a huff. "I didn't ask for *yours*,

but you sure sat here and gave it to me," she threw back.

Chasity let out a groan as she got up from the couch.

Malajia looked at her. "Where are you going, Chasity?"

"I can't deal with Alex's ass right now," Chasity barked, storming upstairs.

"I can't deal with *your* evil ass *either!*" Alex yelled after her.

"Fuck off!" Chasity yelled back from her room.

Fed up, Alex sucked her teeth. "I'm going for a walk," she grumbled, heading for the door. *I need to get out of here before I kill these girls.*

Sidra flinched when the door slammed shut. "That escalated quickly," she commented to Malajia, who grabbed the bowl of popcorn from the table.

"Somebody is gonna slap Alex's ass before the end of the semester, watch," Malajia predicted, shoving some kernels into her mouth.

"Let's hope it doesn't come to that," Sidra sighed.

"Damn this stadium is crowded," Malajia complained, as a few students brushed by her.

"Well, it *is* the homecoming game," Sidra chortled.

"Ahhhhh, I told y'all we was gonna win this game," Mark boasted to some members of the rival team as they passed.

Malajia gave his arm a hard yank. "Boy, will you stop taunting them before they fuck you up," she bit out.

"Ain't nobody scared of them," Mark assured.

Having just watched Jason lead their football team to a victory in his first game back since he'd gotten hurt a year ago, the gang couldn't wait to get out of the stadium and go celebrate.

Malajia craned her neck, scanning through the crowd. "Where's Chaz?"

"Probably giving Jase a congratulatory blow job in the locker room," Mark joked.

Sidra sucked her teeth, while Malajia backhanded him on the arm.

"You are so vulgar," Sidra sneered, folding her arms and looking away.

"Keep my girl and what she does or doesn't do to her man out your damn mind alright," Malajia hissed, backhanding him again.

"I'm just joking," Mark laughed, looking at Malajia. "You wanna give *me* one?"

"Oh God, I just threw up mentally," Sidra complained, putting her hand over her stomach.

Malajia narrowed her eyes at Mark. "No, I *don't*," she sneered. "You didn't do nothin' but piss me off all damn day, you don't *deserve* it."

"Yeah, what else is new?" Mark mumbled, rubbing his head. He put his hands up as he saw Jason walk out. "My homie!" he exclaimed.

"Loud as always," Jason commented, approaching his friends.

"Great game Jase," Sidra gushed, giving him a hug.

"Thanks," Jason said through a forced smile. "Um, I'm gonna skip going out tonight, guys."

"Whatchu' mean?" Mark charged, obviously disappointed.

Jason shook his head. "Just not really in the mood," he replied. "I'll catch y'all later."

"Damn, everybody is dry today," Mark complained as Jason walked off. "I'm gonna go eat up all David's snacks and shit. I'll see y'all later." He halted his departure, turning back to Malajia. "Unless you wanna—"

"Fuck out my face Mark," Malajia spat, glaring daggers at him.

"Just double checking," he mumbled, walking away.

Malajia rolled her eyes at his departing back. Seeing Chasity approach, Malajia pointed at her. "Chaz, you wanna go do something?"

Chasity shook her head. "I'm gonna go chill with Jason,"

she replied, looking at her phone.

"What's up with him?" Sidra asked, curious. "He seemed pretty down. Which is weird since the team just won the game."

Chasity adjusted her pocketbook on her shoulder. "His dad is sick," she revealed and was met with sympathetic looks. They knew how Jason felt when it came to his father's health. "It's the flu, but with his heart and everything...Jase is worried."

Ever since Jason's father had a heart attack over a year and a half ago, Jason had been on pins and needles every time the elder Adams fell ill.

"Totally understandable, give him our love," Sidra said, before Chasity walked off.

Malajia let out a long sigh. "Hope his dad gets well soon," she commented. Sidra nodded in agreement. "Well, Chaz and Jase are out, Mark's on my nerves, we done lost Josh and David in this crowd, Em left, and Alex is somewhere being a bitch..." she paused, looking at Sidra. "You wanna go to a movie?"

Sidra stared at Malajia, slowly placing her hands on her hips. "Why did you have to make it seem like I'm your last resort?" she griped.

Malajia laughed. "Aww, come on Princess, you know you're my favorite...after Chasity."

"Whatever, let's just go," Sidra agreed. "You're buying the popcorn."

"Fine...can I borrow some popcorn money?" Malajia asked as they headed for the exit.

Sidra let out a loud groan.

Chasity was sitting in Jason's room, waiting for him to get out of the shower. She'd arrived at his room just as he was getting in. His cell phone lit up, prompting her to look at it. Seeing that it was his home number, she grabbed the phone and headed for the bathroom. She knocked on the door. "Jason," she called. Hearing the shower water turn off, she knocked again. "Babe, your house is calling."

"Can you answer it for me?" Jason replied from the bathroom.

Chasity hesitated. "You sure?"

"Yeah."

"Okay," she agreed, heading back into his room. Chasity pushed answer, putting the phone to her ear. "Hello?"

There was a pause on the line "Who is this?" the woman hissed.

Chasity rolled her eyes. "It's Chasity, Ms. Nancy," she replied, recognizing the voice.

"Where is my son?"

Chasity's jaw tightened. The tone that Jason's mother was using was just plain nasty. "He's in the shower," she replied, trying her best to keep her true feelings from reflecting in her tone. "Do you want to leave a message for him?"

"No, I *don't* want to leave a message, I want to *speak* to him," Mrs. Adams spat. "And why are you answering his phone? Shouldn't you be in your *own* room somewhere?"

"How do you—" Chasity paused what was about to be a rude remark regarding where her son *could* be, but decided against it.

What Jason didn't need—when he was already stressed—was an argument between his girlfriend and his mother. Chasity pinched the bridge of her nose, trying to keep her temper in check. "Since you don't want to leave him a message, he will call you back when he finishes in the shower." Chasity frowned when she didn't hear a response. She looked down at the phone and saw that Jason's mother had hung up, without so much as a goodbye. "Bitch," she hissed, tossing the phone on the bed.

Jason walked into his room, towel wrapped around his waist. "What did they say?" he asked, putting his toiletries on his dresser.

"It was your mother and she didn't say shit," Chasity bit

out.

Jason caught her harsh tone and looked at her. "What did she say to you?" he asked.

Chasity folded her arms as she struggled with whether to bad mouth his mother to him, or not. "She...she didn't want to leave a message with me, she would rather talk to *you* directly."

Jason eyed her skeptically. "Why do you sound like you're answering phones at a call center?" he asked, noticing her strained, polite tone.

"Because...I'm trying to refrain from telling you that your mother was being a jackass to me," she threw back through clenched teeth.

Jason rubbed his eyes with his hands. *Goddamn it Mom,* he thought. "Chaz, look I'll talk to her again."

Chasity retrieved Jason's phone from his bed and handed it to him. "Don't worry about it, check on your father," she urged.

Jason sighed, grabbing the phone. "She's pissing me off with that shit," he grumbled. "You didn't do shit to her, you don't deserve that."

"It doesn't matter," Chasity said, shaking her head. "And don't say anything about it when you call back. Just...find out about your dad." She headed for the door. "I'll be back."

"Where are you going?" he asked, spinning to face her departing back. The last thing that he wanted was for her to leave.

"I'm gonna go pick up the food I ordered," she answered. "Don't worry, I'm not mad and I'll be back."

"Okay," Jason said. It was mostly to himself; Chasity had already walked out the door. He took a deep breath then pushed redial.

Chapter 21

Emily adjusted her position on her bed, flipping pages in her textbook. After the football game, not in the mood to stick around the stadium with her friends, Emily made her way back to the room with the intentions of taking a nap. But with much on her mind, sleep wasn't happening, so she figured she'd get some studying in. She looked up when the door opened.

"Em, guess what?" Sidra beamed, walking in with Malajia tailing behind.

"Sidra, you ain't even gotta be cheesin' that damn hard," Malajia teased.

Sidra turned around to respond, but jerked her head when she saw how close Malajia was to her. "Can you back up?" she barked, annoyed.

Malajia laughed.

"You're so weird," Sidra grumbled. She looked at Emily. "Anyway, my brother is coming to visit me in a few weeks," she revealed, elated.

Malajia flopped down on Sidra's bed, rolling her eyes in the process. "Marcus was texting her all hype in the middle of the movie," she complained. "I told her to turn the phone off."

"I wasn't turning my phone off while texting my brother, so get over it already," Sidra threw back.

Malajia shook her head. "Yeah?" she challenged. "That's why that flashlight cop was about to throw you out 'cause your phone was all bright."

Sidra waved her hand at Malajia dismissively.

"I'm happy for you Sidra," Emily said, tone tired. "How long is he staying?"

"Probably for just a day," Sidra shrugged. "It doesn't even matter how long, it'll just be good to spend some one on one time with him. Every time I'm home, his time is spent with that...*thing*."

Malajia chuckled at Sidra's change in tone at the mention of Marcus's girlfriend. "Still don't like India, huh?"

Sidra's head snapped towards Malajia. "Don't ever say that raggedy ho's name in my presence," she bit out. "No, she shall be referred to as '*thing*'...or ho...or an instigating, ghetto, manipulative *bitch*."

"Geez Sidra." Emily looked concerned. "Is she really *that* bad?"

Malajia put her hand up as Sidra opened her mouth to speak. "God no, Emily *please* don't get this girl started," she begged. Having heard Sidra's many vent sessions when it came to her brother's relationship, Malajia wasn't in the mood to listen to another one.

Flustered, Sidra ran her hands over her face. "You know what, I'm gonna go make some tea, anybody want some?" she said.

"No thank you," Emily declined as Malajia just shook her head no.

Once Sidra left the room, Malajia looked at Emily. "You left the game early," she mentioned.

Emily leaned her head back. "I know, was just sleepy."

"You're sleepy, but you're not *sleeping*," Malajia pointed out.

"Yeah...can't seem to get any sleep right about now," Emily sighed, closing her book.

Malajia fixed her gaze on Emily. "You look like you want to talk about something," she said.

Emily hesitated for a moment. She did want to express her concerns, just without getting judgment in return. But Emily remembered that she wasn't talking to Alex. "Okay...it's Will," she said.

Malajia frowned slightly. "What's wrong with him?"

"I wouldn't *know* because I haven't *spoken* to him," Emily vented. It was apparent that just the mention of him, was making her upset.

"Time out," Malajia said, adjusting her position on the bed. "You haven't heard from him since he bailed on your date?"

Emily slowly shook her head. "Nope."

"It's been *two* days," Malajia said. "What the hell?"

"I know," Emily sulked.

Malajia paused for a moment, trying to choose her words carefully. "Look—I don't want to be negative right now, because I know Alex has already been on some suspicious bullshit when it comes to him, and I know how much you like him, but...."

"Mel, just say it," Emily said, almost pleading.

"Say what?" Malajia asked.

"Say that he has a girlfriend or he has a double life...*something*," Emily pressed. "I know people think that I can be naïve—"

"No, who says that?" Malajia cut in.

Emily shot her a knowing look. "Come on," she said. Malajia just turned away momentarily. "I mean I *get* it, I guess I *can* be, but what I'm *not* is stupid," Emily continued. "I know things seem off... I guess I just hoped that..." Emily sighed. "I'm starting to think that Alex was right."

Malajia held a sympathetic glance; she felt terrible. Emily seemed sad and confused. She remembered what that felt like. She didn't want to believe that Will was being malicious to Emily, but she couldn't help but think that at this point. "Em—"

"It's okay, I'll be fine," Emily cut in. Her tone was unconvincing. "I have to get back to studying."

Taking that as her que to leave, Malajia stood from the bed. "Sorry Em," she consoled, walking out of the room.

Emily let out a deep sigh. "Me too," she murmured to the empty room.

"I fuckin' hate Spanish," Malajia fumed to herself, hurrying down the steps of the Language and Arts building. Having just finished a test that she was sure she failed, she wasn't in the best of moods. "I need to get Chaz to tutor me again... I need to stop bullshittin'."

Her solo rant fest ceased when she saw Carl heading for the gym. Recalling the conversation that she had with Emily the other day about his cousin, she frowned. "Yo, big head ass Carl!" she hollered.

Carl stopped and turned around. Seeing Malajia walk up to him, he threw his head back and let out a heavy sigh. "Malajia, whatever you heard that I did or said, it's not true," he said, coming face to face with her.

"Boy, ain't nobody thinking 'bout you," Malajia sneered, waving her hand. "What's up with your cousin? I don't appreciate him playing my girl."

Carl looked bewildered. "What are you talking about?"

Malajia flung some of her hair over her shoulders. "I'm *talking* about that bullshit he pulled a few days ago when he took Emily out and then left all of a sudden...talking about he had a damn emergency," she seethed. "He hasn't called her yet. And don't act like you don't know. Guys talk more than women do."

The confusion hadn't left his face. "Malajia, I don't—"

"Does the bastard have a girlfriend somewhere?" Malajia asked, abruptly cutting him off. "I mean, even if he *doesn't,* if he's not interested in her anymore, then he needs to *tell* her." Malajia was too angry to care that she had basically just inserted herself into Emily's business. But seeing how down Emily had been lately, she felt like she had no choice. "Now, *she* might not key up his car, but *I* will, all day…*and* yours."

Carl shook his head. "Keying my car won't be necessary," he bit out, adjusting his gym bag on his shoulder. Malajia rolled her eyes. "Look Will likes Emily, trust me. He talks about her all the time."

"Then what was that whole *leaving* thing about?"

"If you're talking about this past Friday, he really *did* have an emergency."

Malajia sucked her teeth. "Oh please, what was it? He had to go see some bitch?"

"Malajia, Will doesn't have a girlfriend alright," Carl assured, putting his hands up. "He had to go to the *hospital* that night… His son was sick."

Malajia was completely caught off guard and it showed on her face. "His *what*?" she slowly replied.

"Will's two-year-old son had a high fever and they took him to the ER that night," Carl explained. When he noticed the shock still written on Malajia's face, he came to a realization. "Y'all didn't know that he has a child…*did* you?"

"Look at my face," Malajia hissed, pointing to herself. "Does it *look* like I knew?"

Carl ran his hand along the back of his head. "Shit," he grimaced. "Okay look, don't tell Emily okay?"

"Boy you must be crazy," Malajia threw back. "There's no way in hell, I'm keeping this from my girl."

"Fine okay, keep your damn girl code and shit, but don't tell her you heard it from *me*," Carl begged as Malajia walked off.

"Not *only* am I telling her *that*, I'm telling her that *you* told Will not to tell her," Malajia threw over her shoulder.

"Malajia come on, stop playing!" Carl yelled after her. When she didn't respond, he threw his head back. "He's gonna kill me," he groaned.

"Shit, shit, shit," Malajia panicked, sprinting through

campus to her house. *Why did I have to pull an Alex and say something?* She thought, stopping in front of the door. She put her hands on her knees and bent down to catch her breath. "Ugh, I gotta start going back to the gym." She took a deep breath and opened the door to find the other girls in the kitchen.

"Chasity just taste it," Emily giggled, holding a spoon near Chasity's face.

"I'm not eating that shit," Chasity refused, moving Emily's hand away.

"Chaz, it's only banana pudding," Sidra laughed.

"I don't eat no goddamn bananas, y'all know that," Chasity argued.

"I know, but this one doesn't even *taste* like bananas," Emily promised, moving the spoon back near Chasity's face. "I wouldn't lie to you."

"Chasity, she's telling the truth you can't taste the bananas," Alex chimed in, scooping some into her mouth.

Chasity fixed a stern gaze on Emily, ignoring Alex. "Move it or I'll throw up on it," she warned.

Emily quickly moved her hand back, earning a giggle from Sidra.

Malajia decided to cut short the conversation. "Hey," she said, walking over.

"Ooh, you want to try some of this banana pudding that I just bought?" Emily smiled.

Malajia put her hand up. "Not right now Em," she replied. "Um…have you talked to Will yet?"

Emily looked up at Malajia. *That was out of nowhere.* "No, still haven't heard from him," she answered, putting a lid over her pudding container.

Malajia scratched her head. *Damn it.* "Okay well, I have to tell you something," she put out, earning curious looks from the girls. "Do you want to talk in private?"

Emily shook her head. "No, whatever it is, you can say it in front of them," she assured. "What's wrong?"

Malajia let out a long sigh. "Okay…so I pulled an 'Alex'

and I talked to Carl…about *Will*," she drew out hesitantly.

Alex frowned. "What is *that* supposed to mean?" she questioned. Malajia just waved her hand at Alex dismissively.

"Um…I wish you hadn't done that Malajia," Emily chided.

"Trust me, I wish I hadn't either," Malajia laughed nervously.

Emily sighed; there was no need to harp on it. "It's fine, what did Carl say?" she wondered. "I mean…is Will okay?"

"Yeah, spit it out Malajia," Sidra urged, putting one hand on her hip and the other on the counter top.

Malajia put her hands up. "Okay… So I was going off on Carl about what Will did and was just on some…he shouldn't be stringing you along mess, and I told him about how he just cut your date early on Friday." She took a deep breath. "So um…what he said was that um… The reason why he left early was because…he um…he had to take his…his son to the hospital."

The girls all stared at Malajia in disbelief.

"Yep, those are the same looks I gave to Carl when he told me," Malajia confirmed.

"Wait, Will has a child?" Chasity asked, unaware if she heard correctly.

"Yep, he's two and his name is Anthony…" Malajia paused. "Okay, I don't know if his name is *really* Anthony, but he *does* have a two-year-old son."

"Mel, are you sure? I mean you know how Carl lies," Sidra pointed out.

"Sidra, Carl may be an asshole, but I doubt he'd lie about the wellbeing of a child, *especially* one that is related to him," Malajia pointed out.

Emily just stood there speechless and in shock. She couldn't believe what she had just heard.

Alex put her hand on Emily's shoulder. "I'm so sorry Em," she said. "I hate to be the one to say it—"

"Then *don't*," Chasity hissed.

"I told you. I *told* you girls that it seemed like Will was hiding something," Alex boasted, ignoring Chasity's warning. "I mean come on, who talks to someone for *weeks* and only goes out *twice*? I knew that seemed weird. He didn't even have the decency to tell you Emily... Come on, what *else* is going on?"

Emily didn't say anything, she just headed for the door.

"Sweetie, where are you going?" Sidra asked.

Emily grabbed her coat. "I'm going to talk to him," she threw over her shoulder, opening the door.

"You want us to take you?" Sidra offered. She could only imagine how Emily felt.

"Nope, I'll be fine," Emily quickly said, closing the door behind her.

Alex folded her arms, a satisfied look on her face.

Chasity glared at her. "What the fuck are you so happy about?" she hurled, not hiding the disdain in her voice.

"I know right?" Malajia added. "Emily probably feels humiliated, and you're standing here looking all smug and shit."

"I'm not happy that Emily is upset," Alex clarified. "But I *am* happy that she has finally woken up and sees Will for the liar that he is."

Emily hurried off the bus the moment it came to a stop, and stormed into the movie theater in the mall. She saw nothing but red. She was embarrassed, she was confused, and more importantly, she was disappointed. Disappointed in Will for keeping the truth from her. Worse still, she was disappointed in herself for falling for someone who couldn't even be straight with her.

Emily walked up to the counter. "Is Will Palmer here?" she asked the ticket clerk.

The clerk smiled, nodded, then placed a call.

Emily knew that this wasn't a conversation that was to be had over the phone. She needed to see him face to face.

She took a chance coming to the theater to look for him. For all she knew, he could've been out.

She stood at the counter, drumming her finger tips on the top of it. Feeling her eyes well up, Emily let out a groan. When she heard Will call her name, she spun around to face him.

"Hey, what are you doing here?" he asked, both surprised and delighted to see her.

Emily just stared at him; her glistening eyes burrowed through him.

Noting the look on her face and tears filling her eyes, his light smile faded. "What's wrong?"

"Seriously?" she spat. Gathering her composure, she wiped her face with the sleeve of her coat. "Can I talk to you in private please?"

"Sure." Will lead her to his office. Once they got inside and he closed the door, he faced her. "Emily, I'm sorry that I haven't called you," he apologized, sincere. "It had *nothing* to do with you. I've just been dealing with a crisis."

"You mean your son?" she blurted out.

Will frowned. "Who told you that?" he asked, voice stern.

"Doesn't even matter," Emily ground out, folding her arms. "The point is why didn't *you* tell me?"

He ran his hands over his head. "Look, it's complicated."

"How so?" Emily challenged. "I mean, having a child is nothing to be ashamed of. What you *should* be ashamed of is the fact that you had me thinking that you lost interest in me, that you were seeing someone else, when all you had to do was *tell* me."

Will was panicking on the inside. "I didn't tell you because…" he took a deep breath, trying to calm down. "Look, most women who are about to *graduate college* don't want to deal with some guy with a kid, a *young* kid at that," he tried to explain.

"I'm *not* most women," Emily argued.

"How was I supposed to know that?"

"By being honest in the *first* place," Emily threw back.

Will sighed. "Look...this is all new to me okay," he began. "I haven't dated anybody since my son's mother. We broke up when he was a few months old."

"So, you two are just okay with not being together with a child that young?" Emily asked.

"We *were*," he corrected. "We were both in school in North Carolina and we were doing fine sharing the responsibilities." He paused momentarily. "Until she died in a car crash six months ago," he revealed.

The frown left Emily's face. "I um...I'm sorry."

"Thanks," he nodded. "I left school and moved to Virginia with my son to be closer to my family," he continued. "I'm a single father and I need all the help that I can get... I just didn't want to scare you off before you got a chance to know me."

Emily felt some of her anger melt away. "While I get why you felt the need to keep the fact that you had a child from me...you still *shouldn't* have," she chided. "You can't keep things like that from people... I wouldn't expect you to bring your child around me without knowing me, but you should've given me the opportunity to decide for myself if I wanted to get to know you or *not*, knowing *this*."

Will looked down at the floor. "I know I was wrong for keeping you in the dark," he said. "I'm sorry...but like I said, I'm new to this."

Emily just looked away.

"So...is this it?" he asked, not sure if he wanted to know the answer. "Did I mess everything up?"

Emily rubbed her face with her hands as she tried to figure out her emotions. "I um...I like you Will and I haven't had the nerve to say that to anybody...ever. So this is new for me too," she said. "A child is not a reason why I would stop talking to you. I love kids and as long as you're a good father to your child—which I'm sure you *are*—we won't have an issue... But lying to me *is* an issue, so please don't do it again."

Will breathed a sigh of relief. "I hear you loud and clear. Thank you for not running…yet."

Emily stared at him, offering a slight nod.

He put his hand up. "No more secrets, I promise. "

Emily took a deep breath. She believed him. "Okay."

Will grabbed his wallet from his desk. "Here, I want to show you a picture of him," he smiled, walking over to her, holding the photo in front of her face.

"Awww, he's so cute," she gushed, eyeing the dark-skinned, smiling boy in the photo. "How is he?"

"He's better," Will answered, closing his wallet. "He had a pretty bad virus, but he's getting through it. He'll be okay."

Emily smiled back. "Good to hear."

Emily walked into the house almost two hours later and was met with eager looks from the girls; they were in the dining room, getting ready to eat dinner.

"Are you okay?" Malajia asked, eyeing Emily sympathetically. She couldn't help but feel bad that she had to be the one to break the news to Emily about Will's secret child.

"I'm okay," Emily assured, sitting at the table. "I talked to him."

"Well?" Alex pressed.

Malajia put her hand up. "Wait, before you go into all that, what's the boy's name?" she asked. Her question was met with curious and confused stares.

Emily chuckled. "His name *is* Anthony coincidentally," she confirmed, much to Malajia's delight.

Malajia threw her head back and closed her eyes. "Yeeeeessss," she rejoiced loudly.

"Malajia, seriously?" Sidra responded, shaking her head.

"Hey, one of my exaggerations was actually true this time, I'm hype," Malajia joked.

Alex rolled her eyes at Malajia, before turning her

attention back to Emily. "How did he take it when you told him that you weren't gonna see him again?"

Emily frowned at Alex's assumption. "He didn't take it *any* way because I didn't *tell* him that," she returned, much to Alex's confusion.

"I thought you went to find him to break things off," Alex shot back.

"Alex, I never said that," Emily argued. "I just wanted to talk to him and get the truth from him myself... I'm gonna keep seeing him."

"Emily, you're crazy," Alex condemned, throwing her hands up in agitation. Emily rolled her eyes as she fought to keep her rising temper in check. "This man blatantly kept you in the dark, led you on and not to mention he has a *child*," she reminded.

"So *what*? A child is not a deal breaker," Emily stood firm.

Chasity, Sidra, and Malajia sat in silence as Alex and Emily went back and forth.

Alex sucked her teeth. "All I'm saying is, how irresponsible *is* he to have a child at such a young age? ...You don't need that in your life right now."

Chasity raised her hand, unable to keep her mouth shut any further. "Can I just jump in here real quick Em?"

"Sure can, I'm finished anyway," Emily ground out, heading up the steps. She was so over Alex, she couldn't think straight.

"What is it Chasity?" Alex bit out.

"So, you're just gonna sit here and criticize the man for having a baby at a young age...and in so many words tell Emily to look *down* on him because he made a mistake?" Chasity hissed at Alex.

"Aww shit," Malajia mumbled, knowing where this argument was headed.

Alex rolled her eyes. "Chasity come on, would *you* date a man who had a baby while you were in college?"

Chasity glared at Alex. "Lest you forget, you judgmental

bitch," she bit out. "If I wouldn't have had a miscarriage last year, *I* would have a baby right now," she reminded.

Alex, realizing her mistake, closed her eyes and pinched the bridge of her nose.

"Are you telling me that you would look down on *me* and *my* child because of a *mistake?*"

"*You're* different Chasity," Alex argued.

"How so?" Chasity challenged. "Jase and I stupidly had unprotected sex and I got pregnant, shit happens. But that doesn't give you the right to judge someone or make someone *else* judge them because it never happened to *you.*"

"*Exactly,*" Malajia hissed, eying Alex with disdain. Malajia remembered her own unplanned pregnancy situation. And even though hers ended in an abortion and not a miscarriage, the same thing still applied as far as she was concerned. "You can't pick and choose who you look down on if the damn situation is the same. And granted, he didn't tell her right away, but she knows *now* and she's old enough to decide if dealing with him is right for her or not."

"Chaz, while I am truly sorry that you feel that I would think differently of you if you would've had your baby, I still stand by my feelings about Will," Alex responded after a few moments. "She deserves better."

The three girls just shook their heads. Alex was being completely unreasonable and judgmental.

"So…are we gonna eat or continue to argue?" Alex asked.

"I can stand to do *both*, actually," Malajia commented.

Alex made a face at her.

Chapter 22

Alex bundled her coat up to her neck as she approached the gates of the house. She walked up to the door, but as she went to twist the doorknob, the door opened. "Hey Emily," she stammered, looking up.

"Sorry, didn't see you," Emily returned, tone even.

Alex moved around Emily as she entered the house. Every exchange between the two women was awkward, ever since their disagreement over Will the other night. Alex watched as Emily was about to close the door behind her.

"You're not mad at me about the other night, are you?" Alex asked point blank.

Emily stopped in her tracks and looked at Alex. "I'm not upset," Emily huffed; her tone wasn't convincing. "I just want you to stop judging him…and *me* for continuing to see him."

Alex walked over to Emily as she removed her coat. "I'm not trying to judge you," Alex explained. "But I just think that you don't really know what you're getting into."

Emily let out a long sigh as Alex continued to speak.

"You've never been in a relationship before, and this is *not* a good idea for a first one."

"Alex," Emily said, voice calm. "Let's just agree to disagree okay?"

"Emily—"

"Please," Emily interrupted, feeling herself getting upset. "I mean it... I gotta go."

Alex somberly watched as Emily shut the door. "She just doesn't get it," she said to herself.

Alex stopped the blender when it was clear that her smoothie was ready. She poured the pink substance into a tall glass and placed the blender into the sink. She was just getting ready to wash it when she heard a light knock on the door. "Coming!" she called, jogging over to the door.

Her smile faded when she saw Will standing there as she opened the door. "Will," she said, tone void of any cheerfulness.

"Hi," Will returned, ignoring the tone and stern look that Alex was giving him. "I'm here to pick up Emily to take her skating."

"She's not here yet."

"I know, I'm a little early," Will politely returned. "Do you mind if I sit and wait? It's pretty chilly out here and I don't want to run the gas down in my car."

Alex didn't say anything as she stepped aside to let him into the house. She went back to the kitchen and began to wash her dishes as Will sat on the couch. The entire time that he sat there, Alex stared at the back of his head. All that kept running through her mind was that Emily was going to get hurt. As her friend, Alex knew that she couldn't allow that to happen. She abruptly cut the water off.

"Will, can I talk to you for a moment?" she asked.

Will turned around, facing her. "Um...sure. What's up?"

Alex dried her hands on a towel, then walked over to the accent chair and sat down. She folded her arms and looked at him. Will stared back, curious as to what she was about to say.

"Look Will, I know you like Emily and all, but she is like a sister to me, so I'm just gonna come out and say what I have to say."

Will eyed her skeptically, "Okay."

"I just don't think that you're good for Emily," Alex bluntly declared.

Will was taken back by that statement. "Oh really?"

"Yes, really," Alex threw back. "She has too much going on in her life for her to be focusing on what's going on with *you*." Her tone was nasty. "You already put her through enough with your mixed signals and your lying."

"Hold up now," Will ground out. "I never lied to Emily, I just withheld information about my son. Now granted that was wrong, but we talked it out and we're moving forward." He fixed his gaze upon Alex's stern one. "I get you're trying to look out for your friend, but don't you think that you're overstepping just a bit? Emily is old enough to make her own decisions. She doesn't need you speaking for her."

"I've known Emily for years," Alex spat. "*You* just got here, so you don't get to tell me anything about her."

Will shook his head; he couldn't believe what was taking place. This woman that he had only barely exchanged words with, was giving him a lecture.

"Emily may be twenty years old, but she's still a naïve little girl," Alex hissed.

Will became angry. "Naïve?"

"*Naïve*," Alex reiterated. "She spent damn near her whole life being sheltered by her over protective mother, so she knows *nothing* about how people can really be. She's never had a boyfriend, so she has no idea the makings of a healthy relationship. Not to mention that she had a bad experience with a guy in high school who made her think that he cared about her when he was only after her for sex, so yeah, I think she's a little naïve when it comes to you."

Will sat there in disbelief. Not so much at how she was coming at him, but in how she was talking about Emily, talking about her as if she was a child. "I'm going to just wait for her in the car," he grumbled, getting up from the couch.

"I really think you need to leave her alone Will," Alex spat as his back. When he walked out and shut the door without saying another word, Alex just shook her head.

Emily fastened her seatbelt before removing her gloves. "It's way too cold to be fall," she said of the frigid temperatures. Having just left from getting a bite to eat, the pair were headed for the skating rink.

Will was silent as he turned the car on and adjusted the heat. He tried to hide his agitation at dinner. But his conversation with Alex earlier had him fuming; he didn't know how much longer he could go without bringing it up to Emily.

"Will…you're being quiet again," Emily observed. "Everything okay? Is Anthony's fever back?"

Will forced a smile. He was grateful that she was concerned for his son. "No, Anthony is fine," he assured. "It's just um… I had this weird conversation with one of your friends today."

Emily frowned. "What do you mean?" she asked, curious. None of the girls had mentioned any conversation before she left earlier. "*Which* friend?"

"Alex," he revealed, much to Emily's astonishment.

Emily looked at him as her facial expression went from confused to stern. "What did she say?" she asked; her tone was as angry as Will felt.

Emily stormed through the door and slammed it shut, grabbing the attention of Alex and the rest of the girls. "Hey Emily," Alex greeted with caution. Judging by the look on Emily's face, she was not happy.

Emily glared at Alex. After hearing from Will what Alex had said, Emily had finally reached her breaking point and was furious. "Don't 'hey Emily' me, Alex," Emily spat, approaching.

The girls were stunned by Emily's frigid response. Especially Alex, who had just set a cup of water on the counter next to her. "Okay, what's the problem?" Alex asked.

"You talked to Will behind my back?" Emily fumed, coming face to face with her.

"Alex, you did *what?*" Sidra asked, eyeing Alex in complete disbelief and disgust, just as Malajia and Chasity were.

Alex just stared at Emily, whose eyes were drilling through Alex like a laser. Alex put her hand up. "Emily, let me explain."

"There is *nothing* to explain!" Emily erupted.

"Ooh, Alex is about to get cussed out," Malajia commented gleefully. She, Chasity and Sidra darted over to the dining room chairs. The girls quickly faced them forward, so they wouldn't miss a thing. It wasn't every day, or *ever,* that they saw Emily lose her temper.

Alex rolled her eyes at the girls, who were getting comfortable in their seats. "Don't you three have somewhere *else* to be?" she hissed.

"Nope," Chasity spat at the same time that Malajia replied, "We ain't goin' a damn step." Sidra just vigorously shook her head.

Alex shook her head, then faced Emily. "Emily, can we go talk about this in private?" she requested, reaching for Emily's arm.

"Don't touch me," Emily hissed, moving her arm out of Alex's reach. "No we *can't* talk about this in private. You don't care about privacy any *other* time."

"Boom!" Malajia reacted, slapping her leg.

"You need to let me explain *why* I did what I did," Alex said to Emily.

"I've *had* it with you, Alex," Emily fumed.

Alex went to open her mouth, but was drowned out by Malajia's voice.

"Sidra, go get that bag of popcorn out the cabinet, hurry up," she prompted, sending Sidra darting to the kitchen.

"Emily, I only spoke to him because I was concerned for you," Alex reasoned. "I was—"

"Just stop Alex," Emily snapped, interrupting Alex's pointless explanation. "You weren't concerned. You *damn* sure didn't seem concerned when you called me a naïve little girl!"

"Ooh Em said 'damn,' she's pissed," Malajia mumbled to the other girls in delight, grabbing a handful of popcorn from the bag.

"This popcorn is dry as shit, yo," Chasity complained, chewing the popcorn kernels.

"Shhh," Sidra urged, reaching over and giving Chasity's arm a poke.

"I didn't mean it like that," Alex said to Emily.

"You meant it *exactly* how you said it," Emily argued, pointing at her. "You still think of me as that whiny little seventeen-year-old that you met freshman year. That's a damn shame, considering how much I've changed."

While Alex understood why Emily was upset, she wasn't just going to stand there and be yelled at. "Look," she ground out. "You might have gotten older, but you still have a *lot* to learn. You have *no* idea what relationships are like. You never had a *real* one."

"What's your point?!"

"The point *is*, that the *first* guy you go for is some lying baby daddy," Alex threw back, folding her arms. "You go for the *first* guy who looks at you and you just fall blind to all the signs."

"And what signs are those Alex?" Emily fumed, voice filled with sarcasm. "Cheating signs? Is every guy a cheater? Is that what you're saying?"

Alex looked at her wide-eyed. "Are you kidding me right now Emily?" she barked. "You're taking a simple act of concern and turning it into something malicious. I *told* you that I was just looking out for you."

"I don't *need* you to look out for me! I don't need you to be my damn mother!" Emily hollered, standing close to Alex's face.

"Yes! She *finally* said it," Malajia praised. "Now make

fun of her shirt."

Alex's head snapped in the girls' direction. "Shut up Malajia!" she screamed, before turning back to an irate Emily. "*First* off, you need to back up out of my damn face."

"Or what?" Emily taunted.

"You're rubbing off on her Chaz," Malajia commented, giving Chasity a nudge.

"Malajia, shut up!" Emily hollered.

"Yes ma'am," Malajia instantly replied, earning a snicker from Chasity.

"What? You think I'd hit you?" Alex spat. "No, I respect you too much for that, and you need to *respect me* by backing up out of my face."

"Cut the self-righteous crap Alex. You don't respect me, you never *have*," Emily argued, not intimidated by Alex's stare. "Ever since I *met* you, I've been like your child. You talked about my mother, but you're acting *just* like her. Talking for me, trying to control my actions, you are no *better* than Kelly Harris."

Alex cut her eye at the three girls when she heard the confirming noises they made. "You're right, I'm *not* your mother, but please don't stand here and act like you don't still need someone to watch over you," she snarled. "You *clearly* can't make the right decisions, otherwise we wouldn't even be having this conversation."

Emily shook her head. This girl in front of her wasn't listening to anything that she was saying. "Are you bored Alex?" she bit out, earning a narrow-eyed stare from Alex. "Are you so lonely and bitter that you have nothing else better to do than insert your overly judgmental behind in everyone's business?"

"You better watch it," Alex warned.

"No, *you* better watch it," Emily threw back, pointing at Alex. "Go ahead and watch Eric and every other guy you ever come in contact with, walk right out of your miserable life, because you can't get over what *one* guy did."

"Ooh!" Sidra blurted out, then slapped her hand over her

mouth as both Alex and Emily shot her glares. "Sorry, I wasn't expecting that."

"Nobody told *her* to shut up," Malajia grunted, folding her arms.

This time it was Alex who pointed in Emily's face. "Don't you dare," she seethed, feeling herself tear up. "You have *no* idea the heartbreak that I've suffered. You have *no* idea what it's like to be cheated on."

"Get over it!" Emily boomed; she was completely fed up with Alex's pity party over her ex. "So *what* Paul cheated on you? It was *four years* ago! Nobody *cares* anymore! He moved on, *you* need to too!"

"You know what, fuck you Emily!" Alex screamed.

"I have heard worse things said to me Alex," Emily threw back. "You think saying that to me hurts me?!" she yelled. "It *doesn't*! What hurts me is the fact that you went behind my back and talked down about me. What hurts me is the fact that you think so *little* of me... Not to mention you just stuck your nose all *in* my business. You had *no* idea if I told him any of what you said to him about what happened to me."

"Well if your little relationship was so perfect like you *think* it is, then you should've told him your *damn* self," Alex countered, tone nasty.

Emily's eyed widened. "You are unbelievable," she seethed.

Alex put her hands on her hips. "So now you think you got some balls, and can get all swole up at *me* because you got these little two-faced hyenas over there in your corner now?" she fumed.

"If she looks over here, I'm gonna slap the shit outta her," Chasity said in a quiet aside to Malajia and Sidra.

"You know I'll follow up," Malajia cosigned. "I ain't no damn hyena."

"How soon you forget, *I* was the one in your corner when they couldn't *stand* your wimpy, whiny ass," Alex threw out. Emily just stood there, fire in her eyes.

"They may not have liked me at one point in time, and that's okay. But at least they didn't hide behind phony smiles and fake explanations for their screwed-up comments towards and *about* me," Emily returned.

Alex shook her head at Emily. She didn't recognize this person standing in front of her. "You just crossed a line with me, Emily," she ground out, pointing again. "A line that may never be repaired."

"I don't care."

"Well, you might not care *now*," Alex threw back, voice dangerously low. "But you'll care when you can't come crying to me after Will's lying ass screws you and leaves you alone, like the *last* one did."

Alex's nasty comment was met with gasps and horrified looks from the girls on the sidelines. "Are you fuckin' kidding me?" Malajia belted out. She no longer cared about being told to shut up. What Alex just said was vicious.

"Whoa," Sidra commented, astonished.

Emily looked like the wind had been knocked out of her. She couldn't believe that Alex stooped so low to bring up something so hurtful. Completely done, Emily grabbed the cup of water from the counter and flung the contents in Alex's face. Alex let out a scream as Emily threw the cup down on the floor and stormed out of the house, slamming the door behind her.

Alex covered her face with her hands in an effort to stop the water from dripping. "Can one of you bystanders hand me a towel please?" she asked. Her voice sounded like she was beginning to cry.

"Fuck no, you ignorant bitch," Chasity fumed, standing from her seat and heading for the door. "I can't believe you just threw that shit in her face like that," she added, snatching the door open. "You fuckin' disgust me Alex. She should've punched you in your goddamn mouth."

Sidra and Malajia both rose from their seats as Chasity walked out and slammed the door. Alex wiped her face with her shirt sleeve. She looked at Malajia and Sidra with red eyes. "So, what? She gets to throw something in *my* face, and I get dragged through the mud because *I* did it?" she sniffled.

Malajia was completely disgusted with Alex's behavior, not only from a few moments ago, but for the past weeks. She just shook her head. "That was foul, yo," she bit out, before walking out.

Alex put her hands on her head as she tried to keep from sobbing out loud.

Sidra slowly folded her arms. "They're *so* right," Sidra began, angry. "You are *beyond* wrong for that."

"But she—"

"Who gives a fuck *what* she said!" Sidra erupted. "She was a *hundred* percent right about Paul. You're letting something that happened four years ago taint your perception of all men! *We've all* told you that. Hell, your own *mother* told you that!"

Alex let her tears flow as Sidra ripped into her.

"Emily is trying not to let her past affect her views and you criticize her for that?" Sidra argued. "She was *fifteen* when that boy used her, and you stood there and had the *audacity* to throw something like that up in her face, because you're mad that you got told the *truth!*"

Alex stood there unable to speak.

Sidra shook her head. "You have issues that you need to deal with, Alex," she concluded, heading for the door.

Alex watched teary-eyed as Sidra walked out of the house, slamming the door behind her. It was then that Alex put her hands over her face and broke down crying.

Chapter 23

Alex tightened the band around her puff ponytail before giving herself one last onceover in the mirror. Sighing, she grabbed her books from her bed and headed out of the room. She paused when she came face to face with Emily, who was just emerging from her room.

"Hey Em," Alex greeted, hopeful.

Not only did Emily not return Alex's smile, but she rolled her eyes, then proceeded down the steps, without saying a word.

Alex's smile faded and she let out a sigh as she heard the door open and shut. *I hate this.*

Alex headed down the steps and into the kitchen and grabbed a bowl from the cabinet, intent on eating cereal. The door opened and she spun around. "Hey Sid," she said.

Sidra waved slightly, before heading for the steps.

Alex sucked her teeth. "Sidra come on, it's been a week," she blurted out. "Is a wave all I'm going to continue to get from you?"

Sidra paused on the staircase. "For now," she bit out.

Alex shut the cabinet door. Since her spat, although she had not been completely shunned by the other girls, Alex did feel the tension from them. "Is it really necessary for *all* of you to be mad at me, when the argument was between *Emily* and I?"

Sidra raised an eyebrow. "Asks the *same* person who participated in freezing Mark out last semester when he played that prank on David," she threw back.

Alex glanced away.

"Lucky for *you*, we're not going to *that* extreme," Sidra mumbled, running her hand over her hair. She fixed a stern gaze on Alex. "You gotta fix things with Emily, Alex... She's hurt."

Alex sighed, walking over to the staircase. "I *tried* to apologize to her, she won't even *look* at me."

"Do you *blame* her?" Sidra asked point blank.

Alex folded her arms in a huff. She knew that she had messed up, but she refused to take all the blame for their fall out. "Look, like I said, I've tried. I'm *still* trying," Alex argued. "*She* said some nasty stuff to *me too*, you know."

"Because of what *you* did to *her*," Sidra threw back, tempter rising.

Sidra had hoped that the morning after Alex and Emily's confrontation, that Alex would own up to the fact that she was completely in the wrong. Now a week had gone by, and she still hadn't; Sidra was beginning to lose hope that Alex ever would.

"I can't deal with this right now, I have a test to take," Alex grunted, walking out of the house.

"Fine Alex," Sidra sighed, walking up the steps.

Alex stomped down the path towards the History building. She was mad at herself for even goading Sidra; now she'd made herself tense before her test. Seeing Eric heading out of the building, she stopped. Alex was able to keep her feelings at bay when she caught glimpses of him around campus, but now that she had locked eyes with him, she didn't know how to feel.

Eric looked at her momentarily, then just as quickly looked past her. Alex followed his progress as he walked by her. She didn't know why, but she hoped that he would at least say *something* to her. After all, they had shared something before he cut their friendship short. The fact that he didn't speak at all annoyed her.

"Eric," she called.

Eric stopped walking and turned around. "What is it Alex?" he bit out.

Alex approached him. "Damn, I know you're mad, but you can at *least* speak," she fussed. "You walked right by me."

Eric smirked, folding his arms. "I'm not obligated to speak to someone I'm not friends with," he spat.

Alex folded her arms, staring daggers at him. "Your immaturity is showing and it's not cute."

"Yeah well, I'm sure it looks better than your game playing," he bit back.

Alex shook her head in disappointment. "God, you were *such* a waste of my damn time," she snarled. The look on his face made her wish that she could take those words back. She knew that she should never have said it; she definitely didn't mean it.

Eric stared at her for a moment, adjusting his book bag on his shoulder. "If I wasn't convinced before that I did the right thing by letting you go, you just confirmed it now."

Alex's eyes dropped to the ground.

"Bye," he grunted, walking off, leaving her standing there alone.

Alex opened her mouth to call after him, but decided against it. The damage was already done.

"Did you end up passing that Statistics exam?" David asked Emily as the pair ambled through campus on their way to the cafeteria.

Emily nodded. "Yes, and thank you for helping me study," she replied, grateful.

"No problem." He adjusted his bag. "I had that class before, I know how hard those tests can be."

"Yeah," Emily agreed.

David looked over at Emily as they continued their pace. He wondered if he should even bring up what he was about to. But having been in a situation similar last semester, where he was hurt by a close friend, David understood how she felt. "So...how are things between you and Alex?" he asked.

Emily looked at him. Even though the guys had yet to comment on the situation between her and Alex, she figured that they knew about it. "Things aren't good," Emily answered, honest.

"Oh..." was all that he could think of to say.

"How much do you know?" she wondered.

"Enough," he answered. "I know what you're going through."

Emily sighed. "I know," she said. "At least Mark finally admitted that he was wrong."

David put his hand on Emily's shoulder. "I know that Alex will too," he consoled. "Y'all are too close for her *not* to."

Emily scoffed. "Not likely," she said. "Judging by her 'I know I did this but *you*' way of thinking."

Emily had felt like slapping Alex when she gave her a so-called apology through Emily's room door, two days after their argument. She remembered how Alex failed to acknowledge her wrong doing, how she tried to turn it around on her.

"She reminds me of my mother sometimes... It's annoying," Emily vented.

David nodded. Any response that he was about to give was halted when he laid eyes on Nicole, leaving the cafeteria.

Emily, noticing the object of his attention, gently nudged him. "Go talk to her David," she urged.

David shook his head. "No, maybe later," he refused. "You and I were talking about—"

"About something that I don't care to *finish* talking about," Emily cut in, stopping. "Seriously, you should go say something to her."

David took a deep breath as he too stopped walking. "I can't," he admitted.

This time Emily placed a sympathetic hand on David's shoulder. He was afraid; she too knew that feeling.

"Yo yo, y'all coming in here or what?!" Mark bellowed from the cafeteria entrance to Emily and David who stood a few feet from the cafeteria. They walked over.

Josh rubbed his ear. "Right by my ear man," he commented of Mark's loudness.

"Shut up," Mark dismissed.

"Anything good in there?" Emily asked.

"Probably not, but I'm hungry anyway," Mark jeered. Seeing that David's attention was still on Nicole, Mark nudged him.

David looked at him, confused. Mark gestured for David to go over to her, but David just shook his head.

Mark sighed heavily. *This is for your own good bro.* "Nicole!" he called, grabbing David's book bag when David tried to walk away.

"Let go," David demanded through clenched teeth.

"Nah, your bitchin' stops today," Mark threw back. He smiled when Nicole approached.

"Hi Mark, you want me to pass one of your threatening messages to Quincy?" Nicole asked, amusement in her voice.

"Fuck Quincy," Mark joked in return, holding on to David's bag with a vice grip. "I'll threaten him in person when we meet up on the basketball court." Nicole put her hands up in surrender. "No, I called you over here 'cause my friend David here wants to ask you something." Mark then gave David a hard pat on the back, before retreating into the cafeteria.

David stood there, eyes wide. *Damn it Mark!* he seethed as Nicole smiled at him.

Josh gave David the 'okay' sign behind Nicole's back as he and Emily joined Mark inside.

David gave a nervous chuckle as he rubbed the back of his neck.

"Well?" Nicole prompted. "What do you want to ask me?"

David felt his palms sweat as he tried to gather his words. "Um…how are you?" he asked, drawing the words out slowly.

Nicole giggled. *He's so adorable.* "Why do I get the feeling that you're nervous to talk to me?"

Because I am. "Uh, no, not nervous at all," he lied. He fiddled with his hands as Nicole stared at him. "Well—okay… I wanted to um…"

"Just ask her out David, damn!" Mark blurted out, peeking out of the cafeteria door.

Both Nicole and David turned and looked at him, making Mark pull his head back inside. Nicole put her hand over her face and giggled, before facing a horrified David once again.

"Please excuse him, he's a fool," David apologized.

"Is he *wrong*?" Nicole asked. "Do you not want to ask me out?"

David glanced down at his sneakers momentarily. "…No, he's not wrong," he admitted. He took a deep breath. "So yeah…do you want to go out sometime? ...With *me*?"

Nicole titled her head. "Sure," she beamed, much to David's delight. "Any day in particular?"

David was so surprised that Nicole accepted, that he hadn't thought that far in advance. He put his finger up. "That's a good question."

Nicole reached into the pocket of her jeans and retrieved her cell phone. "Tell you what, let's exchange numbers and you can call me when you have a set date," she proposed. "Cool?"

"Cool," David smiled, pulling his phone from a pocket in his book bag. Once numbers were exchanged, Nicole headed off, leaving David to stand there, staring at her departing back.

Hearing someone loudly clear their throat, David turned around. "About time," Mark teased.

David shook his head as Mark, Josh, and Emily approached him.

"Em and I had no idea he was gonna do that," Josh promised, putting his hands up.

"Oh, I know," David assured, adjusting his book bag. "This had 'just Mark' written all over it."

"You're *welcome*," Mark boasted, folding his arms.

David's bright smile could have lit the dreary sky. "Thank you."

Mark clapped his hands together. "See, I'm not a *complete* jackass," he joked, giving David a pat on his back.

"Not all the time, anyway," David returned. Mark sucked his teeth as the four of them ambled inside the cafeteria.

Alex ran her hands over her hair as she sat at her desk in her room. Working on her Calculus problems for the past hour, Alex was at her wits end with her formulas *and* her calculator. *Why I decided to put this class off until my last year is beyond me.*

Picking up her calculator and tapping on it with her finger, she let out a loud groan. "I *hate* this stupid thing," she barked, tossing the dead calculator across the room.

Frustrated, Alex put her head in her hands. "I can't do these stupid problems without a damn calculator," she vented to herself.

Rubbing her hands on her jeans, she stood from her seat. Walking out into the hallway, she listened for voices. Hearing two coming from Chasity's room, she knocked on the door.

Malajia pulled the door open and turned her lip up. "Ugh," she scoffed. "Chaz, you got a wide bitch at your door," she jeered to a visibly annoyed Alex.

"Tell it to slide its ass back across the hall," Chasity threw out from her desk.

Alex sucked her teeth, fixing a glare upon a smirking

Malajia. "I didn't come over here to be insulted," she sneered.

"Then why are you here?" Chasity uttered, even toned.

Alex moved around Malajia, stepping inside and folding her arms. "Look, I just came to see if either one of you would let me borrow your calculator," she said. "I know you both aren't too happy with me right now, but I hope not enough to let me fail my homework."

"Mine is broke," Malajia replied, flopping down on Chasity's bed.

Chasity stopped typing on her laptop and shot Malajia a stern glance. "That 'mine broke' shit is getting really old, Malajia."

Malajia shrugged, laughing in the process.

Alex sighed. "Can I borrow your calculator, Chasity?"

"No." Chasity's response was instantaneous, prompting a snicker from Malajia.

Alex shook her head. "Thanks," she mumbled, walking out the door.

"Just take the damn calculator Alex," Chasity called after her. Alex was right; Chasity may have been annoyed with her, but not enough to see her fail an assignment.

Alex turned back inside and grabbed it from Chasity's desk. "Thank you," she said to a non-responsive Chasity.

"Don't be breathing all hard on it, I'm using it next," Malajia scoffed, shaking her hand in Alex's direction.

"Never said that," Chasity said to Malajia.

Alex clutched the calculator in her hand, standing by the door.

"Why are you still standing here?" Chasity ground out.

Alex thought about just retreating to her room to tackle her dreaded homework. But she felt the need to plead her case. "You know that I only went behind Emily's back because I was looking out for her, right?" she began.

Chasity glanced up, frustrated that her work was being interrupted. "You're telling this to *us*, for *what*?" she spat.

"Right, you need to tell that to Emily," Malajia added.

"*She's* the one who nearly drowned your ass with that cup of water."

Alex rolled her eyes. "Look, I know that you two, Sidra *included*, have *some* influence over Emily's refusing to hear me out," she reasoned. Chasity and Malajia looked at Alex as if she had lost her mind. "Emily has *never* been this petty *or* stubborn. I'm pretty sure if y'all talk to her, she'll let up on me."

"Woooow," Malajia drew out after a long pause. "And you wonder why she ain't fuckin' with you right now."

Chasity turned around in her seat, making sure that her whole body faced Alex. "You *do* realize that Emily has a mind of her own right?" she charged. "We have *nothing* to do with the fact that she's not talking to you."

"You just basically called that girl a follower and didn't even have enough decency to say it to her face," Malajia added, voice filled with disdain.

Alex let out a quick breath. "That's not even how I meant it."

"Alex, kill that 'I didn't mean it' shit. Yes, you *did*," Chasity argued. "You *meant* what you said, you *meant* to do what you did, just like you *always* do. And now the *one* person you thought would *never* get tired of your bullshit, is *tired* of your bullshit."

"And here you two go ganging up on me. Blowing things *way* out of proportion, just like *you* always do," Alex barked back, over the conversation.

"Been holding that animosity for a while now, huh?" Chasity taunted.

Malajia scoffed at Alex. "Weak ass comeback."

Alex slammed Chasity's calculator on the desk, then turned on her heel and stormed out of the room, slamming the door.

Malajia kept her eyes glued to Chasity, who stared at her calculator. Malajia put her hand up; she knew where this was about to go. "Chaz—"

"I know that raggedy bitch did *not* just slam my fuckin'

calculator after I was nice enough to let her broke ass hold it," Chasity snarled.

Malajia watched Chasity make a move to jump from her seat. "Ooh! No, no, chill," Malajia urged. She jumped up and grabbed Chasity's arm as she started for the door. "We slap each other with words, not *hands*," she said.

"Malajia, get off me," Chasity warned.

"No, calm your ass down," Malajia refused. "You wanna get out of this room, you're gonna have to go through me."

Chasity looked at her, fire in her eyes. "You sure you wanna do that? There will be no remorse this time," she threatened.

Malajia made a face at her. "Not necessary," she said, grabbing Chasity's calculator. She showed it to her. "Look, it's not broken."

Chasity snatched it from her.

"Now sit down and finish your homework, so we can go to this stupid movie with the guys." Chasity snatched her arm from Malajia's grasp. "You smell good boo, whatchu' got on?" she mentioned as Chasity sat back in her seat.

"Soap, try using it sometime," Chasity jeered, earning a phony laugh from Malajia followed by a middle finger.

"These doubles are killing me," Will complained, running his hand over his hair as he sat back on one of the cushy chairs in his small office.

"I know," Emily sympathized, giving him a pat on the arm. "You need to take some time off."

Will sighed, placing his hands behind his head. "Can't. I'm still saving up to move."

"Look, staying with your parents for now isn't a bad thing," Emily reminded him.

"I'm a grown ass man, living in a basement." he griped. "It's pathetic."

"You're a young single father who needs help," Emily clarified, voice stern. "You're not pathetic, so stop."

"Yeah well, that's not what your friends think," Will said in a sad attempt at a joke.

Emily shook her head. "It's just *one*," she mumbled. "And she's not exactly being a friend right now."

Will, noticing Emily's sudden mood change, sat up straight. "Damn, I'm sorry Emily," he apologized. Will knew all too well how much Emily's argument with Alex was weighing on her. He recalled how she had called him, furious, after it had taken place. She had cried to him about how she felt betrayed by Alex. "I was only joking."

"I know," she returned, examining the pale pink polish on her finger nails.

As the pair sat in awkward silence for several moments, Will tried to think of something comforting to say to her. "So um…" he ran his hand along the back of his neck. "Listen, I just want to let you know that I have no hard feelings towards Alex," he put out.

"That's nice of you," Emily grumbled.

Will turned in his seat to face her. "No, I'm serious," he insisted. "Alex may have been out of pocket, but now that some time has passed, I realize that she did what she did because she was trying to look out for you."

"Will, I don't *need* anybody to look out for me," Emily snapped, facing him. "I'm tired of people doing crap *thinking* it's in my best interest. I'm not a child and I'm tired of being *treated* like one."

"Do *I* treat you like a child?"

"No, no you don't," Emily assured him. "And truthfully, my other friends really don't *either*… They pushed me to change even before I was ready, but Alex…it's like she took over where my mom left off."

"I guess I can see where that would bother you," Will replied. "From what you've told me about your mom, I mean."

"Yeah well, I'm still not talking to *her* either," Emily griped.

"Hopefully your mom will come around," Will consoled,

rubbing her shoulder.

Emily sighed. "Doubt it."

"Can I make a suggestion?" he asked. Emily nodded. "If Alex tries to apologize again…just hear her out."

"I don't *want* to hear her out, I *want* to slap her," Emily barked, slamming her hand on the arm of the chair. It had gotten to a point where the mere mention of Alex made Emily's blood boil.

Will quickly put his hands up. "Okay, let's talk about something else," he suggested.

Thank God. "Yes, please."

"I want you to meet my son."

Emily's eyes widened with shock. "Huh?"

Will chuckled at her response. "You heard right."

Emily ran her hand through her braids. "Um—are you *sure*? You don't think it's too soon?" she asked. "I mean, we've only been out a handful of times."

"So?" he shrugged.

"Well, *technically* we're not in a relationship," she pointed out.

Will chuckled. "You're so cute when you're trying to dodge," he teased.

Emily playfully tapped his arm. "Don't tease me, I'm being serious."

"Okay I'm sorry," he said. "But just because we decided to take things slow, doesn't mean that I'm moving too fast with introducing you to my son," he reasoned. "If nothing else, you're my friend and I've been more comfortable with *you* in these past few months than I've been with anyone in a long time. So, to answer your initial question: yes, I'm sure that I want you to meet Anthony."

Emily was flattered and nervous; she successfully showed both emotions on her face. "But…what if he doesn't like me?"

Will shook his head in amusement. "He's *two*, just give him a cookie and he'll *love* you," he teased. Emily waved her hand at him and giggled. "Tell you what, I'll wait a little longer if you're still feeling nervous."

"Okay," Emily smiled, sitting back in her seat. "You wanna go get something to eat?"

"As long as it isn't this damn movie popcorn, I'm down," Will joked, earning a laugh from a now relaxed Emily.

Chapter 24

David stared at the phone in his hand. *Just call her, David.* He'd been in the kitchen of his house, leaning against the counter, and staring at the blue cell phone in his hand for the past ten minutes.

The front door opened, prompting David to quickly set the phone down. "What's up guys?" he said to Jason and Mark as they walked in, accompanied by Sidra.

"You not foolin' nobody," Mark teased, tossing his book bag on the floor by the steps. "You still staring at the damn phone, huh?"

"No," David lied.

"You're full of shit," Mark laughed, pointing to the phone on the counter. "The phone is right there."

Jason shook his head at David's embarrassed expression. "Just call her, man," he urged. "She gave you her number and agreed to go out with you," he reminded. "All you gotta do is set it up."

"He being corny," Mark commented, flopping down on the couch.

David waved his hand at the guys dismissively, then opened the refrigerator and stuck his head in.

"You tryna find your courage in there?" Mark mocked, earning a backhand from Sidra. He laughed.

"You guys leave David alone," Sidra chided, putting her

hands on her hips. "Mark, you of all people know how he is
around girls."

"Yeah, I know, his balls draw up," Mark laughed.

David grabbed a container of leftover takeout from the
fridge and slammed the door shut. "I'm right *here* you
know," he fussed.

"We're just messing around," Jason chuckled.

Sidra shook her head, then turned her attention to David.
"Sweetie, you don't have to be nervous," Sidra assured him.
"Like Jase said, she already agreed to a date, you just have to
set it up."

David sighed as he walked over to the dining room table.
"I know," he sulked "I have *no* idea what to do or where to
take her." He sat down in a chair. "It's not like I'm
swimming in money."

"Who says you *have* to be?" Sidra frowned.

Mark sucked his teeth. "Growing up around *your*
spoiled, uppity ass, is where he got that idea," he joked.

Sidra glared at Mark. "You calling me a snob?"

"Oh absolutely," Mark confirmed, as Jason nodded
vigorously.

"Whatever," Sidra huffed. "I'm not a *snob* okay. It just
so happens that my boyfriend is well-off…he also happens to
be older. But that doesn't mean that if I was dating someone
my *own* age, that I would expect expensive restaurants and
carriage rides," she argued.

"Why you gotta bring up carriage rides?" Mark sneered.
"My man is feeling down enough already."

Sidra gave the back of Mark's head a light slap. "Boy,
shut up."

"David look, you and Nicole are both in college, I'm
sure she doesn't expect some fancy date," Jason placated.

David nodded slowly. "Where did you guys go on your
first date with Chasity and Malajia?" he asked.

"I took Chaz to a restaurant," Jason answered.

"Same with me and Mel," Mark added.

"Was it expensive?"

Both Jason and Mark shook their heads. Noticing the dilemma on David's face, Mark sighed loudly. "Look man, if you're scared about having to wash dishes or some shit, just do what Josh does," Mark suggested.

"And what is that?" David asked, scooping some food out of the container.

"Do a picnic or some shit," Mark answered.

David gave Mark a long stare. "The fall isn't *exactly* the best time for a picnic outside," he sneered.

"What he *means*, is, Josh always does stuff with December that doesn't take a lot of money," Jason cut in, seeing the attitude on Mark's face from David's remark. "Take her on a bowling date or something like that; keep it simple."

"Just don't take her none of that dry ass Shack pizza that Josh always be tryna feed December," Mark joked.

Sidra once again shook her head at Mark, *Yeah, Josh is so sweet.* She then smiled to herself as thoughts of Josh flooded her mind. Not coming from much money, Josh always found thoughtful ways to do things for the people he cared about without spending a lot. Sidra rubbed her eyes when she found herself smiling longer than she should.

"Anyway, they have a point," she put in. "Just find out what she likes, do something that doesn't break the bank, go have fun and be yourself."

David smiled. "Thanks guys…and lady," he mused, rising from his seat. "I'm gonna call her… soon."

"Yeah whatever," Mark griped. "Just make sure you brush your teeth before you call her. You don't want that funky ass food you were just eatin' to go through the phone."

It was silent in the room for several seconds.

"That was wack, bro," Jason laughed, prompting laughter from Sidra and David. Mark, unamused, just made a face.

Jason opened his door, phone cradled between his ear

and shoulder, with two bags of clean laundry in his hands. "Is Dad taking his heart pills, like he's supposed to?" he asked, closing the door with his foot.

"He sure is," Mrs. Adams assured.

"Is he still complaining about *having* to take them?" Jason, asked, sitting down on the bed.

"He sure is," Mrs. Adams repeated, annoyed. "Gotta love him."

"Yeah," Jason agreed, pulling clothes from his bag. Jason was finishing up his last loads of clothes at the complex laundry facility, when he received a call from Kyle. After chatting with his little brother for some time, his mother jumped on the line to talk as Jason was on his way back to his room.

"You doing okay?" Mrs. Adams asked. "Practice going well? Grades good? You getting enough sleep?"

"Yes, yes, and yes," Jason chuckled. It wasn't new for his mother to fuss over him. "Everything is good over here Mom."

"Good to hear," she replied, then paused for a moment. "Still with what's her name?"

Jason paused from folding his clothes, frowning. "*Chasity*, and yes," he bit out.

"Just asking," she said, feigning innocence. "You know, just trying to catch up, since you hardly call me anymore."

Jason rolled his eyes. "Please stop," he urged. "Seriously Mom, I've told you before that Chasity isn't going anywhere. The sooner you accept that, the better it'll be for *both* of us."

A loud sigh came through the phone. "I am not going to spend our phone time *arguing*," she huffed.

Jason looked confused. *You started it, though.* Despite how much he wanted to hurl that truth back to his mother, he decided against it. He just shook his head.

"Anyway... While I was out running errands earlier, guess who I ran into?"

Jason folded another item. At this point, he was over the conversation. "Who?" he asked, unenthused.

"Paris."

Jason paused; he wondered if he had heard correctly. "*Who?*"

"Paris," she repeated.

"As in my *ex-girlfriend* Paris?" he asked, perplexed.

A soft chuckle came through the line. "Do we *know* another Paris?" she said. "Anyway, she says 'hi.'"

Jason frowned. His mother seemed much too chipper when referring to his ex, for his liking. "Mom, *why* would you think that I wanted to know that?" he groused.

"What's the harm in telling you what the girl said?" she bit back. "You're being way too sensitive."

"And *you're* being way too happy about it," Jason argued. "Paris and I haven't been together in *years*. So any messages from her to me, I *don't* care about and *don't* need it relayed to me."

There was a pause on the line. "You know what, I'll just let you get back to doing what you're doing," she ground out. Jason rolled his eyes. "Hopefully your attitude will improve by the time we see you next Saturday for your game."

"Yeah, I'm sure it will," Jason spat. "Bye Mom." He hung up, tossing his phone on his bed.

Rubbing his face with his hands, he let out a long sigh. *Shit*, Jason thought. Normally he would be excited for his family to attend his games, but with the tension between his mother and girlfriend, Jason was on edge. *At least Dad can reel her in...somewhat.*

David tossed his cell phone on his bed, jumped up, and ran out of the door. Jogging out of his house and across the way to the girls' house, he busted through the unlocked door. "I did it!" he exclaimed to the living room full of his stunned friends.

"You did *what*?" Malajia asked, confused as she handed Mark a glass of juice.

"I finally called Nicole, we're going on our date," David

beamed, holding his arms up in the air.

"That's awesome," Sidra mused, hugging him as applause rang throughout the room.

"About time," Mark praised, taking a sip of his ice-filled drink. He pulled the cup from his lips and looked at Malajia. "Babe, you put too much ice in—"

"You wanna wear that damn juice, boy?" Malajia threatened, pointing at him.

"Naw, this watery juice is good," he returned, earning a middle finger from Malajia. Mark smirked and blew a kiss at her.

"Anyway," Sidra rolled her eyes at their display. "Where are you taking her, David?"

David smoothed his hand down his shirt as he sat on the arm of the couch. "Well, when we were talking, she mentioned that she grew up near an orchard and—"

"David got himself a county girl," Malajia teased.

David shook his head in amusement. "So, I figured that I would take her to Essex Orchard, which is like an hour from here," he informed, excited. "It's perfect. They have arts and crafts, a farmer's market, games, apple and pumpkin picking...even a hayride. And it's not expensive—"

"No, it certainly *isn't*," Malajia mocked, examining her manicured nails.

"Don't be rude," Sidra scolded, shooting Malajia a glare.

"I'm just joking," Malajia laughed.

"Well...what do you guys think? Do you think she'll like that?" David asked.

"I think she'll love it," Sidra smiled.

"That's a good idea man," Josh put in from the kitchen.

"You know what, I heard about that place," Mark said, tapping his chin with his finger. "It sounds pretty cool too. It *is* fall and they got pumpkin donuts and shit."

Malajia was confused; it showed on her face when she turned around and looked at him. "What are you talking about?"

"I don't know," Mark admitted, rubbing his head with

his hand. "When are y'all going, David?"

"Saturday."

"Cool, we should *all* go," Mark suggested. His suggestion was met with confusion.

David shook his head vigorously. "No, no I don't think—"

"We won't mess up your date, David," Mark cut in, putting his hand up. "We can all ride out together, 'cause let's face it...you're gonna *need* a ride, 'cause ain't no bus going out to no orchard."

David put his hand over his face and shook his head. "Crap!"

"We can split off from you and just meet up later," Mark added, enthused. "It'll be fun."

"No, no it *wouldn't* be," Malajia contradicted. "Don't nobody wanna pick no damn apples."

"You *will* and you'll like it," Mark promised, voice stern.

"Yeah well, I'll only go if Chasity goes," Malajia ground out. "*She'll* be miserable *with* me."

Mark rolled his eyes. "Fine, I'll ask Jason later when they get back from dinner," he said. "*He'll* get her to go."

"Whatever," Malajia grunted, folding her arms. "I still ain't pickin' no fuckin' apples."

"So...we all in?" Mark asked, a wide grin on his face, ignoring Malajia's complaints.

"Is this a couple's thing?" Sidra asked, raising her hand. "'Cause James isn't gonna come visit me for like another few weeks."

"December is going home this weekend," Josh put in.

"Uh guys," David cut in.

"Well, Sid and Josh, y'all each other's stand in's any damn way," Mark said with a wave of his hand.

"Guys," David called once more.

"Um, I'm not sure if Will can get off," Emily said.

Mark shot Emily a skeptical glance. "Uh...that sounds like a personal problem, Emily," he mocked.

Emily's eyes widened as she realized what Mark was referring to. "No! That's not what I meant," she shrieked, embarrassed. "*Work.* I meant work." She glanced over and saw Malajia laughing. "Malajia!"

"It was funny, I'm sorry," Malajia laughed.

"Guys!" David bellowed, grabbing everyone's attention. "Don't *I* get a say so in this?"

"Nope," Mark quickly put out.

David put his hands up in surrender. "Fine," he relented. "But if you guys embarrass me—"

"Chill, we got you, bee," Mark assured him.

David just stood there, amazed at what had just happened. *God, help me.*

Chapter 25

Alex sighed as she wiped off the last of her tables. "I swear, these people get more food on the table, than in their mouths," she griped, tossing the soiled rag in a small pail. Alex gathered her cleaning items and made a beeline for the kitchen. After finishing another long afternoon at The Pizza Shack, Alex was mentally and physically drained.

"Josh, sorry about messing up that last order," Alex apologized, leaning against the counter.

Josh removed his apron and hung it on a hook on a wall. "It's okay, at least we get to take the extra pizza home," he smiled.

"I think we'd do better to leave it here. Nobody seems to want any of our pizza anymore," she joked.

Josh chuckled. "True." Josh's smile faded as he noticed the somber look on Alex's face. "It sucks that you haven't been around much," he said.

Alex let out a long sigh. "I know," she agreed.

"It's weird when the whole group isn't together, you know?"

"Yeah well, with the tension between Em and myself, I feel like I just need to back off a little," Alex replied, sullen, folding her arms. "I wish we could just move past this mess already."

"You can't just expect someone to move past things

when they're not ready to," Josh advised, tone calm. "I mean these things take time."

"Come on Josh, it's been over a week," Alex vented. "And I've already apologized...*tried* to anyway."

Josh gave Alex a long stare. "You think that's *all* you need to do?"

Alex frowned slightly. "That's what people do when they argue, isn't it?" she bit out. "I've done my part, but Emily needs to do *hers*."

Josh shook his head. Having heard what happened from Sidra, he was well aware of what had been said from both women. He tried to stay out of it and remain neutral, but Alex's attitude about the whole thing was making him a tad bit annoyed. "Alex," Josh began, then hesitated. *Do I even want to get into this?* "Okay, I'm just going to say this to you, even though I'm sure you've already heard it."

"I probably have," Alex mumbled, massaging her scalp with her fingers.

"You were dead wrong for what you did to Emily," he put out.

Alex rolled her eyes. "Josh, I can see where everybody thinks that, but—"

"There is no 'but' in this Alex," Josh cut in, voice stern. "If any of us went behind *your* back and down talked you to somebody, you'd be pissed."

"I didn't *down* talk Emily," Alex argued. "Or at least I didn't *mean* to."

Josh shook his head. It was clear that he wasn't getting through. *Welp, I tried.* "Let's get out of here," he urged, turning the light off in the kitchen.

Alex nodded.

Alex waved to Josh, then ran her hand along the back of her neck as she walked in the house after the twenty-minute walk back to campus from work. "God, I don't feel like dealing with this paper tonight," she complained. Setting her books down on the couch, she came face to face with Emily, who was emerging from the kitchen.

The two women stared at each other for several strained moments. "Hi Em," Alex said.

Emily sucked her teeth and headed for the stairs.

Alex let out a loud sigh as she spun around to face Emily's retreating back. "Emily hold on a second," she demanded.

"For *what*, Alex?" Emily sighed, continuing her pace.

"Because I'm trying to resolve this like an adult," Alex fussed, standing with her hands on her hips. "You're making this difficult."

Emily spun around. "*I'm* making this difficult?" she pointed to herself.

"Yes," Alex confirmed. "I've apologized to you like twice already—"

"It was *once*," Emily corrected.

"Doesn't even *matter*, you ignored it *anyway*."

"Because your apology was bull crap," Emily fumed from the stairs.

"Excuse me?" Alex sneered. "What do you want from me Emily? You want me to kiss your ass?"

Emily rolled her eyes. "No, Alex that's not what I want," she answered. "But I can't—" She took a deep breath. "Do you even know what you're sorry *for*?"

Alex folded her arms. "Yes, I hurt your feelings," she admitted.

"*How?*" Emily asked, eyes pleading. Emily hated arguing, but she hated the way that Alex treated her more. And she knew that she couldn't allow things to go back to normal, until Alex owned up to her meddling and overbearing ways.

"I threw up what happened to you in your face," Alex declared.

Emily looked down at the floor and nodded. "*And?*" she pressed.

Alex frowned. "Look Emily, I know you think that me

going behind your back and talking to Will was wrong," she began. Emily just stared at her. "And I admit that I may have over stepped, but—"

"You're doing the 'but' thing again, Alex," Emily pointed out.

Alex grew frustrated. "Emily, I'm just trying to explain—"

"*Again*, you're trying to justify it!" Emily wailed. "You were wrong, point blank, and you *still* can't admit that." When Alex didn't say another word, Emily shook her head. "Goodnight Alex," she mumbled, turning to head back up the steps, leaving Alex to sulk alone.

Chasity gripped the fabric of Jason's shirt as she laid underneath him. The feeling of his lips on her lips and her neck was sending her sex drive into overdrive. Having taken a much-needed study break, the couple was taking advantage of the privacy of Jason's single room and had begun one of their passionate make out sessions.

Jason moved his hand down to the button of Chasity's jeans and unfastened them. Yet the notification from his phone made Chasity grab his hand and pull her lips from his.

"What's wrong?" he asked, perplexed.

"Your loud ass phone keeps beeping," Chasity breathed.

"Fuck that phone," Jason dismissed, placing kisses along her neck.

Chasity shrugged as she relished the feeling, but when the phone beeped again, she tapped his shoulder. "Go check your phone," she urged. "It's probably Kyle."

"Fuck Kyle," he joked. Jason was so worked up, he couldn't care less about what his little brother wanted at that moment. He only cared about what *he* wanted, and what he wanted was laying under him.

Chasity nudged him off of her. "You and that boy have been playing phone tag for like two days," she said, buttoning her jeans.

Jason groaned as he rolled over on his back. "Yeah, I know," he sighed. "My parents are probably cussing his wannabe 'dare devil' ass out."

Chasity sat up and smoothed her disheveled hair with her hand. "Still breaking shit, huh?" she teased.

Jason shook his head as he too sat up. "Yeah, his ass ran into my parents' fence with his bike the other day. Almost knocked it over." Seeing Chasity stand from the bed, he pointed to his desk. "Can you hand me the phone babe?"

Chasity walked over and did as he asked. Glancing at the phone, she saw Kyle's name and giggled. "Yeah, he texted you like three times already."

Jason chuckled as he held his hand out. "Yeah, he got in trouble."

Chasity was getting ready to hand Jason the phone, when another notification popped up. It wasn't the fact that it was an unknown number that caught her eye, it was the message that popped up with it. She frowned.

Jason, noticing the look on Chasity's face, frowned in concern. "What's wrong?"

Chasity directed her gaze at him, eyeing him sternly. "Who the fuck is Paris?" she questioned.

Jason's face turned from concern to confusion. "Who?" he asked, unsure if he heard correctly.

"You *know* you heard me," she spat. Chasity glanced back at the phone screen. "'Hey Jase, its Paris. I ran into your mom a few days ago and she told me how great you were doing. She said your number hasn't changed, I'm happy to hear that. Call me,'" she read, tone not hiding her agitation.

Jason rubbed his hand over his face as Chasity glared daggers at him.

"So, I'll ask you *again* Jason," she hissed, clutching his phone in a firm grip. "Who the fuck is Paris?"

Jason let out a long sigh. *Goddamnit Mom, what the fuck?!* "Paris is my ex-girlfriend," he explained.

Chasity gritted her teeth before shoving the phone into his hand. "Why is she texting you?" she seethed.

"I don't know," Jason admitted.

"Don't play with me."

"I'm *not*, I *don't know*," Jason barked back. Jason took a deep breath and stood up. "Look, my mom told me the other day that she ran into her. I don't know *why* she told me that, because I don't *care*," he assured. "I haven't seen the girl since high school."

Chasity just glared at him as he spoke, not saying a word.

"Chaz, that message don't mean shit to me. I'm not even gonna respond to her," Jason promised, seeing that Chasity's angered expression hadn't changed, he held the phone out to her. "Here, you can delete the message right now."

Chasity pushed his hand out of her face. "Whatever," she bit out.

"No, don't 'whatever' me," Jason returned. "I know you're pissed and *I* would be *too*, but believe me when I say that you have *nothing* to worry about when it comes to her or anybody *else* for that matter."

Chasity still didn't budge.

"Do you honestly think that if I was hiding something, that I would've asked you to grab my phone?" he asked.

Chasity folded her arms and looked away

"I ask you to grab my phone *all the time*," he reasoned, holding his hands out. "You know I have nothing to hide."

Chasity rolled her eyes. *He has a point.*

Jason approached her and wrapped his arms around her waist. "You trust me, right?" he asked, gazing into her eyes.

Chasity tried to hold her angry gaze on him, but it was beginning to fade as he smiled at her. She realized that Jason never gave her any reason to distrust him, why would she start now? "Yeah," she mumbled.

"What was that?" Jason teased, putting his hand to his ear.

"Yes, I trust you," she hissed.

"As you *should*," he replied. "I love you," he crooned, leaning in to kiss her. She stopped him by moving her head back.

"Love you too. Do me a favor," she demanded. Jason looked at her with anticipation. "Respond to that bitch and tell her not to text you no more, okay?" she ordered, before giving him a kiss on his cheek and walking out of the room.

Jason watched Chasity walk out, then looked at his phone, irritated.

Alex grabbed a few waffle cut fries from her plate and dipped them in ketchup. "These fries are ice cold," she complained as she took a bite.

Stacey smirked and shook her head. "Yeah well, we *were* pretty late getting here for lunch," she pointed out. "They probably turned all the food warmers off."

Alex shrugged, taking another bite. Saturday afternoon lunches were normally something that she looked forward to with the group. But this Saturday, Alex elected to just spend some much-needed time with Stacey.

"Thanks again for taking pity on me and coming to lunch today," Alex put out, grateful.

Stacey smiled. "You're welcome." She reached for her turkey and cheese panini. "I may be your last resort, but I still love when I get a chance to hang out with you."

Alex shot Stacey a sympathetic look. "No sweetie, that's not what—"

Stacey put her hand up as she broke into laughter. "I'm joking Mama," she assured.

Alex looked down at the table and sighed. "No, you don't need to joke," she said. "You're partially right."

Stacey took a bite of her food. *I already knew that*, she thought. "So," she asked after a few moments of silence, "where are they now?"

Alex concentrated on the fries on her plate. "Where's *who*?" she asked absently.

"Your friends."

Alex looked up at Stacey. "They're on their way to the

Essex Orchard," she replied, tone not hiding her sadness.

Stacey stared at Alex. "They didn't ask you to go, I take it," she concluded, reaching for her drink.

Alex shrugged. "It was *mentioned*," she sulked. "But I know it was only done so I wouldn't feel so bad. Not that I would've gone anyway, everybody who went was paired off. I'd just be walking around by myself."

"How long has it been?" Stacey asked. "Since your argument."

Alex ran her hands through her hair, scratching her scalp. "Like two weeks...maybe more. I lost track."

"Yeah, I don't think you lost track," Stacey chuckled.

Alex shook her head. *Two weeks, two days, to be exact.* "Stacey, I just don't know what to do," she vented. "I've apologized, and it just doesn't seem to be working."

"Well Alex, I know you gave me bits and pieces, but you gotta tell me the *whole* story," Stacey pressed. "I need to understand, so I can try to help."

"I don't think you *can* help," Alex returned.

"Alex...tell me *everything* that happened." Stacey sat in silence as Alex ran down everything that transpired over the past several weeks. From her conversations to Emily about Will, to his secret, to her confrontation with him, to her blow up with Emily.

Alex took a deep breath once she finished and caught Stacey's shocked stare. "I know, it's a lot to take in," she admitted. "But that's everything."

"Alex..." Stacey pinched the bridge of her nose with two fingers, trying to gather her words. "Okay, can I be honest with you?"

Alex nodded. "Always."

"Girl, you were wrong," Stacey declared. Alex rubbed her face with her hands. "*All* the way wrong."

Alex put her hand up. "I mean yeah, I know I said some hurtful stuff but—"

"Naw sis, you can't justify what you did or what you *said*," Stacey interrupted, voice stern. Alex folded her arms like a child and sat back in her seat as Stacey continued to scold her. "You trash talked someone that Emily cares about, you projected your own insecurities about men onto *her*—"

"No, I did not!" Alex exclaimed.

"Yes, you *did*," Stacey shot back. "You went behind her back and got nasty with the man, then had the nerve to talk shit about *her*."

"I was only—"

Stacey put her hand up to silence Alex's pointless reasoning. "That was foul and disrespectful and you need to stop."

Alex was quiet; she was in complete shock. Never had Stacey gone in on her like this. She'd always been the one to see both sides of things, but not in this case. "So—"

"And don't even try to justify what you said," Stacey cut in, knowing what Alex was about to say. "You treat Emily like she's your child. Hell, on some level you treat *all* of the girls like they are. You're not their mother."

"I'm not *trying* to be anybody's mother," Alex argued. "I just...you guys are so important to me. I love my friends and I want what's best for everybody. I just...I feel like it's my job to be that voice of reason."

Stacey stared blankly at Alex. *She didn't hear a word I said.* "You're not their mother." Stacey drew her words out slowly. "*And* you don't listen."

Alex's mouth fell open.

"How many times have you been cussed out for sticking your nose too far in people's business?" Stacey paused for Alex's answer. "Too many to count," she finished when Alex couldn't recall. "Take heed and chill out girl."

Alex looked up at the ceiling. "I guess you're right."

"That I am," Stacey boasted. "And while I'm at it, I might as well get it *all* out."

"Why not? I already feel like shit," Alex grumbled.

"You need to let this thing with Paul and Victoria go," Stacey stated matter-of-factly.

Alex felt tears fill her eyes. That had been a topic that

she had tried to keep buried in the depths of her mind, but she just couldn't escape it. "What if I can't?"

"You *have* to," Stacey insisted. "You're becoming bitter and quite frankly, it's not cute. If you don't stop comparing every man you come in contact with to Paul's raggedy, cheating ass, you're going to drive them away... Look what happened with Eric."

Alex put her hands over her face and leaned her elbows on the table top. She admitted that Eric was the other thought that she couldn't escape. She'd gone to Stacey the day after her confrontation with Eric at the library and had told her everything. "I messed up with him, didn't I?"

Stacey nodded slightly. "Maybe," she answered honestly. "I mean, you have some repairing to do...but you need to repair *yourself* first."

Alex raised her head as she rubbed her eyes. She felt terrible, broken. "God, I'm such a bad friend," she sniffled.

Stacey reached over and put her hand on Alex's hand. "Just a little," she said.

Alex put her head down on the table. "Oh God," she groaned.

Stacey laughed. "I'm messing with you," she assured her. "You're not a bad friend," she stated. "You just need to adjust how you handle your friendships. I know those girls love you just as much as you love them. You're just on their nerves right now."

Alex managed a chuckle through her tears. "Yeah."

"But it happens with family, you know," Stacey placated. "You don't get along all the time, but the love is there."

Alex nodded as she retrieved a napkin from the middle of the table. For the first time in a long time, Alex was forced to look inside of herself and hold herself accountable for her part in the demise of the relationships around her. "Thank you sis," she said, grateful. "I know that I haven't been around for you much lately, and I'm sorry... I didn't mean for us to grow apart."

"Alex we're still friends," Stacey assured her. "We just run in different circles now. But I still love you."

Alex moved from her seat to the one next to Stacey and wrapped her arms around her in a tight embrace. "Love you too."

Chapter 26

"It's cold as shit out here," Chasity complained, shoving her hands into the pockets of her black coat.

"Your ass is *always* cold," Malajia mocked, adjusting the zipper on her coat.

"Yeah well, I'm anemic, it comes with the territory," Chasity sneered.

"Hey, shut up your whining, we're here to have fun," Mark chided, stepping out of Chasity's car. "Don't scare Nicole off with y'all nonsense."

Chasity narrowed her eyes at him. "You're riding back with Sidra," she ground out.

"Mark stop messing with her so you can ride with me," Malajia hurled to Mark.

"*You* can get in Sidra's car *too*," Chasity commented to Malajia.

"No, they corny in her car," Malajia muttered.

The crisp autumn weather was prominent that afternoon, but seemed to be even more noticeable outside of the city. Having just arrived at the Essex Orchards, the group emerged from their cars and surveyed the atmosphere. Apple trees spanned for what seemed like miles. The pumpkin patches were full of children and parents, the hay rides were moving, the vendor stands were filled with handmade crafts and homemade treats, and activity tables were crowded with patrons.

"I'm so excited," Nicole gushed, standing close to David as she surveyed the grounds. "Reminds me of my childhood. I used to have so much fun."

"I can imagine," Chasity sneered, voice filled with sarcasm. She could think of a million other things to do on a Saturday afternoon, and walking around apple trees all day wasn't one of them.

"Chaz, please?" David pleaded, putting his hands together. The last thing he needed was for Nicole to feel intimidated or insulted. It was bad enough he allowed himself to be talked into turning his date into a group outing in the first place.

Chasity rolled her eyes. "Sorry," she grunted, adjusting the gloves on her hands.

Jason chuckled as he sidled up next to Chasity, placing his arm around her. "Come on cranky, let's go get you some food," he suggested, leading her away from the group.

Mark turned to Malajia, who was examining her nails. "Sugar face, let's go get some of that apple cider," he suggested.

Malajia rolled her eyes. "Don't nobody want that hot ass cider," she griped.

Mark pulled a small water bottle out of his coat pocket. "I got vodka to put in it," he announced.

"Yeeeeesss," Malajia rejoiced, mood suddenly lifted.

Sidra shook her head as she and Josh trailed behind the skipping pair. "If I wasn't convinced before, I'm convinced now; those two belong together," Josh laughed in an aside to Sidra.

"Yeah, two loud, crazy drunks," she joked as they continued their pace.

David, who was still standing near the cars, looked over at Nicole once the rest of the group continued on their way. "Sorry about this," he apologized.

Nicole glanced at him, "Sorry for *what?*"

"For my friends tagging along."

Nicole touched David's arm. "David, like I told you over

the phone, it's fine," she smiled. "How *else* were we going to get all the way out here? Neither one of us has a car."

David returned her bright smile with one of his own. "Welp, might as well explore the place," he said, extending his arm out. Nicole wrapped her hand around his arm as they ambled off.

"This is so messy," Sidra complained, dipping a thin brush into a small container of blue paint.

"Naw, you just can't paint," Josh teased, running a streak of red paint along a small clay bowl. Taking advantage of the empty seats at the crafts table, Josh and Sidra decided to try their hand at painting their own bowls.

"Hush Joshua," Sidra spat, giving his arm a light backhand.

Josh chuckled as he continued with his painting. As some of the paint dripped on a paper towel which sat under his bowl, Josh again chuckled. "Yeah, you're right, it *is* a bit messy."

"See, I told you," Sidra returned, swirling her brush in a nearby cup of water. "This thing is going right into the back of my closet when I get home," she said. "I don't need my neat reputation being tarnished by my terrible paint job."

Josh glanced over at Sidra's work. He had to admit that the blue and purple swirls weren't on Picasso's level, but they didn't look that bad to him. "It's not that bad."

Sidra shrugged.

"I'll probably give mine away," he added, concentrating on painting circles on the clay bowl.

Sidra wiped her hand on a wet napkin. "You could give it to December," she suggested.

Josh was quiet for a moment. "Yeah, I may just do that," he replied. "She likes art and this is art...kind of."

Sidra smiled as she watched Josh paint. "So, I take it that things are good between you two," she assumed.

Josh dipped his brush in yellow paint. "Yeah," he replied

finally after a few moments.

Sidra turned back to her bowl. His hesitation didn't sit right. "Things *are* good with you two, aren't they?"

"Sidra, my relationship is good with her, but can we not talk about it?" Josh quickly put out.

Sidra frowned at his tone. "What's wrong with you?"

"I just don't want to have 'relationship' talk with you," Josh bit out.

"So, you're actually in a full-on relationship?" Sidra asked, completely ignoring Josh's request. She'd heard that December and Josh had been spending a lot more time together, but he never confirmed that he had actually begun a relationship.

Josh hesitated, unsure if he wanted to answer. "Yes, she's my girlfriend now," he admitted.

Sidra looked away momentarily as she felt a knot in the pit of her stomach—a feeling that she was confused by. *What the hell was that about Sidra?* She asked herself. "Well...I'm happy for you," she put out.

Josh nodded slowly. "Thanks."

"Can I ask you something though?" Sidra pressed.

"What's that?"

"How come you didn't tell me?" she asked, curious. Before, Josh was insisting that Sidra talk to him about her relationship, and now he didn't want to talk about *his*. "I mean, after the whole conversation we had about her before my trip—"

"I just *didn't*," Josh cut in. The last thing he wanted to be reminded of was Sidra's birthday trip with James. He was certain that the woman that he still was very much in love with had returned from New York no longer a virgin, and that was something that he still found it hard to wrap his head around. "There was no need to."

Sidra took notice of Josh's sharp tone. "Are you upset with me?"

Yes! I'm pissed that you slept with him! Josh looked at her. "No," he lied. "I just feel that at this point in our friendship, we should keep our relationships out of our conversations."

Sidra nodded. "You're right. I get it," she replied. As Josh went back to painting, Sidra rubbed her stomach; it was still unsettled. "Hey, how about we hurry up with these bowls and go get something to eat," she suggested. *Maybe that's what this feeling is, hunger.*

"Good plan," Josh agreed, putting the lids back on his paint jars.

"Yo, you taking all the liquor, bee," Mark complained, reaching for the half empty bottle. Malajia moved it out of his reach.

"Fuck outta here, it's not my fault you used your half in that one drink," Malajia returned, pouring more of the clear liquid into her jar of cider.

Mark sucked his teeth as he took a sip of his drink. "Wooooo," he grimaced, coughing. "I'm about to be lit."

Malajia shook her head, before taking a sip of hers. "We didn't even *need* the cider," she jeered, fanning herself with her free hand as the burning in her chest subsided.

"Come on, let's go ride the hayrides," Mark suggested.

Malajia rolled her eyes. "We can't get on the ride with the drinks, they'll spill."

Mark rubbed his chin. "Good point, good point," he agreed. "Last one to finish gotta be on top later."

Both of them began downing the strong liquid. Mark was leading, until he started coughing.

Malajia used that opportunity to finish her drink, then celebrated by jumping up and down with her arms in the air. "I win! I win," she cheered.

Mark patted his chest. "Naw, fuck that," he managed between coughs. "My drink went down the wrong pipe."

"Not my problem," Malajia boasted. "You gotta be on top."

"Babe, my back hurts," Mark complained.

"*Again*, not my problem," Malajia teased. "It'll get a good stretch while you gyrate on all this fineness later."

Mark narrowed his eyes at Malajia as she did a sexy dance in a circle. "There's no damn music," he sneered.

Malajia wobbled a bit, feeling the effects of her drink. "You mad you lost," she laughed. "Come on, let's go to the hayride now."

"Fuck that hay," Mark griped, folding his arms like a child.

Malajia sucked her teeth. "Fine baby, what do you wanna do?" she pacified.

"I wanna go to the pumpkin patch," Mark pouted.

Malajia walked over to him and put her hands on his broad chest. "Fine, let's go to the pumpkin patch."

The intoxicated pair made their way to the pumpkin patch. Mark couldn't tell if it was the alcohol or not, but the sight of so many pumpkins in one place was thrilling.

"Chill yo, look at all these," he beamed. Staggering through the patch, Mark stepped on a smashed one in the process. "Shit, my sneaks!" he bellowed, trying to wipe them off.

"You might as well wash them things when you get home," Malajia suggested, swaying.

Mark pointed at her. "Good point," he agreed. He spun around, eyes wide at the sight of the largest pumpkin there. He clapped his hands together. "Yo, I'm leaving here with this damn pumpkin," he promised.

Malajia watched as he walked over to the pumpkin. "Chaz isn't gonna let you put that in her car, fool."

"Mel, if I get this pumpkin, you gotta make like eight pies from it," Mark said, ignoring her warning.

"Boy ain't nobody making no goddamn pumpkin pies," she refused, shaking her hand in his direction.

"You *gonna* make these damn pies, or I ain't gyratin' on *shit* tonight," he mumbled, bending down to lift the massive pumpkin.

Malajia pinched the bridge of her nose as she watched Mark struggle to pick up the large fruit. "All those weights you lift, and you can't pick up the damn thing?" she taunted.

Mark let out a yelp as he toppled over, falling on top of the pumpkin. He laid there, exhausted. "I'm drunk as shit yo," he admitted.

"Clearly," Malajia laughed.

"This pumpkin ice cream is um...different," David said, placing another spoonful of the pale orange ice cream in his mouth.

Nicole chuckled as she licked some of her own ice cream from her cone. "Not a fan, huh?"

"I won't say *that*," he shrugged. "I just have to get used to the taste."

Nicole continued working on her large ice cream cone. After walking the grounds and completing several craft projects, David and Nicole made their way to a bench overlooking the grove of apple trees and decided to take a much-needed rest.

David glanced over at Nicole. "I hope that you're enjoying yourself."

"I am," she assured him. "I told you that this reminds me of where I grew up. It brings back memories."

David nodded. "Did your parents make you pick apples and stuff?" he silently berated himself for what he considered to be a corny question. *Come on with this boring conversation David!*

Nicole looked down briefly. "Um no, but my *grandparents* did," she answered. "My parents died when I was eight years old...a car accident," she revealed, tone filled with sadness. "My grandparents raised me."

David put his hand over his head. *Way to go dickhead.* "I'm so sorry," he sympathetically put out.

Nicole examined the remaining contents of her ice cream

cone. "Thank you," she replied. "I mean it was twelve years ago...but not a day goes by that I don't still miss them, you know?"

David stared at her. He knew that feeling all too well. "I know what you mean," he said, his voice comforting.

Nicole glanced at him in anticipation of his next words.

"My mother died when I was fifteen," he explained.

Nicole's mouth fell open as she reached out and grabbed hold of David's arm. "Oh wow, I'm sorry for you too."

David managed a smile. "Thanks. She was sick for a long time, so I wasn't exactly shocked when it happened but..."

"Of course, you still miss her."

"Every day," David admitted. He took a deep breath. "So this conversation just took a morbid tone," he said at an attempt at a joke.

"I wouldn't say that," Nicole contradicted. "We're getting to know each other, which is a good thing."

David nodded. It was somewhat funny to David, but in both of them revealing their loss, he began to feel more comfortable, less awkward. "It's a *very* good thing," he smiled. "Thanks for agreeing to go out with me."

"Thank you for *asking* me," she giggled. "I was waiting on you to ask me out for a while."

Nicole's revelation took David by surprise, and it showed on his face. "Really?"

"Yes," she confirmed, pushing some of her twists out of her face. "I've been seeing you around, I thought you were cute."

David was once again shocked. "*Really?*" he repeated. It wasn't that David thought of *himself* as unattractive. But with always wearing glasses and being what most considered to be a nerd, he found it hard to believe that women would find him attractive.

"Yes," she replied. "*And* you're smart. I like that in a man."

David's bright smile could've replaced the sun. *Best day*

ever, he thought as the two continued with their conversation.

"How many apples are you gonna pick, Jason?" Chasity chortled, watching Jason pick another large, ripe apple from a tree and place it into a paper bag.

"As many as I can fit in this bag," he replied. "The apples at the grocery store are expensive."

"True," Chasity shrugged, handing him her half-filled bag. "You might as well use mine."

"Cool," he smiled, handing his filled bag to her for her to hold.

Chasity had to admit, walking through the tree-lined path, away from the crowds with Jason, was relaxing to her. Once he filled her bag, she leaned her head on his shoulder. Jason wrapped his arm around her shoulder as they ambled along.

"When we graduate, we should get a house near here," Jason mused, breaking the comfortable silence as they continued to walk.

Chasity smiled at the thought of their future together after graduation. "Nah, I can't take the country life," she returned. "It's nice to visit, but not to live."

"Yeah, I guess you're right. I don't know how long I'll last in the country myself," Jason agreed, running his hand up and down Chasity's arm. "I *do* think that when we get married, we should do it away from the city though."

Chasity lifted her head from his shoulder and glanced up at him. "Married?" she questioned, bringing her pace to a sudden stop.

Jason faced her, a smile on his face. "Yes," he said, then chuckled at the wide-eyed look on her face. "What? You never thought about us getting married?"

Chasity shrugged. "I'm not saying that," she denied. "I mean, of course I *think* about it... I just didn't know if *you* were."

Jason rolled his eyes slightly. "Come on Chaz, I jumped

through fire, dragons, and sharks to be with you—" Chasity let out a little laugh at his description of their courtship. "You don't think I'm going anywhere, do you?"

Chasity stared at him. "Well…if you haven't left *yet*, then I guess I'm stuck with you," she chuckled.

"Exactly," he agreed.

Chasity frowned momentarily. "Just so we're clear, you're not asking me to marry you right *now,* are you?"

Jason shook his head. "Nah, when I *do* propose, we won't be standing around holding bags of apples in our hands," he joked.

"Thank God," Chasity teased, pushing some of her curled hair over her shoulders. What Jason didn't know, is that even if he *did* happen to ask her at that very moment, she wouldn't have cared about the not-so romantic circumstances.

Jason, seizing the opportunity, leaned in and planted a kiss on Chasity's lips. Before they could go deeper with the kiss, they were interrupted by loud, familiar voices.

"God," Jason groaned as the pair parted.

"How the fuck do they always find us?" Chasity fussed to Jason, just as Malajia and Mark made their way over to them.

"Whatch'all doin'?" Mark slurred, holding his arm around Malajia.

Jason rolled his eyes. "What did it *look* like we were doing?" he fussed.

Mark shrugged. "Like y'all were about to get it in, in the middle of these raggedy ass apple trees," he returned, unfazed by Jason's attitude.

"How y'all just gonna go off and leave us like that?" Malajia slurred, leaning into Mark. "Y'all some rude asses."

Chasity frowned. "Are you two drunk?"

"We *hope* so," Mark laughed, holding up an empty jar. "Y'all should've had some of this spiked cider, yo. That shit was good."

"If we *all* drank, who was gonna drive back?" Jason

asked, looking at Mark like he was stupid.

Mark shrugged as he pulled something from his coat pocket. "Y'all corny wit those apples," he teased. "You should go pick some pumpkins," he suggested, holding up a small, lumpy, orange and green item. "Look at this one."

Jason pinched the bridge of his nose as he tried to keep from laughing. Chasity, on the other hand, wasn't so amused. "You think that's a pumpkin?" she asked, voice filled with disdain.

"Duh," Mark returned. "What does it *look* like?"

"It *looks* like a gourd, you fuckin' fool," Chasity bit out, earning a loud snicker from Jason.

Malajia slapped her forehead with the palm of her hand as she moved away from a confused looking Mark, who was closely examining the fruit.

"You mean they not the same thing?" Mark asked, confusion prominent on his face.

Jason shook his head slowly. "No, they *aren't*." He drew his words out slowly.

"Why you always gotta embarrass me?" Malajia fussed, smacking the gourd out of Mark's hand. Mark watched it fall to the ground and roll away. "I *told* you that didn't look like no fuckin' pumpkin. But you just *had* to pick it," she mocked. "Talkin' 'bout 'babe, look it's a mutant pumpkin'."

Mark stared at Malajia as she ranted. "You're so fuckin' sexy when you're mad," he crooned.

The irritation immediately faded from Malajia's face, replaced by a seductive smile. "Really?" she replied, twirling some hair around her finger.

"Oh no," Chasity sneered to Jason, knowing full well what was about to happen next. Just as Chasity expected, Mark and Malajia grabbed hold of one another and began to passionately make out in front of them. "Eww! Come *on*!" Chasity complained as Mark and Malajia unzipped each other's coats.

"Foreal?" Jason fussed. "Y'all just gonna do that right in our face, after you interrupted *us*?"

Mark paused short of pulling one of Malajia's long legs around his hip. "They got a point," he mentioned to Malajia.

Malajia stared up at him. "You wanna do it in the car?" she proposed.

"I'll race you," Mark quickly put out before the pair took off running, leaving Chasity and Jason standing there, bewildered.

"And they talk shit about *us*," Chasity said to him.

Jason's eyes widened as he thought of something. "Baby?"

"Yeah?"

"Didn't we drive *your* car up here?" Jason asked.

Chasity frowned as she came to a realization. "Shit!" she exclaimed, dropping her bag of apples and taking off running, with Jason following suit.

Chapter 27

Alex closed her textbook and was getting ready to turn off her lamp, when she heard a loud thud from across the hall. Standing up from her desk, she headed out of the room and stood in front of a closed door. Taking a deep breath, Alex knocked.

"Everything okay in here?" she asked when Emily opened the door.

Emily folded her arms. Her eyes were void of emotion. "Yes, why?"

"I heard a noise, so I was just checking on you."

Emily glanced back at the textbook lying on the floor near her bed. "My language requirement is getting on my nerves right now, so I threw the book," she replied, tone even.

Alex just nodded. The noise had startled her; she thought that she was alone in the house. She figured that Emily would have gone to the orchard with the rest of the group that day. But seeing her light under her closed door, told her otherwise.

"Is that all, Alex?" Emily bit out, tired of Alex standing there.

"Yeah," Alex mumbled, turning to walk away. But just as Emily was about to close the door, Alex turned back around. "Actually no, that's *not* all," she proclaimed to an agitated Emily, who just pulled the door back open. "You look like you could use a break," she said.

Emily stared at her.

"You want to go take a walk?" Alex suggested.

Emily sighed. "No, not right now," she ground out.

"Please?" Alex begged. "I just—I just wanna talk to you... Please."

Emily smoothed a braid back up into her ponytail. She wanted so badly to slam the door in Alex's face, but seeing her pleading eyes made her soften just a bit. And Emily had to admit, the cool, night air might do her some good. "Okay," she agreed finally. "Let me get my coat."

Alex and Emily walked along a desolate path through campus. The night air was chilly, with a half-moon bright in a cloudless sky. Although the atmosphere was peaceful, it didn't take away from the tension between the two.

"You said you wanted to talk?" Emily reminded after ten minutes along the path.

"Yeah," Alex sighed. "Listen, I want to start off by saying that I'm sorry...for *everything.*"

Emily glanced at her. *Here comes the 'but,'* she thought as they continued their snail like pace.

"I know that I was out of line," Alex continued through Emily's silence.

"Why did you do it?" Emily asked. "After I told you that I could handle things, why did you go behind my back like that?"

Alex ran her hand through her hair. "Because in my own twisted mind, I thought that I was looking out for you. *Protecting* you. Like a friend, or a big sister is *supposed* to," she explained.

"I don't *need* for you to protect me, Alex," Emily sniped. "I'm not a *child*. I've told you that before."

"I know," Alex admitted, shamefully.

"I don't need another overbearing mother," Emily

continued, voice stern. "I'm already irritated with the one that I *have*."

"I know that Em," Alex insisted, placing her hand over her chest. "I get it now and I'm trying to work on changing that part of myself...among *other* things."

"Is one of them, not throwing things up in people's face?" Emily threw out.

Alex stopped walking and faced Emily. "Yes." she replied. "I should have *never* said what I said to you. I can't imagine feeling used at fifteen. You trusted us enough to share that, and for me to throw that in your face just because I was angry with you, was—"

"Foul," Emily finished.

"*Very* foul," Alex agreed. She wiped a tear out of the corner of her eye. "I'm letting my own issues affect how I treat the people I love and that's not cool."

Emily looked away momentarily. "You made me so mad... I've never been that mad before," she said. "I never thought that I could actually *get* that mad... Honestly, I wanted to slap you."

Alex sighed. "I know, I'm sorry," she apologized again. The two women stood in silence for a few moments. "Would you feel better if you *actually* slapped me?" she asked.

The question confused Emily. "Huh?"

"If you slapped me," Alex said, "would it make things better between us?"

Emily frowned. "Maybe," she joked.

Alex took a step forward. "Well, go ahead, slap me," she urged.

Emily let out a laugh. "Alex, I'm not gonna slap you," she refused. "We're fine now."

"No, I don't believe you," Alex replied. "I think that you're still mad and if you get your slap out of your system, we can really get past this."

Emily waved her hand at Alex dismissively. "Don't be silly."

Alex rolled up her coat sleeve and held her bare arm out.

"Here, you can slap my arm."

Emily quickly shook her head.

"Just do it," Alex ordered, her voice firm.

"No, I don't want to," Emily refused, her tone now stern.

Alex let out a loud huff. *Well, I gotta take drastic measures.* "Will you stop being a freakin' punk and just slap—" Alex didn't get to finish her taunt before Emily had delivered a slap to her arm. "Shit!" Alex exclaimed, grabbing her arm with her other hand.

Emily immediately put her hands over her mouth in shock. "God Alex, I'm sorry," she said.

Alex put a finger up. "Just give me a second," she panted, rubbing her arm. The girl slapped harder than Alex expected. Alex rung her hand. "That hurt," she admitted.

"Well, you called me a punk," Emily admitted, amusement in her voice.

"Yeah," Alex agreed, looking for a mark. "Trust me, I regret that decision now."

Emily put her hand over her face and laughed.

Alex held her arms out. "So? Are we good now?"

Emily threw her arms around Alex and the two embraced. "Yeah, we're good now," Emily confirmed.

Alex smiled as she and Emily held their embrace for a few moments longer.

"Are you guys still coming down to the game on Saturday?" Jason asked into his cell phone. He grabbed his gym bag and slung it over his shoulder.

"I wish I *could* Jase," Mr. Adams promised. "But I messed around and caught another cold and I'd hate to get down there and get you sick."

Jason sighed, hoping that his father didn't hear him. "Well your health is more important, so just rest," he said, pushing the gym door open and heading outside.

"I appreciate the understanding," Mr. Adams sniffled. "I hate to miss you play again, but I know you'll do great as always." Jason smiled, even though his father couldn't see him. Mr. Adams never missed an opportunity to let Jason know that his son was his pride and joy. "I know that you killed it in the homecoming game."

Jason let out a little laugh. "I did okay," he humbly replied.

"No need to be modest," Mr. Adams replied, voice filled with laughter. "But even though I won't be able to make it, your mother will fill me in on every detail. She still plans on coming down."

Jason halted his steps along the path back to his house. *Shit!* The last thing he wanted to worry about with his mother's visit was her attitude towards Chasity. "Dad, can you talk to her before she comes here?" Jason pleaded.

"I'll have a word with her."

"Dad, seriously," Jason urged. "You know I will never disrespect Mom, but she's not going to just disrespect Chasity either."

"You have my word, I will talk to her," Mr. Adams promised before coughing. "I hate that she's acting like that."

Jason shook his head. "You and me *both*," he agreed.

"She didn't act like this with your ex," Mr. Adams recalled. "At least *I* didn't see it."

Jason rolled his eyes. Paris had been brought up one too many times for his liking. Jason thought about telling his father about his mother giving Paris his phone number. But he didn't want to cause the man any stress. He knew that his father would be upset just like he was.

"Yeah well, it doesn't matter," Jason said. "Mom just needs to get over it." He glanced at his watch. "I gotta go, get some rest and I'll call you later."

Jason ended the call as he approached the door to his house. Sticking his key in, he dialed a number. "Hey baby," he smiled when Chasity picked up. "What are you doing?... You wanna grab some lunch with me?... Cool, give me like twenty minutes... Love you."

He figured that some alone time would be a good time to

break the news about his mother coming down without his father as the buffer. "God help me," Jason sighed to himself as he walked into his house.

"When is your brother supposed to be arriving, Sidra?" Alex asked, steadying a grocery-filled bag in her hand.

Sidra stuck her key into the door and pushed it open. "The hell?!" she exclaimed, seeing Mark sitting at the dining room table. "Boy, what are you doing in here?"

"Malajia went to class," Mark shrugged, rising from his seat.

Alex and Sidra glanced at each other in confusion, before turning back to Mark. "What does that have to do with you being in here, when none of us were home?" Alex asked, frowning.

Mark sucked his teeth as he removed the bag from Alex's hand, and a smaller bag from Sidra's. "Alex, don't start your shit," he ordered to a stunned Alex. "You just got back on everybody's good side a few days ago."

Alex managed a small laugh as she playfully backhanded Mark on his arm. Having finally reconciled with Emily a few days ago, Alex's mood was lighter. So much so, that Mark's comment didn't bother her.

"Mel said it was cool if I chill," Mark explained, setting the bags on the counter.

Sidra studied his walk. "Why are you limping?" she asked.

"I hit my damn leg on the edge of Malajia's bed," he griped.

"Doing *what*?" Sidra pressed, putting her hand on her hip.

Mark faced both girls. "See, we was trying this new sex position and—"

"Ugh, never mind, we don't need the details," Sidra scoffed, putting her hand up.

"Yeah, we hear *enough* coming from her damn bedroom

every five minutes," Alex added, flopping down on the couch. "You damn rabbits."

"Says the one who ain't gettin' none. Except with your *damn* self," Mark returned, rummaging through the bags. "I'm surprised you can lift your damn finger, wit' your lonely ass."

Refusing to go back and forth with Mark about her nonexistent sex life, and her self-pleasuring activities, Alex just waved her hand at him dismissively.

"Anyway, I heard you talking outside. Sid, Marcus is coming down?" Mark asked, opening a loaf of bread.

Sidra stared at him, watching him pull packs of lunch meat and cheeses from one of the bags. "Are you even gonna *ask?*" she groused.

Mark shot her a quizzical look. "For what? Y'all just gonna say yes anyway," he concluded, reaching for a bottle of mustard in the cabinet.

Sidra shook her head as she sat on the arm of the couch. "Anyway, yes, Marcus is coming down this weekend," she beamed. "He said he'll be down early Saturday."

"Cool, tell him to bring down some of those video games he got," Mark ordered.

Sidra flagged him with her hand. "You can call him and tell him that yourself," she dismissed. "Anyway, he was *supposed* to come down *last* week, but he had an attitude."

Alex glanced at Sidra as she played with some strands of her hair. "An attitude about *what?*"

"Y'all ain't got no chips?" Mark interrupted.

"Boy, will you finish making that damn sandwich and leave?" Alex hurled. Mark flipped her off as he took a bite of his finished sandwich.

"Anyway," Sidra began, pushing some of her hair behind her ear. "He and his raggedy girlfriend got into *another* argument, so his mood was done."

Mark laughed. "Yooo, Marcus *still* dealing with that chick?" he asked, knowing the history between Sidra's oldest brother and his on-again, off-again girlfriend all too well.

Sidra tossed her hands in the air in frustration. "Oh my God, yes!" she wailed. "I swear I can't stand her."

"Well what's wrong with her?" Alex asked as Mark walked over and sat on the arm of the chair she was in. She glanced at him. "Can I have a piece?" she asked him, reaching her hand out.

Mark jerked his arm away. "Don't touch my food, dawg," he returned, breaking a piece.

"Shut up," Alex retorted, retrieving the piece of sandwich from him.

"That girl just loves drama," Sidra complained. "I swear, they break up like every three days. She's *always* picking fights." Sidra rolled her eyes, recalling the many times that Marcus complained to her about the girl. "They have an apartment together, but I swear he's always at my parents' house because when they fight, she puts him out."

"That's crazy," Mark concluded.

"I don't understand why he's still with her if it's that bad," Alex added.

"I ask him that all the time, and he says that he loves her," Sidra sneered. "Which is complete bullshit."

Mark chewed his food. "Nah, for him to put up with that much drama, the sex must be good; she must got a vacuum mouth," he joked.

Sidra turned her nose up. "Ugh," she scoffed.

Jason wiped his mouth with his napkin as he stared across the restaurant booth at Chasity. "Are you gonna say something?" he asked.

Chasity shrugged. "What do you want me to say?" she asked. Having just heard of Mrs. Adams's impending visit from Jason, Chasity wasn't exactly full of words.

"I don't know, *something*," he pressed.

Chasity ran her hands through her hair as she sat back in her seat. "I hope you do well at your game," she deflected.

Jason sighed, reaching for his drink. "Are you still

coming?"

"Of course I'm coming," she frowned. "Don't I come to *all* of them?"

"Yes, you do," Jason admitted.

"Then why did you ask me that?"

"Because I know Mom will be there getting on your damn nerves," Jason replied, taking a sip of his soda.

Chasity smirked. *Yes, yes she will.*

"After everything you've been through, you don't need to be dealing with her bullshit," Jason spat. If Chasity wasn't tired of his mother's shenanigans, Jason sure was.

"Look baby," Chasity began, leaning forward. "Stop worrying about it. I can handle your mother, trust me."

Jason shook his head. "You shouldn't *have* to," he sulked.

"No, no I *shouldn't*," Chasity agreed. "But it is what it is."

Jason ran his hands over his short hair, sighing in the process.

"It's not like we're going to be sitting together or anything. Hell, I don't even have to *see* her," Chasity added.

"I guess you're right," he agreed.

"But…if she *does* piss me off, that just means you have to make it up to me," she proposed.

Jason shot her a knowing look. "Oh *really?*" he challenged. "And what would you have me do?"

Chasity took note of the lust in his eyes, while he anticipated whatever freaky thing he expected her to say. "My laundry," she answered, then broke out laughing at the look of disappointment on his face.

"Real basic request Chasity," he threw back, laughter in his voice.

"You obviously have forgotten how much clothes I have," she chortled.

Jason put his hand over his face, letting out a groan.

"*And* you have to use *your* detergent," she added.

"God no," he complained. "I won't have any left."

"Tell her to leave me alone then," Chastity jeered, patting his arm.

"I hope you got some extra money in your pocket, because I'm starving," Malajia said, looping her arm through Mark's as they made their way across a crowded street.

Mark glanced at Malajia as they approached the front door of a fast food restaurant. "I thought *you* were paying for *my* food this time," he frowned.

Malajia halted her steps, glaring at him. "Please, boy," she sneered. "It's *your* fault I'm hungry any damn way. You ate all my left overs."

Mark smirked as he opened the door. "Yeah, yeah," he jeered, allowing her to enter the restaurant before stepping inside himself.

Malajia glanced up at the menu. "Uh, now I don't know what I want," she complained, scratching her head.

Mark threw is head back in agitation. "God, don't start this shit," he groaned. "You *never* know what you want."

Malajia checked her reply once she felt her phone vibrate in her jeans pocket. "Damn that vibration was powerful," she mused, removing the phone. "That felt better than a *real* one."

Mark shot her a glance. "What the hell you need a damn vibrator for when you got *me*?" he scoffed.

"Huh?" Malajia replied, feigning innocence as she checked her messages.

Mark sucked his teeth. "Yeah a'ight," he mumbled.

"The hell?'" Malajia gasped. "Why is somebody sending me a damn ultrasound picture?" she fumed.

"What?" Mark pounced, peering over her shoulder to see. "Whose number is that?"

Malajia shook her head. "I don't recognize it," she admitted. Seeing a blurry black and white ultrasound picture of what looked like a peanut threw her for a loop. "It's probably a wrong number," she concluded. "I'll just text back and let them know."

Mark stared at Malajia while she sent the message. "You okay?" he asked.

"Yeah, why wouldn't I be?" she replied. She met his eyes and realized the answer to her own question. *Oh!* "Babe, I'm fine," she assured. "I already told you I've come to terms with what I did. Seeing a baby on a picture or in real life doesn't make me sad."

Mark placed his arm around her. He planted a loving kiss on her forehead. Mark wasn't sure if he should believe her or not, but for now, he would take her word. "You know what you want yet?" he asked.

"Nope," she chuckled.

Mark's response was halted once he heard the sound of someone sucking their teeth behind them. He turned around. "You cool bruh?" he sniped.

"Yo, hurry the hell up, some of us have places to go," a fellow patron complained of the hold up.

Mark frowned down the man's length. "Man, shut your hungry ass up, don't rush my lady," he fumed. He turned to Malajia. "Mel, you take as long as you want, fuck him," he said. "I'll read the whole fuckin' menu to you *twice*. He ain't gettin' no burger no time soon."

Malajia shook her head as she tried to conceal a laugh. "Boy, stop it," she chortled. "Just get me the number three." As much as she appreciated Mark defending her, a sandwich wasn't worth fighting over.

"You sure?" Mark asked, staring at the man. "You sure you don't wanna read the menu three more times?"

This time Malajia did laugh. "No fool."

Sidra snatched open the door, eyes narrowed. "Really?" she hissed.

Marcus Howard put his hands up in surrender as he fought to restrain a laugh. "Sis, it wasn't my fault," he explained. "The traffic was a mess. You know y'all got that game today."

Sidra sucked her teeth as she moved aside to let her brother into the house. "I told you to leave earlier," she grumbled, giving him a hug. "We won't have time to go eat. The game starts in like a half hour."

"Chill Princess, we'll go to dinner afterwards," he promised.

Sidra relaxed her frown, letting a smile come through. "Okay fine," she accepted. "It's good to see you, even though you're late."

"Yeah well—" Marcus's words were interrupted by the sounds of chatter and footsteps down the steps. He spun around. "Malajia, Chasity, what's up ladies?"

"Hey," Chasity greeted with a wave.

"Girl, stop playing," he smiled, wrapping his arms around Chasity. "You're too damn close to my sister to not give me a hug."

"You finally made it, huh?" Malajia teased, giving the tall, built, brown-skinned man a hug, once he parted from Chasity.

"You always have something smart to say," Marcus chortled. "I heard you're with Mark now," he said.

"Yeah," Malajia smiled. "Who woulda' thought?"

"Shit, not me," Marcus joked. "I thought *we* were gonna end up together."

Malajia turned her lip up. "You know that was *never* gonna happen," she scoffed. "You work my nerves worse than *he* does."

Marcus chuckled.

"Besides, you seem to like the *crazy* type," Malajia sneered.

"Ouch," Marcus winced, placing his hand over his chest. "That's real cute Simmons."

Hell, she's right though, Sidra thought, but decided against making a comment.

Malajia shook her head, then looked at Chasity. "You ready to go to this game?"

Chasity shot her a frown. "Aren't you supposed to go with Mark?"

"I'm not fuckin' around with him today," Malajia snapped, shaking her hand in Chasity's face.

Chasity stared at Malajia, trying not to laugh.

"He wanna be at the gym for like four hours, I'm not tryna miss out on the good seats," Malajia continued.

"You mad," Chasity laughed.

"'Cause, what is he in the gym for? He already got muscles," Malajia fussed as they headed for the door. "Pissing me off."

"Whatever, just don't get on my nerves," Chasity threw out, walking out of the house.

"I do what the hell I want," Malajia immediately threw back. "My purpose in life is to irritate you, best friend."

Sidra shook her head as Malajia shut the door behind her. "You see what I have to go through?"

Marcus laughed. "Hey, at least they're pretty," he commented.

Sidra squinted. "What does that have to do with anything?"

"I don't know, I just wanted to say it," he shrugged.

Chapter 28

Alex grabbed her bag of popcorn from the concession stand attendee. "I'm so mad they ran out of the caramel popcorn," she complained. "I should've known that as soon as they added something new to the concession stands that it would go fast."

Emily retrieved her soda and hotdog from the attendee. "I've never had caramel popcorn," she mentioned.

Alex gasped. "Seriously?" she asked. Emily giggled at the shock on Alex's face, then nodded. "You my friend, don't know what you're missing."

"I suppose I don't," Emily agreed, squirting ketchup on her hotdog.

"I'll make it my mission to get you some soon," Alex promised. The two women began making their way through the crowd, towards the bleachers. "Did Will have to work today?" Alex asked after a few moments.

Emily shot Alex a side glance.

Alex put her free hand up. "No, I'm not going to say anything bad," she assured, sensing Emily's feelings. "I just figured that maybe with everything that he has going on, maybe he could use a break and would like to hang out with us after the game."

Emily stopped walking and looked at Alex, skeptical. "Oh?" was all that she could get out.

Alex smiled and nodded. "If you're going to be with him, then he should get to know everybody and vice versa," she said. "Besides…I never got a chance to apologize to him for what I said."

Emily let a smile come through. "I'll ask him when the next time he'll have free," she replied. "And he's already forgiven you."

Alex stared at Emily with disbelief. "Really?"

Emily nodded. "Yeah, I think after some time he just got over it," she said. "He was more concerned with you fixing things with *me*, than what you actually said to him."

"Wow…that was big of him."

"Yeah, pretty good for a lying baby daddy, huh?" Emily joked.

Alex put her hand over her face in embarrassment. "Come on Em, don't make me feel bad all over again," she pleaded.

Emily chuckled. "Okay, sorry it's out of my system now."

Alex shook her head in amusement. The humor then left her face. "Look, at the end of the day Em…I'm actually proud of you for snapping on me… Sounds weird, I know."

"A little," Emily admitted.

"No, it just means that I'm happy that you've learned to stand up for yourself," Alex clarified. "I'm proud of all the changes that you've made since I've met you."

"Thank you." Emily's smile was bright. She was happy; despite the fact that she had a falling out with Alex, she was glad that Alex was finally able to see her change as a positive thing, unlike her mother.

"Come on, let's go grab some seats," Alex suggested, giving Emily's shoulder a slight nudge. "If we're lucky, maybe we can save some spots for the others."

As Alex turned around, she spotted Eric through the crowds. She stared as he chatted up some people that he was with.

Noticing the sudden change in Alex's facial expression,

Emily leaned close to her. "When was the last time you talked to him?" she asked.

"Um…it was before you and I made up," she answered, tone sullen. "Didn't go well."

"Did you apologize?" Emily asked.

Alex shook her head as she continued to stare at the man. "I don't think he would believe me, even if I did," she answered honestly. "I treated him like shit."

"Yes, you did," Emily bluntly agreed. "For that reason alone, you need to apologize."

Alex glanced away as his eyes met hers. "Yeah, you're right," she agreed. "Besides, if he doesn't forgive me, it'll serve me right."

Emily stared at her friend with sympathetic eyes. She hated to see Alex down on herself. She may not agree with the things that Alex had done, but she knew that Alex was still a good person and a good friend. Emily put her arm around Alex. "Come on, let's go get those seats."

"I should've worn my heavier coat," Malajia complained of the red coat that she had on. "I love Jason to death, but if this school don't put some heat out here, I'm gonna have to sit out of some of these games."

"Yeah, 'cause they can put heat in an outdoor field," Chasity sneered, eyeing her watch. "The whole damn sky is over top of us…genius."

Malajia rolled her eyes. "Yeah well they need to heat those damn seats or *something*," she grumbled, walking towards the field entrance.

Chasity rolled her eyes as she scanned the grounds.

"You looking for Jase?" Malajia asked, noticing Chasity's roaming gaze.

"Yeah, he wanted me to meet him before they started."

Malajia's response was interrupted by the vibration of her phone. "Ooh," she cooed, removing it from her pocket. "I'm loving this new phone."

Chasity frowned her face in disgust. "Eww, your freak ass is gettin' off from a phone?"

Malajia laughed, placing the phone close to Chasity's arm. "Yo, you gotta feel this."

Chasity jerked her hand away. "Bitch if that phone touches me, I'm snapping it in half," she warned.

Malajia waved her hand dismissively, while looking at the phone. She sucked her teeth loudly. "Why the hell do I keep getting texts from this number?" she griped.

"*What* number?"

"Remember I told you that I got this text of an ultrasound the other day?" Malajia recalled.

Chasity frowned. "Yeah?"

"Well, the same damn number, sent me another message, talking about 'miss you' with a picture of a heart," Malajia informed, showing Chasity the message.

"Delete that shit," Chasity ordered. "They probably have the wrong number."

"I texted that back to them the *last* time," Malajia fussed, deleting the message.

"Block it."

"Doing it now," Malajia assured, pushing buttons. Once finished, she glanced up. "No he didn't," she said, eyeing Mark several feet away, walking with Josh and David. "I thought his ass was still in the gym...Mark!"

Mark spun around at the sound of his name being called. "What you hollering for?!" he yelled back.

"How you gonna leave me? You were supposed to be in the gym!"

"Whatchu' mean? You left *me*!" Mark yelled back.

Chasity put her finger to her ear. "Ya'll *both* loud," she ground out. "Malajia, take your ass over to him before I go deaf."

"I'm gonna kick his ass," Malajia promised, snatching her purse strap on her shoulder. "You still waiting for Jase?"

"Yeah, he just texted me."

"Okay, I'll save a seat for you," Malajia assured, before

heading off in Mark's direction. "Yo, you about to be on couples time out," she barked at Mark.

"How you mad at me when *you* left?" he returned, holding his arms out.

Jason said a silent prayer as he shifted his weight from one cleat-covered foot to the other, waiting near the entrance for Chasity. Having received a phone call from his mother, letting him know that she was on campus and on her way to the game, Jason wanted to see Chasity before his game to make sure she was okay. *Just relax Jason, everything will be fine. Dad said he talked to her.*

Jason's inner pep talk was interrupted when he felt someone tap his shoulder. "Hey babe," he beamed, spinning around. His eyes widened seeing his mother staring back at him. "Oh, hey Mom," he greeted, giving her a hug. "Why aren't you inside? Those seats go fast." The quicker that he got his mother to her seat, the better.

"I know, I know," Mrs. Adams said, parting from their embrace. "I just wanted to get a look at you beforehand. Before you get all dirty," she joked.

Jason chuckled. "Okay," he replied, glancing around. He knew that Chasity would be walking up any minute, and he didn't want that encounter. "So, you've seen me. Now you should go inside. I'll see you afterwards."

"I'm going," she assured, giving her son a pat on his cheek. "But before I do, I have a little surprise."

Jason's eyes perked up. "Was Dad able to come?"

Mrs. Adams shook her head. "No sweetie, he'll be at your next game," she promised. "But since he wasn't able to come, I brought someone *else* with me."

Jason smiled. "Kyle's here?" he asked. "I thought he went camping with his friends this weekend."

"He did," she replied.

Jason's smile faded, replaced by a frown. "Then who did you bring?" he wondered, confused.

Mrs. Adams said nothing, which confused Jason even more. Before he could say anything, someone appeared from around the corner, completely taking him by surprise. "What the fuck?" he blurted out.

The piercing look from his mother at Jason's language didn't faze him. He was too focused on the young woman approaching him.

"Hey Jason," the woman smiled. "You look good, then again you always did."

"Paris," Jason spat, not hiding his displeasure. "What are you *doing* here?"

"Your mom invited me," Paris Taylor revealed, much to the shock and anger of Jason, who just glared at his mother.

"Why would you *do* that?" he barked at her. "Are you insane?"

"Relax Jase," Paris said. "I mentioned how much I used to love watching you play football in high school—"

"Hold up," Jason cut in, putting a hand up at Paris. He faced his mother again. "So you two have been *talking*?" he hissed at her.

"Jase—"

"*Jason*," he hurled at Paris.

Paris however remained unfazed. "Yes, we chatted a few times after we ran into each other a while ago," she informed. "Anyway, I wanted to see you play and your mom needed someone to ride down here with her, so she said that I could come."

"My mother has plenty of mouth on her, and can speak for herself," Jason hissed, eyes not leaving his mother.

"Jason, don't be disrespectful," Mrs. Adams warned.

Jason was in a state of disbelief and it showed on his face. "Are you *serious* right now Mom?" he hurled. "How can you pull this crap?"

Paris sighed. "Come on—"

"I am not talking to *you* Paris," he snarled.

"Jason, just calm down, you're being rude," Mrs. Adams scolded.

"Calm down?!" he exclaimed. "How can—" His rant was interrupted when he heard Chasity calling him. "Shit," he hissed. He spun around and saw her approach. He put his hands up once she was face to face with him. "Baby, just know that I had *nothing* to do with this."

Chasity was confused. "What are you talking about?" she asked. "And why do you look nervous?"

"Hello Chasity," Mrs. Adams said, interrupting the couple's exchange.

Chasity rolled her eyes out of his mother's sight. She had hoped that she wouldn't have to see his mother at all. Moving around Jason, Chasity forced a smile. "Hi," she said, tone even.

"Don't you look pretty," Mrs. Adams replied; her polite tone *and* smile were phony.

Chasity raised an eyebrow. The woman didn't have her normal nasty tone. Chasity wasn't sure how to take that. "Thanks," Chasity returned, same even tone.

Mrs. Adams smirked, then glanced at Paris, who was standing to the side of her. "Let me introduce you to my friend here," she said, pointing.

Chasity glanced over at the tall, slim, brown-skinned girl standing next to Jason's mother.

"Mom, don't," Jason urged, teeth clenched. He grabbed Chasity's hand. "Come on Chaz, let's go."

As Jason went to move Chasity away, Mrs. Adams blurted out, "Chasity, meet Paris."

Chasity halted. She turned around, giving the girl a piercing stare. She remembered that name. "*Who?*" she charged, angry. She then glanced at Jason, who was pinching the bridge of his nose with his fingers.

Paris stepped forward, extending her hand in front of Chasity. "Nice to meet you," she said.

Jason knew that Paris being within striking range of Chasity was a bad idea. Immediately, he squeezed a fuming Chasity's hand, pulling her away and leaving his mother and Paris standing there.

"Maybe this was a bad idea," Paris said in an aside to Mrs. Adams.

Mrs. Adams in turn waved her hand dismissively. "It's fine," she assured.

"Who *was* that?" Paris asked.

Mrs. Adams folded her arms. "Nobody," she spat.

Jason backed Chasity against a wall, out of earshot of his mother and his ex. "I'm so sorry," he said, sincere.

"Jason, what the *fuck* is your ex-girlfriend doing here?" Chasity snapped.

"I have no idea," Jason replied.

"I thought you texted her to tell her to leave you the hell alone."

"I *did*," Jason assured her.

"Then why the fuck is she *here*?!"

"Chasity, I don't know!" Jason boomed. He rubbed his hand over his head, trying to calm down. He completely understood Chasity's frustration with the situation. He was frustrated too. "Chaz, I had *no* idea this was going to happen. My mom fuckin' sprung this shit on me."

"What kind of game is your mother playing?" Chasity fumed.

Jason shook his head as he closed his eyes, trying to block out the lasers that Chasity was glaring through him. "I don't know," he repeated.

Chasity flung her hair over her shoulders. "You better handle this shit," she warned. "And while you're at it, tell that bitch to get off this campus before I *drag* her the fuck off."

Jason went to grab for Chasity's arm as she walked away. "Please don't walk—"

"Don't touch me," she hissed, jerking her arm out of his reach. As Chasity stormed away, she began to feel bad. She was taking her anger for his mother and her antics out on Jason. Clearly, he was just as blindsided as she was. Realizing her error, Chasity stopped walking and turned around, only to see him approaching. "I'm sorry, Jase," she said to him.

"You don't have to apologize," Jason said.

"To *you*, I do," she insisted. "I know this isn't your fault."

Jason sighed. "Thank you… I'll handle it," he promised. "Trust me okay. I got it."

Chasity nodded. "Have a good game. See you later," she said before walking away, leaving Jason to sigh.

"Love you," he said, even though she was no longer standing there. Jason, feeling his temper rise, balled his fists at his sides. If he could avoid injuring himself, he would've punched a hole right through the wall.

Chapter 29

"That was a good game," Marcus commented as he and Sidra made their way down the bleacher steps afterwards. "Your boy was playing hard as shit."

"Yeah, Jason sure played pretty angry," Sidra recalled. She'd seen Jason play in countless football games, but she couldn't help but notice that her friend seemed pretty frustrated during this particular match. "I hope everything is okay."

"Well *whatever* is it, tell him to hold on to it," Marcus joked. "He kicked that other team's ass."

Sidra smirked, shaking her head. As they approached the bottom of the bleachers, Sidra pulled Marcus off to the side. "We gotta wait for the guys; they wanted to catch you before we go out."

Marcus nodded. "You know what, being down here on your campus makes me wish that *I* went to college," he mused, looking around at the hordes of students crowding the field.

"I still wonder why you *didn't*," Sidra said, folding her arms.

Marcus shrugged. "'Cause I had this idea that I wanted to come right out of high school and make money," he reasoned. "I *do* want to take some classes, but—"

"What's stopping you?" Sidra asked.

"I need to concentrate on working right now."

"No, *she* wants you to concentrate on working right now," Sidra corrected. "I swear Marcus, you let that unstable girl dictate your life."

Marcus rolled his eyes. The last thing that he wanted to hear was his sister bash his girlfriend. "Leave India out of this," he demanded. "She doesn't dictate *anything*. I have my own mind."

"Yeah well, you need to *use* it and dump the drama queen and put her out before she cuts up all your stuff again," Sidra urged.

"Look, let's get off *my* relationship and get on *yours*," Marcus deflected. "When is the next time you're gonna see James?"

Sidra was clearly annoyed that the topic of discussion was being brushed aside. "In a few weeks, I guess," she answered.

"You *guess*?"

"It may change, depending on how his trial goes," she shrugged.

Marcus studied her. "Oh okay," he replied. "You seem really nonchalant about seeing your man every few weeks."

"Marcus, James and I are in a long-distance relationship, this is just how things are. But we're making it work," she threw back, clearly agitated.

Marcus put his hands up. "My fault, no need to bite my head off, sis."

Sidra looked around. "Where *are* they? I'm starving."

"You know, to keep it a hundred, I always figured that you would end up with Josh," Marcus put out, much to Sidra's shock.

She looked at him wide-eyed. "What? Why would you say that?"

Marcus gave his sister a knowing look. "Really? You're *really* asking me that?" Sidra rolled her eyes, making her brother laugh. "Come on Sid, you *know* he's in love with you. Hell, you told me your*self*."

"First of all, that was never meant to be *repeated*," Sidra chastised. "That is the *last* time that I tell you anything. Second, he *was*. He says he no longer feels that way."

Marcus twisted his mouth. "Yeah okay, is that what he *said*?"

Sidra opened her mouth to curse her brother out, but a voice behind her stopped her words cold.

"Really Sidra?"

She knew that voice. Sidra slowly turned around and came face to face with an angry December. *Shit!* "December—"

"I saw you over here and wanted to come say hi before I left," December explained.

"What did you hear?" Sidra asked, cautiously.

"Oh, not much," December bit out. "Just the part where you apparently told the guy next to you that Josh was in love with you."

Sidra glared at Marcus, who in turn, shot her an apologetic look. Sidra turned back to December, who now had tears forming in her brown eyes. "Listen December, what you heard was—"

"You lied to me!" December wailed.

"What did I lie about?" Sidra frowned.

"I asked you if anything was going on between you and Josh and you looked me in my face and said 'no'."

"That wasn't a *lie*," Sidra assured her. "Josh and I have *never* been in a relationship."

"You think that makes me feel better?" December hurled, voice trembling. "If Josh loves *you*, that means he wishes that you two were together. Which means that when he's with *me* he's—" She put her hand over her face as she tried to keep from breaking down in front of Sidra.

Sidra stared at December; she felt terrible. "Look, maybe at one point he felt something for me, but he doesn't anymore," she tried to explain. "Josh cares about you."

"Josh is a liar," December spat, wiping her eyes with her hand. "I just wish I'd seen it sooner...*before* I slept with him."

Sidra frowned slightly at December's revelation.

December met Sidra's gaze. "Oh what, does that *bother* you?" she sneered, folding her arms.

Sidra snapped out of whatever trance she was in. "What? No, of *course* not."

"What? You're in love with *him too*?"

"No," Sidra denied. "December please calm—"

"Hey, sorry for the hold up," Josh said, approaching.

"Shit," Sidra grimaced, turning away.

Josh immediately focused on December's tear-streaked face. "What's wrong?" he asked, concerned and reaching out to touch her face.

"Don't touch me, you liar," December snapped, moving away from him.

"Huh?" Josh frowned. "Wait, honey what happened?"

"Ask the woman you're in *love* with," December spat, before hurrying away.

Confusion was prevalent on Josh's face as he turned to Sidra, who had her hands over her mouth. "What happened Sidra? What did you say to her?"

Sidra put her hands up. "Josh, just let me explain—"

"What did you say to her?" Josh barked.

Sidra flinched at the bass in Josh's voice.

Marcus stepped next to Sidra. "Josh man, this is my fault," he explained. Josh glared at Marcus. "I *may* have brought up the fact that you um…are in love with Sidra."

Josh's eyes widened. "What the fuck?!"

Sidra shook her head. "December overheard," she added. "I'm so sorry."

"Why would you tell him that?!"

"Josh, at the time that you and I weren't talking last year, I asked Marcus for advice," Sidra reasoned. "I didn't tell him with the intention to hurt you."

Josh ran his hands over his head. "Shit!" he panicked. "I gotta find her."

"I'm sorry Josh," Sidra repeated.

"Forget it," Josh bit out, turning to walk away. Sidra

grabbed his arm, causing him to spin around and face her.

"You...you're sleeping with her?" Sidra asked. That question shocked both of them.

"Yes, I am...*was*," he returned, voice not hiding his agitation.

"Oh," was all that Sidra could say. *Why do you care, Sidra?*

"Why do you care?" Josh asked, pulling the words from her head.

"What?" she hissed. "I *don't* care."

"Good, you *shouldn't*," he threw back. "Don't ask me about my sex life," he ordered. "I don't ask you about yours with James, *do* I?"

I don't have one. Sidra shook her head. "No. No you don't."

"Let's keep it that way." Josh stormed off, leaving Marcus to console Sidra.

"My fault, sis," Marcus apologized.

"Forget it," Sidra dismissed, tone somber. "Let's just go."

Chasity rinsed her hands in the sink of the stadium ladies' room. "I don't know why I got that sticky ass cotton candy," she griped to Malajia, who was touching up her lipstick in the large mirror.

"The bigger question is why didn't you *share* it?" Malajia replied. "Your stingy ass wasn't even hungry."

Chasity ignored Malajia's rambling. She snatched paper towels from the nearby holder. Seeing that the towels were breaking apart when she pulled them, she slapped the contraption with her hand repeatedly in frustration.

"Girl, will you chill," Malajia urged, moving Chasity's hand away from the holder. "You're either gonna break your hand or the machine."

"Fuck that machine," Chasity barked, attempting to dry her hands on the pieces of paper towel in her hand.

Malajia eyed Chasity with suspicion. "What's wrong with you?"

Chasity tossed the crumbled papers in the trash. "Nothing, I'm fine," she lied.

Malajia stepped in front of Chasity as she tried to walk away. "Oh hell no, bitch," she ground out. "We are waaay beyond this avoidance shit."

Chasity sucked her teeth then frowned down Malajia's length. Malajia returned Chasity's glare with a challenging look.

"We've already established that you don't scare me," Malajia reminded. "Now what has you so mad?"

Chasity let out a loud sigh. "I'm not mad...I'm *annoyed*," she clarified.

"*At?*" Malajia pressed.

Before Chasity could respond, the bathroom door opened and in walked Paris. "Fuck my life," Chasity mumbled to herself.

Noticing Chasity, Paris walked over. "Charity right?" she asked.

"Ooh," Malajia gasped at the name mix up.

Chasity glared at her. "It's *Chasity*," she hissed.

Paris shrugged. "Simple mistake," she stated, nonchalant.

"Yeah, whatever," Chasity threw back.

Malajia stared at the girl in front of her, the girl who clearly had Chasity agitated. *Who is this lanky bitch?* "And *who* are you?" she cut in.

Paris glanced at Malajia. "I'm Paris."

Malajia eyed her, full of attitude. "*And?*"

"*And* she's Jason's ex-girlfriend," Chasity told Malajia, still holding her icy gaze on Paris.

"The hell?!" Malajia exclaimed. "And she's here *why?*"

"'Cause she obviously wants her face cracked," Chasity answered for her.

"I don't know what your problem is," Paris sneered to Chasity. "I just came to see Jason play in his game, something that I don't need *your* permission to do."

Chasity stared at the girl in disbelief. "You *do* know that I'm Jason's *girlfriend*, right?" she snarled.

"You better recognize, heffa," Malajia jumped in. She didn't know what Chasity was going to do, but all Malajia knew was that she was ready to jump in if need be.

Paris folded her arms. "Funny, his mother didn't mention that he was seeing anybody."

Malajia leaned close to Chasity's ear. "You want me to smack her?" she whispered.

Chasity ignored Malajia. *Of course, her petty ass didn't.* "Well, *now* you know," Chasity asserted. "And with that being said, you might wanna get the fuck up out my face right now."

Paris simply rolled her eyes before walking out of the bathroom.

Malajia looked at Chasity. "What the hell was *that* all about?" she pounced. "Do I gotta choke slam a bitch?"

"I can do my *own* choke slamming, thank you," Chasity assured.

"Yes, I know that," Malajia agreed, pushing her hair over her shoulder. "Yo...why is she here? Does she go here or something?"

"No, Jason's fuckin' mother brought her raggedy ass down here," Chasity ranted.

"Why would she do that—"

Chasity gave Malajia a knowing look, cutting her words short.

Malajia frowned. "Damn, I know she doesn't care for you—"

"She *hates* me," Chasity corrected.

"Okay fine, but damn that's...that's a *new* level of petty," Malajia concluded.

Chasity folded her arms, sighing in the process. What she told Jason before wasn't the truth. She couldn't handle this behavior from his mother. Being snippy was one thing, but being malicious and sneaky was another.

Malajia put her hand on Chasity's arm. "Look sweetie, *clearly* that girl can't compare to you," she said. Sure, Paris was an attractive woman, but in Malajia's eyes, not more attractive than Chasity. "I mean, she cute and all, but, she could use a sandwich or three…and she *could* change that hair color. I don't know who told her that blond shit was cute, 'cause it *ain't*."

Chasity clapped her hands in Malajia's face, interrupting her rambling. "Focus," she said.

"I *am*," Malajia said, adjusting her purse on her shoulder. "What does Jason have to say about all of this?"

Chasity ran her hand through her hair. "He said that he'll handle it."

"Do you think he *can*?" Malajia asked, point blank. "I'm sure that the blond train wreck doesn't mean *shit* to him, but…at the end of the day, his mom is his mom and there's only so much that he can say to her."

Chasity successfully hid her worry. "Yeah well, he *better*."

Josh jogged up to December's bedroom in her cluster and started banging on the door.

"Who is it?" December barked through the door.

"It's Josh."

"Go the hell away, Josh!" December yelled.

Josh sighed. "You know I'm not going to do that," he replied, putting his hand on the door knob. "Just open the door please. I need to talk to you."

"Why? So you can lie again?"

Josh let out a sigh as he leaned his forehead against the door. "Please, just open the door," he begged.

After a few moments, December opened the door slightly and held her hand over the entrance, blocking Josh from stepping inside.

"Can I come in?"

"I don't think so," December hissed. "Whatever you

gotta say to me, you say it out here."

"Fair enough," he sighed. He stepped forward and tried to touch her arm.

"Don't touch me," she barked. Her reaction made Josh take a step back and put his hands up in caution. "Is it true? Are you in love with her?"

Josh hesitated. "I'm with *you*," he placated.

"You think that answers my damn question?" she grunted, eyeing Josh as if he was crazy. "Answer the question, Joshua," she spat. "Are you in love with Sidra?"

Josh closed his eyes, then looked down at his sneakers. "I…" he took a deep breath. "Yes," he admitted, regretful.

December looked away as tears filled her eyes. "I *asked* you point blank," she sniffled. "You lied to my face. How could you do that to me?"

"I'm sorry." Josh felt like crawling into a hole and dying. He would've given anything to block out the hurt on December's face.

"Keep your sorry," she hissed, moving to slam the door.

Josh bolted forward and grabbed the door. "December, I didn't mean to hurt you."

"Bullshit!" December wailed, delivering a soft punch to Josh's chest.

"It's true," he insisted, grabbing her hand to prevent her from striking him again. "I care about you and—I wish that these feelings for her would go away but—I've been trying to push them out."

December snatched her hand out of his grasp. "So, you're only with *me* because you can't have *her*." Her words were more of a statement than a question.

Josh stared at her; he felt a knot in his throat. Not only because he'd hurt December, but because he knew that she was right. If Sidra had felt the way he felt for her, he would never have gone out with December.

When Josh didn't answer, that gave December the answer that she sought, the answer that she feared. More tears flowed down her cheeks. "Were you thinking of *her* when you were sleeping with *me*?"

"No, I promise I wasn't."

"Like I'm supposed to believe you," she sniffled. "Your word don't mean shit... You're not the good guy that everyone claims you are."

Josh hated the feeling that was inside of him at that moment. He knew in his heart that he was a good person, but he couldn't help but feel like the scum of the earth then and there. "What can I do? What can I say to you to prove how sorry I am?"

"You can't do shit for me but get out of my house and never talk to me again," December said, voice trembling.

Knowing that there was nothing else that he could do, nothing that he could say, Josh stepped away from the door, allowing December to slam it shut. He stared at the door for a few moments, before sadly turning and heading down the steps.

Chapter 30

Sidra poked at her pasta as she sat across from Marcus at the Italian restaurant across town. Her mind had been clouded with the events of the day.

Marcus, noticing that Sidra was distracted, tapped the table. "I'm sorry again about earlier," he said, voice sincere.

Sidra looked up at him and sighed. "It's not your fault," she assured him. "I mean yeah, you have a big mouth."

Marcus chuckled.

"But you didn't know any of that was going to happen," she added, patting his hand with her own. "It's okay... Josh and I will be okay."

Marcus nodded. "Good, he's a good dude."

"Yeah, he is," Sidra sulked, pushing her plate back.

"Okay, change of subject," Marcus suggested, reaching for his glass of vodka and cranberry. "I actually have something to tell you and you may want to grab your drink for this."

Sidra waved her hand. "No, I'm depressed enough, liquor isn't gonna do me any good," she refused.

"Sid, grab the drink," Marcus insisted.

Sidra hesitated at first, then reached for her glass of red wine. "Fine," she muttered. "What do you need to tell me?"

Marcus held his drink up as Sidra took a sip from her glass. "I'm getting married," he blurted out.

Sidra casually took another sip of her wine. "Yeah okay, stop playing with me boy," she dismissed. "Now what do you want to tell me?"

"I'm serious," Marcus said as Sidra took another long sip. "I asked India to marry me and she said yes."

The news caused Sidra to nearly choke on her wine. She patted her chest as she caught her breath.

"You okay?" Marcus asked, concerned.

"You what?" she barked, ignoring his question. "You—you *what*?"

"I'm getting married," Marcus repeated.

Sidra put her hand over her chest. "Marcus…" This wasn't the news that she was expecting to hear; she was disappointed. "*Why* are you doing this?"

"Sidra," he warned,

"Marcus, your relationship with her—"

"Has its ups and downs, but we love each other," he put out, voice stern. "We've been together for five years… It's time."

Sidra didn't care if they were together *ten* years; she didn't want that woman as a sister-in-law. "And it's five years too *many*," Sidra sneered. "Is she pregnant or something?"

"No, she's not pregnant," Marcus answered. "I need for you to stop."

Sidra ran her hand through her hair. "I can't—I *hate* her."

"Clearly," he said. "But I'm asking you to try *not* to."

Sidra put her hands up. "Sorry, I can't turn my hatred off," she sniped.

Marcus rubbed his face with his hand. "God," he huffed. "I swear, I thought telling Mom was difficult, she was *nothing* compared to you."

Sidra leaned forward. "Wait, you already told Mama?" she charged. Marcus nodded. "She didn't tell me."

"I told her to let *me* do it."

"That doesn't mean shit. She tells me all of you guys'

business, even when you swear her to secrecy," Sidra
revealed, flagging him with her hand. "I *been* knowing about
Martin's car being repossessed before *Daddy* found out."
Marcus shook his head at the revelation. "Wow."
"Wow is right," Sidra uttered, folding her arms. Between
her encounter with December and now this, Sidra's day had
gone from bad to worse.

Chasity zipped up her sweat jacket, then pulled her hair
through her ponytail holder to tighten it before heading down
the steps. Just as she reached the bottom step, Sidra barged
through the door.
"Hey sweetie," Sidra sullenly greeted, shutting the door
behind her.
"Hey," Chasity replied, tone dry.
"I'm glad I caught you before you headed out, I have to
vent to you about something," Sidra huffed.
"What's that?" Chasity asked, tone not changing.
Sidra frowned slightly. "You okay?"
"I'm fine, what do you have to vent about?"
"I just found out that Marcus is getting married," Sidra
revealed.
Chasity held a blank stare. "You don't sound too happy
about that," she pointed out.
"That's because I'm *not*," Sidra fussed. "I *hate* that
stupid trick."
"Oh wow," Chasity commented. As much as she wanted
to be a lending ear for Sidra, she was too busy dealing with
her own thoughts to offer a real response.
"Yeah…" Sidra sulked. "I mean, I love my brother and I
know that he wants my support, but I just can't support this. I
think he's making a big mistake." She sighed. "I'm so
depressed right now. I just wanna eat fattening shit."
"You want me to make you some brownies?" Chasity
offered.
"Please?" Sidra pleaded.

Chasity smirked. "I'll do it when I get back," she promised, heading for the door.

"If you're going to Jason's, tell him that he played a good game as usual," Sidra said, removing her coat. "Angry, but good."

"Okay," Chasity uttered, walking out.

Sidra darted up the steps and knocked on Malajia's door. "Mel, open up! You'll never believe what the hell happened earlier."

"How'd you know I was in here?" Malajia asked through the door.

"I hear noises, plus your light is on," Sidra explained. "Now open up," she demanded, knocking again.

"Stop banging, I already heard you," Malajia griped.

"Don't like it when it's being done to *you*, huh?" Sidra taunted.

After some commotion from inside the room, Malajia opened the door, clad in nothing but a tan towel. Sidra eyed Malajia in disgust. "Did you just get out the shower?" she asked.

Malajia shook her head. "No," she answered.

Sidra frowned. "Then what were you doing?"

Malajia stared at her. "Do you really wanna know?" she challenged.

Sidra looked confused, then glanced past Malajia and saw her laptop on her bed. Having a thought, she made a face. "Eww!" she exclaimed. "Your horny ass was in here playing with yourself!"

Malajia smiled, then reached her hand out to touch Sidra's arm. "You wanted to tell me something, Ponytail?" she asked, voice sweet.

Sidra moved her arm away and slapped Malajia's hand down. "Gross, don't touch me!"

"What's wrong?" Malajia asked, feigning innocence, maneuvering her hand and touching Sidra's hair.

"I hate you, Malajia!" Sidra screamed, making a dash for the bathroom.

Malajia busted out laughing. "Sidra, I'm joking. I wasn't doing anything but studying."

"You're such a liar," Sidra ranted through the closed bathroom door.

"Sid, I'm serious, I *did* get out of the shower before you came in, and I just didn't feel like getting dressed so I kept my towel on." Malajia replied, amusement filling her voice. "You can check my laptop, ain't shit on it but some bullshit that I'm writing for class."

Malajia heard nothing from Sidra, just the water from the sink running. Laughing again, she went to go back into her room. Hearing the front door open, she peered over the banister, seeing Alex walk in. She stood there, waiting for Alex to walk upstairs.

"Girl, why are you walking around in nothing but a towel?" Alex asked, curious.

Not saying a word, Malajia walked up to Alex and touched her hair, then her cheek. A gesture that clearly confused Alex. "Hey friend," Malajia smiled.

Alex looked at Malajia like she had ten heads. "What's gotten into you?" she wondered.

"My fingers," Malajia replied, to which Alex immediately freaked out.

"Oh God, you just touched my face!" she shrieked, running to her room. "You're sick Malajia!"

Malajia broke into laughter once again. "I'm *kidding*," she called after her, holding her hand over her towel covered chest.

Chasity paced Jason's room while she waited on his return. He'd told her to come over and that his room door was open. Letting herself in nearly ten minutes ago, Chasity had moved from sitting on his bed, then to his chair. Finding it hard to sit still, she had resorted to pacing. The longer Chasity waited, the more annoyed she became.

Taking a deep breath, she halted her pace when the door

opened. "Sorry I took so long," Jason apologized, shutting the door behind him. "I didn't expect the line at the store to be so long."

She didn't respond; she just watched him set a bag of food on his desk.

"I picked up that ice cream that you like," he said. Jason had to admit, he didn't know what to expect from Chasity at that moment. He didn't see her after the game ended; not that he expected to after what happened. He let a few hours pass before he called her to come over. He figured that they both needed a moment to decompress. Jason looked over at her; she was staring at him with her eyes narrowed.

"Did you see your mom after your game?" Chasity bit out.

Jason walked over and sat on his bed. "No, I didn't," he replied.

"Oh really?" she sneered. "Well, I saw *Paris* afterwards."

Jason frowned. "What did she say to you?"

"A bunch of bullshit, but one thing that stuck out is that she said your mother neglected to tell her that you have a girlfriend," Chasity revealed.

Jason let out a groan. "This whole thing is some straight bullshit," he grunted.

Chasity folded her arms, then walked over and stood in front of him. She glared down at him. "Did *you* tell her that you had a girlfriend, when you texted her?" she asked.

"Yes," he answered, looking her in the eye. "My text said, 'don't contact me,' then she texted back, 'you don't have to be rude, I just want to see how my friend is.' Then I responded, 'we're not friends and I have a girlfriend, so stop it.'"

Chasity frowned. "You didn't tell me all that."

"Because there was no *need* to, I took care of it…at least I *thought* that I did," Jason replied.

"So clearly she's a fuckin' liar *and* hard of hearing," Chasity hissed. "Maybe I need to punch her a few good times for her to get it through that badly dyed head of hers."

Jason shook his head. "No, you're not fighting," he said, stern. "She's not worth it."

"Since when do I give a fuck about a fight being *worth* it?"

"Chasity, I *mean* it," he maintained.

Chasity shot him a challenging look.

"Paris will drop off the face of the earth eventually," he reasoned. "I blocked her number so don't worry about it."

Chasity shook her head. "Fine," she spat through clenched teeth. "But what are you gonna do about your *mother*?" she pressed. "*She* started this shit."

"I know."

"So *do* something about it," Chasity ordered.

"I *will*," Jason assured her. "She left right after my game. I called her several times and I left her a message. I'm pretty sure she's avoiding me."

"Did you tell your dad what she did?"

"I don't want to upset him," Jason answered.

Chasity rolled her eyes and sat down on the bed next to Jason. "I don't like people messing with me, Jason," she said. "You know how I get."

"Trust me, I know."

"And your mother is *seriously* messing with me, right now," she added, looking at him. "I was fine with dealing with her hatred for me, but this is some *other* shit."

"I know," he agreed, touching her leg.

"Jason…I *don't* want to go off on her, but if she keeps this bullshit up—"

"Chaz, I'm not one of those guys who pacifies his mother," Jason said, looking at Chasity. "I love her and I will always respect her, but I have no problem telling her about herself. I defend you to her and tell her to back the hell off."

Chasity stared at him for a moment. "She's not listening," she pointed out.

Realizing that Chasity had a point, he turned away and let out a long sigh. He put his arm around Chasity's shoulder, pulling her close. Giving her a kiss on her cheek, he grabbed his cell phone and stood from the bed.

Chasity followed him with her eyes as he walked to the door. "Where are you going?"

"Just in the hall," he answered, before walking out and shutting the door behind him. He dialed a number and put it to his ear. Hearing the voicemail, Jason rolled his eyes. *Why am I not surprised?* "Mom, it's me again," he said. "Avoiding this conversation isn't going to change the fact that I'm angry," he continued, as he began to pace. "You and I need to have a serious conversation. Call me back."

Ending the call, he ran his hand over his hair. "Dad, how do you deal with her?" Jason grumbled before heading back into the room.

Chapter 31

"Halloween is in a few days," Mark reminded, opening a can of soda. He sat on a bench in front of the Math building with some of his friends. "What we about to do?"

David fished in his small bag of chips. "We can go to the campus Halloween party," he suggested.

Mark sucked his teeth. "What? You mean that corny ass party in the gym with the purple Christmas lights and paper ghosts on the walls?" he griped. "Fuck outta here."

Malajia nearly spat out her water, trying to hold in her laugh.

"It was only a suggestion," David grumbled, stuffing a chip into his mouth.

"There's always the haunted house at the factory behind Mega-Mart," Malajia suggested.

"Been there, done that, not tryna do it again," Mark quickly shot down.

"Well we can go to the movies," Alex suggested, scratching her head. "There's supposed to be a bunch of horror movies playing."

"Please, it's not like *your* scary ass will be watching it *anyway*," Malajia dismissed. "Peeking behind your fingers and shit."

Alex pointed to Chasity, who was busy playing in her phone. "No, that's *her*," she chortled.

"Mind your damn business, Alex," Chasity grunted, eyes not leaving the screen. Alex giggled.

"Man, we're *always* at the damn movies," Mark barked, full of animation. "Let's do something *else*."

"What the fuck do you wanna *do* then?" Chasity snapped, tired of hearing Mark's complaining. "Just like— pick *something* or shut the hell up."

Jason put his arm around Chasity's shoulder. "Breathe," he laughed.

"His voice is like nails on a goddamn chalkboard," Chasity fussed.

Mark made a face at her. "Jase, give her evil ass some so she'll calm down," he jeered.

Chasity flipped Mark off in lieu of a response.

Jason rubbed her shoulder. "Ignore him," he urged. He then looked at Mark. "And shut the hell up, you *have* been bitchin' since you got out here."

Mark flagged Jason with his hand. "Whatever, I got an idea," he announced to the group. "Let's dress up and go trick-or-treating."

"That sounds stupid, ain't nobody doing that," Malajia blurted out, face not hiding her displeasure.

Mark shot her a glare. "You just gonna play me in front of people?" he sniped. "You're supposed to be on *my* side."

Malajia put her hand on his arm. "I'm sorry babe, that's just my reaction when I hear something stupid," she explained, much to Mark's annoyance.

"Don't touch me," he hissed, causing Malajia to bust out laughing. He turned back to the group. "I don't care *what* y'all say, I think it'll be fun."

"You really think that nine, grown ass college students, going to people's houses at night, dressed like crazy people is a good idea?" Jason asked smartly. "You wanna get shot?"

Mark stared at Jason for several seconds. "You scared, bro?" he taunted.

Jason narrowed his eyes at Mark.

Over the entire conversation, Chasity stood up. "I gotta

go to class."

"Good luck on your test," Jason said to her.

"Thanks."

"You're meeting us afterwards so we can go to lunch, right?" Malajia called after her.

"Yeah," Chasity answered, adjusting her book bag on her shoulder as she kept walking.

Mark turned to the remaining group members. "So, when we gettin' those costumes?"

Jason, Malajia, David and Alex exchanged glances, before simultaneously standing up and walking off.

"Oh alright," Mark hurled at them, watching them leave.

David shifted his books from one arm to the other as he headed through the entrance to the Paradise Terrace dorm. Smiling as he passed by dorm residents, he approached a room door and knocked. His smile brightened when Nicole opened the door.

"Come in," she said, signaling him with her hand.

David complied and shut the door behind him. He waved to Nicole's roommate.

Nicole retrieved a book from her desk and handed it to David. "Here you go."

"Thank you." David breathed a sigh of relief.

"No problem," she returned, sitting on her bed. "Thank you for letting me hold onto it, I can't believe I misplaced mine."

David tucked the book under his arm, along with the others. "No problem, Advanced Chemical Principles is *not* a class that you can get through without the textbook."

Nicole ran a hand along the back of her neck. "Trust me, I know," she agreed. "I'm going to tear this room apart until I find it."

David chuckled a bit. "You *were* finished with it right? I didn't rush you, did I?"

Nicole shook her head. "No, I finished my homework

not too long ago, so you're right on time."

"I mean, you could've held it longer if I didn't have a ton of work to do from it myself," David sputtered.

Nicole smiled. "David, I really appreciate it, but there's no need for that, I'll find my book."

"Okay," he nodded. He watched her move around the room, searching. "I'm surprised you're taking that course *now* as a junior. It's typically a senior course."

"Yeah well, I wanted to get it over with," Nicole said, peering behind her desk. "When I get to my senior year, I want it to be as easy as possible."

"Makes sense," David shrugged. He fumbled with his books as he leaned against Nicole's desk. She chuckled as she pointed to her chair. "You can sit down you know."

"Oh, thanks," David returned, embarrassed. He pulled the swivel chair out and plopped down.

Nicole tilted her head. "You still nervous around me?" she asked. "We've been out on a date already, I think the nervous stage should've passed," she added, voice filled with amusement.

David opened his mouth to speak, but was drowned out by Nicole's roommate.

"And she hasn't stopped *talking* about that date," the dark-skinned curvy woman said, rising from her bed. "*Or* that bracelet that you made her when y'all went to that orchard."

David successfully concealed a laugh, as Nicole cut her eye at her roommate. "Don't you have a study group to get to, Kiana?" she ground out.

"I'm going, I'm going," she assured, grabbing her book bag from her closet door. "See ya."

Nicole shook her head as her roommate left, then focused her attention back on David. "Ignore her, she lives to embarrass me."

"I know the feeling... You've met Mark," David joked.

Nicole laughed. "Yes, yes I have."

The pair sat in comfortable silence for a few moments.

"So, what are you doing for Halloween?" David asked, finally. "I'm not quite sure if this is actually going to happen, but my friends and I *might* be going trick-or-treating."

Nicole stared at him in disbelief. "Really? Adult trick-or-treating?" The amusement was heavy in her voice.

David nodded. "The longer you're around me, the more you'll get used to these weird activities," he promised. "So um, if we *do* go, you wanna come with?"

Nicole winced. "I'm sorry David, as fun as that sounds, I'm going home this weekend."

"Oh," David said, not hiding his disappointment.

"Yeah, it's my grandfather's birthday, so my grandmother is planning this surprise party," Nicole explained. "Which is weird because she knows that he hates surprises."

"It's fine," David assured. "I hope you have fun."

"Thanks, I hope that you have fun and get lots of candy."

"I'll save you some," David beamed. He glanced at his watch. "Well, I better go get started on this assignment, otherwise I won't be going *anywhere*."

Nicole stood from her bed just as David stood from his seat. "See you," she said.

David headed for the door and paused, then faced her. "Hey, when you get back, do you want to go out again?" he proposed, voice hopeful. "This time *without* my friends?"

"Sure, I'd love to," Nicole eagerly accepted.

"Great."

"And your friends weren't bad by the way, they're pretty funny," Nicole added.

"Sometimes," he joked. Offering a wave, David walked out of the room, pulling the door shut behind him.

"Emily, no, I'm not doing it," Malajia grunted, walking down their steps.

Emily trailed behind Malajia, grabbing her braids with one hand. "Malajia, please?" she begged.

Malajia spun around to face Emily. "No! I'm not re-braiding your damn hair."

"I've had these things in for over two months, they look *terrible*," Emily whined, scratching her head.

Malajia turned her lip up in disgust. "If you don't get your scratchin' ass away from me," she sneered. "Flinging your dandruff and shit."

Chasity laughed from the kitchen. "Just take them *out*, Emily," she suggested. "And *leave* them out."

Emily skipped down the last few steps behind Malajia. "My hair is *really* a mess under here," she insisted.

"Just wash it and straighten it," Chasity said, opening a bottle of juice.

Malajia shook her head. "No, she don't have *your* hair. She's gonna need a damn perm," Malajia cut in before Emily could respond.

"No, she's not," Chasity disagreed.

Malajia pointed to Emily's hair. "Have you *seen* these roots?"

"Who *hasn't*?" Chasity jeered.

Emily waved her hands. "Hello? I'm standing right here," she cut in.

"We know, we can see your flakes," Malajia sneered. Chasity almost choked on her juice, trying not to laugh.

Emily shook her head. "Okay, can *one* of you help me take my braids out and the *other* help me wash my hair...and deep condition...and straighten it?"

Malajia and Chasity glanced at each other. "I'll help her take her braids out!" Malajia quickly volunteered, before Chasity could open her mouth.

"Shit!" Chasity barked. She dreaded the task of doing her *own* hair; she definitely wasn't going to be in the mood to do anyone else's.

Emily smiled at Chasity. "I appreciate you," she gushed.

Chasity narrowed her eyes. "Don't irritate me," she hissed.

The front door opened. In walked the rest of the group,

minus Josh. "What's for lunch?" Mark asked, dropping his book bag on the couch.

Alex leaned against the couch. "Ooh, they added stromboli's to the menu at my job, I can go get a couple," she informed, enthused. She looked around and saw all eyes focused on her. "What?"

"Girl, that ain't shit but the same old Shack pizza folded into a pocket," Malajia bit out. Alex broke into laugher. "Nobody wants that. Take it off the menu."

"Hell, *I'll* try one," Mark uttered, grabbing his cell phone from his jeans pocket. "I'll text Josh and tell him to bring two back when he gets off work."

"Who's the other one for?" Alex wondered.

"Shit, they *both* for me," Mark replied.

Sidra stood by the steps, pondering if she should even ask her question. "Hey guys...how has Josh been?" she asked finally. "I haven't talked to him."

David winced. "He's how you'd expect him to be," he answered.

"Yeah, depressed and shit," Mark added. "When he's not in class or at work, his ass is right in that room...moping."

Sidra let out a sigh, running her hand over her hair. She felt like this was all her fault. "Damn," she whispered. In the few days since December dumped Josh, Sidra talked herself out of going over to check on him or even calling him. She just couldn't face him.

"You guys have to just give him some more time," Jason chimed in. "The end of a relationship is never easy. No matter how short it was."

"Nah, fuck that. He ain't getting no more time to himself," Mark threw out. "We need to get him to participate in something fun." He held a finger up. "Which is *why* we need to go trick-or-treating."

"You *still* on that?" Jason asked.

"Wait, what?" Sidra asked, confused.

"Oh, you weren't with us earlier, Sid," Alex recalled. "This fool suggested that we dress up and go trick-or-treating for Halloween."

Sidra frowned in confusion. "But…we're *adults*."

"*So?*" Mark shrugged, agitated. "That don't mean we can't go."

"That's *exactly* what it means," Jason laughed. "Dawg, nobody is gonna give a bunch of grown people, candy."

"I bet you they *will*," Mark boasted. An idea came to mind as he rubbed his hands together. "As a matter of fact, let's make a bet."

"God, please!" Chasity complained. "Why do we let him talk?"

"Hey, you shut your face," Mark threw back. "Anyway," he began, excited. "Let's make a bet to see who can get the most candy while we're out."

"How are we gonna do that? When we're going to the same houses?" Malajia challenged. "*If* we get candy, we'll be getting the same amount."

Mark nodded. "Point made."

"Or," David put in, holding up a finger. "We can split into teams and go to different houses."

Alex stared at David in shock as Mark clapped his hands together. "David, you're *actually* with this?" Alex asked.

David shrugged. "What *else* do we have to do?"

"That's what *I'm* talkin' about," Mark threw out, pleased. "I *knew* those glasses was on my side."

David glared daggers at him. "Seriously?"

Mark laughed. "My fault, force of habit," he reasoned. "But yeah, teams. Teams of three."

"Do we get to *pick* the teams?" Sidra asked, now intrigued. If this would get Josh out of his funk, she would be a willing participant.

"Naw, that's too easy," Mark said, grabbing a notebook from the chair. "Let's pick names out of a bag."

"No, last time I had to pick a name out of a bag for some stupid idea, I ended up acting like Emily for three days," Chasity recalled.

Emily looked at Chasity with shock. "Oh my God, that's

so mean," she said, laughter in her voice.

"*You* know you're corny," Chasity jeered.

Alex pointed at Chasity. "That's right, you *did*." she laughed. "Sophomore year, for my social experiment." She glanced at Malajia. "When Malajia wore a damn mop on her head and a dirty ass sheet for those three days, trying to act like she was me."

"It *was* you," Malajia joked, popping a piece of candy in her mouth.

"Focus banshees," Mark interrupted. He grabbed a plastic bag from under the kitchen sink, and placed the nine pieces of paper that he'd torn inside. "I'll pick three names and put them in one pile, then the second and third pile. That's how we get our teams."

Malajia walked over to him, "Naw, you cheat too damn much," she ground out. "*I'll* pick."

"Girl, nobody trusts *you* either," Sidra chortled, walking over. "*I'll* do it." Sidra grabbed the bag and shook it up. "Okay I'm gonna make three piles, then tell you guys who the teams are."

"Fair enough," Alex said, sitting on one of the accent chairs.

"Watch Alex get the corny team," Malajia teased, nudging Chasity.

"And just *who* would be considered corny?" Alex hissed, while Sidra began choosing and putting the small pieces of paper in three piles.

"Shut up, Sidra's finished," Malajia dismissed, putting a finger up.

The group waited in anticipation as Sidra read the names. "Okay so the first team is…Jason…Malajia—"

Jason closed his eyes and lowered his head, letting out a groan.

Malajia shot him a side eye. "Oh foreal Jason?" she hissed. Jason busted out laughing.

"Annnnd," Sidra turned over the last paper in the pile. "Please be Chaz or Mark, please be Chaz or Mark,"

Malajia mumbled, clasping her hands together.

"Emily," Sidra announced, much to Malajia's displeasure.

Malajia's mouth fell open. "What?! No!" she exclaimed. She spun around to see Emily smiling at her. "Ugh," Malajia scoffed.

"Mel, you're so rude," Sidra chided. She grabbed the first paper on the next pile. "Okay next team is…Mark—"

Mark closed his eyes, holding up crossed fingers on both hands. *Please be someone fun, please!*

Seeing the second name, Sidra laughed. "Miss Chasity," she revealed.

Chasity slammed her hand on the arm of her chair. "Are you fuckin' serious?"

Mark pointed at her, smiling. "Ha haaaaa!" he taunted, voice at maximum octave. "I'm gonna get on your neeerrrrves."

"Malajia, trade with me," Chasity demanded.

"Naw, those aren't the rules," Mark rebutted, shaking his hand in her direction.

Jason put his hand over his face and shook his head as he tried to suppress a laugh. He could almost predict the level of agitation that Chasity would experience at Mark's antics. *God, help her.*

"Stop complaining and deal with it," Mark dismissed.

"David's the third person on your team," Sidra announced.

"Fuck!" Mark bellowed, stomping his foot on the floor. A reaction that wasn't appreciated by David.

"Dude!" David exclaimed, holding his hand out.

Mark erupted with laughter. "My bad."

"So that leaves, myself, Alex and Josh," Sidra concluded, gathering the paper from the table.

"You cheated," Malajia grunted.

"How?" Sidra challenged, folding her arms. "You guys *watched* me choose."

Not having any proof, Malajia simply sucked her teeth.

"Oh and Alex, in case you were wondering—you got the corny team."

Sidra and Alex glared at Malajia, who was unfazed.

Sidra walked up a few steps in the guys' home, then went back down. She headed to the front door, grabbed the knob and let out a sigh, then let it go. Looking back towards the staircase, she sighed once again. "Girl, just go up," she prompted herself. A moment later, Sidra navigated the steps, then stopped in front of Josh's door before giving it a knock.

She bit her bottom lip while waiting for an answer. She held it there even as Josh opened the door and stared at her. "Hey," she said finally.

"Hey," Josh replied, tone dry.

Sidra shifted her weight from one high-heel-covered foot to the other. "Um…can I come in?" she asked, pointing to the inside of his rom.

Josh glanced behind him, then looked back at Sidra. "It's pretty messy in here," he warned.

"That's okay," Sidra promised.

Josh, not saying a word, moved aside to let her pass.

Sidra glanced around the room; it was littered with clothes, books, and papers. "You weren't kidding," she commented.

"Yeah," Josh mumbled, quickly grabbing clothes from his bed and floor and tossing them in a pile near his closet. "I haven't been in the mindset to clean."

"Understandable," she said. Sidra knew on a normal occasion, Josh's cleanliness rivaled hers, but she understood his lack of motivation to keep his room clean.

"You can sit," he offered, gesturing to a spot on his unmade bed.

Sidra sat down. Her eyes lingered on his face as he sat down on his chair; he looked drained. "You look terrible," she said after a moment.

Josh smirked. "Thanks." He rubbed his face. "I'm tired. I

had three tests today, plus I had to work," he explained.

Sidra put her hand up. "I'm sorry, I didn't mean—I'll just be quiet."

Josh leaned back in his seat. "It's fine," he uttered. "Truth is...I know I look terrible because I *feel* terrible."

Sidra stared at him with sympathetic eyes. "Have you talked to her, Josh?"

Josh shook his head. "No."

Sidra glanced down at her hands. "I'm so sorry—"

"It's not your fault," Josh cut in. "It's mine."

"It *is* though," Sidra contradicted. "If I hadn't said anything to Marcus—"

"It wouldn't have changed the fact that I lied," Josh interrupted. Sidra looked away. "I lied to her when I told her that I didn't have feelings for you." He placed his hand on his chest. "And I lied to my*self* thinking I could move *on* from you."

The guys were right. Josh had spent the past few days wallowing in a sea of self-pity, but it wasn't because December broke up with him; he knew that she had every right to. Josh was struggling to come to terms with the fact that he hurt December, because he was trying to run from what he really felt...what he *still* felt.

Sidra glanced at the floor, pushing some of her hair behind her ears. "Josh...I thought you said that you were over your feelings for me."

"I'm not," Josh declared point blank.

Sidra stared at him, eyes wide as she felt her heart fall into the pit of her stomach. "Oh," was all that she could get out. *God, please don't start hating me again.*

"Don't worry, that doesn't mean that I'm gonna get all 'we can't be friends' on you again," he assured, picking up on her inner fears.

Sidra breathed a sigh of relief.

"I know that you and I will never happen," he concluded, sullen. "But, I can't be with anybody *else* right now... I was kidding myself thinking that I could."

"Josh...I don't want to see you be by yourself," Sidra said. Sidra knew that Josh was too good of a man and person in general to be alone.

"I won't be, forever," Josh said, confident. "But... December was a good girlfriend to me and I hurt her..." He glanced down at the floor. "I don't want to do that to anyone else. It's not fair to them."

"December probably hates my guts right now," Sidra assumed.

"Probably," Josh attempted to joke. "No, she hates *me*."

"I just hate the fact that *anybody* could hate you," Sidra pouted.

"I'm not above it," Josh replied. "I'll be okay Sid," he declared, noticing the worry on Sidra's face.

Sidra nodded. She didn't know if she believed him or not. "Are you okay enough to give me a hug?" she asked; she just wanted to comfort him.

Josh managed a smile. "Sure." He held his arms out as Sidra headed over to him. She wrapped her arms around him and squeezed tight. She really didn't want to let him go, but she knew that she had to.

Parting from him, she sat back down on his bed. "So...Mark wants us to go trick-or-treating," she revealed, hoping to break the solemn mood.

"He *would* be the one to think of that," Josh chortled, folding his arms.

"Yeah, we picked teams earlier today," she informed. "We're betting to see which team gets the most candy."

"Interesting," Josh mused. It was the truth; he needed a distraction. "Whose team am *I* on?"

Sidra smiled. "Mine...with Alex." Josh nodded in satisfaction. "You will never guess who's on Mark's team," she added, voice filled with amusement. Josh leaned forward in anticipation. "Chasity."

Josh busted out laughing. "Yoooo, Mark is gonna piss her off to no end," he predicted.

"Yeah, I know, he was already starting with her when I

left the house," Sidra giggled. She held her smile as Josh continued to laugh. Seeing him amused, if even for a moment, was a great sight.

Chapter 32

"I don't understand why we had to go shopping for costumes together," Chasity sneered, adjusting the red horn headband on her head.

Mark tugged at the tattered shirt that he was wearing. "'Cause, we're a team."

"Only for getting some dumbass candy," Chasity recalled, exasperated. "Not to have my whole afternoon wasted in some crowded ass costume store with you and David."

Mark rolled his eyes. Halloween night was finally upon the group; Mark had eagerly dragged his reluctant teammates to the costume store in the mall in an effort to grab the best costumes. Now night had fallen; the group paired off to get changed.

"Hey...shut *up*," Mark spat out, pointing at Chasity. "I didn't trust your ignorant ass to actually go by yourself. You would have come back with *nothing*."

Chasity rolled her eyes.

Mark examined his zombie-like makeup in the mirror. "Damn it!" he barked. "This fake blood shit look all dry."

"It's *supposed* to," Chasity pointed out, voice not hiding her annoyance.

Mark pointed to the cracked faux blood on his face. "Naw, it looks all dumb. Here, do it for me," he proposed.

"I don't wanna touch your damn face," Chasity complained.

Mark pointed the squeeze tube in her direction. "Chasity, I swear fo *God*. If you don't stop battling me, I'm gonna cut your tail off that sexy ass devil costume and smack you with it."

Chasity folded her arms and shot Mark a challenging look.

Mark stomped his foot on the floor. "Sike, I'm just playin'. Can you fix it for me?"

Chasity stared at the pitiful look on Mark's half-made-up face and sucked her teeth. "Just give it here," she demanded through clenched teeth, snatching the tube from him.

She approached him, holding the tube close to his face. "Damn it Chaz!" Mark bellowed as blood squirted all over his face. "You play too much!"

"It was an accident," Chasity laughed.

"What is all the commotion?" David asked, emerging from the bathroom.

Chasity couldn't answer because she was too busy laughing.

"Chaz over here giving me a fuckin' face bath with this funky ass zombie blood—" Mark's rant was interrupted when he looked at David. "Dawg, what the fuck do you have on?" he sneered.

David frowned. "Is all that necessary?" he asked of Mark's attitude.

Mark frowned down David's length, taking in his white lab coat, grey wig, black glasses and his black rubber glove covered hand holding a glass beaker. "What are you supposed to be?"

"A mad scientist," David explained, smiling.

Chasity looked confused. "What's *mad* about it?"

David looked down at his outfit. "My eyes because I can't see out of these glasses."

"Then why you got them *on*?" Mark fumed, smacking his forehead with his palm. "Man, I *knew* I shouldn't have left your ass in that store while I went for donuts. We were supposed to get evil or scary costumes. Why you gotta be the one to get some nerd shit?"

"Man, just fix your damn face...literary," David threw back.

"I still think we should've all gotten matching costumes," Malajia said, walking down the steps of the guys' house.

"They didn't have my size," Emily reminded, maneuvering down the steps with her large, pink butterfly wings. "Why are these things so big?" she complained.

Malajia glanced up at Emily as she continued down the steps. "I told you not to buy those," she said. "You just *had* to be a damn butterfly."

"But they're so pretty," Emily giggled.

Malajia flagged Emily with her hand. "Anyway, I still say we should've all been fairies."

Jason shot Malajia a glare from the couch as the girls walked over. "There was no way I was gonna be a fairy."

"Jason you wear tight pants for *football*, surely you could've worn a pair of fairy tights tonight," Malajia threw back.

Jason pointed a warning finger at her. "I wasn't wearing them," he maintained through clenched teeth.

"Well, at least you look good as a vampire," Malajia mused of Jason's costume.

"You don't look so bad as a..." Jason frowned. "What *are* you anyway?"

"A jester," Malajia smiled, doing a twirl.

Jason opened his mouth to speak, but was interrupted when the door opened.

"Look, my costume is staying on, just get over it," David spat, stepping inside the house with Mark and Chasity in tow.

"Wack ass costume," Mark commented; he looked at Malajia. "Look at my sexy baby," he crooned.

Malajia missed the compliment because she was focused on Mark's face. "You look crazy," she bit out.

Mark immediately pointed to Chasity.

"No, don't blame that shit on me," Chasity countered.

"She jacked up my zombie makeup," Mark fussed.

Malajia narrowed her eyes at Chasity. "You messed up my man's face?"

"Nature already did that," Chasity bit back.

Mark let out a loud, phony laugh. Though on the inside, he thought it was a clever comeback. *Good one Chaz, good one.*

Malajia folded her arms as she gave Chasity's red devil costume a onceover. "You *would* be Satan," she sneered.

"You *would* be a fool," Chasity threw back.

Jason laughed out loud as Emily and David tried to conceal their laughter.

Not wanting to show her amusement to Chasity's comeback, Malajia made a face.

"Alright, look," Mark began, holding his hands up. "We gotta get this bet together—"

The door opened and Sidra barged in with Josh trailing behind her. "Guys—"

"Nice costume, Sid," Emily beamed of Sidra's dark angel costume.

"Thanks Em. Listen you guys, when Alex comes in, just say something nice about her costume," Sidra urged, voice almost a whisper. "She's really excited about it."

"What the hell *is* she?" Chasity asked, curious.

"*You'll* see," Josh snickered, earning a backhand from Sidra.

The group faced the door as Alex walked in. All eyes stared as they tried to register the large, unflattering, puffy orange, yellow, and white cone shaped costume on Alex's thick frame.

"Ta da!" Alex smiled, arms up in the air.

"Uhhhh," Jason began, but couldn't finish his thoughts. He just pinched the bridge of his nose in an attempt to keep from laughing.

"Alex…what the fuck are you supposed to be?" Chasity asked bluntly.

Alex sucked her teeth as snickers registered through the group. "I'm candy corn," she explained.

It was silent for several seconds as the group tried to keep their composure. Sidra shot Chasity a warning look. "Your smart ass better not say anything," she hissed, teeth clenched.

Chasity snickered.

"Your fat ass *would* be some sort of food," Malajia hurled at Alex. Laughter erupted as Sidra stomped her foot on the floor.

"Damn it Malajia," Sidra barked.

"What?" Malajia questioned as Alex put her hands on her hips. "*She* know she look fat and stupid."

"Shut up *fool*," Alex threw back.

"Alright, now that we have some drinks in us, let's get going," Mark urged, before downing the rest of the rum and soda in his glass. The group hung out in the house for the next half hour, partaking in some liquid courage before their much-anticipated excursion through the neighborhoods of Paradise Valley.

"Wait, what's the bet?" Sidra asked, "What do the winners get?"

Alex thought for a moment. "*I* know," she announced, excited. "The winning team gets to have a four-course dinner made—"

"Why you *always* gotta incorporate *food* in shit?" Malajia jeered, throwing her head back in exasperation.

Alex shot Malajia a glare. "Please don't make me slap you tonight," she warned. "Anyway, a four-course dinner of their choice."

"That'll work," Sidra agreed, adjusting her trick-or-treat bag on her wrist.

"That's *corny*," Mark grunted.

"David, Josh, and Emily also agree," Alex pointed out. "So majority rules."

Mark eyed Alex, annoyed as she headed into the kitchen.

While the majority of the group migrated for the kitchen in search of a quick snack, Mark huddled with Malajia, Chasity and Jason. He whispered something, then they headed outside on the front step.

"I don't care *what* Puffy, McCornPuffins says," Mark griped to the others. "That bet is weak."

"Wait, *what* did you just call Alex?" Jason asked, amusement in his voice.

"So stupid," Malajia laughed of Mark, as Chasity shook her head.

"Look, they can have that corny bet," Mark continued. "Why don't *we* make our *own* bet?"

"You mean like a 'couples' bet?" Malajia asked, intrigued.

Mark nodded. "Exactly," he confirmed, rubbing his hands together.

"I'm in," Jason shrugged.

"Of *course* you would be," Chasity sneered.

"You scared?" Jason teased.

"Don't play yourself," Chasity returned.

"Ahhh, the tension is already brewing, I love it," Mark boasted. He pointed to Malajia. "Mel, if my team wins… which we *will*, you gotta give me head every day for a week."

Jason busted out laughing, while Chasity looked disgusted.

Malajia's mouth fell open with shock. "Oh foreal?" she barked, smacking Mark on the arm.

"You were just *waiting* for an opportunity like this, weren't you?" Chasity sniped. "That is such a *man* bet."

"You damn right," Mark threw back, unfazed. "And I don't mean no half-assed nonsense either," he crudely added. "I mean full on neck."

Malajia folded her arms. "You tryna say my head game is half-assed?" she asked, irritated.

"Not at all," Mark assured. "I just know how much of a smart ass you can be."

Malajia held a fiery gaze on her boyfriend as she thought for a moment. "Okay," she nodded. "You got a deal. And I will see that bet and raise you," she challenged.

Mark held his arms out in the air. "Bring it on baby," he dared, confident.

"*When* my team wins, you gotta return that oral pleasure, baby," Malajia said.

"You ain't said nuthin'," Mark returned.

"Ugh, these images are making me wanna vomit," Chasity griped.

Malajia shook her head. "Not just every day...whenever I *want* it for a whole week." Mark's mouth fell open. "And you *know* how much I want it."

Mark shook his hand in her direction. "Nah see—"

"And I don't mean no half-assed nonsense," Malajia interrupted, putting her hand in Mark's face. "I mean you gotta full on use that tornado tongue of yours every... single...time...*whenever* I want it. Which means—" she insisted, putting her finger up. "I don't care if you're watching one of those stupid games, at the gym, playing ball, or *whatever*. You gotta drop what you're doing and do it."

Mark stared at Malajia for several seconds. "Why you gotta show off?" he hissed.

"Oh *I'm* showing off?" Malajia bit back, pointing to herself.

"Forget it, we're wasting time. You got a deal," Mark dismissed, shaking her hand. "You gonna lose anyway."

"Yeah, you wish," Malajia sneered. The couple then looked at Chasity and Jason. The two were just standing there in disbelief at what had just occurred in front of them. "Y'all turn," Malajia prompted.

Jason and Chasity looked at each other. "Ladies first," Jason said, gesturing to Chasity.

Chasity's eyes shifted. "Umm," she began, uncertain.

"And don't say no corny shit either," Malajia put in.

Chasity rolled her eyes.

"I'm not doing your homework," Jason chuckled. "So don't even try it."

"Shit," Chasity joked. "Okay fine... When my team wins, you gotta be my servant for a week," she said.

Jason folded his arms. "And that consists of me doing *what* exactly?" he asked.

"Whatever I *want* you to do," Chasity clarified. "And yes, that *includes* my homework...so get over it."

Jason nodded. "Got you," he returned. He then smiled a taunting smile at her.

Chasity frowned. "Jason, I'm not doing that bullshit every five minutes," she snarled, knowing exactly what was on his mind.

"Yes! Man bet number two," Mark laughed, holding his arms up. Malajia rolled her eyes.

"Fine, I'll make the same bet *you* did," Jason directed to Chasity.

"What, you're gonna make me your servant for a week?" Chasity sneered, folding her arms. "No, come up with your *own* shit."

Jason smirked, shaking his head. "When my team wins, you'll be my *love* servant," he amended.

Chasity narrowed her eyes at him. Mark leaned in close to her, tapping her arm. "Aye yo, he means sex servant—"

"I *know* what the fuck he *means*, out my damn face," Chasity barked at him.

Mark backed up, amused.

Jason held his gaze on Chasity. "So... Anything I want, any *position* I want, any*where* I want...you have to do for a week."

"What do you mean 'anywhere'?" Chasity asked, voice filled with attitude. "Any *place* or any*where*?"

A slow, knowing smile crept across Jason's face.

Chasity's eyes widened. "If you don't take your freak

ass somewhere with all that!" she wailed.

"You scared?" Jason taunted once again. Chasity gritted her teeth.

Mark leaned close to Chasity once again. "Yo, just shake his hand, they gonna lose anyway," he urged.

"Mark, I swear to God, you need to stop breathing on me," Chasity snapped, shooting Mark a glare.

Malajia and Jason both laughed at the silly look on Mark's face. "Oh, this is gonna be fun," Malajia concluded.

Chapter 33

"Guys, can we slow down a little bit?" Alex asked, panting as she walked down a tree-lined block with Josh and Sidra. "This costume is heavy."

Sidra glanced behind her and giggled. "Having second thoughts about buying that thing, huh?" she teased.

"Girl, I had second thoughts as soon as I put this mess *on*," Alex admitted, patting her chest. "But it was on sale."

"I can see *why*," Sidra mumbled.

"Hush," Alex chuckled.

"Okay so whose turn is it to choose the next house?" Josh asked, adjusting the trick-or-treat bag on his arm.

Alex quickly raised her hand. "Ooh, I'll do it," she volunteered.

"Alex, every house you choose has no candy, or they don't open the door," Sidra pointed out. "We wasted time on *five* of your houses, already."

"How am I supposed to know that the house is out of candy?" Alex argued, shifting her costume around her waist.

"I'm guessing the houses with no porch light on, means that they're out," Josh said. "At least that's what that meant in the neighborhood that *I* grew up in."

"Yeah, well I'm from Philly, and we knock *anyway*, 'cause the damn bulb might be broken," Alex said, approaching a house. "Let's go to that one."

Sidra and Josh looked at the house that she pointed to. "You mean the only house on the block with no decorations?" Sidra ground out.

"And they probably have the most candy left," Alex reasoned, leading the way.

"Alex if you make us lose this bet, you're doing all of the cooking," Sidra warned.

"Yeah, yeah," Alex dismissed, approaching the door. She rang the doorbell and flashed a smile at Josh and Sidra who were on the bottom step waiting. When no one answered, Alex rang again.

"Still think their light is just broke?" Josh jeered.

Alex went to say something, but the sound of the door unlocking stopped her. "Ha, see, I *told* you," she boasted.

Sidra and Josh weren't as confident as Alex was; they watched an obviously tired woman open the door.

"Trick or treat," Alex beamed, holding her bag out.

The woman frowned. "I don't have any candy," she spat.

Alex slowly lowered her bag. "Oh. Well—"

"You damn idiots have been ringing my doorbell all night, and this sign on my window *clearly* says 'no candy.'"

Alex glanced at the aforementioned sign taped to the woman's window as Josh approached her.

"We're sorry," he apologized, taking hold of Alex's arm. He guided her down the steps. As the door slammed shut, both he and Sidra glared at Alex.

"So, you didn't see that sign?" Sidra asked.

"Apparently *not*," Alex sulked.

"You're banned from picking houses," Sidra returned, pointing at her. "We need more candy, and I don't want to take any chances, messing around with you."

The group ambled to the next block and their eyes lit up when they noticed a large, heavily decorated house in the middle of the block. "We're going to *that* one," Sidra commanded, pointing. As they headed towards the house, some people ran past them.

"Damn, knock us over already!" Alex hurled at the

culprits.

The trick-or-treaters ran up the steps to the house that their group was approaching. It was then that they recognized the runners. "Seriously?!" Sidra exclaimed.

"Y'all burnt for this house," Malajia boasted, glancing at them.

"No, we saw this house first," Sidra fussed.

"What does that have to do with *us*?" Jason threw back. "How were *we* supposed to know that y'all saw it?"

Alex stared at them in disbelief. "We *clearly* were walking towards it when you nearly ran us over," she argued.

"What *we* saw was a fat ass orange marshmallow, slow walking with a dead angel and a drunk mummy," Malajia countered, folding her arms as she stood firm on the steps.

Sidra slowly folded her arms. "I'm a *dark* angel," she corrected.

"You're a *salty* angel, 'cause y'all ain't getting candy from *this* house," Malajia returned, earning laughter from Emily.

"You might as well hit that dead ass block that we just came from, 'cause we're claiming this block as ours," Jason added.

"Yeeesss, I love you as a teammate," Malajia rejoiced, giving him a high five.

"Me too?" Emily asked, holding her hand up.

"You ain't get us enough candy from the last house," Malajia quickly shot down. "You almost out the group."

Emily shook her head in amusement.

"Fine, keep this house," Alex hissed. "We'll just take the one next door."

"Nope, that's ours too," Jason quickly put out, darting to the next house with Josh trailing behind him.

"Josh, you can run faster than that!" Sidra yelled after them. She smacked her face with her palm as she saw Josh stumble over a piece of his costume, allowing Jason to approach the door with ease.

"Ahhhh, y'all salty," Malajia laughed, relishing the

annoyed looks on both girls' faces.

"Cheatin' asses," Sidra groused, walking away defeated.

"You mad you gotta go to another block," Malajia hurled at their backs. She turned to Emily. "Okay Em, time to work that magic," she said as the two of them approached the door. "And don't get scared and run like you did at the *last* house."

"Hey, that zombie popped out of nowhere," Emily explained. "*You* saw it."

"I *also* saw you nearly smack me in the face with those bug wings when you took off," Malajia recalled.

"Well...you were in my way and I didn't wanna die," Emily joked, knocking on the door.

Both girls waited for an answer as Jason ran up to them. "That house was lit," he mused, holding his bag open.

Malajia peered inside. "Yesssss, look at all that candy," she beamed. "They gave out big candy bars too. You made up for that incident at the last house."

Jason looked confused. "Hey, *I'm* the one who went back for the candy that *you* dropped at the last house," he recalled, pointing to himself.

"I wouldn't have dropped the bag in the first place if *Emily*—"

"Naw, don't blame *her*. She was already half way up the block when you started running," Jason interrupted.

Emily's head snapped towards Malajia. "You ran from the zombie too?"

Malajia rolled her eyes. "No," she spat. "Jason scared me."

Jason's mouth fell open. "That's bullshit!" he exclaimed. "All I said was 'Malajia, look', and you screamed and took off running."

"So nobody saw that old lady with the one leg chasing me?" Malajia asked, serious.

Jason glared at Malajia for several seconds. "*What* lady?" he hissed through clenched teeth.

Malajia held a silly look on her face. "Okay so nobody

was chasing me. Bottom line, that whole thing was Jason's fault."

Jason vigorously rubbed his hand across his face. "Never again," he grumbled. "That's why you lost your stupid hat while you were running."

"Fuck that hat," Malajia fussed, waving her hand dismissively.

Emily knocked once again. This time, the door opened and a middle-aged woman in a witch hat came outside holding a large plastic bin full of candy.

"A little old to be in the trick-or-treating game, don't you think?" she teased.

"Never too old to have fun," Emily smiled.

"You got that right," the lady agreed, distributing candy into their bags.

"Thank you," Emily returned, jogging down the steps with Jason following behind her.

Hearing the home owner bust out laughing, they turned around and saw Malajia grabbing two handfuls of candy out of the bowl.

"Come on, Malajia," Emily urged, gesturing to her.

"Don't rush me Emily, she said I can have some more candy," Malajia barked.

"David, how you gonna lose the fuckin' bag of candy?" Mark fumed, as his team approached a dark street.

"It was an accident," David explained. "I told you that I didn't see that sewer opening."

"And I told *you* to go get it," Mark threw back.

"Man, there was no way in hell I was going into a sewer for some stupid candy," David returned. "You must be crazy."

"Boy stop bitchin'," Chasity said to Mark. "It was like five pieces of candy in that bag. It wouldn't have made a difference."

"Chasity shut—just shut up," Mark snapped. "You ain't

been holding up *your* end the whole *night*."

Chasity stopped walking and spun around to face Mark. "That's bullshit and you know it," she fussed, pointing. "*I'm* the reason we have the candy that we *have* in those two bags you're carrying."

Mark sucked his teeth. "That's only because the houses we went to, were all owned by dirty old men who have a thing for young women, in tight ass devil costumes."

Chasity narrowed her eyes at Mark.

"You could see the drool falling out their mouths while you were staring at them with those freaky colored eyes of yours," Mark griped. "Playing in your hair and shit…you tease."

"Why were you staring that hard at their mouths?" David jeered, amusement in his voice.

Mark pointed at him. "You still not allowed to talk to me with your 'trippin-over-nuthin-droppin-the-bag-in-the-sewer' ass."

David rolled his eyes.

"Whatever," Chasity threw back. "The point is, that I held up *plenty* for this dumbass team, where's *your* damn candy?"

"In the bag that David dropped," Mark mumbled.

"Exactly," Chasity threw back. "Those five lonely ass pieces."

"Look here Devil," Mark hissed. "That wasn't my fault. That house that David picked was stingy with the candy."

David shook his head. "*You* picked that house."

"That's not the point!" Mark bellowed, stomping his foot on the ground. "The point *is*…I'm sick of y'all asses."

"Well the feeling is mutual," David put out. "We've been out here for like two hours, let's go to this last house and head back."

Mark stood close to Chasity and David's face. "We're not heading back 'till I *say* so," he commanded. "We need to win."

"Yo, can you back the *fuck* up out my damn face?" Chasity snapped. Mark had been working on her nerves all night long, and she was nearing her breaking point.

"I wish he *would*," David added.

Mark sucked his teeth. "Let's hit that house over there," he suggested, pointing to an eerily decorated home on the corner of the block.

"I'm not going over to that creepy ass house," Chasity refused.

"It's Halloween, *all* of the houses are creepy," Mark sighed.

"Not *all* of them are on a corner near a damn forest," Chasity returned.

Mark rubbed his forehead with his hand. "Chaz, I don't have time for your shit right now," he said, eerily calm, "Let's just get this candy, so I don't have to go down on Malajia every five minutes, okay."

"Wait, what?" David asked, confused.

"You don't wanna know," Chasity advised.

Mark approached the house with a reluctant Chasity and David following. Eerie music and unsettling sounds grew louder as they walked up the path.

"I feel like someone is breathing on me," David said, rubbing the back of his neck.

Mark looked behind him. "You bitchin' *too*, David?" he mocked.

"No," David mumbled.

Mark went to ring the doorbell, when he heard an ear-piercing scream, causing him to jump.

"Yo Chaz, come knock on this door," he said.

"You must be crazy," Chasity returned, keeping her position behind David.

Mark looked at David, who gestured for him to go ahead. Mark let out a sigh. "Fine, at least hold the bags," he said.

David headed up to him, grabbed the bags, and took a step back.

Punks, Mark thought, before hesitantly ringing the bell. The door slowly opened, revealing nothing but darkness inside. Suddenly, a light shined, and a large man with a bloodied, crazed mask appeared, holding a chainsaw which he revved up.

"Oh shit!" Mark panicked. He turned around to find that Chasity and David had taken off running down the street, leaving him standing there.

"Oh foreal y'all?!" Mark yelled, running after them.

As they ran across the street, David stumbled. As he tried to steady himself, he dropped the bags, sending candy tumbling in the street.

"Damn it David!" Mark hollered, making a dash for the candy. "Shit!" he panicked as he ran back to the sidewalk to avoid a car speeding down the block. The three friends stood and watched as the car ran over the candy and their bags.

Chasity and Mark slowly turned and fixed their angry gaze on David, who stared back at them wide-eyed. "I promise you that I did not see that event transpiring just now," David put out.

"I smiled at perverts for that fuckin' candy," Chasity seethed.

"I had to watch her smile at perverts for that fuckin' candy," Mark added.

David put his hands up, backing away. "There's nothing I can say that will change the fact that I feel like an idiot."

"Your goofy ass *should*," Mark bit out.

"I'm over this shit, I'm going back to campus," Chasity said, frustrated. "I don't give a shit about this stupid ass bet."

"Yeah? When you can't walk straight or sit down for a week, I bet you'll care *then*," Mark ground out.

David was once again confused. "Wait...*what*?"

"Look we can still win this thing... I have an idea," Mark announced, ignoring David's questioning.

"I'm not going to another fuckin' house dressed in this bullshit," Chasity fussed.

"You won't have to," Mark promised.

"I'm so glad to get this thing off," Alex sighed, kicking out of her costume and scooting it to a corner of the living room.

Sidra tossed her glittery black wings on the floor next to the couch. "It's been a long, draining night," she concluded, flopping down on the couch.

Alex took a seat next to her and smoothed her hands down her black tights, then tugged at the baggy grey shirt that she had on. "Tell me about it," she chuckled. "I can't wait to see who won."

"Looks like we won't have to wait to find out," Josh said, opening a can of soda. "I hear the others outside."

Josh barely got the words out of his mouth when the door to the girls' house opened, and the rest of the group trudged in. "Emily, will you take those sharp ass wings off?" Malajia bellowed, snapping her head behind her at Emily. "This is the fifth time you hit me with them."

"I didn't even touch you this time," Emily uttered.

"Guys, it's late, let's just get this show on the road," Alex yawned, stretching.

The group huddled together as the teams dumped their candy in three piles on the floor. Complaints could be heard around the room.

"Naw, how did the driest team get all that candy *and* got in before us?" Mark asked, eyeing the largest pile on the floor.

"When team 'steal houses' ran us off the block," Sidra began, gesturing towards Malajia and Jason. "We hit the next two blocks and they had a lot of candy."

"So...all that shit we went through tonight and *y'all* won," Malajia grunted, Alex nodded enthusiastically. "Ain't this about a bitch?"

"Welp, I guess we'll let y'all know what we want for dinner," Josh laughed, joined by Alex and Sidra. Their celebration was met with glares from the others.

"You laughin' kinda hard Josh," Mark observed. "You should be *cryin'* about that homemade mummy costume you got on."

Josh sucked his teeth as he headed for the door. "You corny *and* mad," he put out, unfazed. "Night y'all."

Sidra waved to him, then retreated for the staircase. "I like my rolls freshly made," she teased on her way up.

"She ain't gettin' no fresh rolls," Malajia mumbled to the others. "I'mma pull that old ass can of rolls out the back of the fridge."

Emily giggled, before retreating for the stairs herself.

"Look, forget them," Mark said. "We still have our couples bet." He started making a pile with the candy.

"Naw, don't touch the candy," Jason hissed. "You're just gonna try to move some from their pile, to yours."

"I would never," Mark laughed. "Okay, let's see who won." Mark examined both piles. "And it looks liiiike...*we* did."

Jason and Malajia glanced at each other, then looked back at Mark, who was celebrating alone because Chasity and David were gesturing for him to stop.

"Hold up zombie man," Malajia cut in, putting her hand up.

Mark spun around. "Whatchu' got to say, loser?" he taunted. "You can't talk your way out of this. You might as well get those jaws relaxed."

"No, I don't think so," Malajia returned, confident.

"How you gonna renege on a bet?" Mark asked, annoyed.

"Do y'all think we're stupid?" Jason asked.

"Is that a trick question?" Chasity sniped, earning a warning finger pointing at her from Jason.

"Sooooo," Malajia paused momentarily as she stared at the pile. "All the houses you went to...had the exact same type of candy?" she asked.

Chasity pinched the bridge of her nose and sighed as

David turned away.

"Oh what, you think that's not possible?" Mark maintained.

"*No* that's not possible, *fool*," Jason sneered. "*Every* single house for *blocks*, had the *same* damn candy? *Really?*" He pointed to the fun sized packs of candy corn bunched into a pile. "You *really* thought you were gonna get away with that?"

Mark's eyes shifted. "I'm sure the Mega-Mart had a sale."

"Oh I'm sure they *did*," Malajia agreed. "'Cause your freakin' receipt is hanging out that trick or treat bag on the floor."

Mark's eyes widened as he scrambled on the floor to retrieve the bag. "Fuck!" he wailed.

"You can't blame this disaster on *me* this time," David laughed. "*You're* the one who stuck the receipt in the bag after you got it from the cashier."

"Why you ain't remind me to take it out?" Mark seethed.

Jason slowly shook his head in disappointment. "You tried to cheat...and *stupidly*."

"I told you this shit wasn't gonna work," Chasity griped at Mark.

"Shut the fuck up Chasity!" Mark snapped, completely over the evening's events. His outburst was amusing to her, though.

"Mark, you need to chill with all that—"

"*You* shut the fuck up *too*, Jason!" Mark hurled at Jason, interrupting his warning.

"Stop acting like a baby and get over it," Malajia bit out. "You lost."

"I ain't lose shit," Mark grumbled. "*They* lost," he said, pointing to David and Chasity.

David shook his head. "I'm done for the night," he said, heading for the door. "Good luck with whatever freaky mess you have going on."

Mark hesitantly glanced at Malajia, who was staring at

him with a wide smile. "Welp—"

"Malajia, ain't nobody doin' that right now," Mark refused.

Malajia shot him a challenging look. "Oh yes the hell you *are*," she contradicted. She smiled a seductive smirk as she ran her hand down her chest. "Watching you lose pitifully, got me all hot and bothered."

Mark slammed his hand on the floor. "Come *on*," he complained.

"Oh, I intend to," Malajia teased.

Mark rolled his eyes. "Can I at least eat some dinner first?" he asked. "I'm starving."

"Oh you'll get plenty to eat in a few minutes," Malajia taunted, grabbing his hand. Mark sucked his teeth.

"You keep walking right into it," Jason commented to Mark.

"He sure does," Malajia chortled, pulling Mark along. "Now come on."

Mark let out a loud groan, stomping up the steps behind Malajia.

Alex shook her head as she followed the couple's progress with her eyes. "Malajia, can you not be extra loud tonight please?" she requested.

"Nope," Malajia bellowed down the steps.

Alex sucked her teeth. "Freaks," she mumbled.

Jason stared at Chasity, who in turn shook her head at him. "I'm *really* not in the mood right now," she mentioned.

Jason shrugged. "Okay, there's always later," he smiled, before removing his vampire cape and heading for the door.

Chasity let out a heavy sigh once Jason walked out the house, closing the door behind him.

Alex laughed. "And what did y'all bet?" she asked.

"Some bullshit that I'm *not* doing," Chasity replied, sitting on the arm of the chair, removing her devil horns. She ran her hand through her hair and scratched her scalp. "I'm gonna sleep so hard tonight."

"Girl, you and me *both*," Alex agreed.

Chasity was about to say something else, but the door opened, stopping her. She and Alex looked up to see Jason, poking his head in the house. "Chasity," he called.

"Huh?" Chasity answered.

"It's later," he taunted.

Shit! Chasity was too exhausted and wasn't in the mood for whatever sexual adventures that Jason had planned for that evening. "Um…I promised Alex that I would help her clean up."

"No you didn't," Alex contradicted, amused.

Chasity shot her a glare. "No? You didn't ask me to help you wash the dishes?"

"Nope."

"To clean the living room?" Chasity pressed.

Alex smiled. "Nope," she maintained.

"To wash that fuckin' dusty ass shirt you got on?" Chasity fumed, annoyed that Alex wasn't going along with her lie.

Alex's eyes became slits. "Isn't your man waiting for you?" she hissed.

Chasity rose from her seat, in a huff. "Is *yours*? Oops," she threw back, heading for the door.

Alex quickly grabbed Chasity's horns from the couch and tossed them in her direction. "Heffa," she sneered. She missed her target, and the horns hit the door as Chasity shut it on her way out. Alone and sitting in silence, Alex's eyes scanned the floor. "I'm not picking up all this damn candy."

Chapter 34

"I swear, I think I bombed on my Early Literature test," Alex complained, stabbing her chicken sandwich with her finger. "This is the *one* course that I seem to be struggling in. I have *no* interest in the 17th century at *all*."

Chasity eyed Alex as if she were crazy. "You trying to kill the damn chicken *again*?" she jeered, reaching for her cup of soda.

Alex chuckled. "No," she replied, reaching for a napkin. "I'm just frustrated... I'm ready for a break." She wiped her hand on the napkin.

Chasity and Alex, having a long break between their next classes, decided to take a trip off campus to the mall for a change of scenery. After walking both massive floors of the mall for what seemed like forever, both girls decided to grab something from the food court.

Alex stared at Chasity as the girl reached for her turkey wrap. "You know what Chaz, I don't think we've hung out one on one like this in a long time," Alex stated.

Chasity paused and shot Alex a glance. "Don't start acting corny Alex," she sneered, earning a laugh from Alex as she playfully tapped Chasity's arm.

"No, I'm serious," Alex insisted. "This is nice."

"Yeah, yeah," Chasity downplayed.

Alex shook her head. "Always the smart ass," she commented. "Anyway," she gave her head a scratch. "I've been meaning to bring up something that I heard."

Chasity rolled her eyes. "Don't," she hissed, having an inkling as to what Alex was referring to. Something that Chasity was trying to keep out of her head.

"Yeah, we both know that's not gonna happen," Alex calmly threw back. "Did Jason's mother really bring his ex-girlfriend down here a few weeks ago?"

Chasity set the rest of her sandwich down and let out a loud sigh. "See, *this* is why I don't hang out with you one on one."

"Come on," Alex urged.

Chasity hesitated for a moment. "Yeah," she answered.

Alex frowned. "But, for *what?*" she asked. "She knows that Jason is with *you*. Why would she do that?"

"She doesn't like me," Chasity stated matter-of-factly.

"So?" Alex fumed. "That doesn't give her a right to act like she's in high school with the petty nonsense." Alex was outraged. If there was one thing she hated, it was for people to mess with her friends. "If anything, she put Jason in an awkward situation."

"Obviously she doesn't give a shit," Chasity fussed.

Alex shook her head. "Well, what did he say to her?"

"Nothing because she's not answering his fuckin' phone calls," Chasity put out, exasperated.

Sensing that Chasity was becoming irritated with the conversation, Alex put her hands up. "I'm sorry, I'll drop it."

"No, it's not you," Chasity assured her. "The shit is just irritating."

"I can imagine," Alex sympathized.

"The damn girl called him again, *after* he told her to leave him alone, and *after* he blocked her number," Chasity vented. The agitation that Chasity tried to keep in was brimming as she remembered the incident a few days ago. While coming back from the gym with Jason, he'd listened to a voice message. And when his normally peaceful face became angry, naturally Chasity inquired what was going on—that's when he had told her who it was. "Sneaky bitch used somebody else's phone."

Alex frowned in confusion. "Is this girl stupid?"

"*Clearly* she is," Chasity fumed, tossing her balled up napkin on the table. "I swear to God, when he told me, I wanted to drive to West Chester and fuck her up."

"Chaz, don't let her take you back to that angry place," Alex consoled. "Jason doesn't want her, and she's gonna realize just how foolish she looks going after him, soon enough."

Chasity ran her hands through her hair. "Yeah, that's what *he* keeps telling me."

"Well, Jase is right," Alex confirmed. Alex reached out and put her hand on the visibly upset Chasity's arm, giving it a rub. "Come on Mama, I'll treat you to an ice cream cone."

Chasity frowned. "What am I gonna do with an ice cream cone in the fall, Alex?" she hissed.

"You're gonna say 'thank you' and *eat* the damn thing," Alex threw back, rising from her seat. She signaled for Chasity to get up. "Come on cranky."

The two girls ambled through the scarce mall crowd on their journey to the ice cream parlor. "Before you know it, this place will be packed for the holidays," Alex mused.

Chasity walked beside Alex in silence. A young woman spun around as the girls walked by her. The girl focused on their departing backs. "Chasity? Alex?" she called.

Chasity and Alex both stopped. They turned around in search of the name caller. Recognizing the woman's face, Chasity went from worn out to enraged. Alex rolled her eyes.

"Great, just great," Alex scoffed. *Just what Chaz needs when she's already pissed off.*

"Jackie," Chasity ground out.

Jackie Stevens smiled, and cautiously approached the annoyed women. "Long time no see," Jackie said.

Alex glanced down at Chasity's hand, which was at her side, balled up. With their history, *all* of their history for that matter, Alex knew that if Jackie came any closer, the result wouldn't be pretty.

Alex put her hand out. "You may wanna stop where you are," she warned.

Jackie sucked her teeth. "Relax, I'm not gonna try anything."

"You really think you'd get the chance to?" Chasity sneered.

Chasity fought and beat Jackie twice her freshman year and would have no problem doing it again. This time around, there was no danger of being kicked out of school; they were far from campus.

"Chasity—" Jackie took another step forward and Alex immediately stepped in front of Chasity. "I'm not here to fight," Jackie assured.

"Why did you call us?" Alex asked. "What do you want?"

"I don't know," Jackie shrugged. "I guess I just wanted to say hi. It's been a while."

Chasity was both annoyed and bewildered as she moved around Alex. "'Hi'?" she fumed. "After all the shit you pulled? After you antagonized me for damn near a whole year? After you jumped my fuckin' friend? After you tried to get me kicked out of school, you wanna come over here and say 'hi'?"

Jackie just stared at Chasity.

"Bitch, are you stupid?" Chasity barked.

Alex reached out and grabbed Chasity's arm. "Come on, let's just go," she urged.

Chasity snapped her head in Alex's direction, glaring daggers at her. "*Don't*," she warned.

Alex let go.

"Look, I meant what I said," Jackie said, tone alluding to her agitation. "I just wanted to say hi. It's been a long time. In case you haven't noticed, I haven't been on campus. I left school sophomore year."

"*Why* would I give a fuck?" Chasity sniped.

"Why did you leave school?" Alex asked. Jackie may have not been one of Alex's favorite people, in fact she despised the girl. But education was important to her, and she was curious as to why Jackie would leave.

"Just wasn't for me at the time," Jackie answered. "Anyway, I gotta go. You girls take care."

Chasity flipped Jackie off, before looking at Alex as Jackie sauntered off.

Catching Chasity's angry stare, Alex's eyes widened. "What?" she questioned. "I don't *like* the girl, but I don't see why anybody would just leave school without a good reason." she explained.

Chasity stared at Alex, resisting the urge to fire off a smart remark. "Just come on and get me my damn ice cream," she demanded, walking off.

Alex laughed. "Keep it up rude ass, you won't get shit but a cone full of sprinkles."

"And *you'll* eat 'em," Chasity promised.

Jason punched the buttons on his cell phone as he waited in the hall of the Math building. "I swear to God, I'm about to go off," he grumbled to himself. He placed his phone to his ear. Listening to the phone ring, he sucked his teeth when the voicemail came on. Rubbing his forehead with his hand, he dialed another number. He patiently waited for someone to answer. "Dad, hey, is Mom around?" He quickly put out. "How convenient... No, everything's fine, just been trying to talk to her for a while... No, it's not important, no need to worry. I'll just catch her another time... Okay, yeah I'm sure... Talk to you later."

Jason looked at the phone once the call with his father ended. "Yeah, Mom, you're busy all right," he grunted to himself.

The hustle and bustle of students around him made Jason put his solo rant session on pause. He looked up and saw the guys approaching.

Mark held his open notebook in Jason's face. "Tell me that the answer to this calculus equation is minus twenty-five," Mark hoped, putting his hand up.

Jason glanced at it. He shook his head after mentally calculating. "It's fifty," he confirmed.

Mark threw his head back in exasperation. "Fuck!" he bellowed, shoving his notebook in his book bag. "Well, if that answer was like any of the *other* ones I just gave on that Calc test, I just bombed." He sucked his teeth. "I *knew* I should've taken this course when I was supposed to sophomore year, instead of putting it off."

Jason wanted to crack a smile, but couldn't; he was too upset. As he was leaving his Advanced Machine Assembly class, he had received yet another text from Paris. He had immediately deleted it and tried calling his mother, to no avail.

"I'm sure you did fine on the problems," Jason consoled, tone bland.

"Man fuck that test," Mark griped, adjusting his book bag from one shoulder to the other.

"Yeah, keep that attitude," Jason replied, sarcastic.

Mark ignored Jason's comment. "Let's go grab some lunch right quick."

David looked at his watch. "Can't, I promised Nicole that I'd help her study for her Chem test."

"Code for 'I'm about to smash'," Mark teased.

David rolled his eyes. "Not everyone has that on the brain," he threw back. "Anyway, I gotta go. See you guys later."

"Yeah sure, just remember where you gotta put it," Mark called after David, who in turn flipped Mark off.

"You're such a jackass," Josh chuckled.

"Hey, I'm just tryna help my boy out," Mark shrugged. He turned to Jason. "So? Lunch?"

"Um…no, I'm not hungry," Jason dryly put out.

Mark sucked his teeth as Jason proceeded to walk off. "The hell is wrong wit you dawg?" he barked. "You sound all dry."

"Nothing, I'll catch y'all for dinner," Jason threw back, continuing on his way.

Mark rubbed the back of his neck and looked at Josh, who was looking back at him.

"Why does it look like you're disappointed that I'm the only one left?" Josh chortled.

"'Cause, you corny bee," Mark joked.

Josh shook his head and walked off, leaving Mark to bust out laughing as he followed.

Sidra turned her car off and grabbed bags off the passenger seat, before heading for the house. Seeing a single red rose with a note attached on the front step, she bent down, retrieved it, and glanced at the note before going inside. "Hey Mel, someone left this on the step for you," she announced.

Malajia, who was sitting at the dining room table with books sprawled in front of her, glanced up. "Ooh, a rose, I love roses," she smiled as Sidra handed it to her. She removed the card from the rose and read it. "Aww, Mark is so sweet," she cooed.

"What does it say?" Sidra asked, curious.

Malajia was all smiles as she read the small card. "'Enjoy your day beautiful, I miss you'," she gushed. "He's so dramatic, I just saw him earlier," she joked. "I wonder why he didn't sign it though."

"He probably forgot," Sidra shrugged.

"Yeah, he *is* forgetful about shit," Malajia agreed.

"Now how are you gonna talk bad about him after he did something so thoughtful?" Sidra chuckled.

"'Cause I wouldn't be me if I didn't," Malajia replied, nonchalant.

Before Sidra could say another word, the door opened. "You would never guess who we ran into today," Alex blurted out as soon as she and Chasity entered the house.

"Who?" Sidra asked.

"Jackie," Alex answered.

"Eww," Malajia grimaced.

"My thoughts exactly," Chasity replied, sitting in an empty seat at the table.

"She didn't breathe her ugly on you, did she?" Malajia directed to Chasity, reaching her hand towards her face. "Here, let me look at your face, you know she was scaly. Did she spit a zit on you?"

Chasity laughed, smacking Malajia's hand down.

Alex stood with her hands on her hips, watching her friends break into laughter. "You people are terrible," Alex chided, successfully holding her own laughter in.

"Come on, you *know* she ugly," Malajia said, reaching for her pencil.

Alex shook her head as she sat down on the couch. "She's not necessarily *ugly*. She's…"

"Ugly," Chasity bit out.

"Beauty is in the eyes of the beholder," Alex reminded, pointing.

"And the beholder knows she's ugly," Chasity returned, earning hysterical laughter from Malajia.

"A damn shame," Alex chortled. "Anyway, where's Emily?"

"She's hanging out with Will," Malajia answered. She abruptly tossed her pencil down. "I can't deal with these books anymore. I need to release some stress."

"You wanna go do something fun?" Alex asked.

"Yeah, but not with *you*," Malajia answered, grabbing her cell phone from the table. After quickly punching some buttons, she put the phone to her ear. "Hey lover," she crooned into the phone. "Guess what *I'm* in the mood for? …Oh yes the hell you *are*, your week ain't up yet brotha… Don't play with me… I'll be over in five minutes… Yes, I'll bring some chips over."

"God, you still on that Halloween bet?" Alex giggled as Malajia hung up her phone.

"You damn right," Malajia confirmed, standing from her seat, with her rose and card in hand.

"Mark is gonna get sick of your nonsense," Sidra predicted.

"Please," Malajia scoffed, retrieving an opened bag of chips from the cabinet. "If I had lost, best believe he'd have my face in his lap every chance he got... Don't feel sorry for him."

Sidra shook her head as Malajia hurried for the door. "Later freak," she teased.

"Later dryness," Malajia shot back, shutting the door behind her.

Sidra sucked her teeth, then turned to Chasity. "What about *you?*" she asked, earning a confused look from Chasity. "Jason still keep you tied to the headboard at night for his bet?"

"No, and you sound like you *need* to be," Chasity threw back.

Sidra hung her head in shame as she whined. "God, I *want* to be," she joked, earning laughter from both Alex and Chasity.

Malajia twirled the lush red rose in her hand as she sat on Mark's bed, waiting for him to return from the bathroom. When his room door opened, she glanced up at him, frowning. "Took you long enough, shitty."

Mark sucked his teeth. "I wasn't doing *that,* nasty ass," he returned. "I was trying to get this damn ink off my hands." He showed Malajia the light ink marks on his hands. "I swear I'mma stop using those damn pens my mom brought me. They keep leaking."

"Stop acting like you wasn't writing on yourself on purpose," Malajia joked earning a glare from Mark. His stare made her laugh. "I'm playing."

"Real funny," he sniped.

Malajia rose from his bed and walked over to him.

"Aww, somebody's gotten all sensitive on me," she teased, wrapping her arms around his neck.

"Naw, not me," he denied, pulling her closer by her waist.

Malajia giggled. "Well, at least you're sensitive when it *counts*," she smiled, holding her rose in front of his face. "Thank you for my flower."

"*What* flower?" Mark was clearly confused.

Malajia frowned, holding the rose closer to his face. "This one that I'm holding here," she said. When he still looked confused, Malajia sucked her teeth. "The one that you left on the front step of my house?... You left a note and everything."

"Babe, I didn't leave you a flower *or* a note," Mark insisted.

Malajia looked at the rose skeptically. Parting from Mark's embrace, she retrieved the note from his bed. "So you didn't leave this?" she asked, handing him the card.

Mark opened the little white card and read it. He immediately became agitated. "No, I *didn't*," he bit out. "But I'd like to know who the hell *did*?"

"Hell if *I* know," Malajia said, clearly creeped out.

Mark balled the paper up. "Yo, I swear if that damn Praz sent you this, I'mma smack him right in the chin," he fumed, remembering the popular, dark-skinned upperclassmen who had become Malajia's friend her freshman year.

Malajia rolled her eyes. "Praz graduated in June."

Mark twisted his lip up. "We *both* know he ain't graduate."

Malajia managed a chuckle, despite the eerie feeling that she had. "Yeah, he *did*." She tossed the rose in the waste paper basket. "Forget that stupid flower."

Mark shook his head. He was pleased when he saw Malajia throw the rose in the trash. Yet he began to feel bad, because it wasn't him who bought it for her. "You want me to get you flowers?" he asked, pulling her close to him once again.

Malajia stared blankly off to the side. *If Mark didn't send me that, who the hell did?* "Huh?" she answered when she heard him call her name.

"You want me to buy you flowers?" he repeated.

"Well...*yes*," Malajia sneered.

Mark laughed and kissed her cheek, then moved down to her neck. Malajia, mind plagued with questions, moved his head from her neck. "Chill," she put out.

"What's wrong?"

"I'm not in the mood anymore," she returned. "I gotta finish studying anyway."

Mark watched her move around him and walk to his door. "Go get your books and come over and study with me," he suggested.

"Okay," she replied, shutting the door behind her.

As Malajia walked down the steps, she frowned. Not knowing who the flower came from wasn't sitting right with her. *I barely smile at other dudes now, who the hell would miss me?* she thought, continuing her pace out of the house.

Chapter 35

"Yo, I swear I'm gonna find out who gave Malajia that damn flower," Mark vented to Jason as he passed the basketball to him.

"And just *how* are you gonna do that?" Jason asked, dribbling the ball as he maneuvered around Mark. Mark sucked his teeth when Jason made a basket. "No guy on this campus is going to admit that they sent your girlfriend a flower, they're not stupid."

Mark let out a loud sigh.

After his morning class, Mark talked Jason into playing a one on one game of basketball at the gym to kill some time before his afternoon class. That, and he felt the need to vent to one of his brothers about Malajia's unexpected gift.

"I'll figure out a way," Mark fussed, retrieving the bouncing ball. "That's some disrespectful bullshit."

Jason nodded. "It is," he agreed. "But, you said that Mel threw it away and again, you have no idea who sent it. So terrorizing the campus to find out isn't gonna do anything."

"So if some random dickhead sent Chaz a flower and a card talking 'bout 'I miss you,' you wouldn't be pissed?" Mark challenged, passing him the ball.

Jason held the caught ball for a moment. "I didn't say that I *wouldn't* be. Hell, if I *knew* who sent it, I'm not gonna say that I wouldn't go handle him," he admitted, tossing it back. "But at the end of the day, my lady is beautiful and will have admirers, and I can't fight every man who has a crush on her. Besides, she'll never entertain any other man, so I don't have anything to worry about…and neither will Malajia."

Mark tossed the ball back and forth between his hands. "I guess you got a point. My baby *is* sexy," he agreed, before sighing. "Okay fine, I'll let that shit go this time. But if it happens again, I'm tearing this campus a new ass."

"If it happens again, do what you gotta do," Jason chuckled. "I need a time out." He headed over to the bench to retrieve his towel and water bottle.

"What, you can't handle this beatin'?" Mark teased, following him.

Jason frowned in confusion. "I'm winning seven to four," he pointed out.

"Didn't nobody ask you for specifics," Mark jeered, shaking his hand in Jason's direction as he sat down on the bench next to him.

Jason shook his head. "I sometimes wonder if you were dropped on your head as a child," he grunted, wiping the back of his neck with his towel.

Mark laughed. "I wonder the same thing sometimes." Hearing his phone beep, Mark retrieved it from his gym bag. After reading the message, he sucked his teeth. "Goddamn it Malajia," he huffed. "Yo, she trippin' with this bet shit. It's every fuckin' five minutes with her."

This time, Jason busted out laughing. "You only got like two days left," he placated.

"Naw, this shit ends *today*," Mark fussed, tossing the phone back in his bag. "That damn mysterious flower killed her mood before, so I was off the hook. I'm about to send her ass another one."

"Bro, you know if *you* would've won, you wouldn't cut your week short," Jason pointed out, amusement in his voice.

"You can't tell me what I would do," Mark returned. "Her ass gonna wait," he mumbled after a few moments, taking a sip from his water bottle. "I'm surprised you don't have Chaz held up in a damn room somewhere."

Jason sighed. "No, classes have her stressed out this week... Besides, I'm not that petty." That was the half-truth. Jason didn't want to admit it to Mark, but he sensed a strain between him and Chasity over the whole Paris and his mother situation. A strain that had neither one of them in the mood for anything sexual. "Look, I gotta go. I have to meet Chaz at the library," he said, standing from the bench.

"So we just not gonna finish the game, bee?" Mark called after him.

"No," Jason returned, not turning around. "Stop stalling before Mel comes and finds you."

Mark sucked his teeth, even though Jason was no longer in ear shot. "Yeah, I'll go when I'm good and ready," he mumbled. A second later, his phone rang. Seeing Malajia's number flash on the caller ID, he groaned as he answered. "What?! I'm coming, damn!" he snapped, hopping to his feet.

Chasity highlighted a few lines in her textbook and rubbed the back of her neck with her free hand. She glanced up when she saw Jason walk into the private room she was secluded in.

"Sorry I'm late," he smiled, leaning in to give her a kiss on her cheek, but Chasity moved her head, eyes not leaving her book. Jason frowned in confusion before moving to the seat across from her and setting his book bag on the table.

He held his gaze on her as he got settled. "You okay?" he asked, hesitantly.

"Um hmm," she muttered, still not making eye contact.

Jason reached across the table to touch her hand, but Chasity moved it out of reach. "Okay, what's going on with you?" he pressed. "What did I do?"

Chasity sat back in her seat, tossing her highlighter on the textbook.

Jason held a stern gaze. "Talk to me."

"You remember asking me to grab your mail for you when I got mine?" she spat.

"Yeah," he replied.

"Well, I grabbed it for you."

What the hell? She has an attitude because I asked her to grab my mail for me? "Um...okay," he put out.

Chasity reached under her textbook, retrieving a small yellow envelope. She tossed it in his direction. "You may want to check it," she hissed.

Jason frowned as he picked up the letter. Eyeing the return address in the left-hand corner, he closed his eyes and rubbed them with his fingertips.

"Who's that pretty little envelope from?" Chasity quizzed.

Jason hesitated to speak; he was sure that she already knew the answer to the question. "Chaz—"

"Who is it from?" Chasity's tone was menacing and slow.

Jason let out a sigh. "It's from Paris." *Fuck! Why won't this girl just go away, already?*

"Oh, *is* it?" Chasity sneered, folding her arms. "You wanna open it and see what's inside?"

"Not really," Jason answered honestly.

"That's not a request," Chasity threw back. Jason rolled his eyes. "Open it."

The fact that the letter was sent to him in the first place, coupled with knowing that Chasity saw the letter and was now her full-on angry self, made his stress level hit an all-time high. Reluctantly, he opened the letter as Chasity held her fiery gaze on him. Laying eyes on a few old pictures tucked under a note, Jason sucked his teeth. He immediately went to rip them up, but was caught off guard when Chasity reached across the small table and snatched them from him. "Babe, you don't need to see those."

Chasity ignored him as she flipped through the three pictures of Jason and Paris. "Oh look how cute, she *actually* kept this picture after all this time," she bit out, holding a picture of Jason and Paris kissing on the steps of their old high school.

"Chasity, those pictures don't mean shit to me," Jason promised, putting his hand up.

"Look and she wrote you a note," Chasity seethed, reading it. "'Jason, I thought you would enjoy these memories. Look at how happy we were.'"

"She's fuckin' crazy," Jason barked.

Chasity, not interested in hearing Jason's excuses, immediately tore the pictures up and pushed the pieces in Jason's direction.

"This isn't my fault," he said.

"You're so full of shit," she argued.

Jason looked around as Chasity's voice carried. Luckily their room had a door, and it was shut. "Chasity how could I have known that she was going to send these old ass pictures?"

"No the *real* question is, why does this bitch think it's okay to do shit like this?" Chasity barked.

"It's probably my mom feeding her bullshit."

"No, fuck that," Chasity returned. "What are *you* saying to her?"

Jason's eyes widened in shock. "I'm not saying *shit* to her," he argued, matching her angry tone with one of his own. "I don't entertain this crap. I told her to leave me alone."

"So you want me to believe that she's *that* crazy?" Chasity questioned in disbelief. "She's chasing after a guy who dumped her, and who *clearly* is unavailable... She's *that* crazy, huh?"

Jason rubbed his face with his hands. "I'm telling you baby, the girl loves drama. She always *has*," Jason tried to explain.

Chasity shook her head. "So, what are you gonna say to me *now*?" she mocked. "You gonna tell me that you'll take care of it?"

"I *will*."

"Yeah, 'cause you've taken *such* good care of the situation so far," Chasity sniped, tone dripping with sarcasm.

"I don't know what else I can do," Jason sighed. "I've told her to back off. I've been trying to get ahold of my mom to tell her to cut her shit, but she's avoiding me."

Chasity pinched the bridge of her nose with two fingers as she tried to calm herself down. "Jason, if you wanted to get in touch with your mother, you *could*," she pointed out. "That cell phone that she has isn't the *only* damn way to reach her."

Jason frowned. "What are you trying to say?" he ground out.

"Nothing, forget it," Chasity threw back, slamming her textbook shut.

"No, you think that if I could stop this, I *wouldn't?*" Jason pressed. "You think I *want* this drama?"

Chasity stared at Jason for several seconds. She didn't know if she actually believed what she was thinking. She did trust him, but she was angry. "I just know that right now, I need to get away from you," she answered as she stood up.

Jason watched as Chasity quickly gathered her belongings and walked out of the room. Frustrated, he pounded his fist on the table repeatedly before pushing his book bag to the floor.

Alex opened a bag of freshly popped popcorn, pouring it into a bowl. "So Sid, are you going home for Thanksgiving this year?" she asked Sidra from the kitchen.

Sidra raised an inquisitive eyebrow. "As opposed to where?"

Alex shrugged. "Just wondering if maybe you might go to DC to spend it with James."

Sidra shook her head, then examined the pale blue polish on her nails. "No, James said that he might be in California for Thanksgiving... His sister lives there and she wants the family to come down."

Alex walked over and set the bowl on the coffee table, taking a seat next to Sidra on the couch. "He didn't invite you to go?" she pressed.

"He did," Sidra answered. "But, I'd rather be back on this end, you know?"

Alex nodded. "Maybe next year you guys can spend it together." Her voice was full of hope. "You will be out of school and you'll have more time to travel."

Sidra stared at the movie playing on the TV screen in front of her. "Yeah," she replied, tone unenthused.

Alex, picking up on Sidra's tone, glanced at her. "You don't sound too happy about that," she observed.

"No, that's not it. I'd love to spend more time with James," Sidra clarified. "I just...I don't know. I guess I just have some other stuff on my mind, that's all... Like the fact that I have to spend Thanksgiving with my soon to be raggedy sister-in-law," she spat. "God, I hate saying that."

"When is the wedding?"

"Next year," Sidra answered, tone flat.

Alex gave Sidra's shoulder a rub. "Let's talk about something else," she placated, picking up on Sidra's attitude.

"Sure," Sidra muttered.

"Back to Thanksgiving—" Alex paused when the front door swung open.

"I can't take these braids anymore!" Emily wailed, vigorously scratching her head. "Is Malajia here?"

Alex and Sidra fought to contain their laughter at the deranged look on Emily's face. "No, she's in the library," Sidra answered.

"She promised to help me take these out," Emily pouted, flopping down on the couch.

This time Alex did laugh as she pushed the coffee table forward with her slipper covered foot. "Come on, sit down and I'll help you start taking them out," she offered.

"God, I love you," Emily gushed, hopping on the floor in

front of Alex's legs. "I can't wait to get some shampoo on this mess."

Sidra giggled. "I would help, but I just did my nails."

"I'll repaint them for you when we're done," Emily threw out. "Come on, team work."

Sidra stared at the grin on Emily's face. "Fine," she huffed, scooting closer to Alex on the couch. "Only because I hate to see you suffer."

The girls worked diligently to remove the long, individual braids from Emily's hair. "So, Em, what are your plans for Thanksgiving this year?" Alex asked after about a half hour of silence.

Emily removed another braid and set it on her lap. "Um, I don't really know," she answered, a trace of sadness in her voice. "My Dad said that he'd try to see if he could avoid traveling so we can spend Thanksgiving together, but…who knows." She scratched her head. "I might go to Jersey to spend it with my brothers."

Alex nodded. "Well, sweetie, you know you're always welcome at *my* house."

"Mine too," Sidra put in.

Emily smiled. "Thanks girls." Her smile quickly faded. The last thing that Emily wanted to think of was the holidays, especially since, once again, she would be spending it without one of the most important people in her life.

"But Em, if you come to *my* house, be prepared to be in the presence of a mutant," Sidra spat, much to Emily's confusion.

"Huh?" Emily frowned.

"Sidra, that's horrible," Alex chortled, tapping Sidra on the leg.

"Ouch!" Sidra shrieked, snatching her hand back. "Em that damn hair just cut my finger!"

Alex busted out laughing as the front door opened. Malajia stepped foot inside, took one look at the hair removing process happening in the living room, and immediately walked back out, only to bump into Chasity who was walking up behind her. "Chaz move, before they see me!" she barked.

"What are you doing?" Chasity snapped, trying to move around Malajia to get into the house.

"Uh uh, Malajia, you might as well get in here and help," Alex called, signaling for her. "You promised Em that you'd help her."

Malajia stomped her foot on the floor. "Damn it Chaz," Malajia complained, walking back into the house. "If you would've just moved, I wouldn't be in this mess."

Chasity shut the door behind her once she walked into the house. Still upset over her argument with Jason earlier that day, Chasity was in no mood to go back and forth with Malajia over nonsense.

Malajia flopped down on the couch on the other side of Alex. She glanced up at Chasity, watching her head up the steps without saying a word. "Naw bitch, you gotta help too," she ordered.

Chasity stopped in the middle of the staircase and glared at Malajia. "*I'm* the one who gotta wash that mess when you're done, so I'm not helping with *shit*," she barked.

Sidra made a face at Chasity's nasty tone. "Chasity, your horns are showing."

Chasity rolled her eyes and adjusted the book bag on her shoulders. She knew her tone was a bit uncalled for.

"You okay sweetie?" Alex asked, pausing mid braid.

"No, not really," Chasity quickly put out. "But give me a minute and I'll be fine." She continued her pace up the steps, leaving the four remaining girls perplexed.

"Do you know what's wrong with her?" Sidra asked Malajia.

"I think she had a fight with Jason earlier," Malajia answered, grabbing a few of Emily's braids.

"About *what*?" Sidra asked, curious. For Jason and Chasity to have an argument was rare. Unlike Malajia and

Mark's relationship, where they seemed to fight every five minutes.

"I'm not sure," Malajia answered. She did in fact know what the argument was about. While walking back to the house, Chasity had given Malajia an overview of it. But knowing how Chasity felt about sharing her business with everyone, and making strides to change the blabbermouth part of herself, Malajia deciding against going into any further detail.

"Oh," Sidra returned, examining her finger.

Malajia dropped Emily's braids and began rubbing her face vigorously. "There're so *many* of them!" she wailed.

"How do you think *I* feel?" Emily laughed.

Chasity tapped several keys on her laptop while staring blankly at the screen. *I just don't feel like doing this shit right now*, she thought of her programming assignment. Being a Computer Science major, with a focus on website design, Chasity was normally excited to prefect her craft. But the argument had left her unable to think clearly.

She sighed loudly. "Focus Parker, focus," she prompted herself.

Her phone ringing almost made her snap. Grabbing it from her desk and glancing at the caller id, Chasity rolled her eyes.

"What Jason?" she hissed, setting the phone down and putting the call on speaker. "What?" her tone was sharp.

"Chaz can you come take a walk with me?" Jason asked after a brief pause.

"No, it's cold," Chasity returned.

"I know if I try to come over there, you're not gonna let me in, so I'm asking you to just take a walk with me." Although Jason was pleading, his tone was stern. "We need to talk this out."

Chasity stared at the phone with disgust. She had every

intention of disconnecting the call. But she remembered that her old way of handling things wasn't necessarily the best way. She stomped her foot on the floor repeatedly. "Fine," Chasity bit out through clenched teeth. "Give me ten minutes."

"Okay, I'll meet you outside," Jason replied.

Chasity didn't offer another response before hanging up the phone. She sat in silence for a moment, before rising from her seat, grabbing her coat and heading out of the room. Chasity made her way downstairs and stood at the bottom of the steps, facing the girls, who were still working on Emily's hair.

"Can I run something by y'all real quick?" Chasity asked, much to the shock of the girls.

"Sure," Alex beamed, adjusting herself on her seat to face Chasity. "What's on your mind?"

Chasity moved closer to the couch. "I wanted to ask your opinion on something."

"Is this about the argument that you had with Jason earlier?" Sidra asked.

Chasity shot Malajia a glare, as Malajia's mouth fell open with shock.

"Sidra, you always snitchin'!" Malajia belted out, pointing at her stunned friend.

"What did I do?" Sidra asked, pointing to herself. "I didn't know it was a secret."

"You always starting shit," Malajia fussed, waving her hand at Sidra. "Now I'm pissed. I'm not taking out no more of these old ass braids."

"Wait! Why am *I* being penalized?" Emily asked, shocked.

"'Cause 'Big mouth Howard' is *your* damn roommate," Malajia griped. She looked at Chasity, whose eyes were still fixed upon Malajia in a death stare. "In my defense...I didn't give them any details."

Chasity shook her head. "I don't even care," she grumbled.

The girls sat, eyes fixed and engaged as Chasity gave them an overview of the day's events. Emily sat with her mouth open.

"What's *wrong* with her?" Emily asked of Paris.

Chasity didn't blink as she stared at Emily's half-braided head. "I'm sorry, but it's really hard for me to pay attention to what you're asking when you look crazy."

Emily put her hand over her face. "I know," she admitted, laughter in her voice.

"But to answer your question, she's fuckin' disrespectful," Chasity fumed.

"I say we trash her," Malajia threw out.

"I *want* to, but Jason keeps telling me not to worry about her," Chasity complained.

"Then you *shouldn't*," Alex said.

"Alex, I'm trying *not* to, but this shit is starting to get to me," Chasity admitted. The tone in her voice sounded as if she was trying to keep from screaming. "I don't know, maybe I'm overreacting. Do you guys think that I'm wrong for being mad at *him*?"

"Hell no!" Malajia exclaimed. "You're not overreacting. He needs to handle that shit...before *we* do."

Alex put her hand up. "No, hold on a—"

"Alex, I'm not tryna hear it, I know Chaz can fight, but I'm ridin'," Malajia argued, shaking her hand in Alex's face. "I'll follow up *real* quick."

Alex narrowed her eyes at Malajia. "First of all, calm your hyper butt down," she ordered Malajia. "Second," she began, facing Chasity. "I don't think that you should be mad at Jason," she placated. "After all, it's not his fault that the girl keeps coming after him."

Malajia held a confused look as Chasity rolled her eyes. "*True*, but he's not doing enough to prevent the shit *either*," Malajia reasoned.

"What *else* is he supposed to *do*?" Alex argued. "I mean from what you've told me Chaz, he's told her over and over to leave him alone, right?"

"So he says," Chasity mumbled, glancing at her manicured hand.

Sidra stared at Chasity. "What, you don't believe him?" she wondered.

"I don't know," Chasity admitted. "I'm starting to wonder if he likes the attention."

"Chaz, don't start doubting him," Alex advised. "Once you start questioning everything that he does, then you start to lose trust and that's a recipe for disaster."

Malajia slammed her hand on the arm of the couch. She was annoyed that Alex wasn't backing up Chasity's feelings. "Why you gotta say *recipe*?" she barked. "You always thinkin' 'bout food."

"Why do you always have to start with me?" Alex hurled, tossing some braid hair at Malajia; she blocked it from hitting her face.

"'Cause, you tryna make her feel bad for her feelings and shit," Malajia argued. "What happened to 'man hating' Alex?"

"She's trying to *change*," Alex spat.

Sidra shook her head at the byplay. "Chill children," she chided. Then looked at Chasity, who seemed to be deep in thought. "Look Chaz, I agree that Jason has no control over this girl but—" Sidra took a deep breath. "Sweetie, you *know* who started all of this... Jase needs to deal with *her*."

"Yeah well, he can't seem to contact her so—" Chasity brushed off, putting on her coat. "Anyway, thanks. I gotta go."

"Everything will work out Chaz," Emily said as Chasity headed out the door.

"Thanks," Chasity threw over her shoulder, before shutting the door.

Malajia frowned at Emily, who in turn looked back at her wide-eyed.

"What?" Emily asked.

"That wasn't comforting," Malajia hissed. "You should've said, 'we'll whoop her ass for you Chaz'."

Emily flagged Malajia with her hand, before grabbing another braid.

Jason glanced over at Chasity, who was walking in stride beside him. They'd been walking through the campus in silence ever since he met her outside of her house nearly twenty minutes ago. "So, are we going to talk, or are we going to just play the silent game?" Jason asked, some bite in his voice.

"I'm not playing," Chasity mumbled.

Jason sucked his teeth. After a beat, he stopped walking and moved around Chasity to stand in front of her.

Chasity shot him a warning look. "What are you doing?" she hissed. "I'm fuckin' freezing."

"The sooner we get this conversation going, the sooner you can get back in the house," Jason promised.

Chasity narrowed her eyes at him.

"You want me to start?" he asked.

"No," she ground out. She folded her arms to her chest, taking a deep breath. "Do I have anything to worry about with you and her?" she blurted out.

Jason frowned. "What do you mean?"

"I mean…" she rubbed her forehead with her hand. "Is there *any* chance of you and her getting back together?"

Jason stared at her in disbelief. "You seriously just asked me that?"

"Do you *blame* me?" Chasity threw back. Jason let out a groan. "What am I supposed to think when some girl that you used to sleep with keeps popping the fuck back up?"

"You're supposed to trust me."

"I'm not saying that I *don't* trust you," Chasity argued. "But… Look, I never had to deal with this shit before, okay."

Jason ran his hand over his hair. He hated this. He hated the fact that his woman was feeling threatened because of his ex's antics and his mother. He hated that the arguments between the two of them were increasing. And now, he was sensing that Chasity's trust and faith in him was being chipped away, and that was killing him.

He took both of her hands in his and held them. "Chaz, I promise you. You have *nothing* to worry about when it comes to me and Paris ever getting back together."

Chasity looked away momentarily.

"I don't want her," Jason assured, tone sincere, caring. "I don't love her. I love *you*. I'm with *you*. You have to trust me babe."

Chasity stared at him. She heard his words, and while she appreciated them and wanted to believe them, she admitted to herself that for the first time in a long time, she felt insecure. The idea that Chasity wasn't enough to keep Jason's past feelings for his ex from resurfacing, was putting her in a bad headspace. But instead of harping on it, she just nodded. "Okay," she said finally.

Jason pulled Chasity in for a hug and a quick kiss. "I promise, this shit will be over soon," he said, holding her in his arms. "I'm going to give my mom an earful when I see her over Thanksgiving. And the best way to deal with Paris is just to ignore her. I've been giving her too much damn attention by responding to her."

"Yeah well, hopefully you're right," Chasity said, holding on to him.

Me too, he thought. Jason said a silent prayer hoping that his promise to Chasity would be true. "Come on, let's get you out of this cold," he said, guiding her to the path leading to their houses.

Chapter 36

"I have an idea of what we can do for Thanksgiving," Emily blurted out, sitting in the booth of a fast food restaurant with the girls.

"You screamed all in my ear," Malajia fussed, reaching for a taco from the tray in front of her.

Emily stared at Malajia in confusion. "I didn't even scream," she denied.

"And, she's not even sitting *next* to you," Alex laughed. The look on Malajia's face was of pure silliness.

"Well…whatever," Malajia grumbled, reaching for a packet of taco sauce from Chasity's tray.

"Girl, get your dumbass hand off my damn sauce," Chasity hissed, smacking the packet out of Malajia's hand.

"Come on bitch! You know I can't eat no damn tacos without the sauce," Malajia bellowed, slapping her hand on the table.

"It's not *my* fault that you used all of yours on one damn taco," Chasity spat, opening her packet and pouring the sauce on her own taco.

Malajia stared at the red sauce dripping on to the taco. "So you just gonna use it right in my damn face?" she asked, voice dripping with disdain.

"Yup," Chasity shot back.

Sidra chuckled, shaking the sauce pack in her own hand.

"I swear you two argue like you're real life sisters," she commented.

"She *is* my sister, even though I hate her ass half the time," Malajia grunted, turning to Sidra who was sitting next to her.

"The feeling is mutual...the hate part," Chasity sneered.

"Girls, you want to hear my idea?" Emily put in.

"Sure," Sidra smiled, then immediately frowned when Malajia yanked the sauce packet from her hand. "You are such an asshole," Sidra snapped.

"Malajia, why are you always on ten?" Alex shook her head, handing Sidra one of hers. "You need to chill sometimes."

"*Some*times?" Sidra scoffed.

"Anyway." Emily put her hands up, hoping to cut short the bickering. "I was just thinking that this is really going to be our last Thanksgiving in college."

"Yeah?" Malajia questioned, confused.

Emily pushed some loose hair strands up into her high bun. "Which means that this will be our last Thanksgiving *together*," she added.

Alex glanced at Emily, while taking a sip of her drink. "That's not necessarily true Em," she contradicted. "I'm sure we'll all make an effort to get together for the holidays once we graduate."

"What if we *can't*?" Emily asked, tone sullen. "I mean, some of us might move away, you know... All I'm saying is that I think that we should do something together...here." Emily looked around at the girls. "...on campus."

"Time out," Malajia said, putting her hands up. "Instead of us going *home* for the break, you want us to stay here on this dry ass campus?"

Sidra tried to suppress a laugh, but was unsuccessful. "It *would* be pretty dull here for those four days."

"Besides, I was gonna spend Thanksgiving with my family—"

"What, you actually *want* to spend it with the

Simmons's?" Alex teased Malajia, knowing the many complaints that Malajia gave in the past about going home for the holidays.

"Yeah well…I like them now," Malajia joked. "Then I was gonna go to Chaz's house the next—"

"No the hell you *wasn't*," Chasity quickly denied. "You keep your ass *home*."

Malajia's mouth fell open in shock. "But it's tradition," she argued. "I *always* come over on the holidays."

"And you *always* get on my damn nerves," Chasity barked.

Emily let out a sigh as she put her hands up in surrender. "Okay, it was just a suggestion," she sulked.

Alex had a thought. "I thought your brothers wanted to spend the holiday with you, Emily," she said, grabbing another taco from her tray.

"They do, but they'll be working most of the holiday and I'll just be up in Jersey, sitting there waiting for them to get off…looking stupid," Emily replied, tone somber. What she didn't want to say was that, as much as she wanted to spend the holiday with her brothers, it would be hard being back in her home town. Especially knowing that her mother was merely minutes away, yet Emily would be unable to see her. Despite the fact that the women weren't on the best of terms, Emily still missed her mother.

"Well, like I said before, you can always come to Philly," Alex offered, smiling.

"Don't nobody wanna sit up in that hood ass row house of yours," Malajia teased. "Laying all on that dirty ass air mattress and shit."

Alex picked up a balled-up napkin and threw it at the laughing Malajia. "Don't talk about my house," she fumed.

"I'm just messing with you," Malajia promised, amused. "You know I love your mini ass house."

Sidra nearly spat out her soda from laughing as Chasity shook her head.

"Alex, you should smack the shit outta her," Chasity

instigated, gesturing to Malajia, who was still laughing.
"I'm *about* to," Alex grumbled.

"Carl, I'm not tutoring you in Advanced Calculus
again," Jason refused, slinging his gym bag over his
shoulder. "I've tried to help you before."

Carl wiped his face with a towel, before resting it on his
shoulder. After an intense football practice, the teammates
were packing up to leave the stadium.

"It's just taking me time to get the hang of that shit,"
Carl reasoned, shrugging.

Jason gave him a blank stare. "Dawg, you failed the
class *twice* already," he pointed out. "You're making me look
bad."

Carl laughed slightly. "Look, I need to pass the rest of
these tests, *including* the damn final, so I can pass this class.
I'm tryna graduate with you guys in the spring," he
explained, retrieving his gym bag from the floor. "Help a
linebacker out."

Jason shook his head as he and Carl made their way
towards the exit. "Fine," he reluctantly agreed. "But I swear
if you play around again, you're on your own."

Carl put both hands up. "You got my word, I'm gonna
focus this time," he promised.

"Fine, I gotta stop by the Math department to make sure
I don't have any other tutoring sessions today," Jason replied.

Carl raised an eyebrow. "Since when do you do tutor
sessions for the math department?"

"Since the department head asked me to help fill in for
the regular tutor while they're taking care of other stuff,"
Jason answered. "It's only for like a week, so I don't mind.
But if I don't, we can get started today."

Carl looked at Jason. "Today?" he asked. "It's Friday.
We can't start *tomorrow*?"

Jason stopped walking and stared daggers at his amused
teammate. "Never mind," he griped.

"I'm just joking," Carl laughed. "Just hit me up when you find out a time."

Jason nodded as he and Carl parted ways. After returning to his room to freshen up, Jason made his way to the Math building. He headed inside and made a beeline for the department office. "Do I have any tutoring sessions scheduled for today?" he politely asked the young, work-study student.

After doing a brief search on the laptop in front of her, she looked up and smiled. "No Jason, you're all clear for today," she informed. "Enjoy your weekend."

Jason returned her smile with one of his own. His response in kind was interrupted when he heard a familiar voice from across the room. *No, it can't be*, he thought, shaking his head. Turning to walk out of the office, he heard the voice again. Spinning around to face the sound, Jason's eyes widened at the sight of Paris emerging from a small office with the department head. "Oh fuck no!" he barked, gaining attention and frowns from the room.

"Mr. Adams, that language is not acceptable in this office," the department head scolded.

Jason's frown was fixed on Paris's smiling face as he tried to keep his temper in check. "I'm sorry about that Dr. Curtis," he apologized, before walking over to Paris and catching her by the arm. "Excuse us," he said, guiding her out of the office and across the hall.

"You could've just said 'hi,'" Paris sniped, jerking her arm from Jason's tight grip.

"What are you doing here?" Jason fumed. He had no intention of exchanging any pleasantries.

"You know what? Being rude is unbecoming of you," Paris snarled, folding her arms.

"Answer the damn question, Paris," he demanded.

Paris sucked her teeth. "I'm here to check out your school," she informed.

"For *what*?" Jason's patience was wearing thin.

"I'm thinking about transferring."

Jason's eyes widened in horror. "You *what*?" he snapped.

"I'm getting tired of WC University," she explained, unfazed by Jason's horrified reaction to her news. "They don't even have *dorms* there. I'm commuting back and forth from my parents' house... I want to have the whole college experience and...I like this school."

"You came to that conclusion from those few hours that you were here *weeks* ago?" Jason sneered, folding his arms. He knew Paris well enough to know that she had an ulterior motive. "What kind of bullshit are you trying to pull? What? I ignore you and now you show up at my school? The fuck is wrong with you?"

"Don't talk to me like that," Paris barked, pointing at him. Despite her reaction, Paris was actually enjoying the back and forth with Jason. *Damn, I almost forgot how sexy he is when he gets all intense.*

"You need to get your ass off of this campus," Jason ordered.

Paris stared at him, defiant. "You don't own the damn school, you can't kick me off."

Jason clasped his hands together in an effort to remain calm. "You heard what I said," he bristled, tone low and menacing. "And I mean *now*."

Paris stared at Jason's departing back, a scowl prominent on her face.

Upon exiting the building, Jason felt a knot in his stomach. "Shit," he fussed to himself.

Chapter 37

"What are we gonna do tonight?" Malajia asked, swirling some spaghetti onto a fork. "It's Friday and I'm bored."

"I'm going to go hang out with Will," Emily informed, grabbing a forkful of pasta from Malajia's plate.

"Don't touch my food," Malajia spat, pushing Emily's hand away.

"You're so stingy with food," Emily chuckled before placing the food into her mouth.

"As much food as she eats off the rest of our plates, she needs to stop," Alex commented, sitting at the dining room table with Malajia and Emily. Malajia simply rolled her eyes as she went back to eating. "Anyway," Alex began, placing her fork on Malajia's plate.

"What the hell, man!" Malajia barked, mouth full.

"Oh shut up," Alex ordered, retrieving some noodles. "And stop spitting on the table."

"I'll spit on *you*, how about *that*?" Malajia returned, reaching for a napkin. "Y'all dry as shit, where's Sidra and Chasity?"

"Sidra is at Mega-Mart and I think Chaz is at the gym," Alex answered.

Malajia tossed her fork down onto her plate. "Her skinny ass don't need to be at no damn gym, she *need* to be here rescuing me from *y'all* wack asses," Malajia spat. "And Sid know she don't need shit else from no damn Mega-Mart."

Emily shook her head. "Malajia, it's amazing how comfortable you are with insulting us while we're sitting right here," she said, laughter in her voice.

"She's triflin' isn't she?" Alex directed to Emily as she gestured her head towards Malajia.

"Hey, I don't sugar coat shit," Malajia threw back with a wave of her hand.

"Mel, please go call that man of yours so y'all can find something to do together," Alex begged, placing her head on the table. The sound of Malajia's voice was working her last nerve. "Spare us, please."

Pushing herself back from the table, Malajia sucked her teeth. "Fine, I could use some penis anyway," she jeered.

"Oh come on!" Alex loudly complained, jerking her head up at the same time that Emily busted out laughing. "God, you're such a freak."

Malajia laughed as she headed for the staircase.

"Carl, on second thought, we can start tutoring tomorrow," Jason said into his cell phone as he sat at his desk. "Okay cool. Later." Ending the call, Jason tossed the phone on his desk and ran his hand over his head. After unexpectantly running into Paris earlier that afternoon, and his inability to reach his mother again by phone, Jason was in no shape to concentrate on Advanced Calculus. "Fuck, I gotta tell Chaz," he griped to himself, putting his face in his hands. This was the last thing that he needed after his repeated efforts of reassuring Chasity that Paris wouldn't be a problem.

He rose from his seat and reached for his coat, when he heard a knock on his door. "Yeah?" he called. When no one answered, curiosity got the best of him and he headed for the door, opening it. "I swear to God," he fumed.

"Oh, you thought I was going to just leave without

telling you about yourself?" Paris said, pushing her way into the room.

Jason looked panicked. *Shit!* "How did you find out where I live?"

Paris gave a knowing look. "It's amazing how easy it is to find out where one of the most popular guys on this campus lives just by *asking* someone."

"Yo, you need to stop this!" Jason exploded. "First the texts and phone calls, then you send me packages, and *now* you show back up on my campus, talking about transferring. What the hell is *wrong* with you?!"

Paris put her hands up. "Okay...truth is...seeing you after all this time made me realize how much I miss you," she admitted much to Jason's confusion.

"I have a *girlfriend*," he reminded her, tone sharp. "And even if I *didn't*, I would *never* get back with you. After everything that you put me through, after what you've *done*."

"You mean to tell me that after *three years* of being together, you've *never* thought about what it would be like to get back together?" Paris asked. "I find that hard to believe."

"I don't give a shit *what* you believe," Jason threw back. "It's the truth. We were broken up a whole *year* before I left for college. That's *plenty* of time to get over someone. Not to mention that mentally, I was over your ass *before* we broke up."

"Oh please, we both know that's not true," Paris bristled. "You're just saying that because you're in your little *relationship* now," she taunted. "A shame she doesn't know that she's a rebound."

"Don't fuckin' bring my lady up," Jason seethed. "She was *never* a rebound. I already told you, I *been* over you."

Paris let out a quick sigh. *He never defended me like that*, she thought. "Look...I know you're still mad about what happened—"

"It doesn't even fuckin' matter," Jason argued.

"So, you're not even going to let me *apologize*?" she barked.

"For *what*? I don't *give* a fuck, just leave me alone," he barked back.

Paris folded her arms, staring at him.

Malajia, who was across the hall in Mark's room, frowned. After leaving Alex and Emily at her house nearly an hour ago, she was hanging out with Mark in his room, watching a movie. Hearing Jason's elevated voice from across the hall, she was curious as to what was going on. "Is Jason arguing with somebody?" she asked Mark, who was focused on the TV screen in front of him.

Mark shrugged. "Don't know."

Hearing a female voice arguing back, Malajia jumped up from the bed. "That don't sound like Chasity," she said.

"Maybe her voice changes when she gets mad," Mark replied, tone nonchalant.

Malajia stared at Mark in disbelief. "What?" she asked in confusion. "You sound stupid." She reached for her phone.

"What are you doing? We gotta finish watching the movie," Mark complained.

"Fuck that movie," Malajia hissed, waving her hand at him. She dialed a number and put her ear to the phone. "Chaz?" she said once the line picked up. "Where you at?... Oh yeah? Well bitch, you need to get your ass over here to the guys' house... Jason is arguing with some chick...Yes... I'm on it, get here."

"Not Chaz?" Mark assumed as Malajia disconnected the call.

"Nope," she answered, making a beeline for the door.

Mark hopped up from the bed. "Where are you going?"

"I'm about to see who the bitch is," Malajia spat. Mark, knowing how quickly the situation could escalate, grabbed Malajia from the door. "What the hell are you doing?" she fumed.

"Stay in here," Mark ordered, opening the door.

Malajia sucked her teeth. "Boy you got me chopped,"

she persisted, reaching for the doorknob.

"Malajia, I'm not playing, stay your ass in this room," Mark ordered with a seriousness that Malajia didn't expect. "Let me check out the situation."

Malajia was too annoyed to speak, but she complied and watched as Mark walked out of the room, shutting the door behind him.

Mark walked across the hall and stood outside of Jason's door. "Bro, you cool?" he asked.

Jason's face was red with anger. "No," he answered.

Mark peeked his head inside and saw a woman who was not Chasity, in Jason's room. "Uhhh," he began, unsure of what to say or what was going on.

"She was just leaving," Jason assured, reaching for Paris's arm.

"I'm not going *anywhere*," Paris refused, moving her arm out of Jason's reach. "We have shit to talk about."

Jason looked like he was about to explode. He heard the front door open, then heard someone running up the steps, but didn't pay it any mind; all he was focused on was getting Paris out of his room. "Paris, I swear to God, if you don't—" His words were interrupted when Chasity pushed past Mark and barged into the room. Clad in black leggings, black sweat jacket, sneakers and her hair pulled back in a ponytail, Chasity was already in fight mode. "Shit," Jason panicked. "Baby it's not—"

Chasity ignored Jason as she charged right for a startled Paris. Jason immediately moved in front of Chasity, backing her up against a wall. Mark, trying to keep the fight from happening, barged into the room and stood between Jason and Paris.

"Sis, I don't know who you are or what you *want*, but I suggest you move," Mark advised Paris.

"Oh really? You're gonna block me?!" Chasity yelled at Jason, putting her finger in his face. "You protecting this bitch?'"

"That's *not* what I'm doing," Jason argued, putting his hands out.

Hearing his room door open, Mark put his hand over his face. "Fuuuck," he groaned. He darted out of the room just in time to see Malajia charging. He grabbed hold of her and held on. "Naw, chill Mel. Chill!" he ordered, tightening his grip.

"Chasity, is it that damn Paris in there?!" Malajia yelled, repeatedly slapping Mark's hand in hopes that he would let go.

"Everybody chill out!" Jason boomed. "Paris, get the fuck out!'"

"You think I'm scared of her?" Paris questioned, approaching Jason's back.

"The bitch is walkin' up on her, she walkin' up on her!" Malajia bellowed, trying to get out of Mark's grip.

"Malajia, stop tryna bite me!" Mark hollered.

Chasity slapped Jason's hand away from her. "Move!" she ordered.

"No, I'm not letting you fight," he fumed.

"I said *move* goddamn it!" Chasity screamed, elbowing him in the stomach, causing him to double over. Seizing her opportunity, Chasity moved around him and stood in Paris's face. She frowned down the girls' length. As much as she wanted to drag Paris up and down the room at that exact moment, Chasity needed answers first.

"Before I fuck you up, you need to tell me *why* the hell you keep popping up," Chasity ordered, tone furious.

Paris smirked and folded her arms. "You seem like *such* an angry person," she observed. "That can't be healthy for your relationship."

"Don't concern yourself with *my* fuckin' relationship," Chasity barked. When Paris rolled her eyes, Chasity put her hand up. "That's right, Jason is in a relationship with *me*. So whatever you had in the past is over."

"If you believe that, why does my coming around make

you so mad?" Paris asked.

Chasity balled her fists up. "Because you're being disrespectful, you fuckin' weird ass bitch," she hurled back. "What kind of desperate shit are you on to keep pulling this? He doesn't want you. That should've been clear when he broke up with you."

"Jason didn't break up with me, I broke up with *him*," Paris revealed.

What the fuck?! He didn't tell me that shit! Chasity fumed. Despite the words in her head, she didn't let her confusion show. "That's not the goddamn point," she argued. "Stay the fuck away from my man! I'm *two* seconds from ringing your fuckin' neck."

"You think fighting me is going to solve your problem?" Paris barked.

"Sure will," Chasity assured.

"No, I don't think so," Paris confidently contradicted. "See you don't want anybody to know this, but you're insecure."

Chasity held a piercing look on her face, but didn't speak.

Gotcha, Paris thought. "Wow...I'm right huh?... It's a shame, you're too pretty to be insecure... But I get it," she taunted. "You see, you have to go around knowing that *I* was the first one to have Jason... That's right, *I* was his first. You have to sleep with him knowing that everything he's doing to *you*, *I* taught him."

Chasity felt like she was about to explode as her breathing became heavier and her hands started shaking. Chasity ignored the commotion from the hallway as Mark tried to keep Malajia contained; she ignored Jason's yelling at Paris to shut up and get out, she even ignored the fact that one of her arms was in Jason's grip. All she could see was Paris's smug face as she talked about her past with Jason. All she saw was red.

Paris laughed, "Poor baby... See, one never forgets their first love, and unfortunately for *you*, I'm very memorable."

Before Paris knew what was happening, Chasity's hand had reached out and grabbed hold of her neck. Snatching her other arm from Jason, Chasity closed her other hand over Paris's neck, gripping tight. Paris gasped for air, while trying to pry Chasity's hands off of her neck, only making Chasity squeeze harder. She didn't just want to beat her up; in that moment, Chasity wanted to kill her.

Shit, Mark thought. As mad as Chasity was, if they didn't get Chasity out of there, she would do something that she wouldn't be able to undo. Mark let go of Malajia and rushed over to help pry Chasity's hands from Paris's neck, while Jason grabbed Chasity from behind.

Mark, acting quickly, nudged the gasping Paris into Jason's closet, closing the door. Not for Chasity's safety, but for her own.

Jason backed Chasity against the wall once again; he was desperately trying to calm Chasity down, but wasn't succeeding. "Let go of me!" Chasity yelled at him.

Malajia stood by the door. In that moment, she forgot about Paris. She charged over to Jason and nudged him. "Let go of her," she ordered. When Jason didn't comply, and Chasity continued to scream and swing at him, Malajia gave Jason a hard shove with both of her hands. "Jason, let go of her!" she yelled.

"No! You just want her to fight," Jason argued.

"*No*, I *want* to get her out of here. She's pissed the fuck off you asshole!" Malajia hollered back, grabbing Chasity's arm and pulling her away from Jason when he finally released her. As much as Malajia was down to fight, she realized in that moment that it was in her best friend's best interest to be removed from the situation. "Let's go," Malajia ordered, tone stern.

Jason watched with agony as Malajia practically pushed the enraged Chasity out of his room. He was seething; he could have torn his entire house apart. Seeing Paris emerge from the closet, Jason stormed in her direction.

Mark, seeing the rage in Jason's eyes, blocked his path.

"Naw, you need to go cool off, bro,"

"I'm not gonna put my hands on her," Jason assured.

Mark put his hands up in surrender and moved aside.

Jason stared at Paris as she clutched her neck; she seemed like she was still struggling to catch her breath. "Get...the...fuck...out." He drew his words out slowly.

Paris reached her hand out to try to touch his arm. "Jason—"

"Now!" Jason yelled, jerking his hand out of her reach. The bass in his voice startled both Paris *and* Mark, who was still in the room with them.

"Well, damn," Mark commented, putting his hand over his chest.

"If you *ever* contact me, my *mother,* or come in contact with my girlfriend again, I *promise* you, I will fuck your life up," Jason hissed to Paris.

Paris just stood there, desperation on her face.

"Play with me if you want to," he threatened, before storming out of the room, leaving her and Mark standing there.

Paris glanced over at Mark, who shrugged. "You might wanna get to leavin'," he advised.

Chasity sat on her bed with her room door closed and her face in her hands. After being coerced away from her target and escorted by Malajia back to their house, Chasity went straight to her room, ignoring the concern and questions that the girls were hurling at her. She left it to Malajia to give them a briefing of the events.

Chasity's leg bounced the way it usually did when she was worked up. She felt angry, she felt powerless, she felt out of control, which were emotions that she was no stranger to. Feeling tears sting her eyes, she reached for her phone and dialed a number. Chasity wiped the tears away as the line rang.

"Mom?" she said, voice trembling. "Um...are you going

anywhere this weekend? ...I'm gonna come home
...Tonight... No, I'm not okay," she admitted, as more
tears fell. "I just need to come home for a few days... No, I
can drive... Okay, see you."

Once she ended the call with her mother, she just held
the phone tight. Chasity sat in silence as she heard a light tap
on the door.

"Chasity?" Jason softly called from the other side.

She closed her eyes and shook her head, not intending on
answering.

"The girls say that you're in here," he said. "Can you
just talk to me please?"

I should just leave and not even tell him, Chasity thought
as Jason knocked once again. Before she made up her mind
to answer, the doorknob twisted and Jason opened the door.

"I figured I'd give that a try," he said, walking in and
shutting the door behind him.

Chasity could've kicked herself for not locking her door.

Jason stood by the door, resisting the urge to go over and
sit next to Chasity, who wasn't making eye contact with him.
He just stared at her. "Chaz?" he called to her.

Chasity looked up at him. In that moment, Jason could
see the tears glistening in her eyes. He felt his heart drop.
"God...I'm so sorry," he said, putting his hand on his chest.
He moved to approach, but Chasity put her hand out.

"Don't," she ordered, tone filled with pain. Jason obeyed
her command and stood back against the door. "I have a
question," she began.

"Ask me," he prompted.

Chasity hesitated as she ran her hand over ponytail. "If
she didn't break up with you...would we even be together
right now?" she asked, unsure if she really wanted an answer.

Jason took a deep breath. "If she hadn't broken up with
me, I would've broken up with *her*," he assured. "The
relationship was already over...she just beat me to it."

Chasity just stared at him as he continued to speak.

"We were together throughout high school...Well, *most*

of it," he explained. "It started out okay, but as the relationship went on, I started seeing how immature she was—how *entitled*... Her parents had money, so she never felt that she had to work for anything, including *attention*. She hated when I did anything that didn't include her... She would start acting out by doing shit to make me jealous, that included flirting with other guys just to get a rise out of me." He took a deep breath. Jason hated even reliving his past relationship—he'd put it behind him and moved on— but he figured he needed to at that moment.

"Junior year, I really started focusing more on school and football... I knew that I had the opportunity to get a scholarship my senior year, so I wanted to make sure that I did everything that I could to get it... Paris didn't approve of that because that meant that the more time I focused on my future, the less time I had for her...and to get back at me...she cheated." Jason shook his head. "When I found out, on one hand I was angry but...in a way, I was *relieved* because it gave me the out that I was looking for... She was no good for me, and I gave her more time than she deserved.... When Paris realized that I knew what she had done, she panicked and figured she'd look better in the end if she was the one to end the relationship first, so that's what she did."

Chasity still sat in silence.

Jason studied her, wondering if she was going to respond. When Chasity didn't, he took another deep breath. "You were *never* my rebound baby... I'd *been* over her when I started pursuing you."

Chasity shook her head. "It was a simple 'yes' or 'no' question," she hissed. "Why are you telling me all of this?"

"I'm just trying to make you understand that I have *no* feelings for her," Jason stressed.

"It doesn't even matter at this point Jason. If it's not *her*, it'll be someone *else*," Chasity fumed.

Jason frowned. "You really believe that I would cheat on you?"

"I'm not saying—" Chasity sighed, wiping the wetness from her face. "This whole mess, started with your mother," she reminded. "She has it out for me. She brought Paris here to fuck shit up for us... It'll just be a matter of time before she pulls something like this again...and she *will* because she just *doesn't* want us to be together." More tears spilled. "Which means that as long as I'm with you, I have to watch my back, and I'm tired of doing that."

Jason just stood there taking everything that Chasity was throwing at him, trying to contain his own emotions as she poured out hers.

"I have been through *so* much shit in my life and I have been angry for *so* long and I've been trying to change," Chasity said. "I'm *trying* to just allow myself to be happy, but it's like every time I'm in a good place, something else happens that pulls me back to that angry, guarded, bitch that you and everybody *else* on this damn campus met four years ago." She took a breath as her voice broke. "I'm tired... I'm only twenty-one years old and I'm fuckin' *tired*. I don't want to keep having to deal with stupid shit...and I can't put myself in situations where I *have* to... I have to just back off."

Jason stood there, feeling a knot form in his throat as a dreaded thought roared in his head. "Chaz...are you breaking up with me?"

Chasity turned away from him. "I um...I just need time to think about things," she answered vaguely. "So I'm gonna go home for a few days... I'm leaving tonight."

Jason took a step towards her.

"I said *don't*," she spat, once again stopping him in his tracks.

"Please, don't do this," Jason begged. "I know that you're upset, and rightfully so. But I can fix this...I just—"

"Jason, you can't control anything," Chasity said. "I know you *want* to, but you *can't*. That has been made obvious and I have to think about *my* sanity right now."

"I get that, but don't *leave*," Jason pleaded. "You can't

just go without trying to resolve this... We're in a relationship and... I don't want to lose you—I'm *not* gonna lose you over no bullshit."

"Jason—"

"Don't leave," he interrupted. "At least not today."

Chasity felt a breakdown nearing. "I *have* to," she said, voice trembling. "Because if I don't get away from this campus, from *you* right now...I'm going to say something to you that we both may regret... You can take that however you want."

Jason stood there, feeling the sting of tears behind his eyes. Fortunately for him, they didn't surface. Not wanting to push Chasity any farther away than she already was, he decided to back off. He simply nodded before walking out the door, closing it behind him.

Chapter 38

"What are your plans for Thanksgiving?" Emily asked Will as they walked out of the movie theater. "It's next week."

"I hope to be securing an apartment," Will answered, resting his arm on Emily's shoulder as the pair strolled through the mall food court. Emily, deciding not to spend her Saturday just milling around the house, journeyed to Will's job and waited for him to get off.

Emily's smile was bright. "Seriously? You found a place?" she beamed. She knew how much Will was looking forward to getting a place for him and his son.

"I've been looking at a couple," he admitted, pointing to an empty table where they both walked over to. "Just trying to figure out what I can afford, you know?"

Emily nodded as she sat in the seat across from him. "Yeah, I get it," she said, running her hand along the edge of the table. "Just don't rush into anything. I'm sure your parents won't mind you staying longer if you need to"

"My parents already want me to stay," Will said. "But the little man and I need our own space."

"I understand," Emily replied, folding her arms on the table. "Well, when you move, maybe I could help you decorate."

Will smiled at the thought. "When I move, maybe I can cook for you," he proposed.

"You don't cook," she teased, earning a deep laugh from him.

"I can learn though," he chuckled. The pair sat in silence for a few moments. "Speaking of Thanksgiving, what are *your* plans?"

Emily sighed heavily. "I um…I think I'm just going to stay on campus for the break."

Will looked confused. "Why would you do that?" he asked. "I thought you were planning on spending the break with your brothers," he added, recalling a conversation with Emily on the subject weeks ago.

Emily shrugged. "I just don't really feel like being in Jersey."

"None of your friends invited you to stay with them?"

"*Sure* they did. I was at Alex's house *last* year," she replied, tone sullen.

"But?" Will prompted.

Emily hesitated; she wondered if she should even say what she was thinking. "Truth is…I miss my Mom, and being in Jersey for the holiday…" She rubbed her arm. "I just feel like…if I'm back home I should be able to go see her and I can't… My Dad has to travel, and I'd just rather stay on campus."

Will tilted his head as he shot Emily a sympathetic look. "I'm sorry Em," he said.

"I'm fine," she assured. "I just wish my friends would stay with me you know? I tried asking them, but I don't think it's gonna happen."

"Did you tell them the reason why you're staying?" he asked. "The *real* reason?"

Emily slowly shook her head. "They might think I'm crazy…or stupid."

"I think you should give them more credit," Will advised. "If you're honest, they might change their minds about going home."

Emily pushed some of her hair behind her ears as she shrugged again.

Will reached out and touched Emily's arm. "Maybe I can come by and keep you company for a little bit one of those days. I could pick up dinner," he offered.

Emily managed a smile. She had to admit, the chance to spend some more time with Will was making her feel much better about her decision to stay. "That sounds good," she said.

Jason, clad in his football uniform, paced the floor of the stadium locker room. He'd been going over the same path for the past half hour.

"Jase, you're gonna burn a hole in the floor," Carl joked, following Jason's stride with his eyes.

Jason ignored his teammate as he continued to pace.

Carl set his shoulder pads on a bench. "So we lost the game…it wasn't the first."

Jason halted his pace. "It's the first game that we lost all season," he seethed, kicking a trashcan over.

"Bro, it *happens*," Carl tried to console him. "The other team was just better."

Jason started pacing again. He knew that was only half the reason for their loss. "It's *my* fault."

"Nobody believes that," Carl assured him.

"I don't care *what* they believe," Jason fussed. "It's the truth."

After the blow up the previous evening, and after Chasity left campus for the weekend, Jason found himself unable to focus, unable to function, unable to sleep. He had spent the rest of Friday night locked in his room, held up in his bed until the sunlight peered through the blinds and forced him from his bed the next morning. Jason didn't have the endurance or the mindset to effectively play in the football game that afternoon. His distraction was a contributing factor in a loss for the team.

"Look, we have another game in two weeks, then the season will be over," Carl pointed out. "Fresh start next season."

Jason shot Carl a glance. "This is my *last* season, remember?" he reminded him. "I graduate next semester."

"Oh yeah," Carl replied, scratching his head. "You know if you fail a couple of those classes, you can drag this football thing out another season," he attempted to joke.

Jason ignored Carl's pointless comment as he continued to pace. He couldn't figure out what was worse: the fact that he lost the game in the first place, or the fact that he lost the game in front of his father, who had finally been able to make it out. Jason glanced over at the door as his coach stuck his head inside. "Jason, your father is out here. He wants to speak to you."

Jason let out a sigh; he had hoped that his father would have just left right away. He wasn't in the mood to talk to anybody at that point. "You can send him in," he said. The coach nodded and signaled for the remaining players to leave the room to give Jason some privacy.

Jason removed his shoulder pads and set them on the floor next to his locker, as his father walked in. He stared at his father and folded his arms, unable to say anything.

"Are you okay?" Mr. Adams asked, voice filled with concern.

Jason shook his head. "Can't say that I am," he answered honestly.

Mr. Adams sighed as he ran his hand along the back of his neck. "It's okay to lose sometimes," he replied. "It's not the end of the world."

"I see that Mom didn't come with you," he spat, completely ignoring his father's consoling.

"No...she said she had some things to do."

"Sure, because it would've been too much for her to face me after doing what she did," Jason sneered, much to his father's confusion.

"What are you talking about?" he asked.

"I wasn't going to tell you this because...I thought it would be better if you didn't know what your wife was up to, but I don't really care anymore."

"Why are you talking about your mother like that?" Mr. Adams asked, voice stern.

"My *mother* has made it clear that she doesn't give a damn about me," Jason hissed. "You know what she did? That game that you couldn't make weeks ago, the one where you said Mom was coming alone?"

Mr. Adams nodded.

"Well she *didn't* come alone," Jason revealed. "No, she managed to pull Paris out of a hole somewhere and she brought *her*."

Mr. Adams's eyes widened. "Paris?" he asked. "As in your ex?"

"That's the same, damn one," Jason vented. "She brought her up here to cause a rift between me and Chasity...and it worked. I don't think that Chasity even wants to *be* with me anymore."

Mr. Adams, in disbelief that his wife of twenty-five years would ever pull something like this, especially on their son, reached for his cell phone.

"Dad, you're wasting your time calling her, I have nothing to say."

"No? Well, *I* do," Mr. Adams fumed as he called his wife

Jason smirked as his father waited for the line to pick up. "Let me guess, no answer," he said as he watched his father put the phone back into his pocket.

"Nope."

"Yeah, figured. She knows you're with *me*," Jason spat, retrieving his keys from his locker. "When you go home, just be sure to tell Mom that I said, thank you for ruining my life and I hope that she's happy."

Mr. Adams faced Jason's departing back as he watched his son make his way towards the door. "Jason—"

Jason sighed as he turned around. "Dad please don't try to justify anything," he said.

"I wasn't *going* to."

"And I don't need any advice either," Jason added. He looked away as his father held a sympathetic gaze on him. "I'm sorry… I don't mean to be mean, but I just need to be alone right now… Have a safe trip home." Jason didn't give his father the chance to respond as he left the locker room.

Trisha picked up her mimosa and took a quick sip, before setting the glass back down on the table. "Are you going to touch your food?" she asked Chasity, who was in the seat across from her.

"I *did*," Chasity replied, tone dry as she poked at her French toast with her fork.

"Are you going to *eat* it?" Trisha corrected.

"Eventually," Chasity replied. Her appetite was nonexistent. She'd returned home the previous evening after her blow up with Paris, and dreaded conversation with Jason. Chasity spent most of the evening being held by her mother as she cried out her frustrations. The next afternoon, Trisha—determined to get Chasity to cheer up—had dragged her to brunch at an upscale restaurant in Center City.

Trisha grabbed Chasity's glass of mimosa and pushed it in her direction. "Here, sip on this," she urged.

Chasity reluctantly took the glass and took a sip.

Trisha folded her arms on the table as she stared at Chasity. "So…I know you didn't want to talk about what had you so upset last night," she began. "But, I think it's time you tell me *now*." Trisha recalled the helplessness that she felt as she held Chasity in her arms the night before. She had tried to get Chasity to tell her what was wrong, but she never got an answer; all she got was tears.

Chasity took a deep breath. "Long story short…Jason's mother hates me so she brought his ex-girlfriend to school for one of Jason's games to get to me. The stupid bitch kept contacting him after that, sending him old photos and shit… Yesterday she came back to the school; she and I got into it, then I argued with Jason and left."

Trisha sat in stunned silence at Chasity's revelation. She admitted that she hadn't kept as many tabs on Chasity's life as she had in the past, due to trying to cope with her loss. But she never imagined that she could miss so much.

"Wait…what?" she replied finally, reaching for her glass. "I need another damn sip of this," she said.

Chasity shook her head.

Trisha clasped her hands together in an effort to keep her composure once she set her glass back down. "Okay, *first* of all, what is his mother's issue with you?"

"She doesn't want me with Jason," Chasity replied honestly.

"Why not?" Trisha fumed.

"She thinks I'm just bad for him," Chasity answered.

"She needs to carry her ass to hell with that shit," Trisha seethed. "What does *Jason* say about that? What does he *do* about that?"

"He can't do much," Chasity said, shrugging. "At the end of the day, he can't change her mind… He tries to be a buffer between us but…sometimes he just can't."

"Okay, I'll get back to his mom in a minute," Trisha said, putting her hand up. "I want to know the deal with this damn ex of his."

"I just told you," Chasity replied, voice tired. "She kept contacting him, he told her to stop and she wouldn't. Jason told me not to worry about it, but then the bitch showed up at school and…she taunted me and I lost it."

"You fought her?"

Chasity hesitated for a moment. "I choked her a little…a *lot* before they broke it up," she revealed.

Trisha pinched the bridge of her nose as she tried to gather her thoughts. This was all too much at once. "I'm going to give you some advice that I want you to *really* listen to," she began.

Chasity sat in anticipation.

"There will *always* be girls who show an interest in your man," Trisha stated matter-of-factly. "That is the downside to being with a man that not *only* is physically attractive, but is loving, attentive *and* educated… They will come out of the woodworks…that being *said*, don't fight a girl over it."

Chasity frowned in confusion. "Say *what* now?"

"You heard me."

"So, I'm just supposed to let these damn girls disrespect me like that?" Chasity asked in disbelief.

"They're not worth it," Trisha pressed, voice stern. "Now as far as Jase's little triflin' ex, if the girl got in your face, then you did what you had to do… But just know that these girls out here will *always* test you, but you can't feed into that shit," she advised. "You have come *too* far and have *too* bright a future to stoop to their level… As disrespectful as it is to go after someone else's man…and it *is* disrespectful…those girls don't owe you shit. They're not your family, they're not your friends… The *only* person who owes it to you to be faithful and to not disrespect you, is Jason."

Chasity rolled her eyes as she listened to Trisha continue.

"As long as *he* doesn't entertain that shit, and as long as you have trust and a solid relationship, you don't have anything to worry about."

"That's easier said than done," Chasity argued. "It's not in my nature to let shit slide like that."

"If you want peace…you *have* to learn how to," Trisha advised. "Everything doesn't need a raging reaction, baby."

Chasity folded her arms and sighed as she sat back in her seat.

"You don't think that Jason has to deal with guys liking *you*?" Trisha asked.

"None of them ever texted me, or got in his damn face," Chasity shot back. "'Cause I'd shut that shit down immediately."

"I hear what you're saying," Trisha assured. "I get your frustration with him. You feel that he could've handled the whole thing better."

"Somewhat."

"You may be right… Or maybe, he did all that he *could* do. And I'm sure that at this very moment, Jason feels just as upset as *you* are over all of this," Trisha said. "He loves you Chasity, and you love him. This is not the time to break your relationship apart."

"I hear what you're saying," Chasity replied. "I just need…a minute."

Trisha nodded. "Take your minute, but talk to him."

"I will," Chasity promised.

"Now…back to his mother," Trisha began, bitterness in her voice. "Now *that* right there, is unacceptable. A random bitch trying to come between you two is one thing, but his own *mother*? …No. Now I know that Jason doesn't want to snap out on his mother, but *I'll* have no problem doing it."

"I'll deal with it."

"Oh no you *won't*," Trisha denied. "If Jason can't handle it, *I'll* handle it. She's not gonna keep messing with you," she fumed. "Yeah, I think me and *Mrs. Adams* need to have a little chat, mother to mother. I'm not playing games here. I'll slap her."

"What happened to not stooping to no levels?" Chasity jeered.

"*You* don't. *I've* reached my full potential already. I'm able to stoop as low as I want," Trisha returned. "Just say the word and I'll check her ass."

Chasity smirked.

Trisha pointed to Chasity's uneaten food with her fork. "Now eat your food, before I check *you*," she ordered.

Jason laid in his bed Sunday evening. The images on the TV screen near him were steady moving, but Jason wasn't paying attention; he was too busy staring up at the ceiling. After having just ended a two-hour long conversation with his father moments before, Jason was mentally drained.

He sat up in bed when he heard a knock. "Come in," he

called, putting the TV on mute. He was skeptical when he saw Malajia walk in, holding a foil-covered plate.

"Hey Jase, you look terrible," Malajia bluntly stated.

"Thanks," Jason jeered, adjusting his white t-shirt. "What brings you by?"

Malajia looked down at the plate in her hands. "We made burritos over at the house, so I brought you some," she replied, holding the plate out in front of her. "The guys said you barely left the room...so I figured you haven't eaten much."

Jason managed a half smile as he took the plate from Malajia's hand. "I haven't," he admitted.

Malajia nodded. "Yeah, and if Chaz were here, she'd bring you something, so I'm just filling in for her right now."

If Chaz was here, I wouldn't be feeling this low, he thought. "Thanks. I appreciate it," he replied.

Malajia gave a nod as she turned to walk out the room, but stopped. She turned around to face him as he started removing the foil from the plate.

"Look, my bad for hitting you the other day," she began. Jason glanced up at her. "...and for calling you an asshole...and for making faces at you and calling you a stupid idiot," she apologized.

Jason frowned. "When did you make faces at me and call me a stupid idiot?" he wondered.

Malajia held a blank stare on her face for a moment. "Oh, that part was behind your back," she recalled, snapping her fingers.

Jason shook his head. "Listen, I get why you did...we're cool."

Malajia took a deep breath. "Cool," she looked down at her hands. "I'm just gonna say this and I'm gonna go."

Jason stared up at her. "Okay."

"In my opinion...things didn't have to go that far," Malajia started. "I feel like things could've been handled *way* before it got to this point. You can't put Chaz in situations like that. You wouldn't want that done to *you*."

"What exactly do you think I *did*?" Jason asked, curious, earning an eye roll from Malajia. "Despite what you *think*, I wasn't entertaining that. I wasn't leading her on. I was telling her to back off and I have told my mom to back off in the past... I tried."

Malajia put her hands up in surrender. "Okay...I hear you," she relented.

"I *do* get why you feel that way though," Jason replied. There was no point being upset with Malajia. He knew that it was coming from a loving place. "I know you're just being a good friend to Chasity."

"I'm *your* friend *too*," Malajia clarified. "I don't want to see *you* hurt or upset *either*. But even though I may be wrong in what I feel, I just had to say something," she explained. "You know I gotta check y'all asses every now and then... This group don't know how to act."

Jason chuckled. "Thanks again for the food," he said, grateful. "I'll bring your plate back when I'm done."

Malajia waved her hand at him. "Boy, ain't nobody thinkin' 'bout that scraped up, plastic ass plate," she jeered.

As Malajia went to walk out, Jason called her, so she turned back around. "Have you talked to her?" he asked.

Malajia stared at him and opened her mouth to speak, but then closed it.

Jason, knowing what that meant, just looked down at his plate. "If you talk to her again, can you tell her..." he sighed. "Never mind, I'll wait until I see her."

"Okay," Malajia replied, fiddling with her fingers. She felt bad; Jason looked broken to her. "She said she'll probably be back before her first class tomorrow," she revealed.

Jason gave a nod as Malajia walked out the door. He let out a long, deep sigh, before removing the rest of the foil from the plate.

Chapter 39

"Two more muthafuckin' days to go before break!" Mark bellowed as he emerged from the History building after his last class of the day.

"Was all that necessary?" Alex asked, not hiding her annoyance as she headed down the building steps.

"Yep, I'm over these damn classes...and I'm ready for some good food," Mark replied.

"Greedy," Alex laughed. "I take it you're going home for break?"

Mark glanced at Alex as the two friends navigated the crowded path through campus. "Why *wouldn't* I?" he scoffed. "I do it every year... Why? You're *not*?"

Alex shrugged, glancing up at the clear blue sky. "I don't know yet," she answered honestly. "Emily kind of suggested that we stay on campus and spend the holiday together, since it will be our last one in college."

Mark made a face. "Why would she want to stay *here*?" he asked. "This campus gonna be dead as shit... Nobody but the damn Dean will be here, 'cause you know he don't have a damn life."

Alex snickered as she playfully backhanded Mark on his chest. "Leave that lonely man alone," she teased. "No, but I think Em is on to something here," she added, pushing some hair from her face. "We always end up spending part of

Thanksgiving break together *anyway*…well most of the time. What's wrong with spending the full break together?"

"The lack of that good ole *home cooking* is what's wrong," Mark countered, gesturing to a nearby classmate. "Y'all girls can't cook like my mom."

Alex shot him a challenging look as she placed a hand on her hip. "I'm pretty sure if we all stayed, we could throw a Thanksgiving dinner together."

"See, you already fuckin' shit up," Mark rebuffed, shaking his hand in her direction. "You can't just *throw* Thanksgiving dinner together."

Alex sucked her teeth as she waved a dismissive hand at him. "Whatever," she grumbled as they continued on. "I still say we should try it."

Emily brushed her straightened hair off of her face and pulled it back into a low ponytail, before going back to writing in her notebook. "Can't believe I have a test the week of Thanksgiving," she fussed to herself, surveying the paragraphs on the paper in front of her. "I hate World History."

The door flew open and Malajia barged in. "Hey Harris, I need to use your stapler real quick," she announced.

Emily glanced up at her once the initial startle wore off. "You almost gave me a heart attack," she griped, holding her hand to her sweatshirt-covered chest.

"My bad," Malajia giggled.

Emily reached for the pink stapler on her desk. "What happened to *yours*? I saw you with it yesterday."

"I ran out of staples, Miss twenty questions," Malajia griped.

Perplexity masked Emily's face. "I only asked *one*, though," she replied.

"Less talking, more handing me the stapler," Malajia urged, holding her hand out. Emily shook her head, placing the stapler in Malajia's hand. "Thanks, I won't be long with it," Malajia promised. "I just need to staple this stupid homework that I have to turn in to stupid Professor Miller, for my stupid Business Ethics class," she groused.

Emily held a blank stare as Malajia ranted.

"The whole idea of doing this much work before the holiday is—"

"Stupid?" Emily finished, laughter in her voice.

"Yeah, *exactly*," Malajia complained. Before Malajia could say another word, Sidra barged through the door, tossed her books and purse on the floor, then kicked them across the room.

Her actions had Emily and Malajia baffled; they were both wide-eyed. "Um…you cool Princess?" Malajia asked finally.

Sidra spun around, placing her hands on her hips in a huff. "No, no Malajia, I'm *not* cool."

Malajia made a face at Sidra's tone. "Um, eww to your funky ass response," she sniped.

Emily tapped Malajia on her arm in an effort to keep her quiet. "What's wrong Sid?" she asked, tone caring.

Sidra let out a sigh. "Let's just say that I'll be staying here with *you* on campus for Thanksgiving," she revealed.

Emily let out a yelp of excitement at Sidra's news, before immediately regretting it. "Sorry…um…*why?*"

Sidra flopped down on her bed. "My mother—*my* mother, invited that…she-devil to my house for Thanksgiving dinner," she fumed.

"Ooooh, Marcus's little fiancé, huh?" Malajia assumed, leaning up against Sidra's desk. "He's still planning on marrying her?"

"Unfortunately, *yes*," Sidra sneered.

"Well Sid, you already said that you might see her there anyway," Malajia pointed out, recalling one of their previous conversations on the subject.

"Yes, I know, but Mama actually *invited* her," Sidra hissed. "I expected Marcus to sneak her over but…" she let out a loud sigh. "Look, me and Mama were in agreement, we *both* hated her. And *now* she wants to have that bitch in *my* house, up in *my* face for Thanksgiving…in *my* kitchen, baking pies and shit."

"Well Sidra, I'm sure your mother is only trying to make peace with India because she'll be her daughter-in-law," Emily pointed out.

"*I'm* her only damn daughter!" Sidra erupted, slapping her hand on her bed. "*I'm* the only one that should be baking pies in my kitchen… *I* make the damn pies!"

Emily glanced at Malajia, who had her hand over her face, laughing. "Malajia," Emily warned.

Malajia put her hands up as she tried to stop laughing. She then walked over and sat next to Sidra and put her arms around her. "Aww, somebody's jealous," she teased.

"That's not it, and you *know* that," Sidra ground out. "She's bad for my brother."

Malajia pulled Sidra close to her. "Yes…but sweetie, you know that Marcus is gonna do what he wants to do anyway… He's going to marry that train wreck and you just have to be supportive."

Sidra leaned her head on Malajia's shoulder. "I don't *wanna* be supportive… I *wanna* be mean...and petty," she pouted, earning a snicker from Emily. "I hate my brother's choices in women." Sidra lifted her head. "Emily, are you and Will in an *actual* relationship or just casually dating?"

Emily eyed Sidra, skeptical. "We're good friends," she answered. It was true, she and Will never established relationship status. As they discussed previously, both were comfortable just building their friendship for the time being.

Sidra adjusted her position on her bed. "Okay so, since you're technically still single, why don't you date one of my other brothers, so I can have a normal sister-in-law."

Emily's eyes widened. "Uh…no," she refused.

Sidra sighed. "Maybe I can see if Alex—"

"Sidra, nobody wants to date your brothers," Malajia quickly and bluntly stated.

Sidra couldn't help but chuckle at Malajia's honesty. She

tossed her arms in the air. "Fine... So Em, it's me and you on campus."

"Yay," Emily squealed, clapping her hands together. She turned to Malajia. "Mel, you might as well stay too," she smiled, hopeful.

Malajia glanced from Emily to Sidra, disgust on her face. "Ugh," she scoffed.

"Sidra called, she asked us to come over to their house," David informed the other guys as they sat in their living room.

"I don't feel like leaving," Mark muttered. "What the hell do they want?"

"Who knows," David shrugged. "Shall we go?"

"*You* go," Mark refused, flagging David with his hand. "*I'm* chillin'."

Josh stood up and stretched. "Just come on, you already know we're gonna get yelled at if we don't go," he pointed out.

Mark flipped Josh the finger. "Nope."

Josh rolled his eyes and looked at Jason. "You coming Jase?"

Jason shook his head, staring at the TV screen. "No," he sulked. Jason was in no mood for whatever Sidra had planned. He was upset that Chasity had returned to campus earlier that morning and he hadn't seen or talked to her. He wasn't sure if he was more upset at *her* for not calling him, or at him*self* for being too afraid to call *her*.

Josh shrugged as he and David headed for the door. Before they could open it, the doorknob turned, and Chasity strolled in.

"Chaz, what's up?" Josh stammered, seeing the annoyed look on her face.

Jason immediately sat up straight and looked in her direction when he heard her name.

"Sidra said get y'all asses over to the house before she

comes over and starts screaming," Chasity ground out, gesturing towards the door.

Mark sucked his teeth as Josh and David walked out of the door. "Man, I'm not scared of no damn Sidra," he grunted, remaining seated. "They can tell me what she wants later."

Chasity folded her arms, fixing a stern gaze on Mark. "Yeah we thought you might say that," she replied. "That's why Malajia said if you don't take your black ass across that damn street, she's holding out for a week."

Mark immediately jumped up from the couch. "She always gotta go overboard," he fussed, darting out of the house and leaving Jason and Chasity alone.

Chasity shook her head as she shut the door behind Mark. Jason stood up and they faced each other. "You got back earlier?" he asked after a few moments of silence.

Chasity nodded.

Jason looked down at the floor for a moment. "Did you get what you needed when you left?" he asked.

Chasity once again nodded.

Jason didn't know what to make of Chasity's silence. He didn't know if he should be angry or scared of what decision she had made during her weekend away. "So...are we...okay?"

Chasity looked down at her hands for what seemed like forever. She realized after getting a reality check from her mother, that her energy should be focused on continuing to strengthen their relationship, and not on the people who try to weaken it. Chasity, after fixing her gaze upon a desperate looking Jason, nodded a third time.

Jason let out a sigh of relief. He held his arms out and on instinct, Chasity crossed the room and the couple embraced.

"I'm sorry about everything," Jason said, burying his face in her hair. "I never wanted to put you in that situation."

"I know," Chasity replied, holding on to him as she felt his arms tighten around her. "I know it's not your fault."

Jason closed his eyes as he held on to her. Hearing her

say that she didn't blame him, which was something that he had been carrying around with him, was a relief. He doubted Chasity really knew how much of a relief it was to him.

"Just because *y'all* wanna stay on campus for Thanksgiving, you expect the *rest* of us to?" Mark bristled as Malajia squeezed next to him on the couch.

Sidra rolled her eyes. "Why do you always have to be so damn difficult?" she hissed.

"'Cause you know it's gonna be corny here," Mark countered. Mark regretted leaving the comfort of his couch, just to go to the girls' house to be coerced into forfeiting Thanksgiving at home, to stay on campus instead.

Emily placed her cup of soda on the table in front of her, and sat down in the seat. "Come on, I don't think it'll be that bad," she said.

"Please," Mark scoffed, folding his arms.

Sidra sucked her teeth at Mark. "Whatever. Look, Alex and Josh already agreed to stay with me and Emily," she informed. "We just need the rest of you guys to get on board."

"Of *course* Josh's whipped ass did," Mark hissed.

Josh, who was seated on the arm of the couch, reached over and smacked Mark in the back of the head. "Shut your ignorant ass up," he scolded as Mark let out a yelp. "I usually spend Thanksgiving with you guys *anyway*, so I figured staying would be best."

Mark gestured to Josh with his thumb, as he directed his gaze to the rest of the group. "Naw, he stayin' 'cause Sidra said so and shit," he jeered.

Josh sucked his teeth.

"Look," Alex put in, tired of Mark's comments. "I think—" The door opening interrupted her words. The group turned around to see Chasity and Jason walking in, holding hands.

"Awww, you two made up?" Emily gushed.

"Yeah," Jason smiled, shutting the door behind them.

"About time," Mark commented. "I was tired of seeing you mope around the damn house," he said to Jason.

"And we were tired of hating you, Jase," Malajia added.

"Well damn," Jason chortled.

"Jason, ignore her, nobody hated you," Alex assured. "We may have been *annoyed* at that little ex—"

"How about we just don't mention that bitch, okay," Chasity quickly said, sitting on a chair.

"Yes, *please*," Jason added. If he didn't hear about Paris for the rest of his life, it would be too soon for him.

"Just so you know Chaz, I was all for you choking that bitch," Malajia said.

"Malajia, just drop it alright," Chasity requested. She was tired of the entire situation.

Malajia put her hands up. "You got it, boo."

"Anyway, glad that things are back to normal," Sidra said. "Jase, some of us are staying on campus for Thanksgiving and we're trying to get the rest of you guys to stay."

Jason shrugged. "I'll stay," he answered, much to the shock of some and delight of others.

"Really?" Alex asked.

"Yeah...I'm not in the mood to be home right now," he put out. Although he wouldn't mind being home with his father and little brother, the tension between him and his mother overruled any thoughts of doing so.

David pushed his glasses up on his nose. "You guys know I'm in," he smiled, he rubbed the back of his neck. "Can I invite Nicole? ...She's staying too. Her grandparents are traveling."

"Naw, ain't no extras," Mark denied, pointing at David.

"You're not even *staying*, so what does it matter?" David threw back.

"He's staying," Malajia promised.

Mark shot her a glance. "How you gonna speak for me?" he spat.

Malajia poked him in the forehead. "If *I'm* staying, *you're* staying," she demanded. "Just get over it."

Mark folded his arms and let out a quick huff.

"Who's whipped *now*?" Josh mocked, folding his arms. Mark made a face at him in retaliation.

"So, you *did* decide to stay after all, huh?" Emily asked Malajia.

"Yeah, man," Malajia huffed, then turned to Chasity. "*You* might as well stay too."

Chasity ran her hands through her hair. "Fine," she sighed. A response that caught them off guard.

"What? No arguing, no cussing? No throwing stuff?" Alex reacted, amused. Chasity stared at her. "I can honestly say that I am speechless Parker."

"You sure about that?" Chasity sniped. "I can't tell by the running of your wide ass mouth."

Alex laughed.

"Anyway, it's not like I have anywhere special to be."

"So, it's settled, we're all staying," Emily gushed. *This is just what I need, right now.*

"We'll go to the store sometime tomorrow and get the stuff we need to make a full Thanksgiving dinner," Alex beamed. Like Emily, she was excited to be staying on campus to spend the holiday with her second family. "The works, turkey, baked mac and cheese—"

"The turkey ain't even gonna be *thawed* in time," Mark complained, running his hand over his head.

Malajia snickered as she drank some of her water.

Alex rolled her eyes. "God, you know what? Fine, we can go *today* and get one, so it can start thawing," she hissed. "Always whining." She put a hand up. "We can all pick a dish and make it—"

"I pick cranberry sauce," Malajia quickly stated, her hand shooting up.

"Malajia, no," Alex shot down. "That doesn't require anything but opening those cans."

Malajia made a face. "No, I'm gonna try to make it from

scratch," she clarified. "Who still eats that nasty ass jelly mold from a can?"

"Alex," Chasity jeered. "Can grooves be all in it and shit."

Jason snickered.

Alex put her hand up. "Wait, so you mean to tell me that nobody else eats cranberry sauce out of the can?" she wondered.

"I don't even *like* the stuff," Sidra said. "But even if I *did*...I wouldn't."

"Alex eat cranberry flavored gelatin and shit," Mark laughed. "Ole poor ass."

"Stop it guys, plenty of people eat it," Emily put in. "*I* eat it, and I actually like it."

"It's *nasty,*" Malajia barked. "So, like I said, I got cranberry sauce."

"Just don't put carrots in it," Chasity sneered to Malajia. "You know how your people do."

Malajia opened her mouth to speak, then dissolved into laughter. "I have no comeback 'cause it's true. Mom stays trying to put carrots in shit."

"Hey wait a minute, how about the losing trick or treat teams, make every-damn-thing since you guys owe us a victory meal *anyway,*" Sidra proposed; her suggestion was met with disdain.

"Bullshit bitch," Chasity snarled.

"Yeah, you can't pick Thanksgiving dinner as a victory dinner," Jason added.

"Naw, that ain't happenin'," Mark refused.

"She tryna get out of doing shit 'cause she mad her Mom ain't let her make the pies this year and shit," Malajia put in.

Sidra's eyes widened. "That was uncalled for," she ground out through clenched teeth.

"Hey, hey!" Alex interrupted, standing from her seat. "We're not gonna do this. No arguing," she chided. "While I *do* agree that you guys still owe us a victory dinner, Thanksgiving is *not* the time to do it. We're going to do this

together. Agreed?"
"Agreed," Emily smiled.

Chapter 40

"Emily! Alex is down here messing with your stuffing!" Malajia shouted from the kitchen.

"I didn't touch it!" Alex wailed.

Trotting down the stairs, Emily let out a small laugh. "What is all the hollering about?" she asked.

"Alex is down here fuckin' with people's food," Malajia told, taking the lid off of her cranberry sauce which was simmering on the stove.

Thanksgiving morning was finally upon the group, and instead of being at their respective homes helping their families' cook the meal, the group was on campus, in their house, preparing the meal themselves. The process was turning out to be more difficult than they'd imagined. It was only one o'clock in the afternoon, and they were already fed up.

Alex tossed a discarded piece of raw cabbage at the back of Malajia's head. "You're always lying," she ground out.

Emily walked over to the counter and peered into a large bowl that she had previously filled with her stuffing ingredients before heading upstairs. "I don't see anything different about it," she shrugged.

"That's because she's *lying*, Emily," Alex spat, rinsing the last of her chopped cabbage in the sink. "I didn't go *near* your stuffing."

Malajia sucked her teeth as she walked over to Chasity, who was putting the last of her shredded cheese into her large pan of baked macaroni and cheese. Malajia examined the pan and pointed to it. "That ain't enough cheese," she griped.

Chasity stopped what she was doing and regarded Malajia with anger. She wasn't in the mood for Malajia's critique on her food. Having had to run to the store just that morning for extra cheese, Chasity could have stuffed the plastic bags that the cheese came in down Malajia's throat.

"Get the fuck away from me Malajia," Chasity grunted after a few seconds.

"Malajia, leave the girl alone," Alex advised. "*You're* the reason she had to go to that store earlier. You just *had* to have tacos last night."

Malajia rolled her eyes as Chasity grabbed the heavy pan off of the counter. "Mind your business and add some more salt to that bland ass cabbage you got over there," she mocked.

"You might not want to talk about food, because we have *yet* to taste that cranberry sauce you call yourself making," Alex countered.

"Don't you worry, that sauce is gonna be hittin'," Malajia said, confident. "I'm adding my own spin on the recipe and everything."

"Didn't the recipe call for orange juice?" Chasity asked, recalling what Malajia showed her the night before.

"So?" Malajia wondered.

"There's no damn orange juice in the house."

"And?" Malajia barked. "We got *oranges*, I told you, I got this."

Emily giggled. "Chaz, don't you have to put your mac and cheese in the guys' oven?" she asked.

"I'm going, I'm going," Chasity assured, tone unenthused.

"Ahhh, that's why you gotta go out in the cold," Malajia teased.

Chasity glanced over at Malajia's pot; it had started smoking. "Your cranberries are burning."

"Ooh!" Malajia panicked, rushing over to stir the sauce.

Mark walked in as Chasity was walking out. "Ooh, is

that the baked mac and cheese?" Mark asked, leaning close to the pan.

"Move," Chasity barked, continuing on her way.

Unfazed by Chasity's reaction, Mark strolled in and headed right for Alex's pot of cabbage. He frowned. "No greens?!" he bellowed.

Alex nudged him with her elbow. "No. All the ones left over at the store looked horrible," she explained.

"Man, it ain't Thanksgiving without *greens*," Mark complained.

Emily glanced up, while mixing her stuffing. "Um, are you guys okay with Will stopping by for a plate?"

"Of course we are," Alex smiled, placing a lid on the top.

"Is he bringing dessert?" Mark asked.

"I can *ask* him to," Emily answered. "I'm sure he wouldn't mind."

"Cool, cool," Mark relented. He then stretched. "God, let me go get started on these damn yams," he griped.

Malajia looked confused. "I thought Jason was making the candied yams," she said.

Mark shook his head. "He *was*, but I lost at cards last night so now *I* gotta make 'em," he informed. "He's doing the mashed potatoes."

Malajia smacked her forehead with her palm. "Babe, don't mess 'em up," she ordered.

"Chill, I got this bee," Mark stated, confident. "I called Mom and she told me how to make 'em."

"Was she mad that you didn't come home this year?" Alex asked.

Mark scratched his head. "No, as a matter of fact, she was too damn happy for my liking," he hissed. "Talkin' 'bout her and Pop were going to Florida anyway...make me sick."

Malajia laughed as Mark walked out of the house.

Sidra came darting down the stairs. "How's my turkey looking ladies?" she asked.

Alex pulled the oven open and peered inside. "Looks good, Sid," she smiled.

Sidra walked into the kitchen. "Good," she breathed. She grabbed the baster and began tending to her bird. "I had Mama on the phone with me the entire time I was cleaning and seasoning this thing." She smiled at the golden-brown bird. "It's almost finished."

"Yeah well, it just better be good," Malajia jumped in, removing her sauce from the stove. She grabbed a bowl from the cabinet. "You make that potato salad?"

"No," Sidra answered, still basting. "I told you since I was doing the turkey, I wasn't making the salad."

Malajia sucked her teeth as she poured the contents into the bowl.

Alex peered into the bowl. "Can I taste it?" she asked of the sauce.

Malajia shot her a glance. "Everybody will taste it at the same time at dinner," she spat. "Put some more damn salt in that cabbage and get out my bowl."

"Yo *why* are these damn yams so hard to peel?" Mark complained, trying to peel the sweet potato.

Jason looked up from the white potatoes on his cutting board. "Didn't your mom tell you to boil them first so that they would be easy to peel?"

"Man, I wasn't tryna peel no hot ass potatoes," Mark bristled. "I just wanted to get it over with."

"That's what you get for not following instructions," Josh said from the living room couch. Just as the girls were preparing their dishes at their house, the guys were in their own home, preparing theirs.

Mark looked into the living room. "Man shut up," he bit out. "You talking shit when all you gotta make is rice."

"Well...that's all I know how to make," Josh muttered.

"I heard you can't even make *that*," Chasity teased.

After taking advantage of the guys' free oven space for her macaroni and cheese, Chasity decided instead of heading back to her house, that she'd be better off staying there so that she could keep an eye on it.

"Who told you that?" Josh wondered.

Chasity pointed to Jason, who started laughing.

Josh glared at Jason. "Bro."

"Josh I'm sorry, but the last time we had you make rice, you damn near set the kitchen on fire," Jason reasoned.

"That was *one* time," Josh argued. "The times before that, it was fine."

"Nah, the times before *that* it was soggy as shit," Mark chimed in, still peeling his yams. "We were secretly happy when you burnt it the last time, because we knew we wouldn't have to eat it."

Josh made a face. Hearing Chasity laugh from the dining room table, he sucked his teeth. "I'm not the only guy who can't cook," he grumbled.

"David is making biscuits from *scratch*, me and Jase are making shit from *scratch*, you're making rice out of a *bag*," Mark threw back.

"Mark, all the shit you *make* is out of a bag," Josh pointed out. "French fries, burgers—"

"Burgers come in a *box* dickhead," Mark interrupted. "Shit!" he bellowed when the yam that he was holding slipped out of his hand and onto the floor. He watched it roll near the stove.

"That's what you get," Josh jeered.

Mark sucked his teeth as he bent down to pick it up. He went to toss it in the bowl.

"Throw it the hell away," Jason barked at him. Mark stopped in his tracks. "You didn't even *attempt* to wash it off."

"Jason, watch him before he gives us food poisoning," Chasity said.

"I'm on it," Jason promised, placing his potatoes into a pot.

Mark just sucked his teeth as he tossed the spud in the trash.

"Sidra, you could've basted this turkey more," Malajia jeered, chewing her piece of turkey.

"Hush, I basted it *plenty*," Sidra bit back, scooping some stuffing onto her fork.

A few hours later, food fully prepared, the group was finally able to sit down in the girls' house and enjoy their hard work.

"I think the turkey is good," Alex beamed, pouring gravy on to her food.

"I'm not paying her any mind Alex, she's just mad because she messed up the cranberry sauce," Sidra commented, waving her hand.

"I *didn't* mess it up," Malajia defended.

"It tastes like orange peels," Chasity bristled, earning snickers from the group.

"The recipe called for oranges," Malajia argued.

"A cup of orange *juice*, like I *said*," Chasity threw back. "Not a cup of orange peels. The shit is bitter."

Malajia flagged Chasity with her hand. "Y'all trippin', it just needed to settle a bit more. It's good." She scooped some up with her fork and placed it into her mouth. She immediately made a face and spit it out. "Goddamn it," she complained of the bitter taste, reaching for her glass of juice. She quickly downed it as laughter erupted around her. "Ugh...I can still taste it," she complained, then broke into laughter. "Yeah, I can't defend this shit, I apologize."

Mark chuckled. "At least you tried," he consoled.

"Nah Mark, I appreciate it, but that shit is *horrible*," Malajia said, wiping her mouth.

Mark shrugged, then glanced at the table. "Hey, how come nobody's eating those yams?" he asked.

"'Cause they're burnt," Jason laughed.

Mark rolled his eyes. He realized that he'd left his dish

in the oven a little longer than he expected when he saw smoke come from the oven. "Y'all coulda' still tried them," he grumbled, placing food into his mouth.

"My *rice* isn't burnt," Josh teased.

"You better leave my man's food alone," Malajia ordered, then turned to face a mopey Mark. "It's okay, at least you tried."

"Are *you* gonna try them?" Mark asked her, voice and eyes full of hope.

"Uh uh," Malajia replied, turning away, earning snickers from the room and a head shake from Mark.

David emerged from the kitchen with a glass of soda, and handed it to Nicole. He was happy when she accepted his invitation to have dinner with him and his friends.

"Thank you," Nicole smiled, taking a bite of her biscuit. "David, these are so good," she said between chews.

David was smiling from ear to ear. "Thank you," he replied. "It was my mother's recipe."

Nicole rubbed his shoulder. "Well she'd be proud."

"Nicole, please stop complimenting him before his face freezes like that," Mark teased of David's wide smile.

Nicole giggled; David ignored him.

Sidra scooped a serving of baked macaroni and cheese on to her plate. "So what do—"

"Sidra, you don't get no more baked mac," Malajia abruptly cut in. "Everybody ain't get seconds yet."

Sidra stared at Malajia with confusion. "You just finished your *third* serving!" she exclaimed.

"Why you monitoring my food?" Malajia hurled back.

Sidra stared at Malajia, a blank expression on her face. "Chasity, welcome to the club of Malajia wants your dish all to herself."

"Nah, don't put Chasity's mac and cheese in that dry ass turkey's category," Malajia ground out, breaking a biscuit.

"I was *talking* about—you know what, never mind it's not even worth it," Sidra flashed back. "Anyway, what does everybody want to do tomorrow?" she asked. "Want to go to the mall?"

"With *what* money?" Alex muttered, stirring her cabbage around on her plate.

Mark smirked. "I see you ain't eatin' that raggedy cabbage," he mocked. "Bet you wished you had those greens right now."

Alex narrowed her eyes at him. "Will you and your burnt yams shut up?" she snapped. Between Mark criticizing her choice in vegetable, and the fact that he had been nitpicking with her and the other girls while they cooked, Alex was at her wits end.

"How the yams gonna shut up? They not even talking," Mark threw back.

Alex slammed her hand on the table as laughter resonated throughout the room. "I swear I'm so tired of you," she grunted.

"She mad 'cause she told a starch to shut up and shit," Mark mocked.

Emily took a sip of her juice, then set the cup back down and looked around the room at her chattering friends. Although she was happy that she had all of her friends in one place for what could be their last Thanksgiving holiday together, her mood was still slightly sour.

"Em, you haven't said much," Sidra pointed out. "Everything okay?"

Emily offered a smile. *I miss my mom*, she thought. "I'm fine, just tired," she replied. "It's been a long day."

"Is Will still coming over?" Alex asked.

Emily nodded. "Yeah, he should be here soon." Emily was a bit nervous. This would be the first time that Will would be hanging out in the presence of all her friends. *I hope he doesn't feel uncomfortable.*

"Is he still bringing dessert?" Mark asked.

Emily winced. "No, he said that what was left at the store looked picked over," she answered much to Mark's disappointment. "But he said he'll bring a bottle of wine."

Mark clapped his hands. "That'll do," he rejoiced.

"I just want to thank you guys for letting me chill with you today," Nicole put in. "With my roommate gone, I would've been pretty bored in my room."

"No need to thank them," David assured. "You were *more* than welcome."

Before anybody could say anything else, they heard a knock on the door. Emily jumped up from her seat and darted past Malajia, brushing her shoulder in the process. Malajia let out a yelp and slid off the chair. "Damn Em!" she barked, grabbing her shoulder.

"Girl!" Alex snapped, both amused and annoyed at Malajia's theatrics.

"Get your dumb ass off the floor," Chasity hissed. Malajia let out a loud huff as she rose from the floor.

Ignoring the commotion behind her, Emily opened the door and smiled brightly as she laid eyes on Will. "You made it," she breathed.

Will returned her smile, stepping inside. He gave Emily a hug before waving to the group. "Hey guys." The gang eagerly greeted him in return.

"You got that wine, bee?" Mark asked, standing from his seat.

"Got it right here," Will replied, handing it to Mark before shaking the guys' hands.

Alex rose from her seat and hesitantly walked over. That was the first time that she had been face to face with Will since she'd insulted him and Emily. "Will, I just want to say that I'm sorry for—"

"It's forgotten," Will assured, giving a quick hug to the grateful Alex.

"You gave in too quick," Malajia joked. "You shoulda' made her suffer some more."

Alex glowered at Malajia.

"Will, what's in that other bag?" Josh asked, pointing to the brown plastic bag gripped in Will's other hand.

He quickly glanced down at it. "Oh," he reacted, excited. "Well the discount toy store near the movie theater is going out of business, so they had all of these little bean bags for like fifty cents," he smiled, holding the bag out for someone to take.

Mark slowly grabbed the bag, as Emily fought to contain her laughter at the blank look on his face. Mark peered into the bag and retrieved one of the tiny, colorful, bean filled squares. He then glanced back at the rest of the group and put his hand up. "I got it," he said, when someone went to open their mouth.

Will stood with a bright smile as Mark faced him.

Mark let out a loud sigh and pinched the bridge of his nose. "Will...bruh—"

"Mark, please don't," Emily begged, voice trembling with amusement.

"Naw Em, I gotta say it," Mark protested, holding his hand up. "Will, if you gonna be in the group..." he rubbed his forehead. "You can't be showing up with corny ass gifts like this, yo," he jeered, inciting snickers from around the room.

Will busted out laughing. "Pretty silly, huh?" he agreed, running his hand over the top of his freshly cut hair. "Just figured y'all can use them to play a game or something. Emily said you guys always make up fun stuff to do."

"Aww, it was a sweet gesture," Emily pouted, patting Will's shoulder. "Mark, leave him alone."

"Naw Em, Mark's right," Malajia chortled.

"I mean, who thinks to bring *bean bags* to dinner and shit," Mark ranted.

Alex sucked her teeth as she placed a spoon in the bowl of cabbage. "God boy, will you leave him alone?" she barked at Mark, who frowned at her. "I swear, you've been on my last nerve all damn day."

Mark just stood there in silence as Alex continued her rant.

"Either sit your annoying ass down and eat, or go the hell home and take your burnt yams with you."

The room fell silent for a moment. "Babe, you gonna let nappy roots talk to you like that?" Malajia egged on, earning an eye roll from Alex.

Mark looked down at the bean bag in his hand, then glanced at Will. "On second thought," he muttered, before tossing the square directly at the bowl of cabbage. To his delight and Alex's fury, the bag hit its target, landing in the bowl with a thud. Sending cabbage pieces and juice flying on the table. While some of the group was stunned at what just happened, Malajia screamed at the top of her lungs with laughter.

"You stupid dickhead!" Alex exploded, jumping back from the table.

Chasity, who had just finished taking a sip of wine cooler, spit it all over Jason's shirt as she busted out laughing at Alex's reaction.

"Baby come *on!*" Jason complained, holding the wet fabric away from his skin.

"I'm sorry," Chasity laughed, putting her hands over her face. She had never heard Alex use that term before, and that, paired with the anger in her voice, was hilarious.

"That's what you get for talking shit," Mark hurled at Alex, who grabbed the wooden spoon from the bowl and began chasing him around the room. "Shit! She tryna hit me wit a spoon!" he yelped, darting up the steps.

"Get the hell out!" Alex screamed, in pursuit.

Malajia cringed when she heard Mark scream. "Alex, don't hit him in the penis okay!" she yelled up the steps. "I need that."

Placing her hands on her hips, Sidra shot a disgusted look Malajia's way. "You could've kept that to yourself."

Unfazed, Malajia shrugged.

"Ouch! You ain't have to hit me on the damn knuckles!" Mark yelled from upstairs.

David shook his head. "He can never behave himself," he commented.

"This has got to be *the* funniest dinner that I've ever been to," Nicole concluded, reaching for another biscuit.

Emily put her hand over her face and shook her head.

"Will, next time, just stick with the wine," she joked to an amused Will.

"I'll keep that in mind," he promised, putting his arm around her.

Chapter 41

Sidra walked out of the English building and proceeded down the steps. Having just finished her last final of the semester, she was eager to get back to her room and finish packing. Finals week nearly over, students were leaving campus for winter break, little by little. Sidra planned on leaving the next day.

As she walked down the path Sidra glanced over and saw Malajia sitting on a bench, slumped over. Both confused and concerned, she darted over.

"Malajia, are you okay?" Sidra asked, shaking her arm.

Malajia glanced up and started whining. Sidra shook her again. "Stop it," Malajia grunted, smacking her hand away.

"You want to tell me why you're sitting out here in the cold, looking crazy?" Sidra asked.

"I failed my Spanish final," Malajia complained.

Sidra frowned. "You *what*?" she scoffed. "What is *with* you and this damn language?"

"I *hate* it!" Malajia belted out, placing her hands on her head. "I studied, I really *did*."

Sidra folded her arms, shooting Malajia a knowing look. "*When* did you study for it exactly?"

Malajia's eyes shifted. "This morning."

Sidra shook her head. "Mel—" she put her hand up. "Okay, maybe you didn't do as bad as you think."

Malajia stared at her. "Sidra there were twenty questions. I only answered five and the answer that I wrote for all *five* was 'eggs'."

Sidra tried hard not to laugh, but it was coming through when she tried to speak. "Well umm...did you at least write 'huevos'?"

"No, I wrote fuckin' '*eggs*', e-g-g-s," Malajia snapped. "*None* of the questions asked about eggs."

Sidra could no longer hold it in; she erupted with laughter.

"It's not funny," Malajia huffed.

"How do you not think so?" Sidra laughed. "Come on, you *know* you should've studied."

Malajia folded her arms. "Well, now I gotta repeat the damn class next semester," she ground out. "Which means I'll be taking an extra freakin' class so I can graduate on time."

Sidra patted Malajia on the arm. "At least you're going to suck it up and do it."

"Save your pity," Malajia grumbled. She started repeatedly stomping her feet on the ground, whining out loud in the process. "I'm sick of school."

"I know sweetie, but we only have one more semester to go," Sidra placated, reaching for Malajia's arm. "Now come on, let's go so you can pack your stuff."

"I still have one more final tomorrow," Malajia whined, sliding down the bench.

Sidra grabbed Malajia's arm. "Girl, will you stop embarrassing yourself?" she snapped, giving Malajia's arm a yank. "Get up, *now*."

Malajia sucked her teeth, then slowly picked herself up. She stood in front of Sidra, smoothing her coat down.

Sidra couldn't help but chuckle at Malajia's poked out lips. "Fix your face Malajia Lakeshia Simmons," she ordered. "You'll do better next semester."

"Yeah, yeah," Malajia grumbled as Sidra put her arm around her.

As Sidra went to take a step, she saw December in the distance, walking up the path. Sidra turned to Malajia. "Shit," she muttered.

Malajia frowned. "What, we fighting?" she asked. "I just failed a final, I'm ready to let off some steam."

Sidra rolled her eyes; she grabbed Malajia's hand to stop her from shrugging out of her coat. "No, nobody is fighting," Sidra assured. "I just feel weird seeing her after what happened."

"That's on *Josh*, not on you," Malajia pointed out.

"Still…" Sidra sighed.

"You want to walk in the other direction?" Malajia asked.

Sidra shook her head. "This way is faster."

Malajia gave an approving smile. "That's right, your parents ain't raise no punk," she approved. Sidra chuckled. Both girls began walking down the path.

December eyed both girls, then looked at Malajia. "Hi Malajia," she said, then shot Sidra a side-glance as she continued past.

Sidra rolled her eyes as she continued walking.

"Brrrr," Malajia jeered of the cold exchange.

"It's whatever," Sidra dismissed. "I didn't exactly expect her to speak to me."

"Shit, she didn't have to speak to *me* either," Malajia grunted. "We ain't cool like that."

Sidra gave Malajia a nudge. "Don't freeze the girl out, she's not in the wrong."

Malajia scoffed. "Too late."

Jason tossed some clothes in his suitcase. "How do you think you did on your finals?" he asked Chasity.

Chasity handed him another of his folded shirts. Finished with her own packing, she decided to head over to Jason's room to help him with his. "Passed, that's all I care about at this point," she said.

"Yeah, I hear you," Jason replied. He let out a sigh.

"You okay?" she asked.

"Yeah, I'm good," he answered. He hesitated for a moment. "Can I ask you a question?"

Chasity looked at him. "Yeah."

"Do you think your mom would mind if I crashed for a few days at your house when we get back?" he asked.

"Shouldn't be an issue," she answered. "Don't want to be home?"

Jason shook his head. "I don't want to see her face right now," he spoke of his mother.

"Understandable," Chasity consoled.

"I mean, I know that I have to talk to her eventually, and I *will*," he added, rubbing his face. "But…"

"You need a minute, I get it." Chasity understood all too well the need to separate herself from those who had hurt her. "You can stay as long as you want."

"Don't worry, I'm not gonna move in," Jason joked.

"Fuck it, you *could*, I'm normally in there by myself anyway," she chortled.

Jason smiled. "Thanks." He tossed something else in his bag, then walked over and sat next to her on the bed.

Chasity looked over at him. "What does your dad have to say about all of this?" she wondered.

"Oh, he's pissed at her," Jason confirmed. "No doubt."

Chasity shook her head. She wanted so badly to comment, but decided against it. While she took joy in the fact that Mrs. Adams was told off by her husband for doing what she did, she knew that Jason was hurt by the entire situation. So, she wanted to make sure that she showed him nothing but support.

Chasity put her hand on his leg. "Sorry," she sympathized.

"You don't have to be sorry," he said, taking her hand. He gave it a kiss.

"You wanna do something to take your mind off of it?" she proposed.

Jason smiled at her. "What do you have in mind?"

Chasity pointed to his suitcase. "Finish packing so you can pack up the car."

Jason laughed. "You—that's the *second* time you played me."

Chasity too laughed. "'Cause it's so easy, your horny ass walks *right* into it."

"Funny, funny," Jason smirked. He leaned in for a kiss.

Chasity moved her head back. "I said finish packing," she chortled.

"You *really* want me to do that right now?" he crooned, eyeing her.

Hormones in overdrive, she shook her head. "Nope."

Just as Jason kissed her, the door swung open, startling them both. "Fuck, Mark!" Jason yelled when Mark barged in.

"Y'all getting ready to leave, just bang in the car later," Mark jeered.

Chasity rolled her eyes as she stood up from the bed.

"Where are you going?" Jason asked her.

"His face killed my mood," she grunted, walking out the door.

Jason glared at Mark, who was holding up a container of food. "I should punch you in your face."

"My bad bro," Mark said. He pointed to the container in his hand. "Yo…you still want this left-over spaghetti that you were saving?"

Jason looked at him as if he had lost his mind.

"I'm hungry and there's nothing else down there."

Jason stood from his bed, then pushed past Mark to get out of his room. He wasn't in the mood for Mark's nonsense; he wanted to finish what he started with Chasity.

"Jase, the food though," Mark called after him. When Jason didn't respond on his way down the steps, Mark sucked his teeth. "Fuck you then."

Jason spun around, and ran back up the steps at full speed.

Seeing the anger on Jason's face, Mark tossed the

container on the floor, and darted for his room. "Never mind about the food!" he belted out.

"You weren't lying, this is really good," Emily mused, shoving a few kernels of caramel popcorn into her mouth.

Alex giggled. "I *told* you."

Finishing up a final, Alex and Emily walked to a nearby convenience store, where Alex finally treated Emily to some caramel popcorn.

"The fresh kind does taste better than the bagged though," Alex added.

Emily grabbed more from her bag, while chewing what was already in her mouth. "Good to know."

"So...you ready for break?" Alex asked, walking in stride with Emily through campus.

"Yeah," Emily answered. "My dad has some time off, so we get to hang out."

"That's good," Alex smiled. "Have you told your dad that you have a boyfriend yet?"

"Will is not my boyfriend," Emily replied, taking more popcorn.

Alex looked over at her. "Why not?"

"I'm okay with him being just a friend right now," she said. "I mean, maybe one day, but—"

Alex touched Emily's shoulder. "You don't need to explain, I shouldn't have asked," she said. "I'm still learning to back off."

"Alex, you can still ask me questions," Emily chuckled.

"Can I give you some advice too?"

Emily nodded.

"Take all the time you need," Alex said. "As long as you two are on the same page, everything will work itself out...slow is good."

"Yeah?" Emily wondered.

Alex nodded. "I think it's great that you two are using this time to strengthen your friendship," she praised. "The best relationships start from friendships, so you're on the right track."

Emily smiled. "Thanks."

"You're welcome," Alex replied. Passing by a building, Alex stopped.

Emily noticed, and stopped along with her. "You okay?" she asked.

"Yeah," Alex uttered, staring at the entrance. "This is umm...Eric lives here."

"Oooohhh," Emily put out. She held her gaze on Alex. "Can I give *you* some advice?"

"Sure."

"Talk to him...now," Emily urged.

Alex glanced down at the ground. "I *want* to Em, I do. I miss him but—" She sighed. "I can't."

"Yes, you *can*, Alex," Emily insisted. "You're just scared and that's okay. But you still *have* to."

Alex looked at Emily, she felt like crying. "What do I say?"

"What you feel," Emily shrugged.

"What if he doesn't forgive me?"

"Then...at least you can say that you tried," Emily placated.

Alex knew that Emily was right. She gave a nod. "Okay."

Emily smiled, then handed Alex the rest of the popcorn. "Maybe you can break the ice by offering him some."

Alex put a hand up, letting a laugh come through. "Thanks, but I think I should do this without food in my hands."

"Makes sense," Emily agreed. She gave Alex a hug. "Good luck."

"Thanks...see you back at the house." Alex watched Emily walk off, before turning her attention back to the complex. After standing there a few more minutes, Alex made her way inside the building. She stood in front of Eric's door. After hesitating for a few moments, she knocked.

Maybe he went home already, she thought when he didn't answer. *Try one more time.* She knocked a second time, and hearing commotion from inside, held her breath.

She finally let the air out of her lungs when the door opened. Eric looked at her, face void of emotion.

"H—hi Eric," she stammered.

Eric held his gaze. "I'm trying to finish packing, so—"

"I won't keep you, I just—" Alex wasn't surprised by his tart tone. She was just happy that he hadn't slammed the door in her face. "Do you mind if I come in?"

"Yes, I do mind," Eric bit out.

Alex glanced down at the floor, shifting her position from one foot to the other. "Fair enough," she muttered. Gathering her courage, she took a deep breath, looking him in the eye. "Listen…I wanted to come over here to apologize to you," she began. "I know that I gave you a lot of mixed signals…sleeping with you after I told you that I couldn't do the causal thing was wrong… I hurt you and I know that."

He folded his arms, but didn't say anything.

"Saying that you were a waste of my time…couldn't be further from the truth," she continued. "I was just mad; I should never have said it… My time with you was amazing. You're an amazing man and I was just too stupid to see it."

Eric still didn't speak as Alex poured her heart out.

Alex didn't care that he wasn't responding; in fact she was glad that he wasn't. She needed to get everything out, and she felt that if he started talking that she would break her focus.

"Eric, me saying that I couldn't date you because of school was a lie… Yes, I want to focus on school, but the real reason is that I have trust issues when it comes to men… I'm still hurt by what my ex did and I know that I should be over it already, but—I'm trying to move past it, I really am, but until then, I just have to be by myself."

Eric tilted his head slightly, still holding his gaze on her.

"I hope you can understand that," she said, eyes pleading. "And I know that just being my friend isn't what

you want, but I hope that one day you can try because..."
tears welled up in her eyes. "I *need* your friendship. I care
about you and I *miss* you and I hate that I can't pick up the
phone and talk to you." She knew that it was time to go
before she broke all the way down. Alex wiped her face.
"So...I'll let you get back to packing, umm...have a safe
break." Alex walked off.

Eric watched her walk towards the exit. "Alex," he
called, just as she grabbed the knob.

Alex spun around.

Eric's face was no longer masked with frustration. He
looked relaxed. "You have a safe break too," he said after a
moment. "And...thank you for the apology. I appreciate it."

Alex gave a slight smile through her tears. No, he didn't
say that he accepted her apology or agreed to be her friend
again, but at least he didn't seem angry anymore. In Alex's
mind, that was a start. "See you next semester, Eric."

"See you," he replied as she walked out.

Chapter 42

"Try not to work too much," Emily said into her cell phone as she put her seatbelt on. "I'll see you in a few weeks...and say hi to Anthony for me." Her smile was bright as she adjusted the heat in her father's car. "I know, maybe next semester... Okay, bye." Emily glanced over at the driver's side as the door opened.

"You ready to get this show on the road, baby girl?" Mr. Harris asked, settling in his seat, putting the late model sedan in gear.

Emily nodded eagerly. "The last time I went skiing was sophomore year," she recalled. "And I didn't even do any *actual* skiing." After a trying semester, Emily was glad to finally be on winter break. More importantly, she was glad to be able to spend the first week of break with her father, on a much-needed ski trip.

A deep chuckle flowed through Mr. Harris as he pulled out of the driveway of his home. "Yeah, I figure since I finally have some time off, I can do some making up for missing Thanksgiving...again."

Emily shot him a sympathetic look, removing the pink gloves from her hands.

He glanced over at Emily once they approached a stop light. "So...you were on the phone for a while earlier," he said.

Emily glanced out of the window. "Yeah," she sighed.

"Was it that boy?"

His question caught Emily off guard. "Huh?" she stammered, shooting him a wide-eyed glance. *How did he know*?

"Yeah, your tone sounded a little different than when you talk to one of the girls," he chuckled, maneuvering the car through the streets.

Emily smiled as she shook her head. "Which one of them told you?"

"Dru."

A soft laugh erupted from Emily. "He is such a tattle tale."

When she told Brad and Dru of her friendship with Will, she knew in the back of her mind that the news would eventually get back to her father. She just wasn't sure of when. "Yes, it was my friend, Will," she confirmed.

Mr. Harris nodded slowly as he processed Emily's words. "So…what's he like?"

Emily pushed some hair behind her ear. "Daddy."

"Now come on, you already knew I was going to ask," he chuckled.

Emily took a deep breath. "Well, he's really nice and hard working—"

"Is he in school?"

"Not at the moment, he, um…he had to drop out for a little while to get some stuff in order," she vaguely responded. "As a matter of fact, that's why we're not dating really… We're just friends. He has stuff going on and I'm really not ready for a relationship."

"That's understandable," her father replied. "You don't want to rush into something that you're not ready for."

Tell me about it, she thought.

"What stuff does he have going on?"

Emily snapped out of the little daze that she was just in. "Um…he's working a lot of hours right now, trying to save for a place." She rubbed the back of her neck. "He's staying with his parents for now. He went to look at a place around

Thanksgiving, but it wasn't what he wanted for him and his um...son."

Mr. Harris's eyes widened. "He has a child?" he asked, tone calm.

Emily nodded. "Yeah, he's two," she replied. "His child's mother died and now he's raising him alone." Emily sighed. "Go ahead and say it, Daddy."

"What do you think that I'm about to say?"

"That I'm wasting my time getting to know Will," she assumed. "That he's irresponsible for having a child that young. That I don't need that in my life when I'm about to graduate college." She looked down at her hands. "At least that's what Mommy would say," she sulked.

Mr. Harris smirked after a few seconds. "Well, *clearly* I'm not your mother," he joked. Emily forced a smile. "We all make mistakes in our life and lest you forget, your mother and I were your age when we had Dru. As long as the young man is handling his responsibilities as a man and a father, I can respect him."

Emily fixed her eyes on her father, sitting in silence as he continued to speak to her.

"Look baby girl, I can't tell you what to do with your life. Do I have a vision of how I see it going? Sure," he said. "But I know that you are more than capable of making the right decisions for yourself."

Emily looked at her father in awe. He was the total opposite from her mother. He trusted her decisions as an adult, and instead of talking at her, he talked *to* her. She had so much respect for him. "Thank you, Daddy."

"Anytime," he returned. "Speaking of your mother...I wanted to tell you that she called me the other day."

Emily felt her heart drop. "Oh yeah?"

"Yeah. She actually called to check on you."

Emily shook her head. *Why doesn't she just call me?!* "What did you tell her?"

"That you were doing wonderful, of course," he replied, pulling into the airport parking lot. "I *also* told her that she should call you and ask you *herself*."

Emily scoffed. "Yeah, she's never going to do that."

Mr. Harris found a parking spot and pulled in. Turning the car off, he glanced at his sad daughter. "I know that you miss her," he consoled.

Emily nodded.

"She's your mother and the only one that you will have… It's okay to miss her."

"I *hate* that she's not talking to me," she said. "I want things to be okay between us, but I just—I can't be the one to call her…I *won't*. She hurt me, and she has to apologize… and *change*."

Mr. Harris nodded in agreement. "Hopefully she will come to her senses, sooner than later," he hoped, giving Emily's hand a pat. He took a deep breath as he removed his seatbelt. "Ready?"

Emily took one look at the huge smile on his face and pushed her somber thoughts to the back of her mind. "Yes, let's go," she beamed.

"What time do you have to go to work?" Sidra asked, playing with the strings on a throw blanket.

Josh glanced at his watch as he leaned back on the couch in Sidra's living room. "I have to leave in about twenty minutes," he replied, stifling a yawn.

Sidra stared at the side of his face. "You look tired," she sympathized.

Josh nodded in agreement. "Yeah, I didn't get much sleep last night," he informed.

"Stuff on your mind?"

"Kind of," he answered. What Josh didn't reveal to Sidra was that he was kept up late because December called him about something of his that she found while she was cleaning out her cluster room. The conversation, a simple request for him to get his stuff, turned into a full-on verbal lashing from her. That just wasn't something that he wanted to share with

Sidra.

Sidra patted his shoulder. "Well, I was going to ask you if you wanted to go to the movies after you got off, but you should probably sleep afterwards."

Josh rubbed the top of his head. "I'm actually going to hang out with Sarah," he revealed, much to Sidra's surprise and delight.

"Oh wow," she gushed, grabbing his arm.

Josh smiled. "Yeah, I think it's time we started hanging out again," he said. "She's been really trying to rebuild our relationship you know... She's even been giving me money when she can, to try to repay what she stole."

"That's wonderful Josh," Sidra beamed. "I'm glad that you forgave her...and that she's trying to repay you...even though trying to repay thousands of dollars will take a while."

Josh chuckled. "Tell me about it," he agreed. "But it's a start... I have to admit, I missed having a big sister you know."

Sidra just smiled. She couldn't help but feel extra excited about Josh's family healing. She knew firsthand how the drama affected him.

As Josh rested his head on the back of the couch, Sidra held on to his arm and found herself staring at him as he dozed off. *He's so adorable when he's sleeping.* She shook her head to rid her inner thoughts.

"Josh," she called, giving him a slight shake. "If you fall asleep now, you won't get up in time," she added when he jerked awake.

Josh sat up straight and rubbed his eyes. "You're right," he murmured. "Thanks."

Sidra turned and faced the staircase when she heard her mother's voice. "Princess, you're not going anywhere within the next few minutes, are you?" Mrs. Howard asked.

"Um, no I don't think so," Sidra answered. "Why?"

"Just checking," Mrs. Howard smiled, placing both hands on the arm of a nearby accent chair.

Sidra shot her smiling mother a skeptical look. "Mama?" she questioned. "What are you up to?"

"Nothing," she replied.

Josh glanced at Mrs. Howard. He let out a small laugh, then turned to Sidra. "Yeah she's up to something," he joked.

"I *know* she is," Sidra agreed, eyes not leaving her mother. "You're not gonna make me go pick up a dish or something from Mark's mother again, are you?" she asked. "You know how you get about your casserole dishes."

Mrs. Howard giggled. "That's cute, smarty pants," she returned, amused. "Although now that you mention it—"

"*Mama*," Sidra cut it, her tone a warning.

"I'm joking."

Sidra closed her eyes as she had a thought. "*Please* don't tell me that India is coming over here right now," she hissed. When Mrs. Howard stared at her, Sidra sucked her teeth. "Mama, I'm *not* playing nice with her," she whined, stomping her foot on the floor.

Her mother narrowed her eyes. "Are you finished?"

Sidra rolled her eyes and folded her arms. Before Sidra could ask another question, there was a knock at the door.

"Get that for me please?" Mrs. Howard smiled.

Sidra, still holding a gaze of confusion, did as she was asked. Sidra's eyes almost popped out of her head, they'd gotten so big. "James!" she exclaimed at the sight of him standing there, holding a bouquet of flowers. "What are you doing here?"

"Surprise," James announced, before giving her a quick kiss on the lips. Sidra stepped aside and let him in. He gave her mother a warm hug before extending his hand to Josh, who had just stood up from the couch. "Good to see you again, man."

"You too," Josh returned, shaking James's outstretched hand in a firm grip. He then glanced at Sidra. "I'm gonna head out."

"Okay," Sidra returned, tone more sullen than she'd realized. "Get some rest tonight," she urged at Josh's departing back. Josh nodded and put up the 'okay' sign as he walked out of the door.

"You look beautiful as usual," James cooed, removing his coat and hanging it on the coat rack near the door.

Sidra was so busy staring at the door that she didn't hear him initially. "Huh?" she said when he repeated it. "Oh, thanks," she blushed, facing James. She retrieved the flowers from his hand. "What are you doing here? I thought you were going to be in Boston for your case this week."

"I just got back today," he answered. "My case settled, so I have a few days of rest and I wanted to surprise you with a little Christmas visit."

Sidra faced her mother, who was standing with her hands clasped together, a grin plastered on her face. "You knew about this, didn't you?" she assumed, sitting the flowers on the coffee table.

Mrs. Howard nodded. "How was the drive from the airport James?" she asked. "The roads weren't too icy were they?"

"No ma'am, they were just fine," James replied. He turned to Sidra once Mrs. Howard retreated to the kitchen to allow them some privacy. With Sidra's mother out of sight, James was free to greet his girlfriend in the manner with which he really wanted to. Moving closer to her, he wrapped his arms around her and planted a passionate kiss upon her, one that she returned. Feeling a warmth coming over her, she gently placed her hand on his chest and nudged him away.

"You want my dad to walk in and have a heart attack?" she asked, trying to catch her breath.

James laughed as he ran his hand across his forehead. "Good point," he agreed. "I missed you."

"Missed you too," she returned, sitting on the couch. She patted the cushion next to her and he sat down.

"I'm sorry that I haven't come to see you more often in the past few months," he apologized.

"It's fine," Sidra said. "I know that you've been busy." She patted his leg. "At least we talk all the time."

"Yeah but talking isn't the same as spending *actual time* together," he pointed out, tone sincere.

Sidra looked away momentarily. Surprisingly, she found herself to be fine with how things were.

"I promise that I'll make more of an effort to make time for you," he vowed.

Sidra looked at him. "Okay," she replied.

"As a matter of fact," he began. "I was thinking that maybe I can take you back to DC with me for the rest of the week," he proposed.

Sidra's eyes widened. "Um…"

"Don't worry, I'll have you back by Christmas," he chortled. "I know how important it is for you to spend it with your family."

"No, it's not that," she assured. "It's um…I just don't…" James stared at her as she continued to stammer. "I'm not—"

"Sidra, just like the New York trip…I don't expect for us to sleep together," he said.

Sidra sighed. "I just want to make sure that you know that I'm *still* not ready and have no idea when I *will* be." Sidra had come to terms with her decision not to sleep with James. And although she still wasn't sure what exactly in her subconscious made her change her mind at the last minute, she knew that she had made the right decision.

"I know," James assured. "And I'll tell you now, like I told you *then*…I'm fine with that. I'm not going anywhere."

Sidra smiled. *He's such a good man*, she thought. *But why am I not as excited as I used to be about spending time with him?*

"You want to leave today?" James asked, interrupting Sidra's questions to herself.

"Um, sure," she replied, tone more eager than her mind was. "Give me some time to pack."

James sat back on the couch in satisfaction as she headed for the steps. "Knowing how you are with packing, I say we'll be leaving in about five hours," he teased.

She laughed. "More like *six* hours," she returned,

earning a deep laugh from him. Her smile faded as she reached the top of the staircase. *I wonder if Josh made it to work okay*, she thought.

Chapter 43

"Girl, what have you done to your room?" Alex chuckled, glancing around Stacey's bedroom in her parents' home. "It looks like a crayon box threw up in here," she joked of the colorful walls and bedding.

"Funny," Stacey giggled, tossing a pillow at a laughing Alex. "I told you that I'm experimenting with colors… you've seen my hair."

Alex retrieved the pillow from the floor and tossed it back to Stacey. "I expect nothing *less* from an Art major," she quipped. "I like the red tips on your hair better than the green that you had last month by the way."

"Yeah, that might have been a bit too much," Stacey agreed, amused. "Thank God for wash out dye and hair weaves."

"I hear that, girl," Alex chortled. Having gotten off work merely an hour earlier, Alex decided not to go straight home as she had originally planned, but opted instead to visit Stacey for a bit. Alex plopped down at the end of Stacey's bed. "So, Ma will probably be calling your mom a little later, but I figured I'd tell *you* now," she began, playing with the strings on the comforter. "She wants you guys to have Christmas dinner with us again, this year."

Stacey smiled. The last time that she had Christmas dinner with Alex's family was her freshman year. "I can speak for my parents when I say that we'd love to come."

Alex clasped her hands together. "Great."

"I'm sure Mom will be thrilled, knowing that she doesn't have to cook," Stacey replied, enthused. Her smile faded as she looked down at the bed. "Um, we might be a bit late though...well, *Mom* will be."

"That's fine, you know my family rarely starts anything on time," Alex joked.

Stacey looked at Alex. "Yeah well, she'll be stopping at Mr. and Mrs. James's house first."

Alex's easy expression hardened. "Um...o-kay."

Stacey felt bad for even saying anything. "Yeah, Mrs. James asked for help with a few things, so she's gonna stop over."

Alex sat for a moment in silence, then her facial expression softened. "Look Stace," she began, patting Stacey's leg. "I know that your mom and Mrs. James are still cool. I mean just because *my* mom isn't speaking to her, doesn't mean that everyone else's can't... After all, Victoria didn't betray *her* daughter."

"She did when she betrayed *you*," Stacey clarified.

Alex smiled. "I appreciate that," she replied. "But you know what..." Alex looked at the ceiling and took a deep breath. "Maybe you should try to forgive her." Stacey looked confused. "I mean...I don't know."

Stacey shot Alex a skeptical look. "If that's what you *want*... But a few months ago, you were ready to take my head off because you thought I still spoke to her."

"Yeah well, after getting raked over the damn coals for how bitter I am, I figured I would try to change that," Alex replied.

"Could *you* ever forgive her?"

Alex shook her head. "I...don't *know*," she admitted. "I mean, I definitely would *never* trust her again. I'd *never* be friends with her again, but... I know that forgiveness would be more for *me*, than her...well *them*."

"I understand," Stacey said. "But don't feel *obligated*. You can work on bettering yourself *without* it for now."

Alex just nodded.

Stacey hopped up from the bed. "Come on, let's go get some burgers," she suggested.

"Girl, I just left a damn burger place," Alex declined. "Hell, I still *smell* like them."

"That you *do*," Stacey teased, earning a playful backhand from Alex. "We won't go to *your* diner, we can go to the one up the street."

Alex let out a huff. "Fine," she relented, standing up. "But *you're* treating."

"Very well," Stacey agreed.

Both women trotted out of the house and into the biting cold.

"Let's walk to my house really quick," Alex prompted. "I can't take this damn work uniform another minute."

Stacey nodded in agreement. After a few moments, they turned down Alex's block. "I think it's supposed to start snowing later this week,"

Alex rolled her eyes. "God, I hope not," she muttered, wrapping her scarf around her neck a second time. "Christmas is only two days away, it just needs to hold off until after."

Stacey giggled. Then, as quickly as the amusement showed on her face, it was gone. "Shit," she mumbled as they approached the steps to Alex's house.

"What's wrong?" Alex asked, eyes focused on her coat pocket as she dug around for her house keys.

"Nothing," Stacey returned.

Alex glanced up at Stacey. "Then why did you say 'shit'?" she asked, amusement in her voice. Before Stacey could offer a response, they heard a man's voice.

"Hey ladies," the voice nervously said.

Both Alex and Stacey were stunned to see Paul standing in front of them.

"Shit," Alex whispered. *I gotta start wearing a disguise*

when I come outside, she thought.

"Paul, you *know* that you can take Peach street to get to your block," Stacey hissed, seeing the distressed look on Alex's face. "There's *no* need for you to come down here."

"I know, I was *about* to but—" He scratched his head. "Look, I was on my way to work when I saw you coming down the block so... I just wanted to um—"

Paul seemed to be quivering under the tense gaze from Alex's eyes. If he could have slid under a rock at that very moment, he would have. He scratched his knit-hat-covered head once again.

Alex shook her head. She recognized Paul's movements; the constant scratching of his head meant that he was nervous.

"Yeah, you *should* be nervous," Alex hissed.

"Alex, can I just talk to you for a minute, please?" Paul begged.

"Nope," Stacey immediately interjected. Paul sighed as he looked at the ground.

Both Alex and Stacey turned to head into the house, but Alex stopped, midway up the steps. She looked at Stacey. "Stace, can you wait for me inside, please?" she asked, handing her the house key.

Stacey regarded Alex with shock. "You sure?"

"No," Alex answered honestly. Tapping Stacey's arm, she took a deep breath. "It's fine, I'll be in, in a sec."

Stacey gave Alex a long look, then looked at Paul and rolled her eyes before doing as Alex asked. Once the door shut, Alex focused her attention back on Paul. Folding her arms across her chest, she shot him a challenging look. "You have two minutes," she spat.

Paul stood there, not saying a word for seconds. It was as if he didn't actually expect her to agree to talk.

"Boy don't waste my time. If you have something to say, then say it," Alex bit out, her impatience prevalent.

"Okay, okay," Paul murmured, putting his hands out in surrender. "Look, I know that you hate me...and probably will for the rest of your life, but..." he scratched his head once more. "I never got to tell you face to face that I was sorry—*am* sorry, for what I've done to you."

Alex rolled her eyes. "Is that it?"

Paul stared at her momentarily. "It's not," he said. Alex sucked her teeth as she looked at the watch on her wrist. "I cheated on you because I was mad..." he continued. "You were moving on with your life...doing something that I *should* have been doing and I wasn't able to...and I know that that was my *own* fault."

Alex was silent.

"You pushed me because you saw in me what I didn't see in myself... I failed and I took it out on *you*... I will forever have to live with what I did and who I did it *with,* and I guess I'm paying for it by being forever tied to a woman who I kinda despise."

"Tuh," Alex spat, somewhat amused.

"Yeah I know," Paul agreed, shaking his head. "Anyway, like I said, you may always hate me, and you may not care, but just know that I wish the best for you... You're a good woman Alexandra, and you deserve someone who will treat you how you deserve to be treated... someone who's the *opposite* of me."

When Alex didn't respond, Paul just sighed. He had said what he wanted to say, finally. Even if Alex didn't accept it, he still felt a bit lighter. "Have a merry Christmas," he said, turning to walk off.

Alex had every intention of retreating inside the comfort of her home, satisfied with not saying a word to him. But as she turned, something in her stopped her. Glancing back at Paul's retreating figure, she took a deep breath. "Paul," she called.

He immediately stopped and spun around to face her. Both fear and anticipation were written on his face. Alex stood there, thoughts running through her head. Thoughts of everything that she had been through with him. However, one thought that stood out in her head was that she was no longer *with* him. No longer in a relationship that was toxic. Alex was in a position to find true happiness. But she knew that if she was ever going to be able to do that, she would have to heal herself.

"I don't hate you…anymore," she put out after moments of silence.

Paul looked stunned, and that is how Alex left him as she walked into the house.

Stacey, who had been peering out of the window at the two of them, stared at Alex.

"You heard?" Alex assumed.

Stacey nodded. "I'm nosey," she joked as Alex removed her coat. "You okay?"

"Yeah," Alex answered.

"You think you'll *forgive* him?"

Alex thought for a moment. "Baby steps sis…baby steps."

Jason removed a bottle of juice from the refrigerator and opened it. "Yeah, I'm about to grab some more stuff and I'll be over later," he said into his cell phone. "Yeah, I'm okay, it was fine… You still want to go grab something to eat later? …Okay cool, I'll see you soon."

Jason took a sip of his juice as he ended his phone call. Closing the refrigerator, he moved to walk out of the kitchen, only to see his mother standing there. *Great, just freakin' great*, he thought as she stared at him.

"Judging by your conversation, I take it that you're leaving again?" Mrs. Adams asked, fiddling with her shirt.

Jason didn't answer.

The tension in the room was not missed by Mrs. Adams, who tilted her head. "You've been MIA since you've been back on break… I don't know where you've been, but—"

"I'm sure you know *exactly* where I've been," Jason spat, tone stern but even.

Mrs. Adams looked away momentarily. He was right;

she knew that he'd been at Chasity's house pretty much every day since he'd been back on winter break, nearly a week ago. She expected that Jason was still upset, but never imagined that he would just completely stay away.

"Yeah…yeah, I suppose I *do*," she admitted. "Look Jase," she began, taking a deep breath. "Why don't you just stay, okay? I mean it's *Christmas* after all."

Jason fought the urge to roll his eyes at his mother. "Mom, Christmas was *yesterday*. I was here all day yesterday and even spent the night," he ground out. "Christmas is over and now I have to go."

Mrs. Adams stood in Jason's way as he tried to walk out of the kitchen. Frustrated, Jason rubbed his face with his hands.

"Mom, can you *please* not do this right now?" he asked, feeling his patience shorten.

"So, you're really just going to walk out, again?" she hissed, ignoring his request. "You're disappointing—"

"Disappointing *who*? *You*?" Jason spat. "'Cause it's not Dad and Kyle, because they know *exactly* why I haven't been around. It's *you* who doesn't seem to get it."

"Don't talk to me like that," Mrs. Adams demanded.

"Oh *stop* it, already," Jason ground out. He put a hand up. "You know what, this is a waste of my time, I gotta get out of here."

"What, are you going to be mad at me forever?" she asked, angry.

"Yup," Jason threw back, defiant.

She folded her arms in a huff. "Jason…we need to talk about this," she insisted.

"Talk about *what*?" he challenged. "About the fact that you were so blinded by your hatred for my girlfriend that you dug up my ex just to cause problems? About the fact that you damn near ruined my relationship? My *life*?"

Mrs. Adams, seeing the hurt in her oldest son's eyes, put her hands up in surrender. "Okay, okay Jason," she placated, voice calm. "I know that I didn't handle that well… I was wrong for that and I did tell Paris to leave you alone."

"Before or *after* she came *back* to my school talking about transferring?" he questioned, folding his arms. "Before or *after* she showed up to my room and refused to leave? Before or *after* Chasity had to put hands on her? Before or *after* Dad yelled at you about it?"

His mother looked down at the floor momentarily in shame. She recalled the verbal lashing that she had received from her normally calm and laid-back husband, the day that Jason confessed to his father everything that had been going on. She remembered the look of pure disappointment that was on his face, and in his voice, when he told her point blank that she was deliberately hurting their son.

"Jason, I'm sorry," she said.

"Sorry that your plan didn't *work*?" Jason threw back. "Because it *didn't*, Chasity and I are *still* together."

"I know you are," she replied. "And no, I'm not sorry that my plan didn't work. I'm sorry that I hurt you."

"You disrespected me and you disrespected my relationship," he corrected matter-of-factly. "All because you don't like who I'm with."

"Jason, I just feel like she's going to hurt you."

"*You're* hurting me!" Jason exploded.

Mrs. Adams put her hand up again. "Jason—"

"No, I'm *tired* Mom," Jason cut in, angry.

"I feel like she puts you *through* too much," Mrs. Adams reasoned.

Jason was astounded. "As opposed to *who*? Paris?" he questioned. "The girl who *cheated* on me?"

Mrs. Adams frowned. "She *what*?!" she exclaimed. "Baby, you never told me—"

"It doesn't even matter," he hissed. "I shouldn't have *had* to because this should have never *happened*."

Mrs. Adams put her hands over her face. If she didn't feel terrible before, she certainly did now. If she had known that Paris had hurt her son, she would have never spoken to Paris when she ran into her, let alone brought his ex back around. "I didn't know Jason... I didn't know because I didn't *see* it. I didn't *see* you upset, I didn't *see* you depressed... I *saw* that with Chasity."

Jason shook his head. His mother was right about one thing: when he was with Paris, Jason rarely let it show when he was angry. He knew that the reason why Chasity affected him so much more than Paris was because of how deep his feelings ran for Chasity. With Paris, it was infatuation, leading to indifference. With Chasity, it was love.

"You of all people should know that a relationship, a *real* one, is not going to be all sunshine every single day," he argued. "I've heard you and dad argue on *more* than one occasion growing up, and never *once* did anybody say that you two shouldn't be together."

"I just think that Chasity has issues," she reasoned.

Jason narrowed his eyes. "I think it's been made pretty clear...it's *you* who has the issues," he hissed.

Mrs. Adams was taken back and it showed on her face. "I just want what's best for you, son."

"No, you don't," Jason immediately returned, before moving around her to walk out.

Seeing him leave made her want to break into pieces. She hated the rift that had been forming between her and her son. A rift that she knew, if she didn't fix it, would break their bond forever. Spinning around to face his departing back, she raised her voice. "What do I have to do to make you stop hating me?" her tone was pleading.

Jason stopped in his tracks but didn't turn around.

"What? Do you want me to apologize to you again? Fine, I'm *sorry* baby... Do you want me to apologize to Chasity? Fine, I'll do that too. Call her over here."

Jason sighed. As much as Chasity deserved an apology from his mother for all that she had done, he knew that she would only be doing it to get back in his good graces. His mother would still be holding on to her grudge against Chasity. He made a promise to himself that he would always protect her, even if it was from his own mother.

"Mom, unless you plan on *sincerely* apologizing and putting this mess behind you…you're not getting anywhere *near* her," Jason said, tone dangerously low. "And until then, even though I do love you and always *will*…we're not going to be on good terms."

Mrs. Adams's face fell, along with her heart, as she watched her son walk out of the kitchen.

As Jason passed the entryway, he locked eyes with his father, who had been listening out of sight. Jason felt the need to say something to him; he wasn't sure how he felt about his tone and the words that he'd spewed at the woman who had birthed him. "Dad—"

Mr. Adams put his hand up to silence him. "You're good," he confirmed, much to Jason's relief. Not saying another word, Jason just nodded and headed up the steps.

Mr. Adams followed his progress for a moment. He was proud. Jason stood up for himself and the woman that he loved. He prided himself on making sure that his sons knew the importance of doing that. He walked into the kitchen and stared at his wife, who was standing there with her hand over her head. She looked back at him with tear-filled eyes.

"I messed up," she sniffled.

Mr. Adams held his arms out and she hurried over to him. He wrapped his arms around her. "Yes, yes you did," he agreed. "Fix it."

Chapter 44

"Chasity, you should really go visit your grandmother," Trisha urged, folding her coat on top of her suitcase.

Chasity leaned over the couch and clasped her hands together. "I know," she agreed. "I'll make sure I go over there."

"And I mean a *real* visit," Trisha clarified. "For a *few hours*. You know she misses you."

Chasity glanced down at her hands. "I know, I'll go," she promised. "After you guys get back from your little mother-daughter trip."

Trisha put her hands on her hips. "I still don't understand why you turned down a trip to the Bahamas in the dead of winter, to stay *here*."

"'Cause I'd rather stay here with Jason," Chasity bluntly responded.

Trisha put her hand on her chest. "Ouch," she pouted. She presented Chasity with the opportunity to go to the Bahamas for the week with her and her mother a few days ago. She had to admit that she was a bit hurt when Chasity told her that she didn't want to go.

Chasity laughed. "No, I'm joking," she clarified. "Y'all need this trip for just the two of you. Besides, I'm not trying to sit on that plane when it takes off and she starts singing gospel songs. You know how she is."

Trisha busted out laughing. "God, don't remind me," she said, putting her hand over her face. "My momma. Gotta love her sanctified self."

Chasity chuckled.

"Anyway, my flight leaves in a few hours so I should get going," she said, looking at her watch. "Is Jason on his way back over?" Chasity nodded. "How was it for him being around his Mom?"

"Um, he wasn't too thrilled about being there," Chasity replied. "But he survived."

"Did he tell her off?"

"Kind of."

"Oh?" Trisha pressed. "What did he say?"

"I'll tell you later," Chasity replied. She wanted to keep her mind off of Jason's mother as much as possible.

"Okay…can you just tell me if I need to check her?"

Chasity shot her a warning look. "Mom," she spat.

Trisha put a hand up. "Okay fine… But just know that the conversation between me and Nancy, *will* happen eventually," she promised. "She's gonna see *exactly* who *you* get *your* attitude from."

"Go catch your flight," Chasity ordered.

"Don't rush me," Trisha returned, wrapping her scarf around her neck. "Do you need for me to leave you some money?"

"No."

"Condoms?" she teased.

Chasity narrowed her eyes. "No," she spat.

"Just making sure," Trisha said, unfazed by Chasity's reaction. "I still don't understand why you're not on the pill."

Chasity rolled her eyes. "I don't like taking pills, you already know that."

"How about the shot?"

"How about no?" Chasity returned. "I tried that already and it had my system acting all stupid."

"Was that before or *after* you got pregnant last year?" Trisha jeered.

"After," Chasity hissed. "Look, how about you stop worrying about *my* sex life, and get *yourself* one."

Trisha's mouth fell open. "Excuse me, smart ass?" she barked. "My sex life is just fine, thank you."

Chasity shot Trisha a skeptical look. "You haven't been on any dates in forever."

"You don't know *what* the hell I've been doing," she argued.

"*Have* you?" Chasity asked, folding her arms.

"No," Trisha muttered. "Fine, I'll admit, my love life has been a bit dry lately," she admitted, amusement in her voice. "I just haven't had much time to date."

"Your business is doing just fine, you *have* time," Chasity pointed out. "You're making excuses."

Trisha flagged Chasity with her hand. "Whatever," she dismissed.

"Mom, I'll be graduating in the spring, which means that I will be moving out soon after… You need a life that doesn't revolve around *me*," Chasity stated.

"You don't *have* to move out, you know. This house is big enough for you and Jason to raise a family in," Trisha proposed.

Chasity held a look of disgust on her face. "Are you crazy?" she blurted out, earning a laugh from Trisha.

"I'm just playing," Trisha assured, still laughing. "You should see your face."

"That's not funny."

"It *was*," Trisha maintained, laughter subsiding. "I hear you though… I just hate dating, but I agree I need to start going on them again."

"Uh huh," Chasity agreed.

Trisha chuckled. She glanced over at the slim box sitting on the coffee table. She gestured to it. "That the gift from your father?"

Chasity cut her eye at it. "Mm hmm," she muttered.

"What is it?" Trisha wondered.

"A bracelet," Chasity answered, nonchalant.

"Diamond?"

"Yup."

Trisha nodded. "I take it that you don't want it?"

"Nope," Chasity spat.

Trisha sighed. When the package was delivered to her house a few days ago, addressed to Chasity and from Derrick, Trisha didn't know how Chasity would receive it. She knew that Chasity still wasn't ready to communicate with her father.

"Did he tell you that I texted him back?" Chasity asked, cutting into Trisha's thoughts.

Trisha looked surprised. She had no idea. "You did?" she asked.

Chasity nodded. "It wasn't too long after I went back to school," she said. "He texted me asking me how I was doing. I was going to ignore it, but after talking to Jason and thinking about that damn letter from Brenda, begging me to talk to him if he reached out, I responded." She was getting annoyed just thinking about it. "I didn't *want* to, but I did."

Trisha held a sympathetic gaze. "What did you say?"

"I told him that I was doing fine. He goes on to say that he really wants to rebuild a relationship with me, and asked me how he can go about doing that," she vented. "I told him that if he was serious, we could start by talking, and I said that if he called me, I'd at least speak to him."

"Chasity, that's big of you honey," Trisha praised. "At least you're giving him a chance."

Chasity fixed her gaze on Trisha. "Do you really think he called me after that?" she ground out.

Trisha frowned. "What do you mean?"

"He never called me," Chasity reiterated. "No texts, *nothing*. Then sends this bullshit present to me, like that's supposed to make up for anything."

Trisha rubbed her face with her hands. She was angry at Derrick; she was tired of him dismissing their daughter. But because Chasity was already upset, she had to remain a calming force. "I'm sorry," she consoled, touching her arm.

"I don't know—If he has the opportunity to talk to you like he claimed he *wanted* all this time, I don't get that *now* that he has the green light from you, why he won't step up and *do* it."

"Because your baby daddy is full of *shit*," Chasity spat. "It's easy to blame *me* for us not talking, 'cause he gets to go around and say how much he's *trying* and have people feel bad for him. But the truth is, he doesn't *care*. As long as he can throw his damn money at me without doing any damn work, he's fine with it."

Trisha sighed once again. "Do you want me to talk to him?" she asked. "Sorry, I used the wrong word, I meant cuss him the fuck out?"

"Don't bother," Chasity returned. "He's not worth the time or vocal cords."

Trisha moved in and hugged Chasity; she held her daughter for a long moment. It was comforting for Chasity.

Chasity broke from the embrace and glanced at her watch. "You need to go so you won't miss your flight."

"I know, I'm going," Trisha said, giving Chasity a kiss on her cheek. "I left a gift under the tree for Jason."

"I know, I opened it," Chasity replied.

Trisha laughed. "I knew you would, nosey," she said. Trisha hurried over to her suitcase and grabbed the handle. "I'll be sure to send that bracelet back to Derrick when I get back. You don't need to do it."

"Okay," Chasity said, grateful.

"Call me if you need me."

"I will," Chasity promised.

"Love you baby," Trisha said, heading for the door.

"Love you too," Chasity called after her.

"I swear, for school to be out, it's too many damn people in this damn office," Malajia griped, fidgeting in the seat on which she sat.

"Fall semester may be out, but winter classes are still

going on," Mark yawned.

Malajia shot him a glare. "Didn't nobody ask you that," she spat, earning a side glance from an annoyed Mark.

"Don't catch an attitude with *me* baby," he threw back, pointing to her. "You're lucky I drove your ass back down here in the *first* damn place."

Malajia rolled her eyes as she spun around in her seat. Malajia couldn't help her mood. Getting confirmation that she had failed Spanish 201 via an email of her grades from the school, days before New Year's, and the reality that she would need to take it again, had her on edge.

"Naw, you think I drove five hours, *and* agreed to wait with you while you register early for some damn language class, just to catch your bullshit?" Mark added, fixing a stern gaze on her. "You better get some damn act right."

"Who the fuck are you talking to, bruh?" Malajia barked, holding her finger to his temple.

"Somebody who's about to be on couple *and* dick timeout if she don't stop trippin'," Mark returned.

Malajia's mouth fell open. "You ain't even gotta act like that," she said, tone now calm. She sat back in her seat and patted Mark's leg. "Sorry," she said.

"Um hmm," Mark mumbled. "Why are you registering early anyway?"

"'Cause I don't want the same damn professor that I had this past semester," Malajia replied. "She was trippin' hard with those damn tests." Mark chuckled. "Nah, I'm taking Professor Bell's easy ass class… Her class fills up fast."

"Makes sense," Mark shrugged.

Seeing the door open to the Business department head office, Malajia sighed. "God, Dr. Fairway is gonna cuss my black ass out," she grumbled.

Mark laughed. "Didn't he tell you that he was tired of you playing around with those easy classes?"

"Yes. Yes he did." As soon as Dr. Fairway spotted Malajia siting on the chair, he signaled for her to come to him. Malajia sucked her teeth. "This isn't my fault," she whined, hopping up from her seat.

"What is with you and these language requirements?" Dr. Fairway spat, allowing her to walk past him and into his office.

"I don't even know, sir," Malajia answered, as he shut the door behind them.

Malajia opened the office door twenty minutes later with her class registrations in hand. "Dr. Fairway, I *promise* I'm gonna graduate on time," she called into the room, before walking out. "'Cause I damn sure don't want to see *your* bald ass any longer than I have to," she mumbled.

"What did you say?" Dr. Fairway asked, hearing sounds coming from her.

"Huh?" Malajia panicked, quickly shutting the door. She stifled a laugh as she headed over to the chairs where she and Mark were sitting. She frowned when she didn't see him there. *Where the hell did he go?* "He better not have gone to get food without me," she muttered to herself. As Malajia moved to head towards the exit, she collided with someone.

Both women steadied themselves and went to offer a quick apology in passing, when they recognized each other.

"The fuck?" Malajia barked.

"Nice to see you *too*, Malajia," Jackie returned, adjusting her purse strap on her shoulder.

Malajia rolled her eyes. *Great, just what I need right now.* "What are you doing here? Didn't your funny looking, friend jumpin', getting your ass beat *twice*, slackin' ass, drop out of school like two years ago?"

Jackie folded her arms and frowned at the venom that Malajia spewed from her glossed lips. "Was all that *really* necessary?"

"Abso-fuckin-lutley," Malajia hissed. Luckily for her, most of the crowd had cleared from the office, leaving Malajia free to use her profanity without repercussions.

"Whatever," Jackie returned. "Not that I owe you a

damn explanation, but I'm registering for classes for next semester."

Malajia stood there, a mask of anger frozen on her face.

"I'm coming back to school…part time," Jackie added.

"Can't you *wait* until I graduate?" Malajia ground out. "I was getting used to not seeing your triflin' ass around."

"Look Malajia, like I told Chasity and Alex when I saw them at the mall that day, I'm not gonna start any trouble. You don't have to worry."

"Bitch ain't nobody worried 'bout your ass," Malajia barked.

"I'm just trying to get my life back on track."

"Jackie, I can speak for Chasity, Sidra, Alex, Emily and the *rest* of this campus, when I say that nobody gives a *shit* about your life and what you've been doing with it," Malajia hurled. "You're a shit starter and you will never change."

Jackie shook her head. "I'm not proud of what I used to do," she replied.

Malajia rolled her eyes. "Spare me," she bit out, moving around Jackie to walk away.

Jackie spun around. "Malajia, you act like you've never done anything that you're ashamed of," she hurled at Malajia's back.

"No bitch, I *haven't*," Malajia returned, still walking.

"You sure about that?" Jackie countered.

The challenging question made Malajia stop in her tracks and immediately turn around to face Jackie. "And just what the hell is *that* supposed to mean?"

Jackie took a step towards Malajia. "All I'm saying is that you should be careful about throwing up people's past regrets. You wouldn't want *yours* thrown in your face, now *would* you?"

Malajia stood there speechless as Jackie stared at her with a smug look. *What the hell is this raggedy bitch trying to get at?* Before Malajia could vocalize her question, she heard Dr. Fairway call Jackie's name.

"I gotta go, see you around," Jackie said, before walking

into the office.

Malajia followed Jackie's progress and stared at her departing back, until the office door closed. She was confused; she was annoyed. *I freakin' hate her, I swear.*

"Sugar face, you all done?" Mark asked, strolling up to her.

Malajia was so preoccupied with her own thoughts that she just stood there, quiet.

"Mel," Mark chuckled, waving his hand in front of her face.

"What?" she spat.

"You done? I'm tryna go eat."

Malajia pushed some of her hair behind her ear. "Yeah," she murmured. "Yeah, let's go."

Mark placed his arm around her shoulder as they walked out of the office. Heading out to the parking lot, Malajia bundled her coat to her neck. "Mark, I'm not tryna walk all the way over to the other side of the parking lot," she complained. "Can you please go bring the car around?"

"Yeah," Mark agreed, before heading off.

Malajia quickly dialed a number on her cell phone and put it to her ear. "Chaz, what are you doing?" she asked when the line picked up. "Eww, you freak. Anyway real quick, guess who I saw down here at school …Jackie's ratchet ass… Girl, yes, and as usual she got on my damn nerves…apparently she's bringing her ashy ass back to school…hold on."

Malajia pulled the phone away from her ear and checked a text message. Frowning, Malajia eyed the words, "Happy Holidays baby" accompanied with a heart emoji. *What the fuck is this damn number?* She wondered of the unrecognizable phone number, then put the phone back to her ear. "Sis let me call you back."

Malajia ended the call and started texting the number back. "You have the wrong number," she read aloud, before hitting send. Malajia lifted her head up in time to see a familiar sedan slowly drive through the parking lot. Staring, eyes wide and full of fright, she looked to see if she could see the driver, but the tinted windows kept anything from view.

As the car drove out of sight, Malajia closed her eyes and shook her head. "Stop it Malajia, stop," she whispered to herself. "There are ten thousand cars that look just like that."

Folding her arms to her chest, she was relieved when she saw Mark pull up. Not waiting for him to get out and open the door for her, Malajia hurried over to the car and hopped in.

"Let's get the hell off this damn campus," she ordered, putting her seatbelt on.

"You got it," Mark said as he pulled off.

College life 402;

Undergrad Completion

Book Eight

The College Life Series

Coming soon!

CPSIA information can be obtained
at www.ICGtesting.com
Printed in the USA
LVHW011630090919
630427LV00012B/899